To my dad, who taught me the art of silliness —E.C.B.

Dedicated to Stephanie Hays. A DRAGON-SIZED thank you for adding your unique sparkle with every step of this adventure. You're a true glitter-boost of inspiration to this art troll in his creative cave! —L.F.

Etch and Clarion Books are imprints of HarperCollins Publishers.

The Sparkle Dragons

For information address HarperCollins Children's Books, a division of HarperCollins Publishers, 195 Broadway, New York, NY 10007.
clarionbooks.com

Library of Congress Cataloging-in-Publication Data has been applied for.

ISBN: 978-0-358-53809-7 hardcover
ISBN: 978-0-358-53808-0 paperback

The illustrations in this book were done in Photoshop with digital brushes ...and a dash of dragon sparkles too.
The text was set in Jacoby.
The display text was set in Maduki.
Cover and interior design by Stephanie Hays

Manufactured in Spain
EP 10 9 8 7 6 5 4 3 2 1
4500842198

First Edition

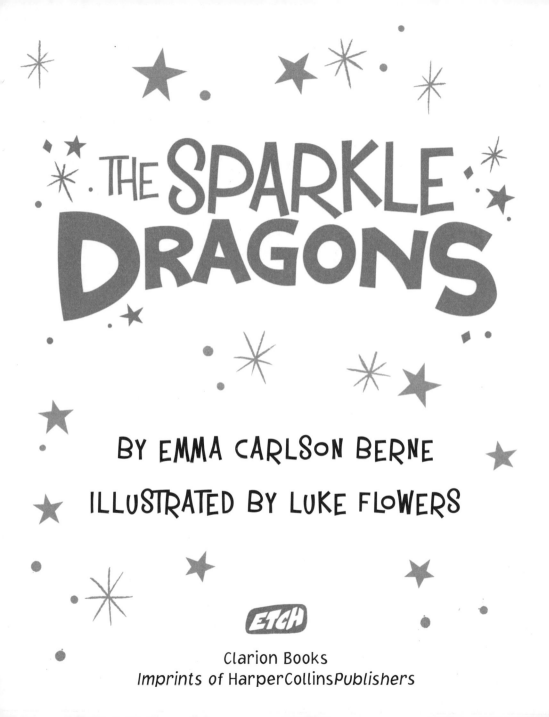

THE SPARKLE DRAGONS

BY EMMA CARLSON BERNE

ILLUSTRATED BY LUKE FLOWERS

ETCH

Clarion Books
Imprints of HarperCollinsPublishers

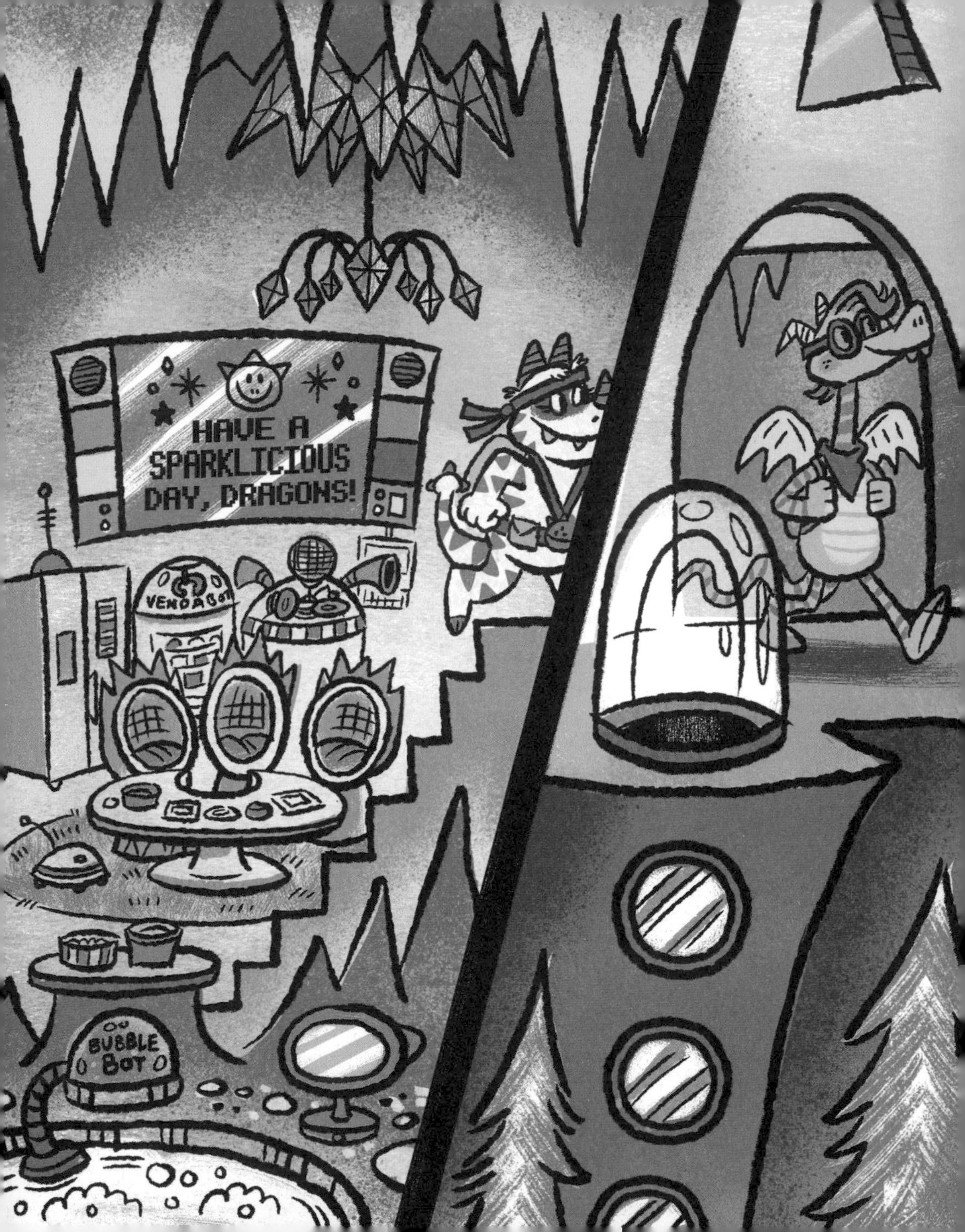
HAVE A SPARKLICIOUS DAY, DRAGONS!
VENDABOT
BUBBLE BOT

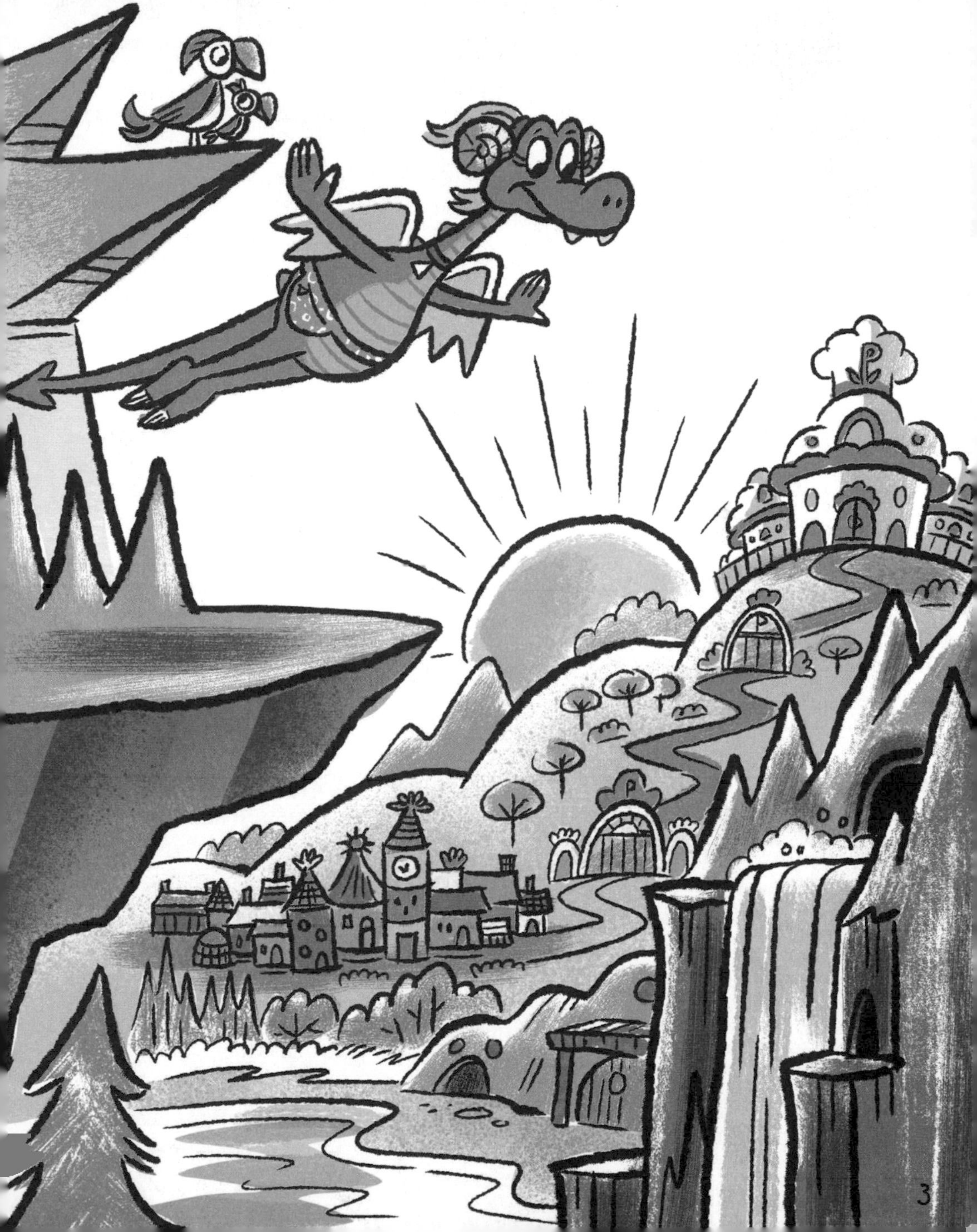

INTRODUCING

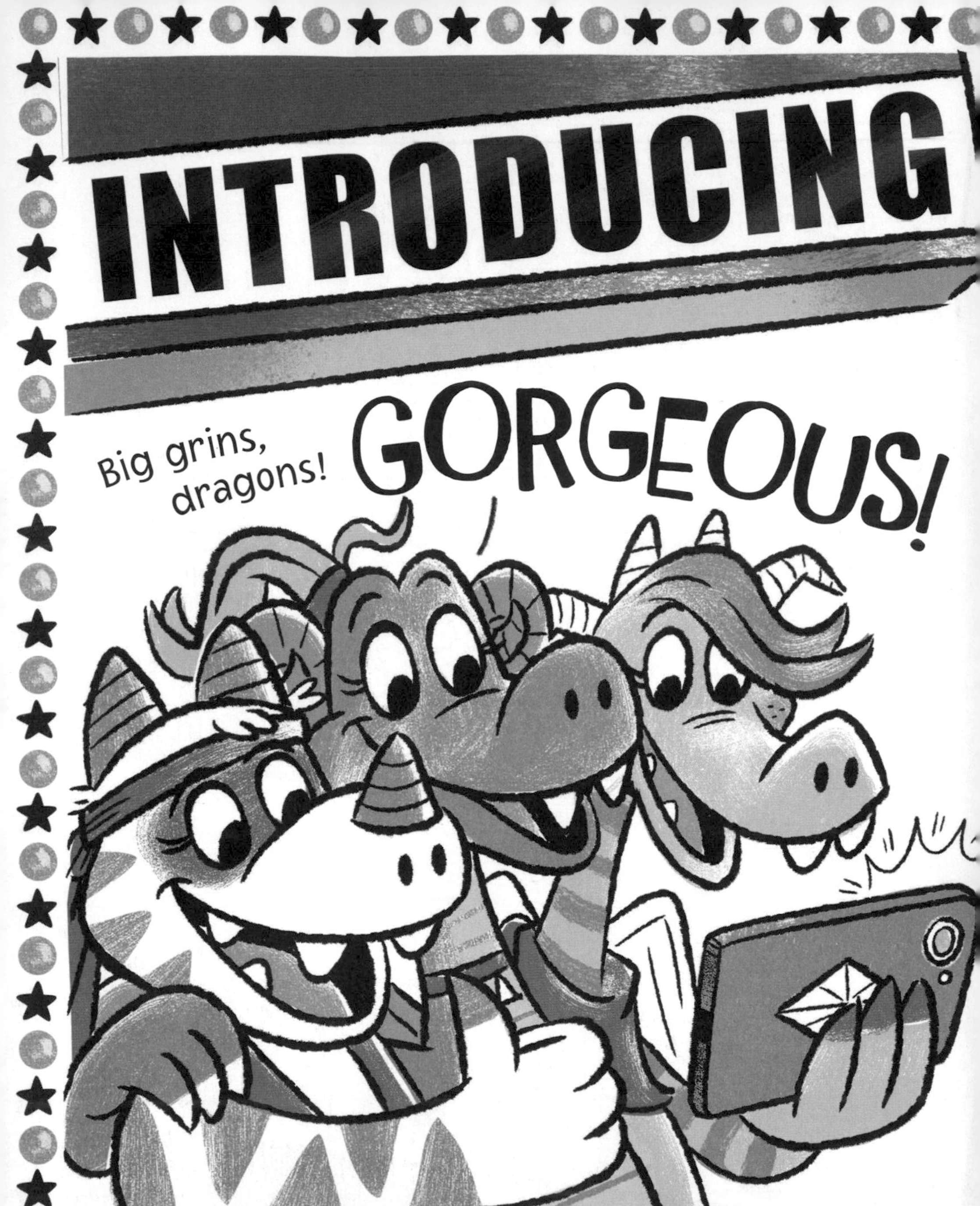
Big grins, dragons!
GORGEOUS!

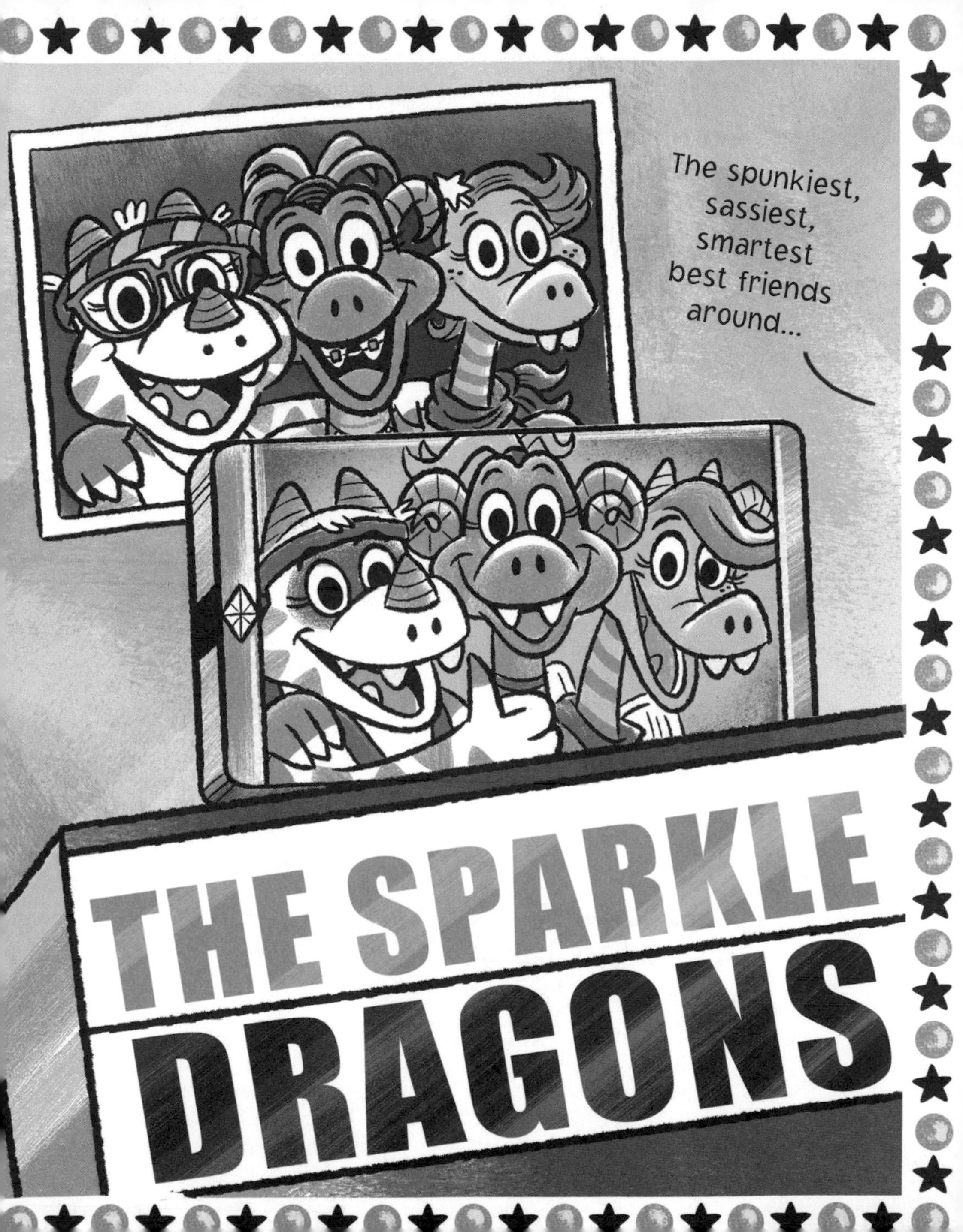
The spunkiest, sassiest, smartest best friends around...
THE SPARKLE DRAGONS

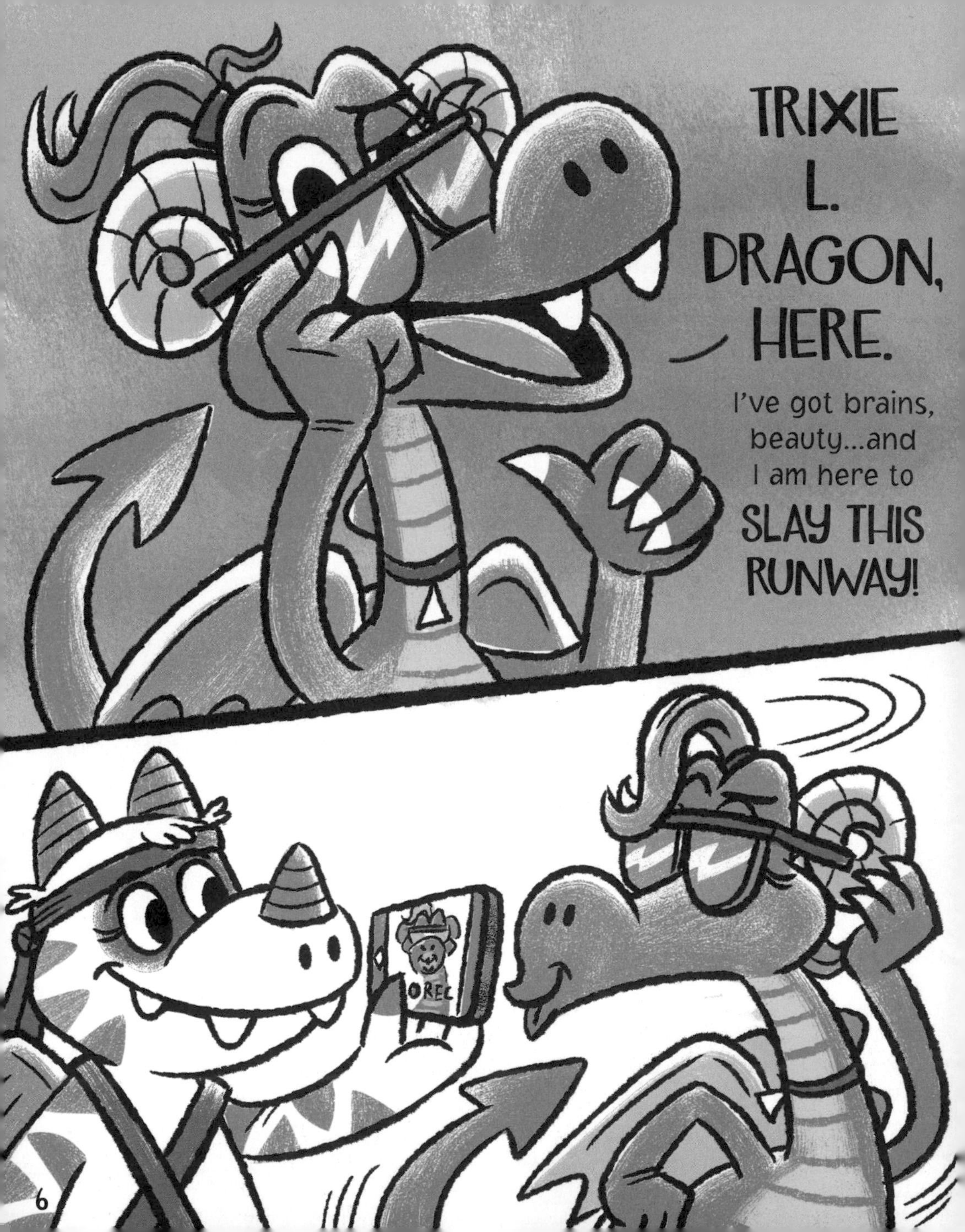
TRIXIE L. DRAGON, HERE.
I've got brains, beauty...and I am here to SLAY THIS RUNWAY!
REC

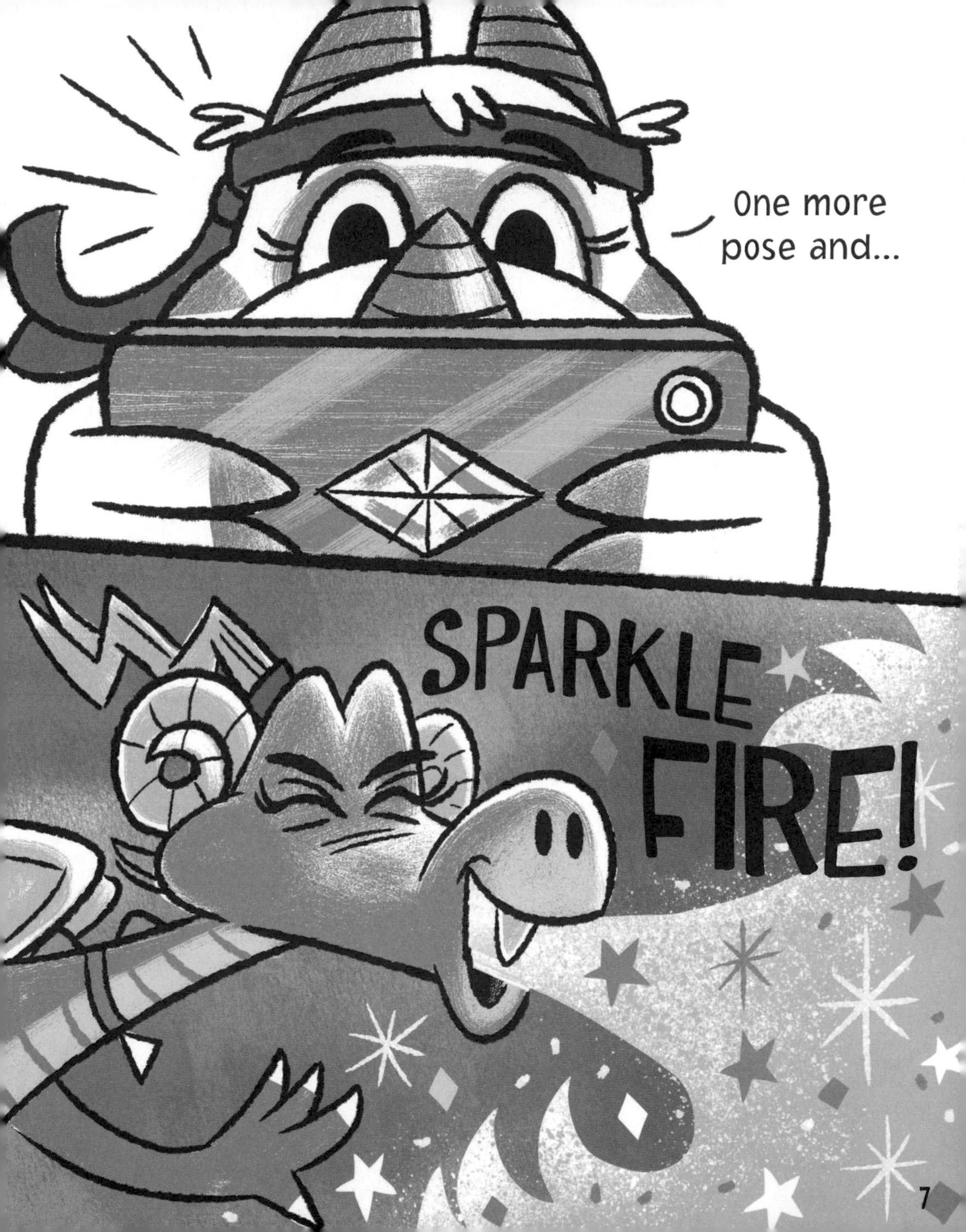
One more pose and...
SPARKLE FIRE!

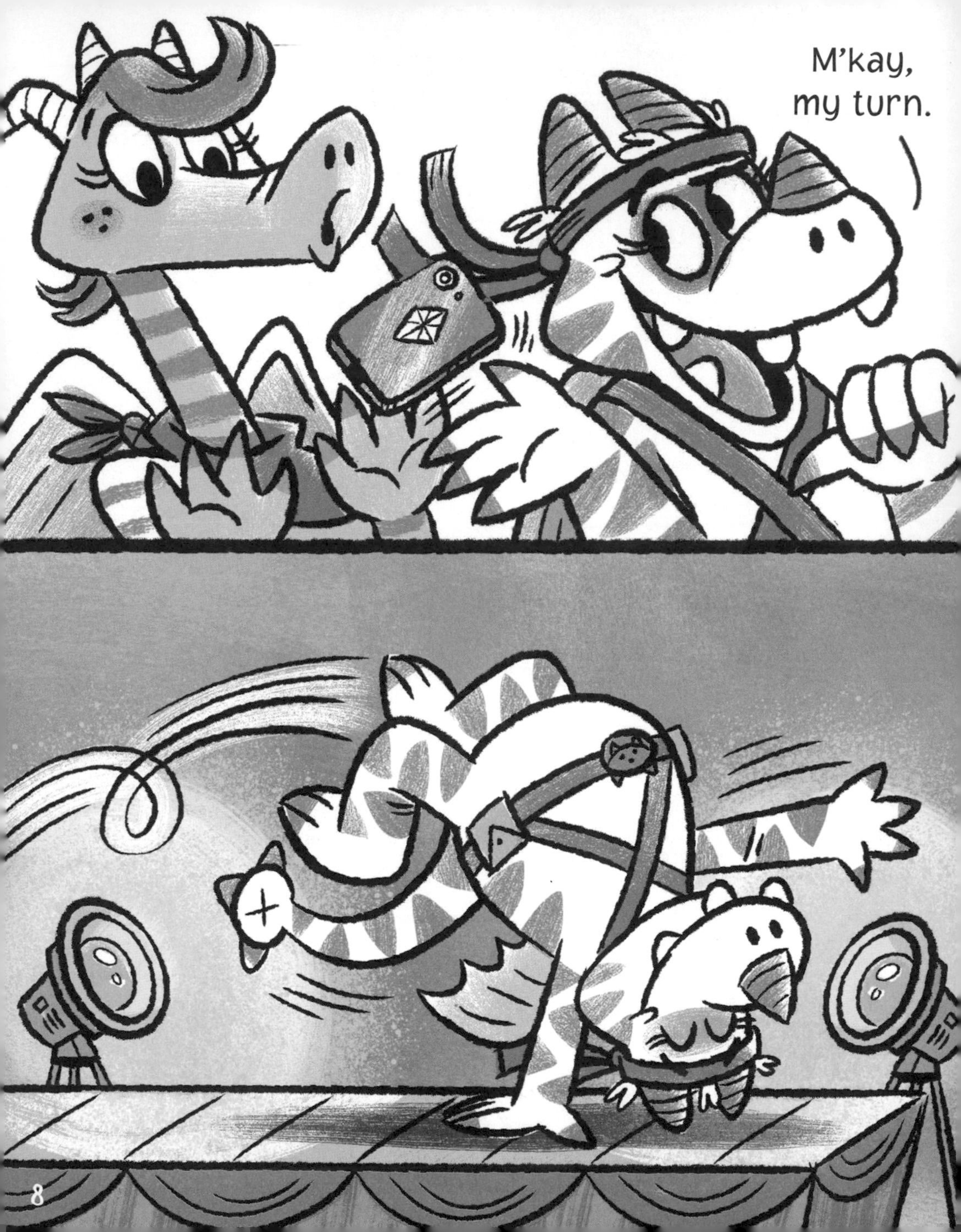
M'kay,
my turn.

HELLO, WORLD!

Rue here. I'm feisty, fierce, sharp as a dragon's tooth, and dedicated to fighting for good with my BFFs.

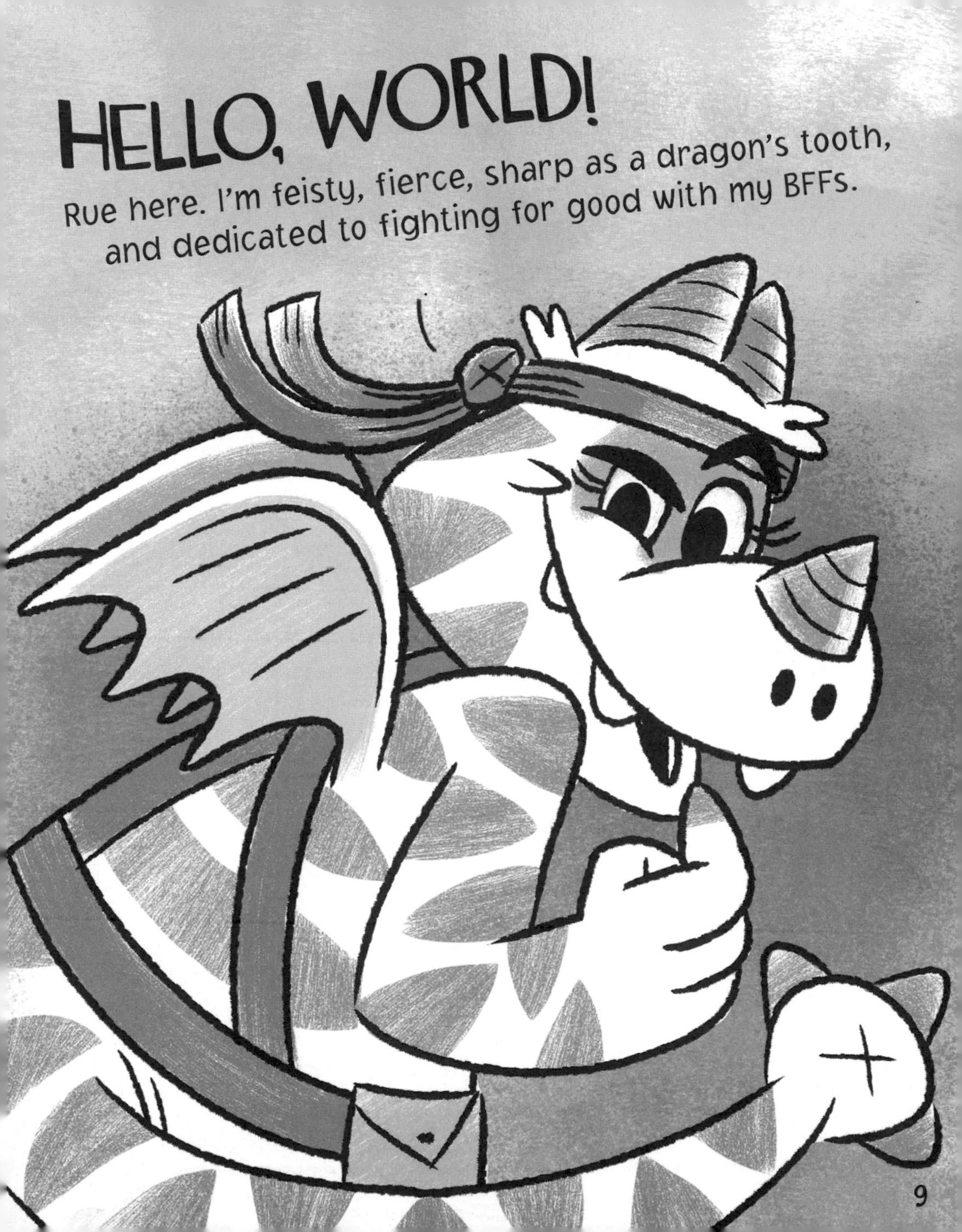

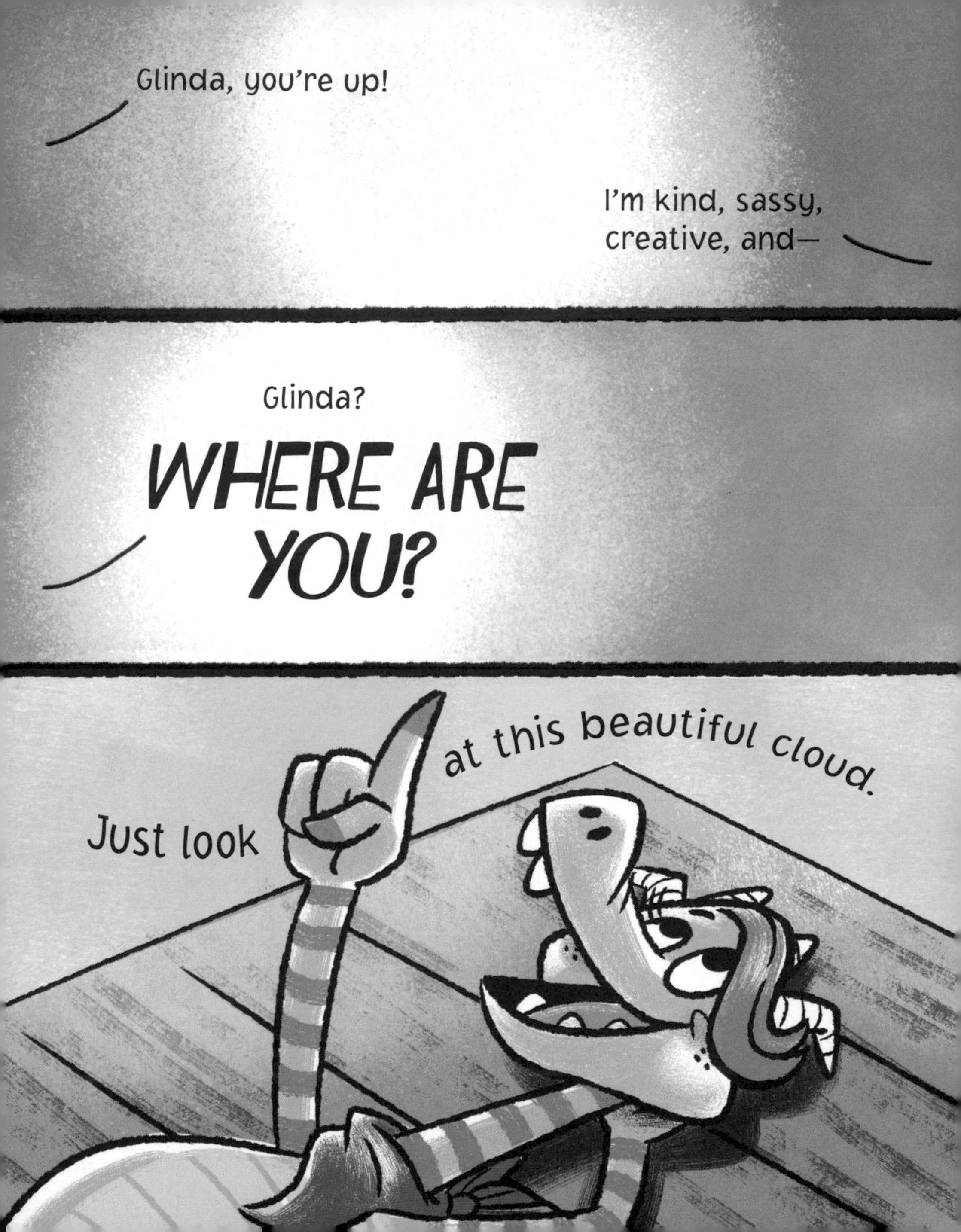
Glinda, you're up!
I'm kind, sassy, creative, and—
Glinda?
WHERE ARE YOU?
Just look
at this beautiful cloud.

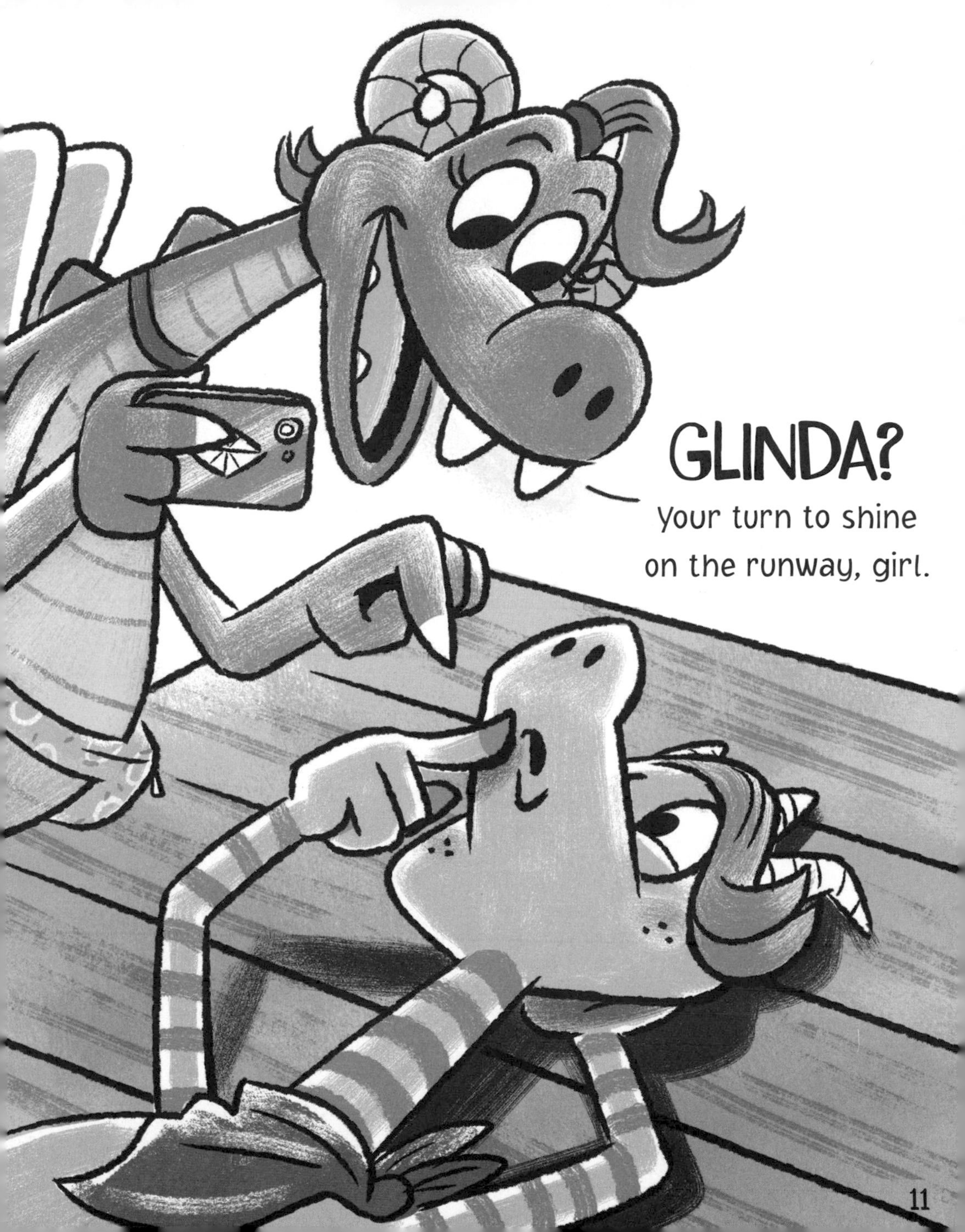
GLINDA?
Your turn to shine
on the runway, girl.

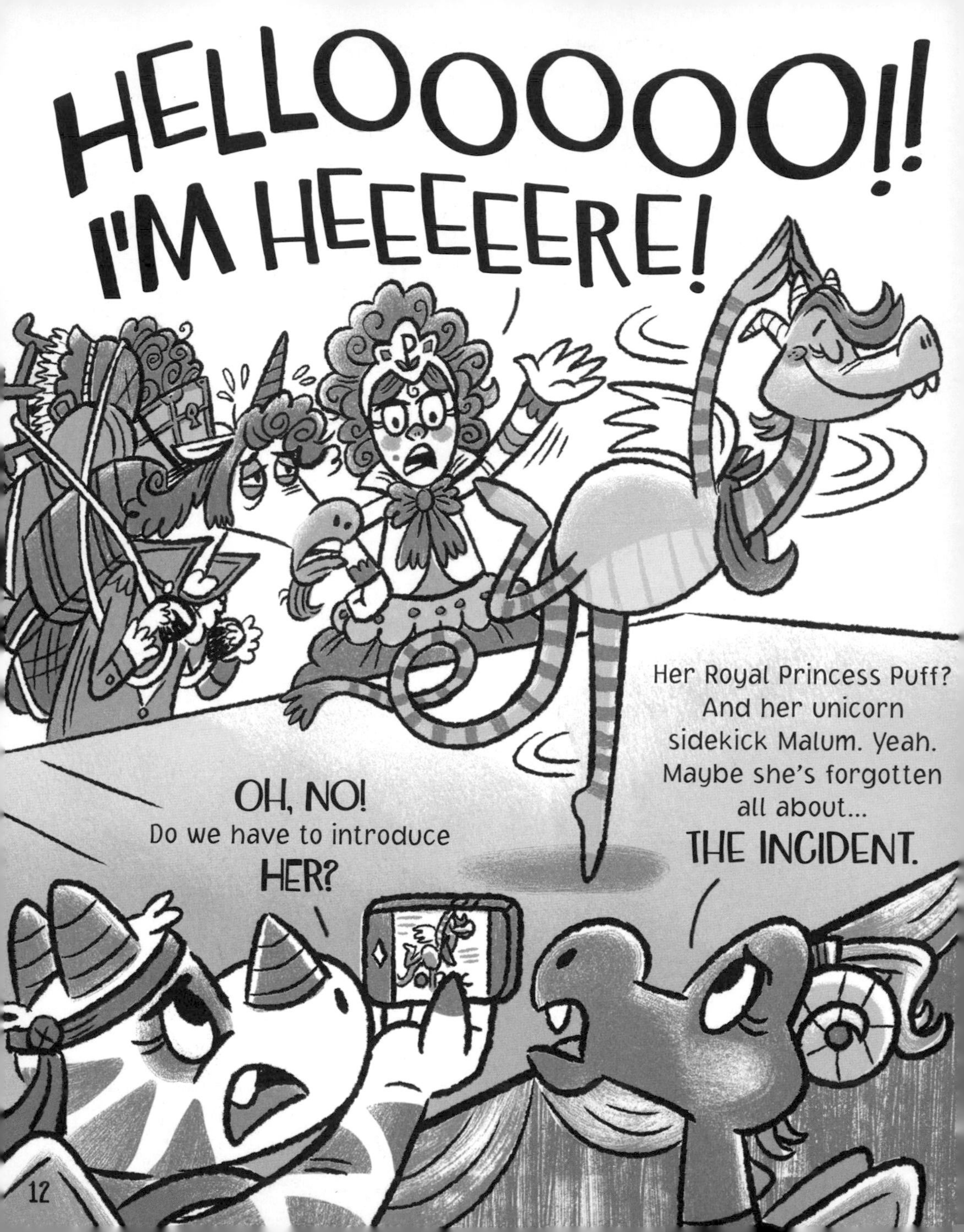
HELLOOOOO!! I'M HEEEEERE!
OH, NO! Do we have to introduce HER?
Her Royal Princess Puff? And her unicorn sidekick Malum. Yeah. Maybe she's forgotten all about...
THE INCIDENT.

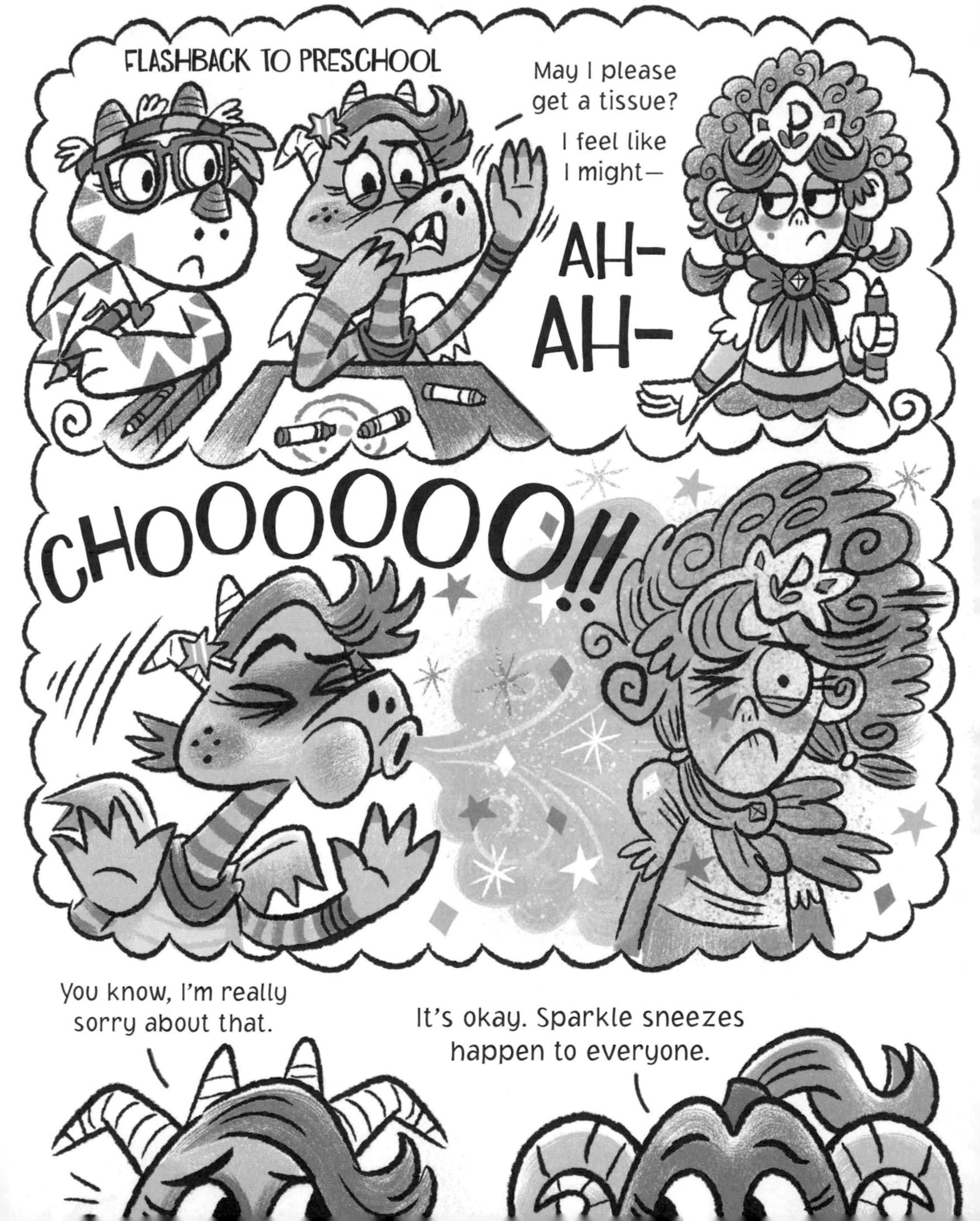
FLASHBACK TO PRESCHOOL
May I please get a tissue?
I feel like I might—
AH-
AH-
CHOOOOOOO!!
You know, I'm really sorry about that.
It's okay. Sparkle sneezes happen to everyone.

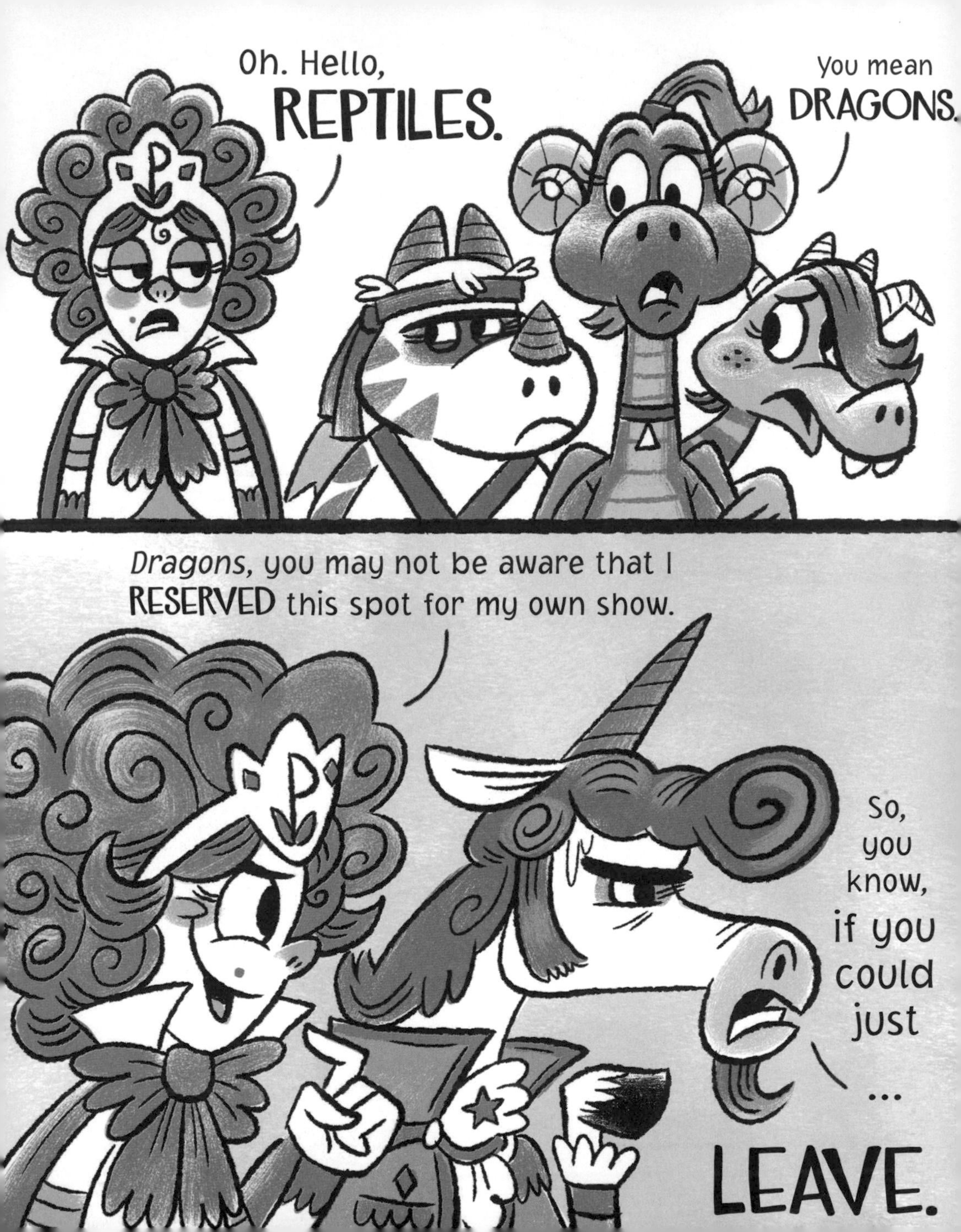
Oh. Hello, REPTILES.
You mean DRAGONS.
Dragons, you may not be aware that I RESERVED this spot for my own show.
So, you know, if you could just ... LEAVE.

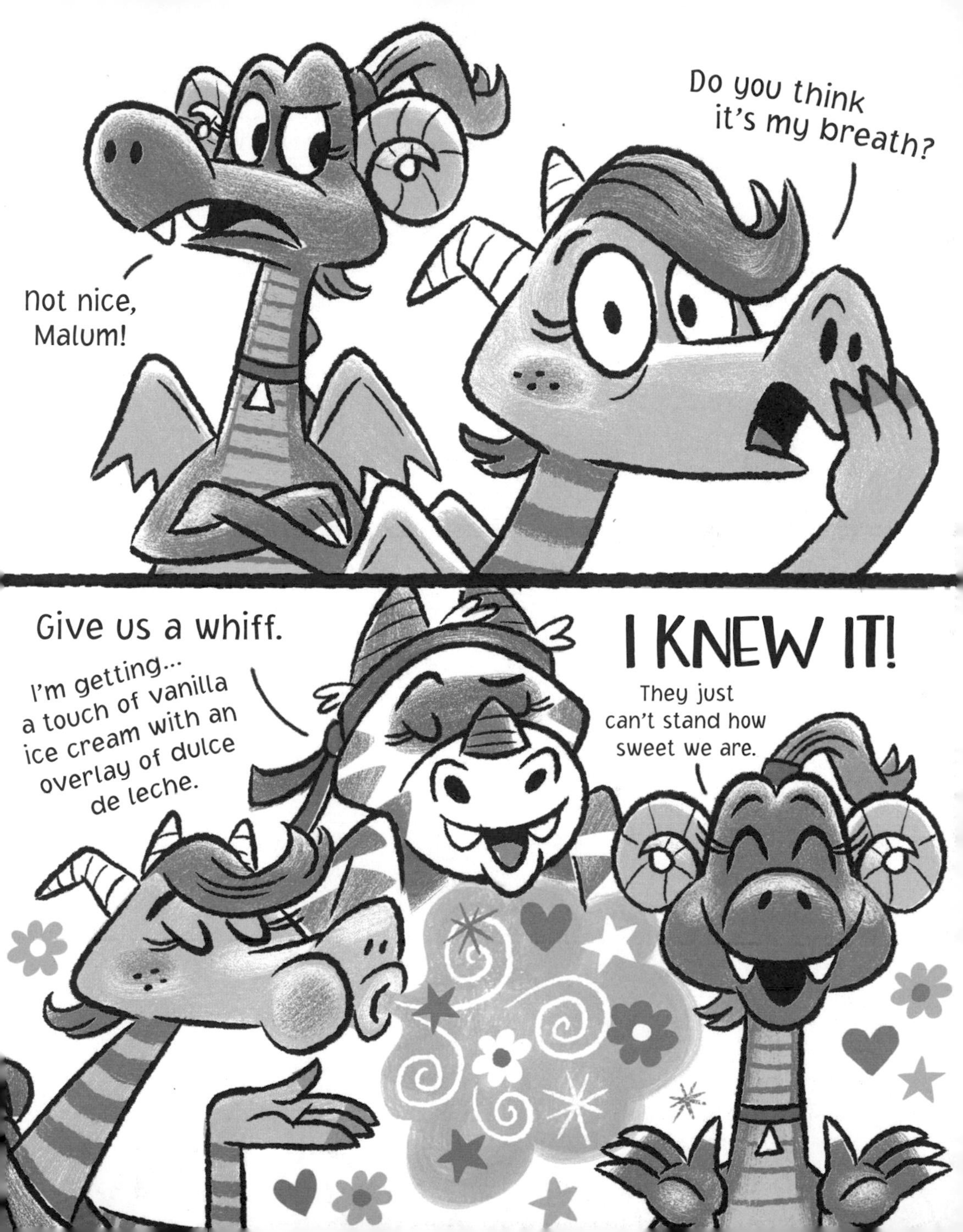

Not nice, Malum!
Do you think it's my breath?
Give us a whiff.
I'm getting... a touch of vanilla ice cream with an overlay of dulce de leche.
I KNEW IT!
They just can't stand how sweet we are.

CHAPTER ONE
A VERY PUFFY PAGENT

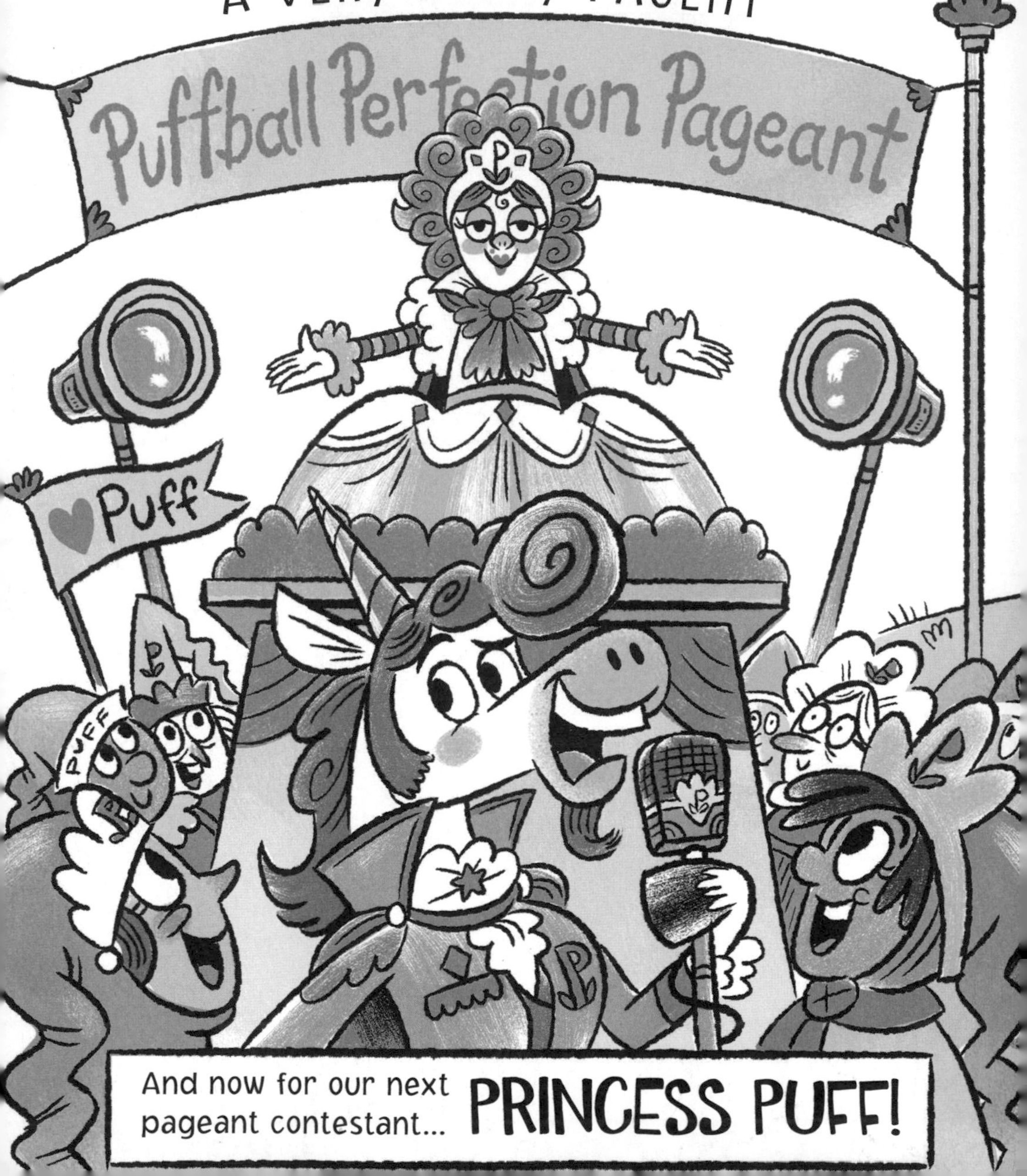
Puffball Perfection Pageant
Puff
PUFF
And now for our next pageant contestant...
PRINCESS PUFF!

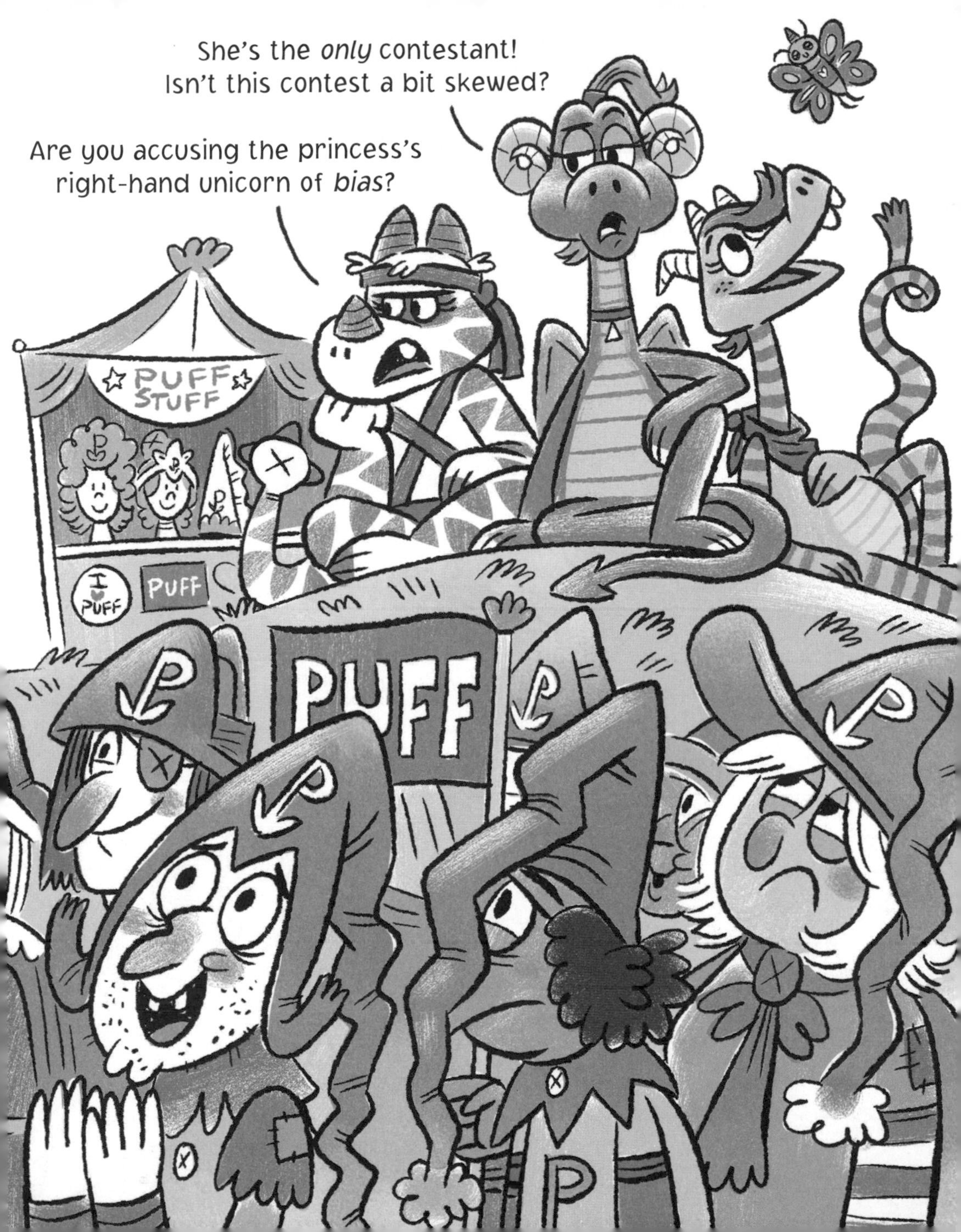
She's the *only* contestant!
Isn't this contest a bit skewed?
Are you accusing the princess's
right-hand unicorn of *bias*?
PUFF STUFF
I ♥ PUFF
PUFF
PUFF

And now we have...

PRINCESS PUFF!

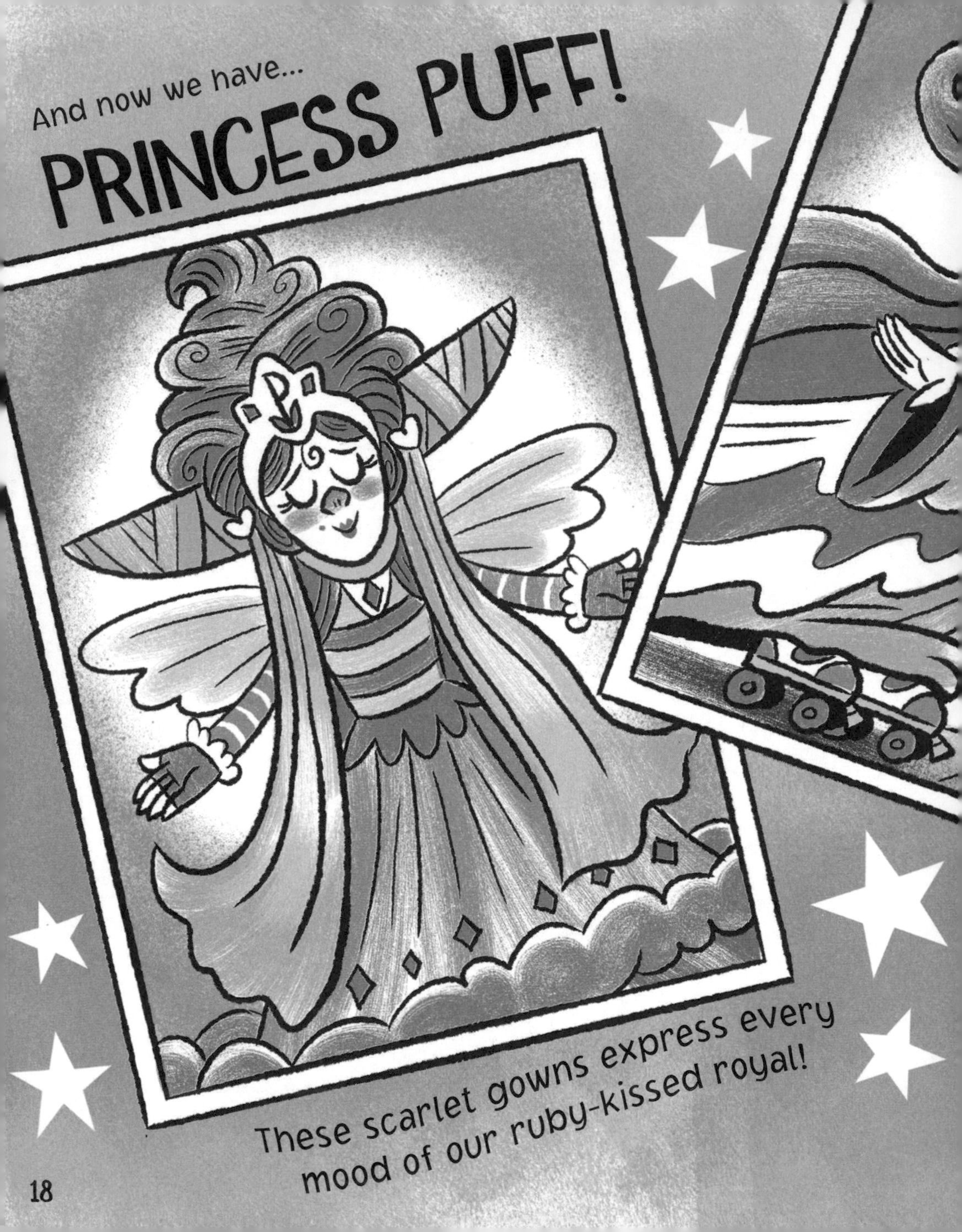

These scarlet gowns express every mood of our ruby-kissed royal!

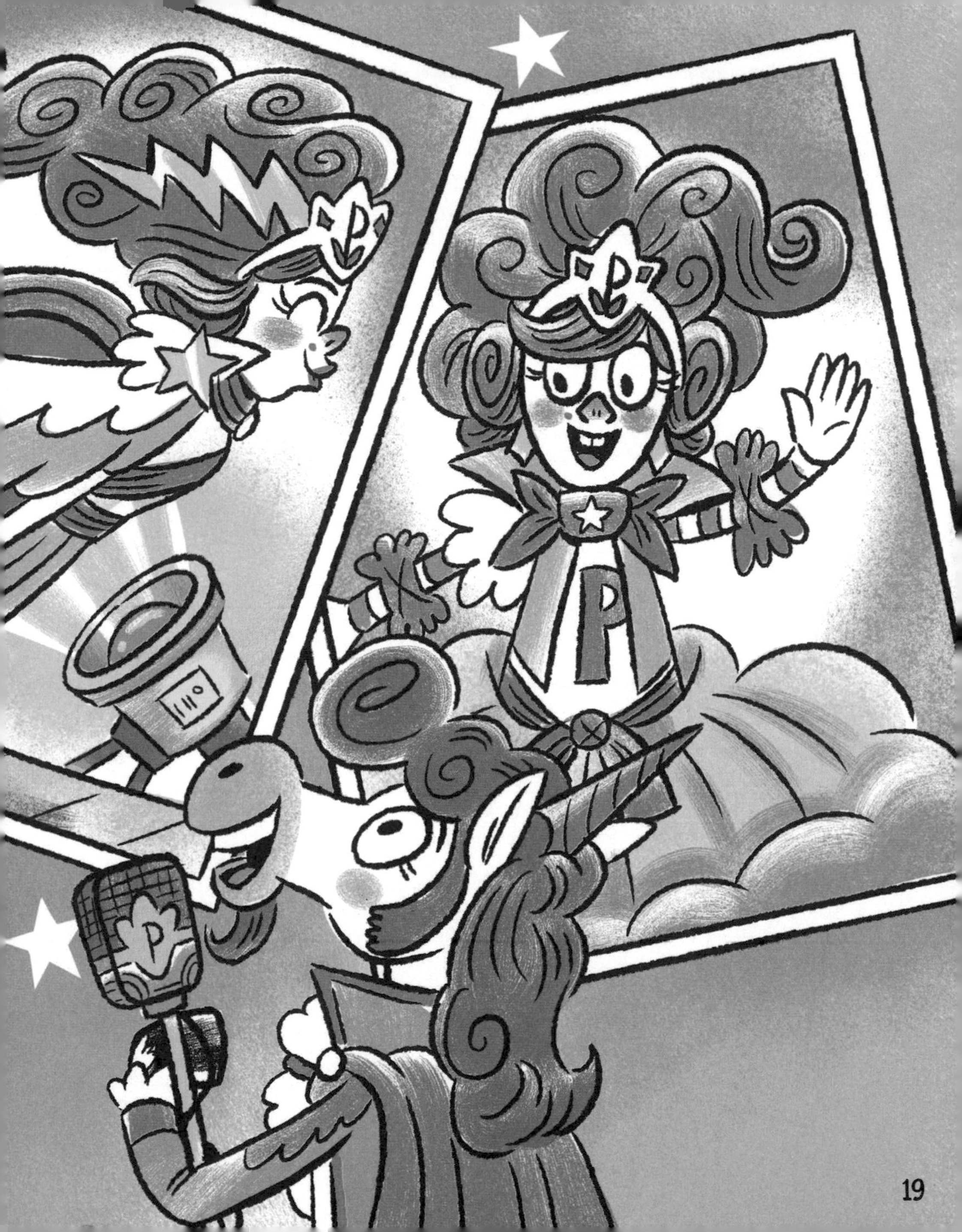

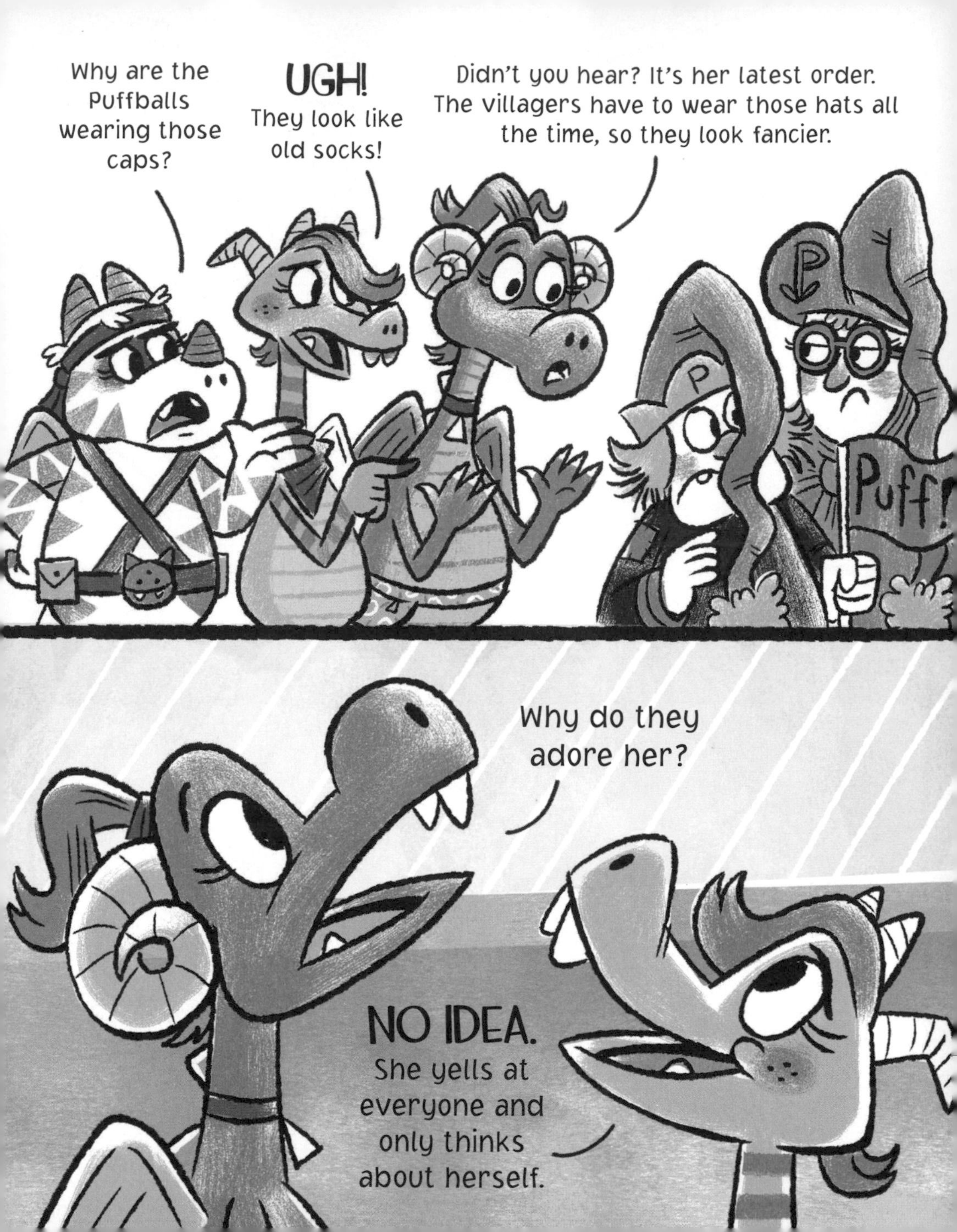
Why are the Puffballs wearing those caps?
UGH! They look like old socks!
Didn't you hear? It's her latest order. The villagers have to wear those hats all the time, so they look fancier.
P
P
Puff!
Why do they adore her?
NO IDEA. She yells at everyone and only thinks about herself.

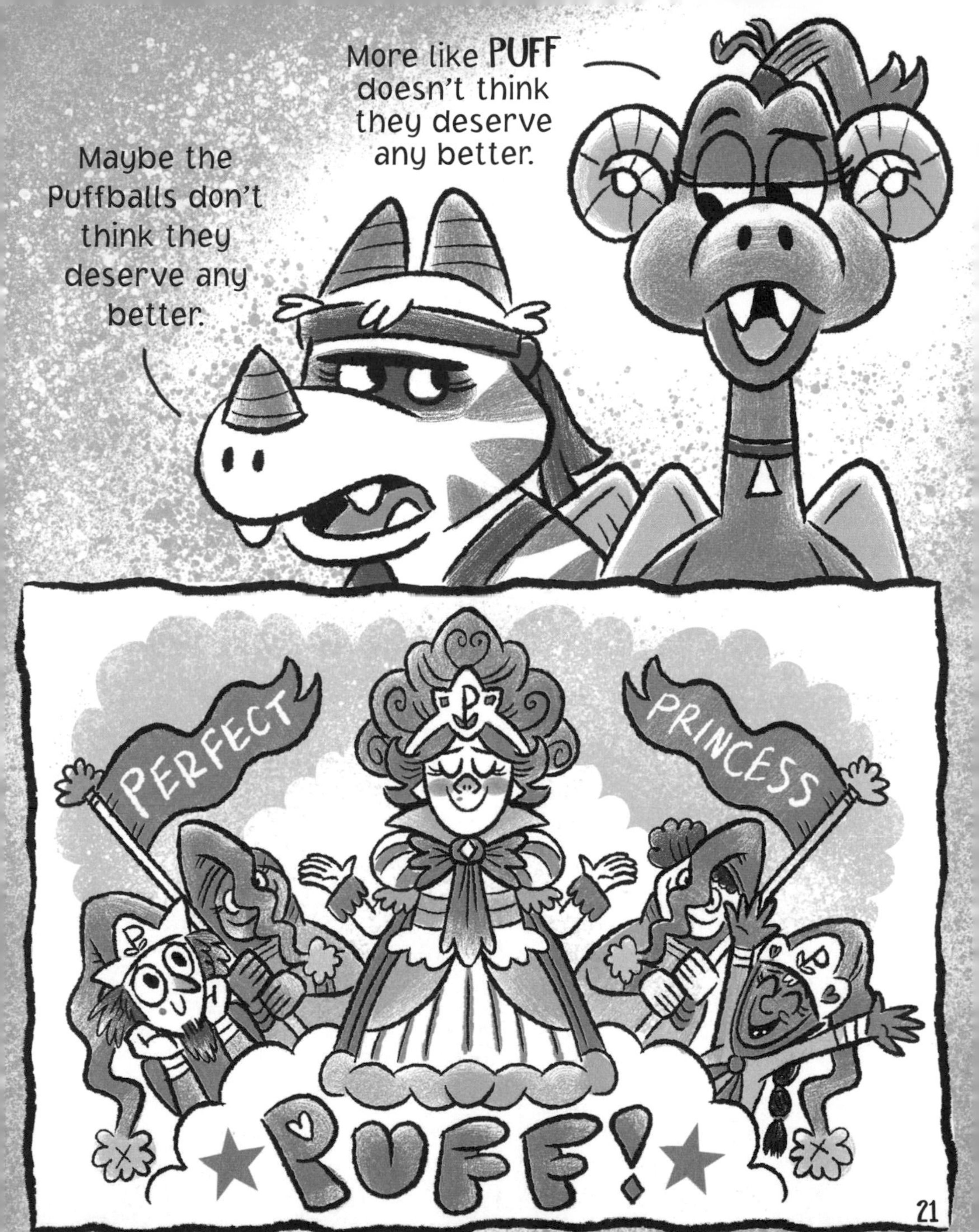
Maybe the Puffballs don't think they deserve any better.
More like PUFF doesn't think they deserve any better.
PERFECT
PRINCESS
PUFF!

CHAPTER TWO
WIGMANIA

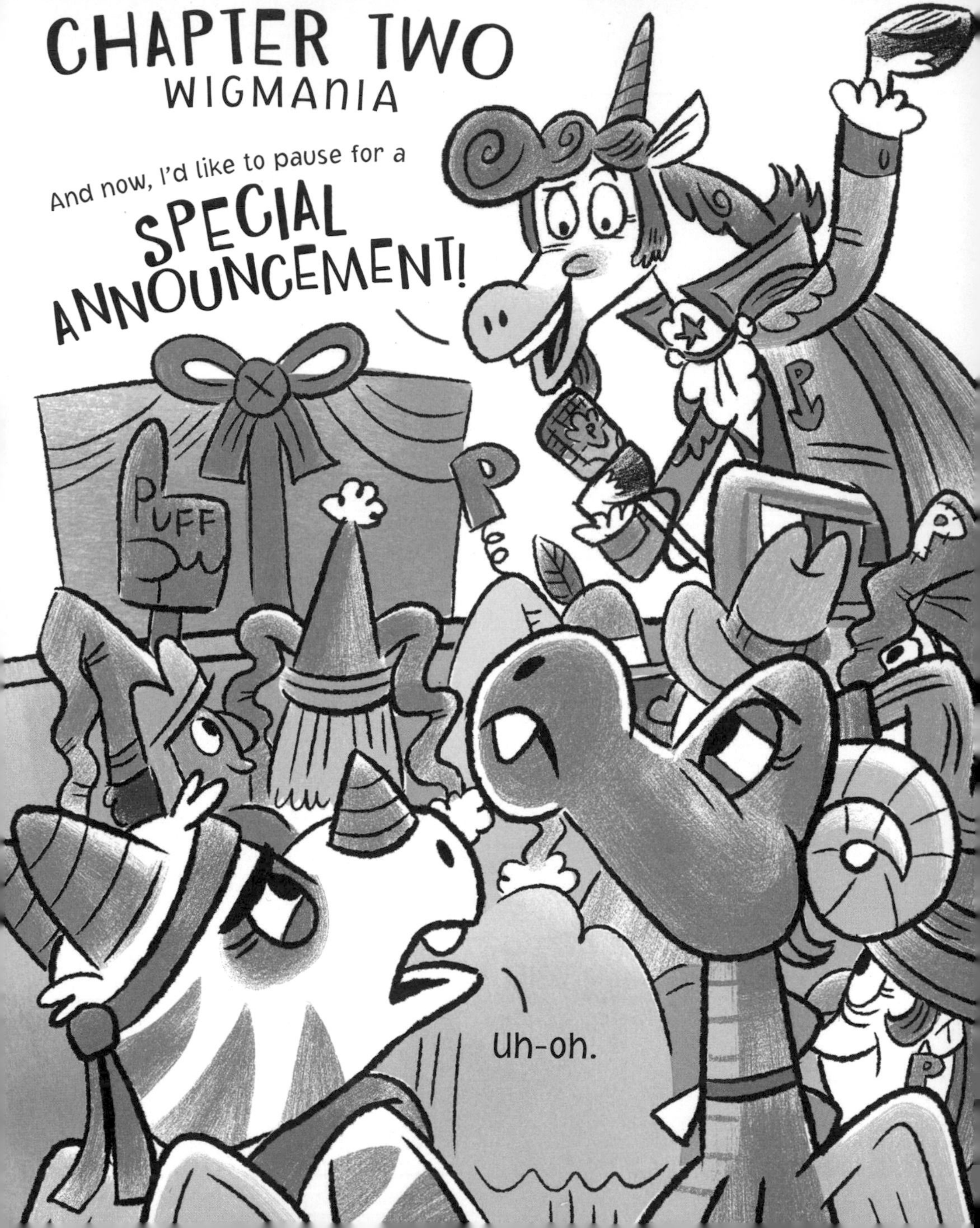
And now, I'd like to pause for a SPECIAL ANNOUNCEMENT!
PUFF
Uh-oh.

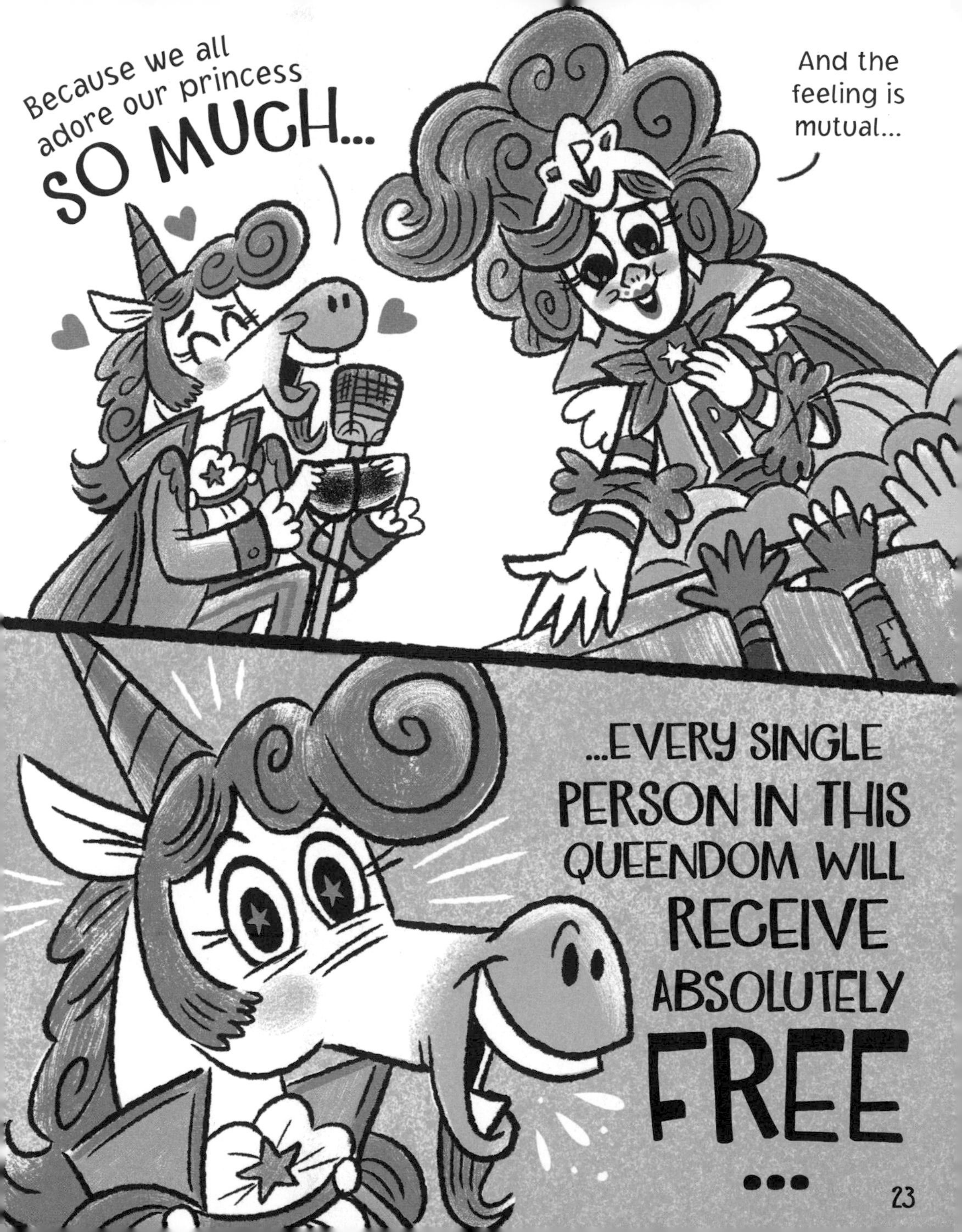
Because we all adore our princess SO MUCH...
And the feeling is mutual...
...EVERY SINGLE PERSON IN THIS QUEENDOM WILL RECEIVE ABSOLUTELY FREE
...

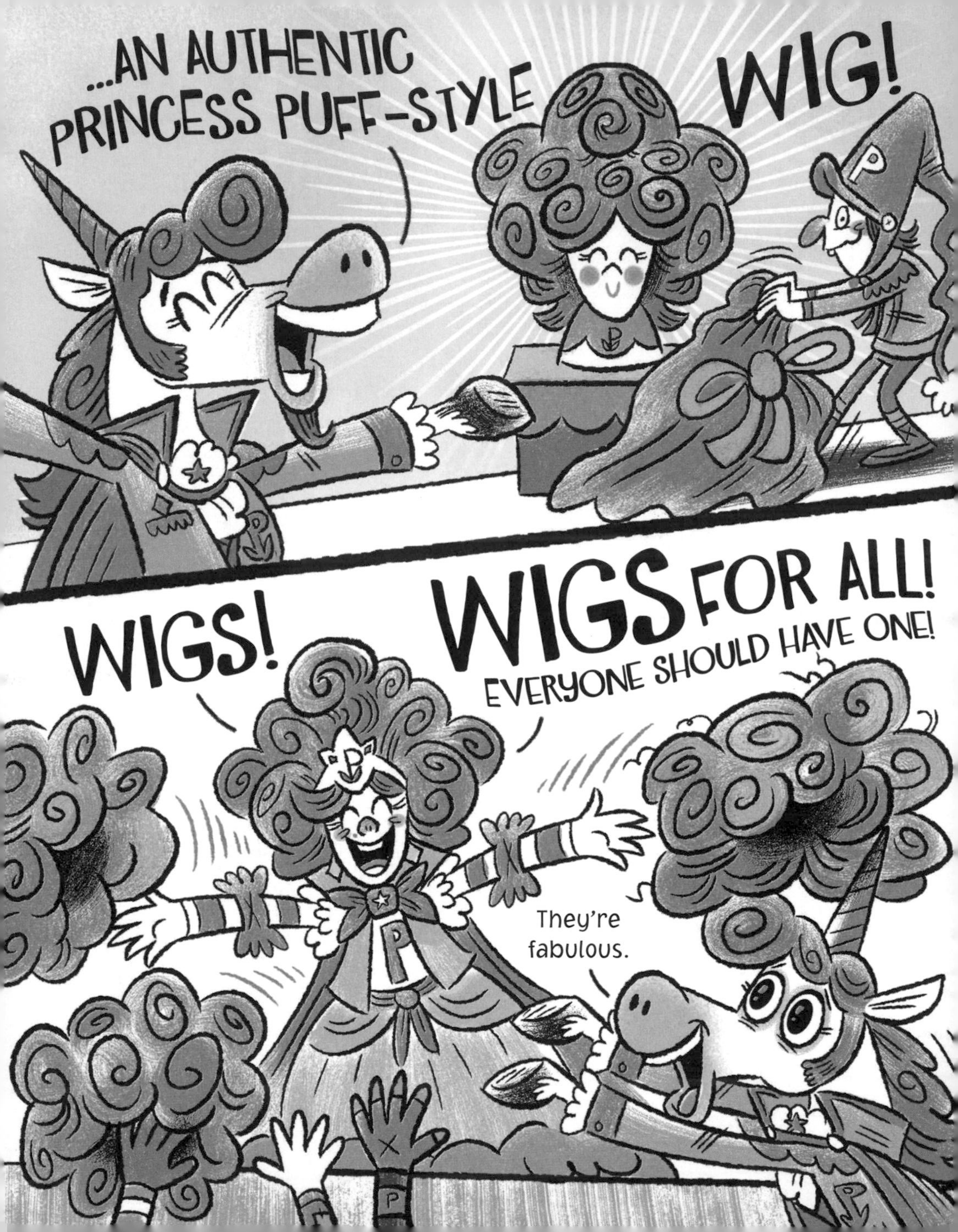
...AN AUTHENTIC PRINCESS PUFF-STYLE WIG!
WIGS! WIGS FOR ALL! EVERYONE SHOULD HAVE ONE!
They're fabulous.

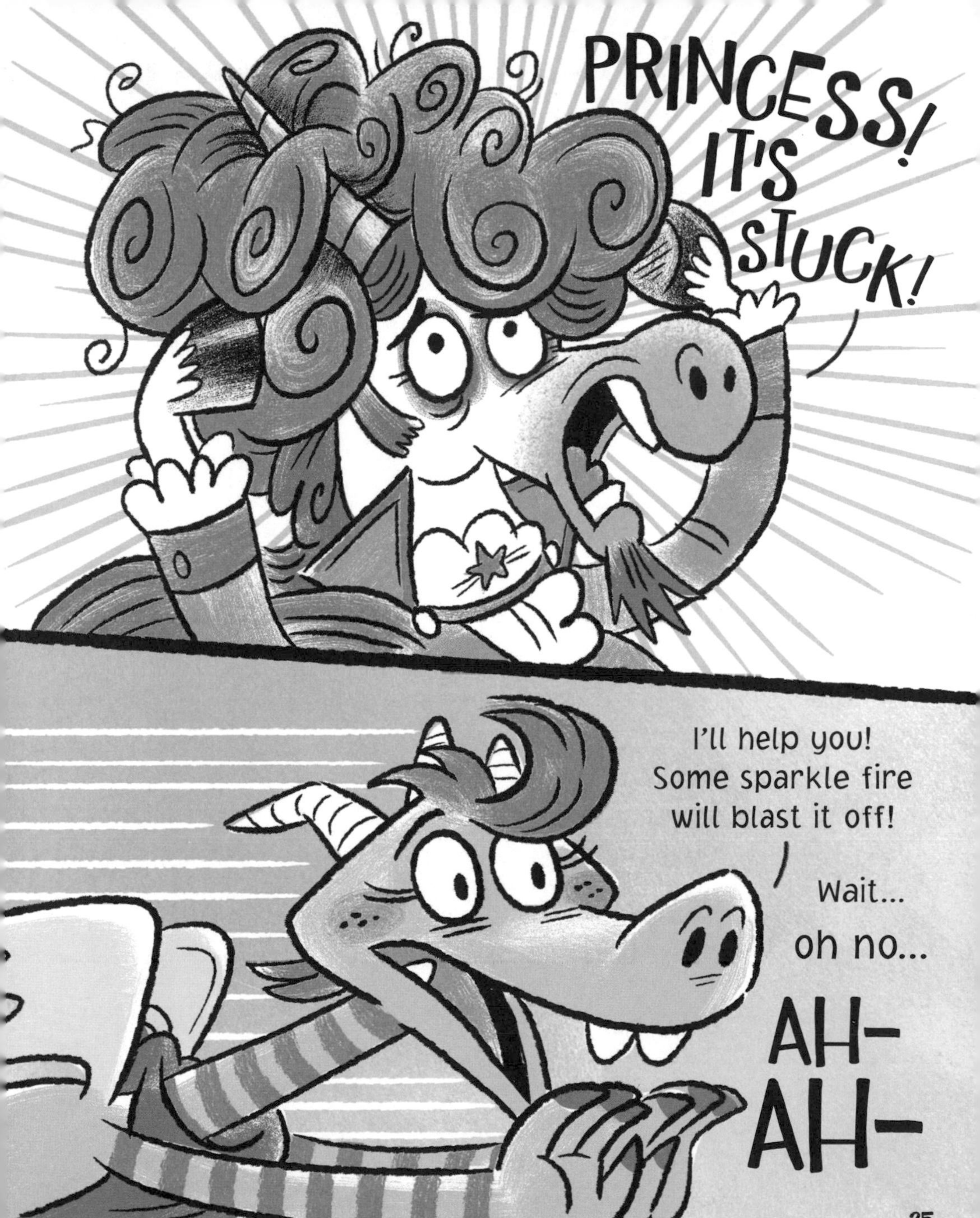
PRINCESS! IT'S STUCK!
I'll help you! Some sparkle fire will blast it off!
Wait... oh no...
AH-AH-

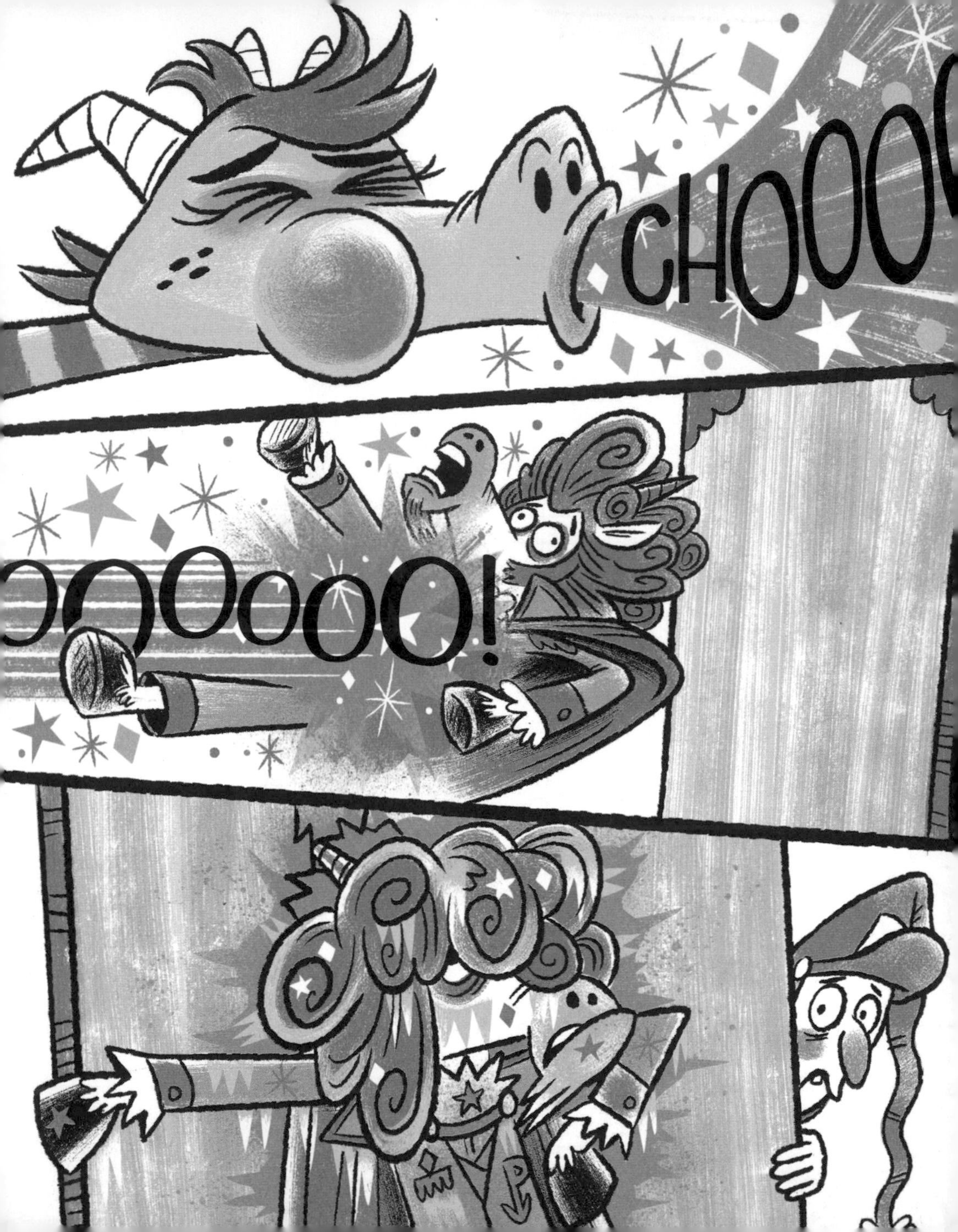
CHOOOO
OOOOOO!

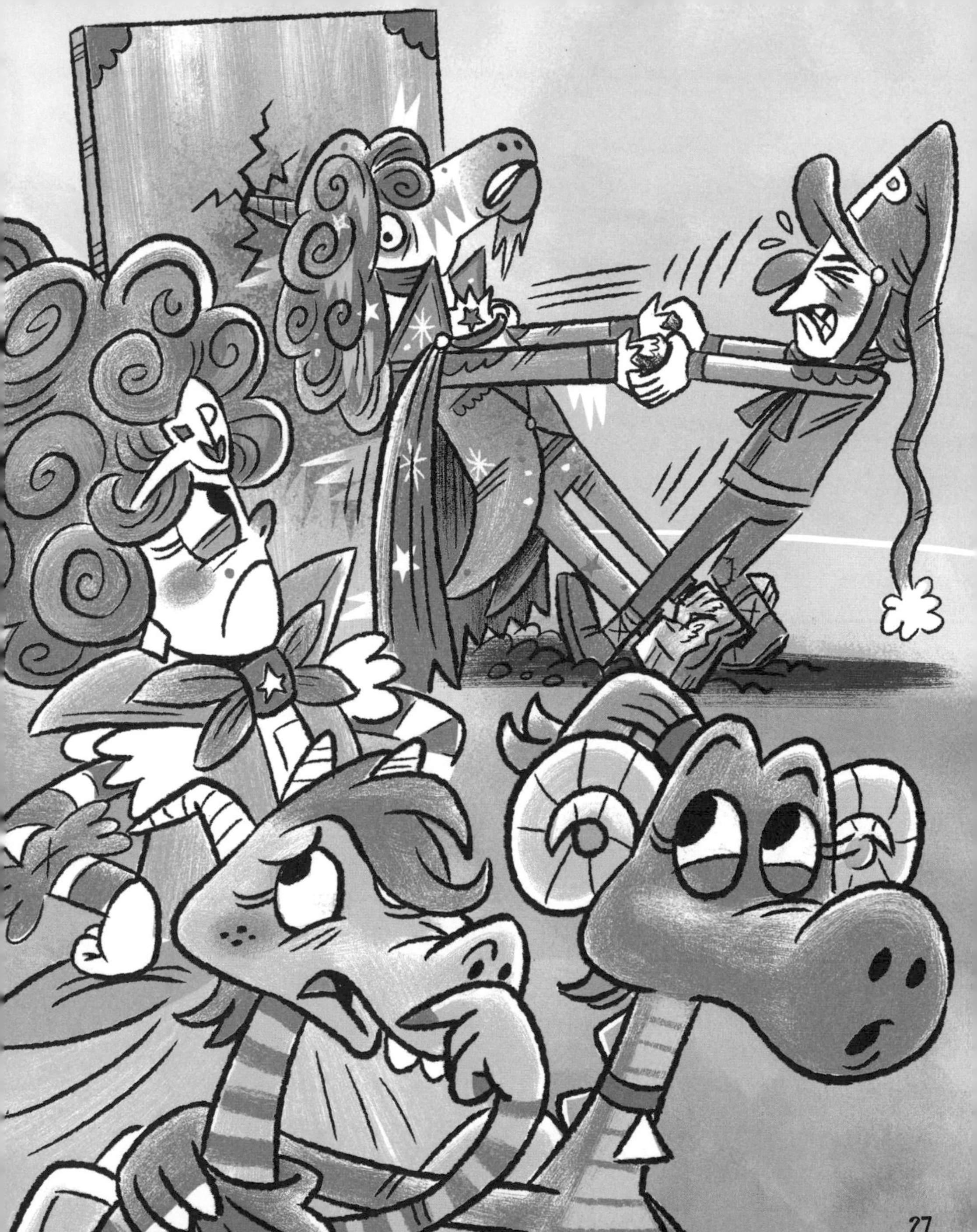

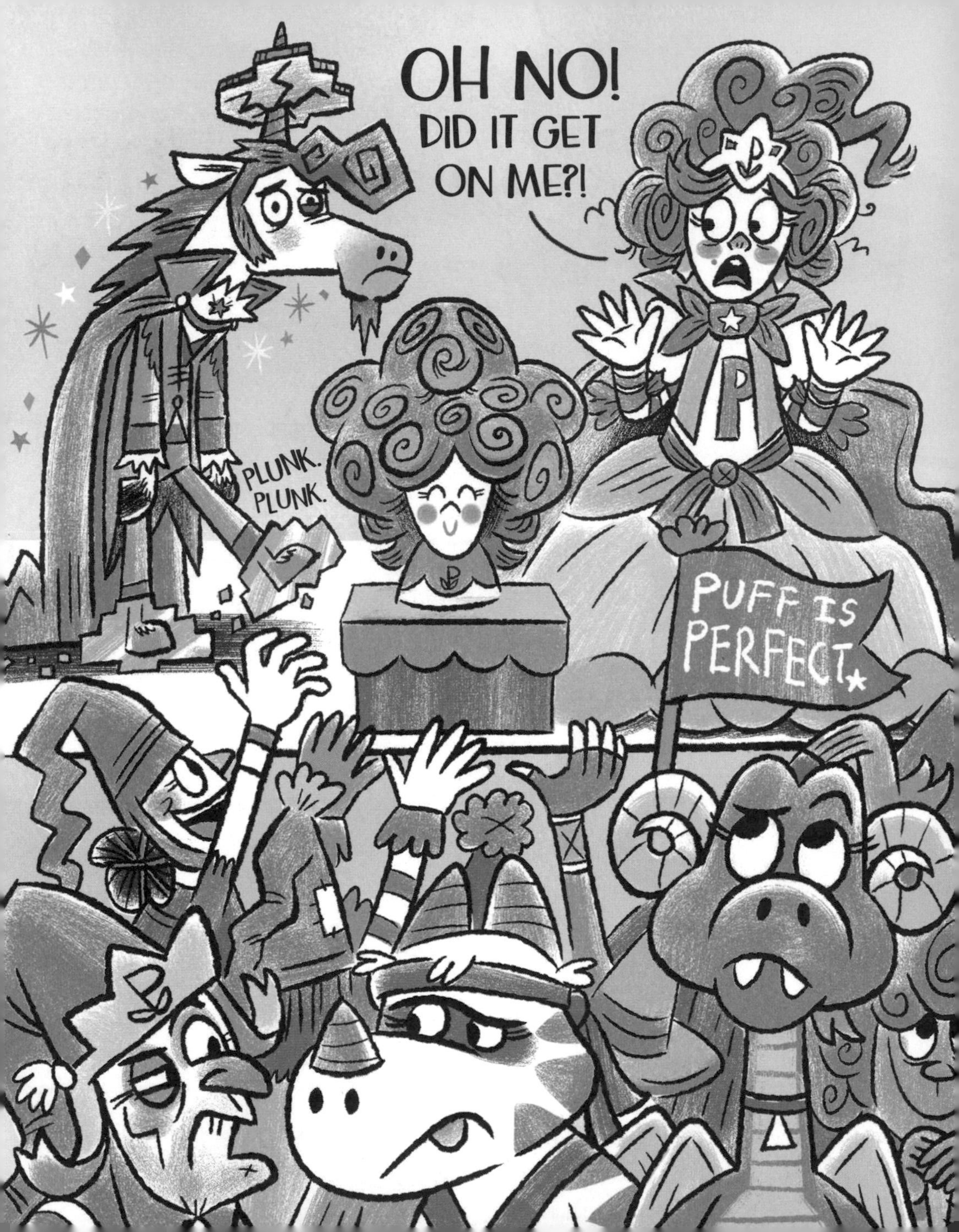
OH NO!
DID IT GET
ON ME?!
PLUNK.
PLUNK.
PUFF IS
PERFECT.

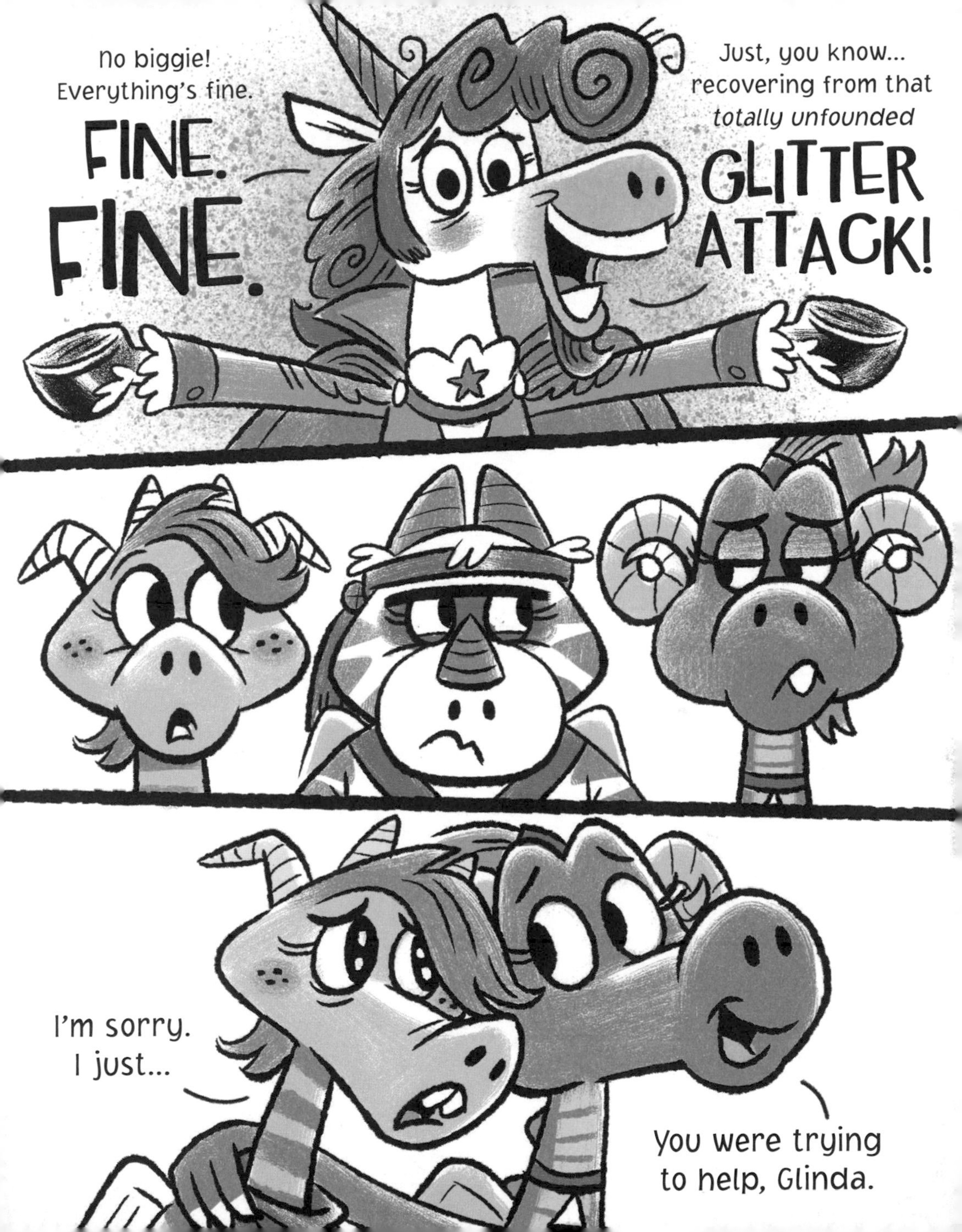
No biggie!
Everything's fine.
FINE. FINE.
Just, you know...
recovering from that
totally unfounded
GLITTER ATTACK!
I'm sorry.
I just...
You were trying
to help, Glinda.

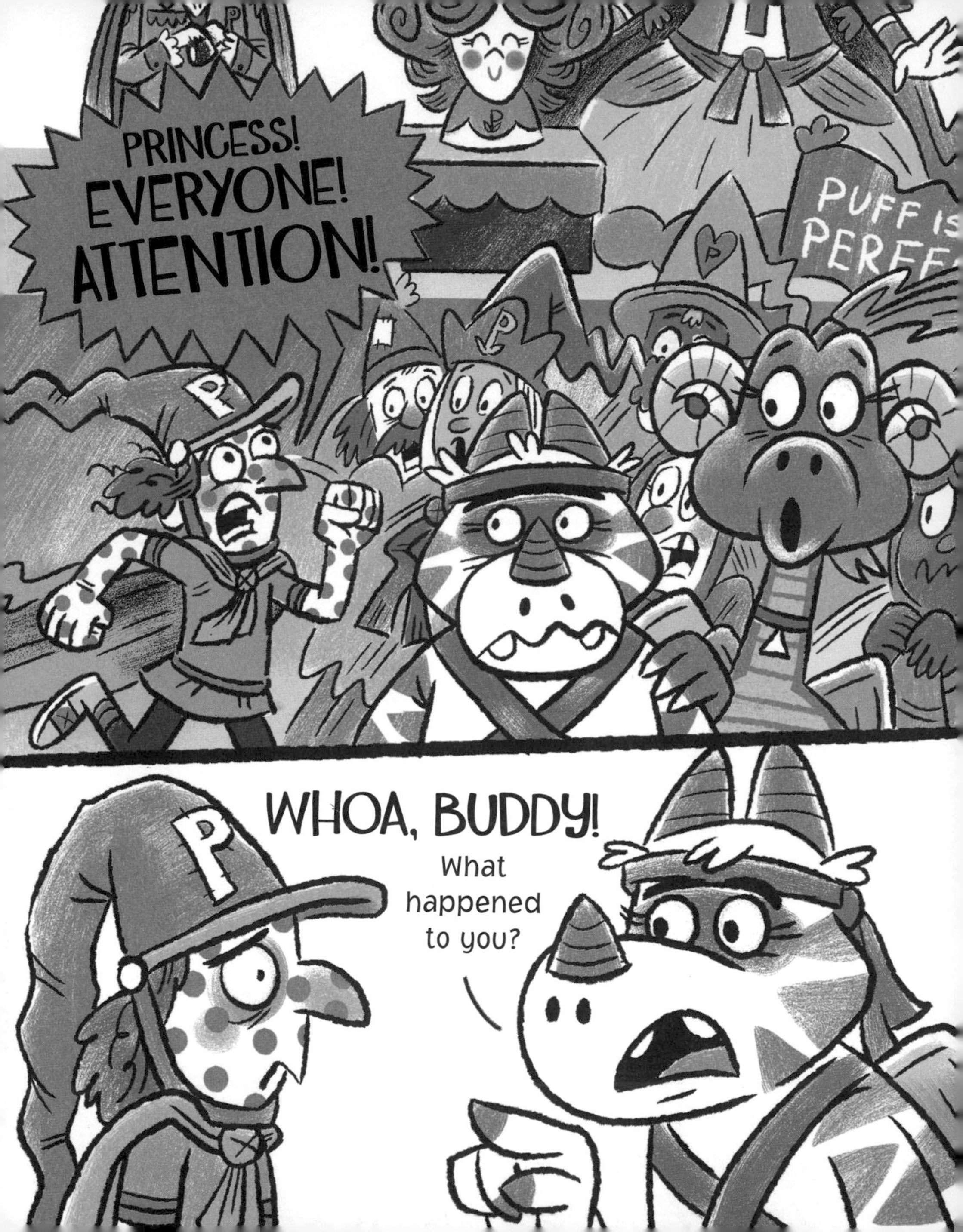
PRINCESS! EVERYONE! ATTENTION!
PUFF IS
WHOA, BUDDY!
What happened to you?

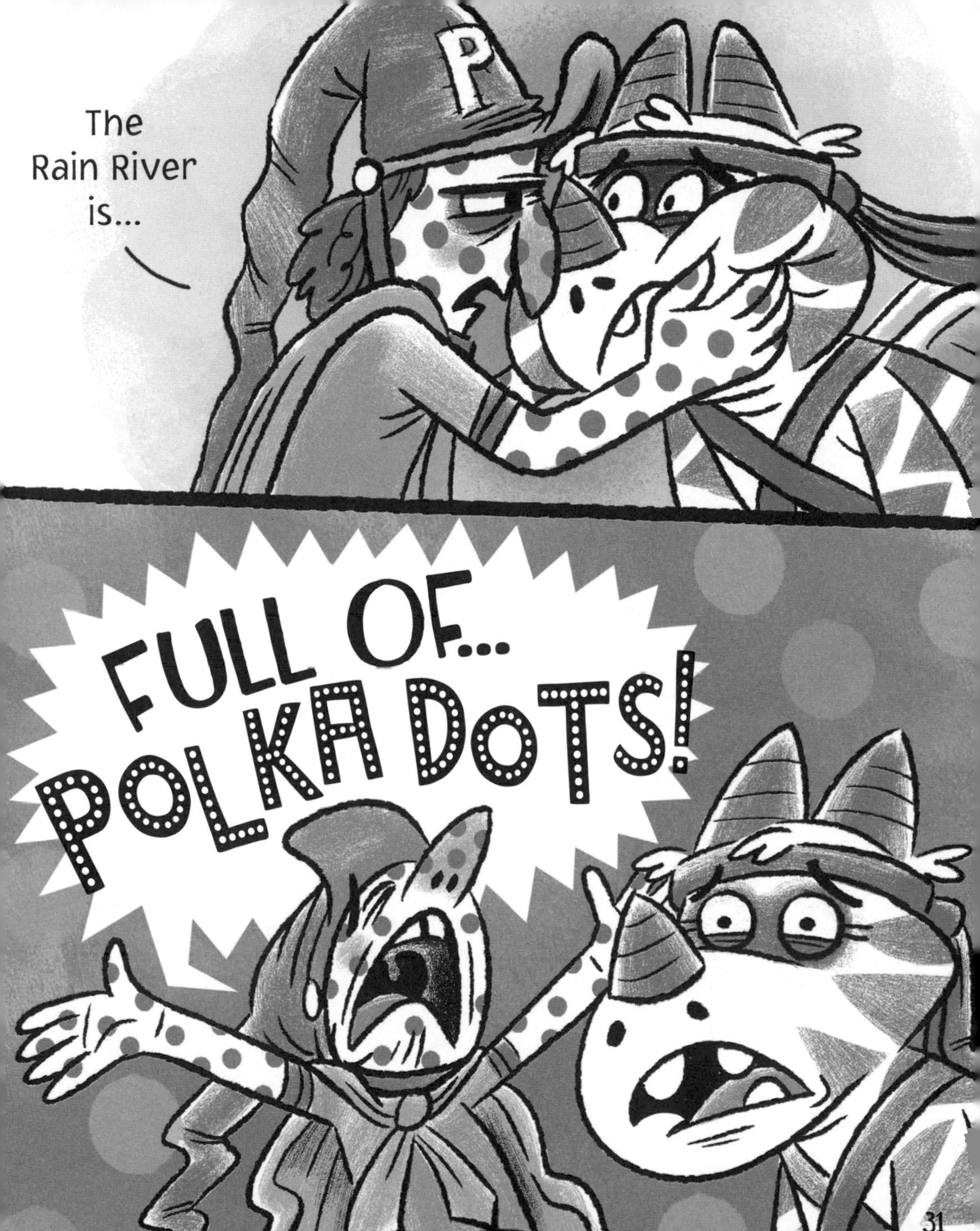
The Rain River is...
FULL OF... POLKA DOTS!

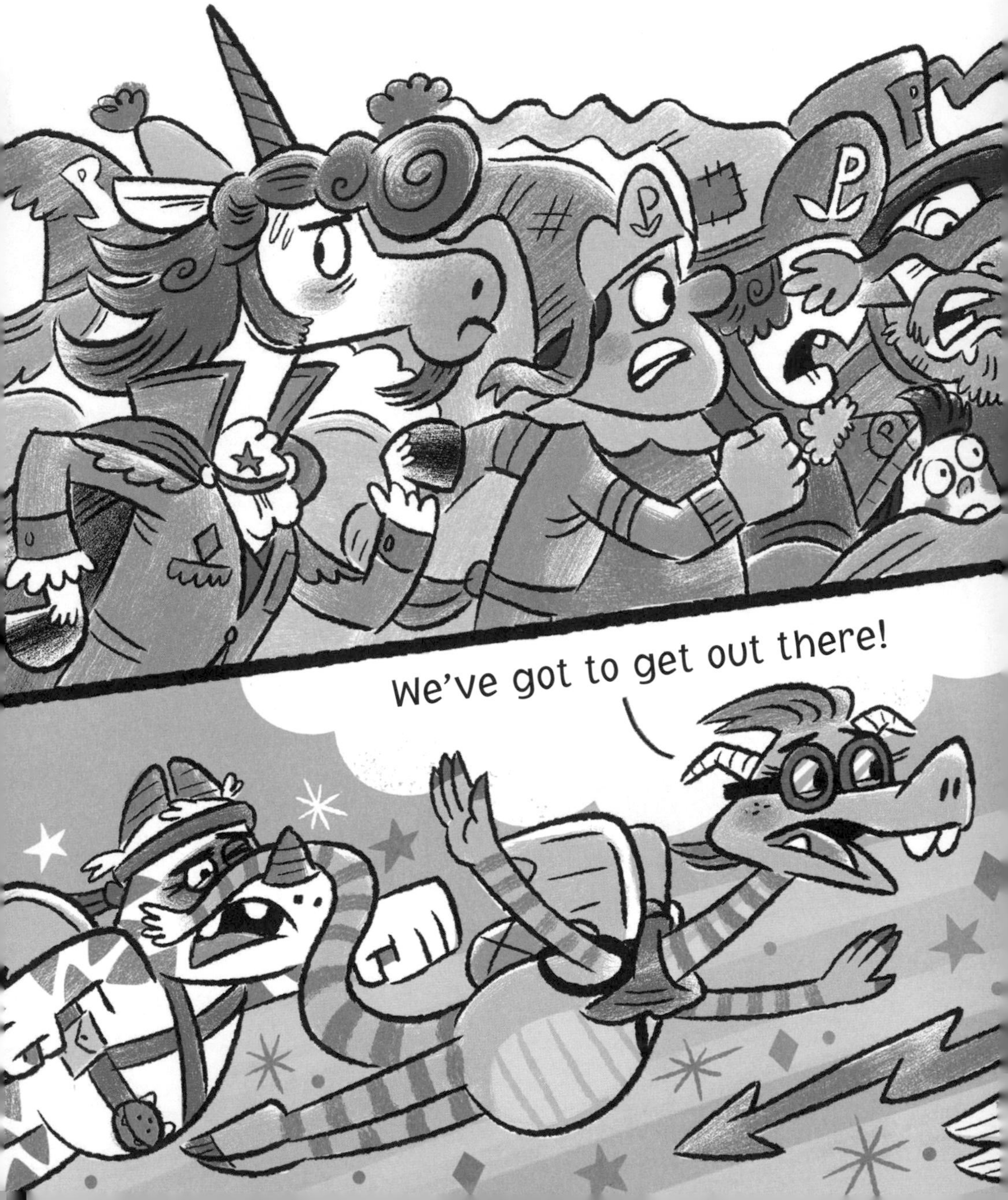
We've got to get out there!

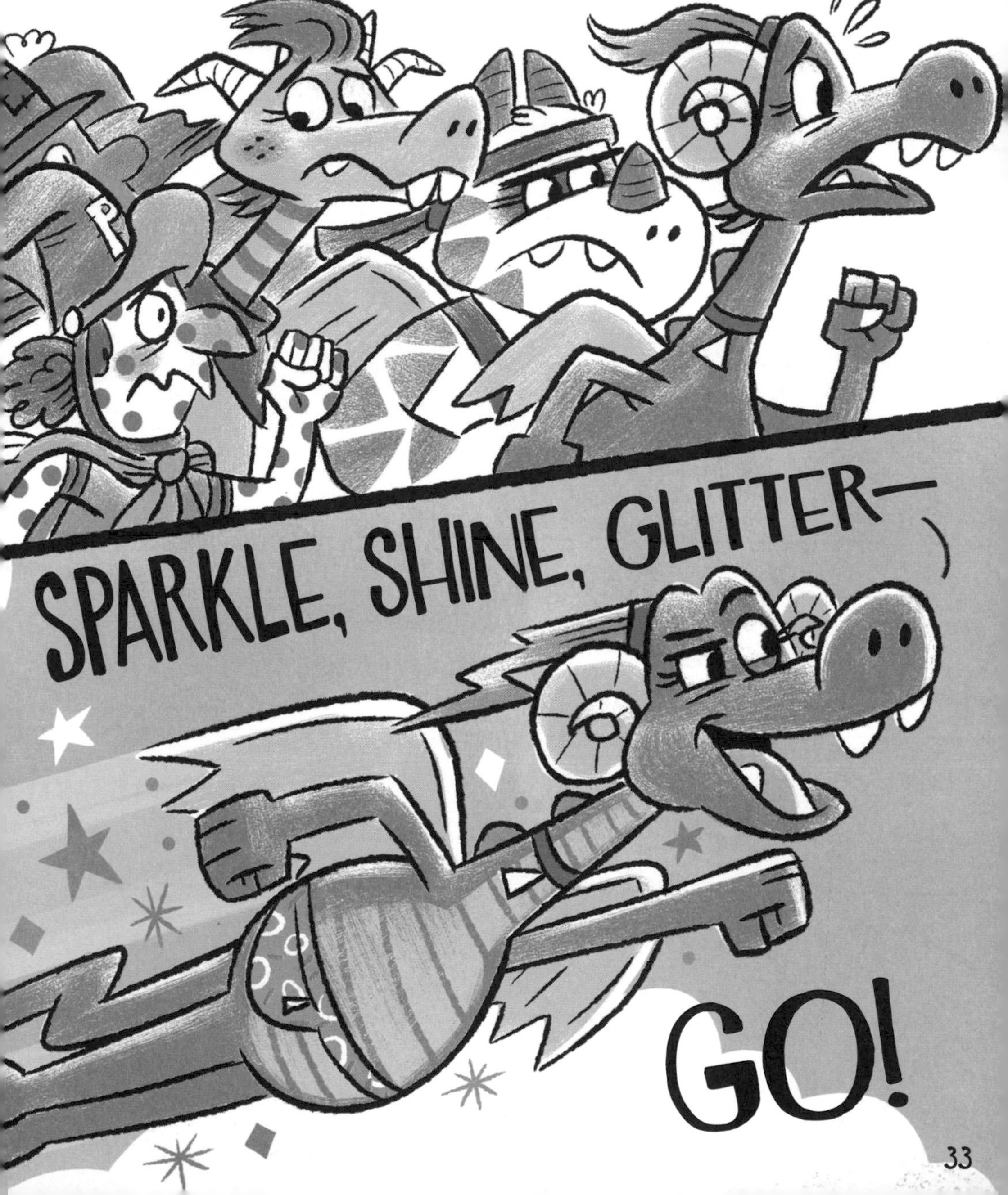
SPARKLE, SHINE, GLITTER—
GO!

CHAPTER THREE
DOTS, DOTS EVERYWHERE

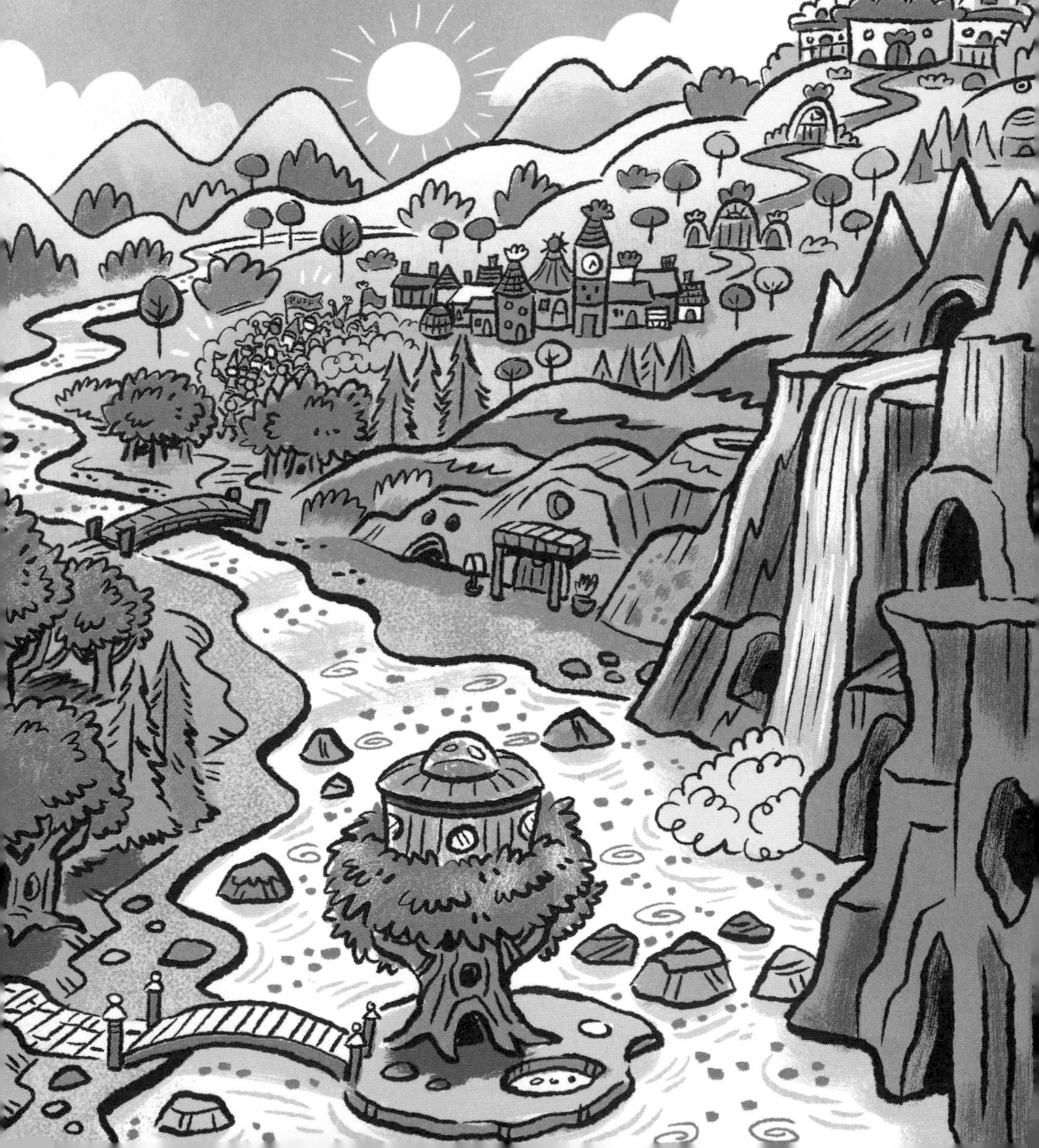

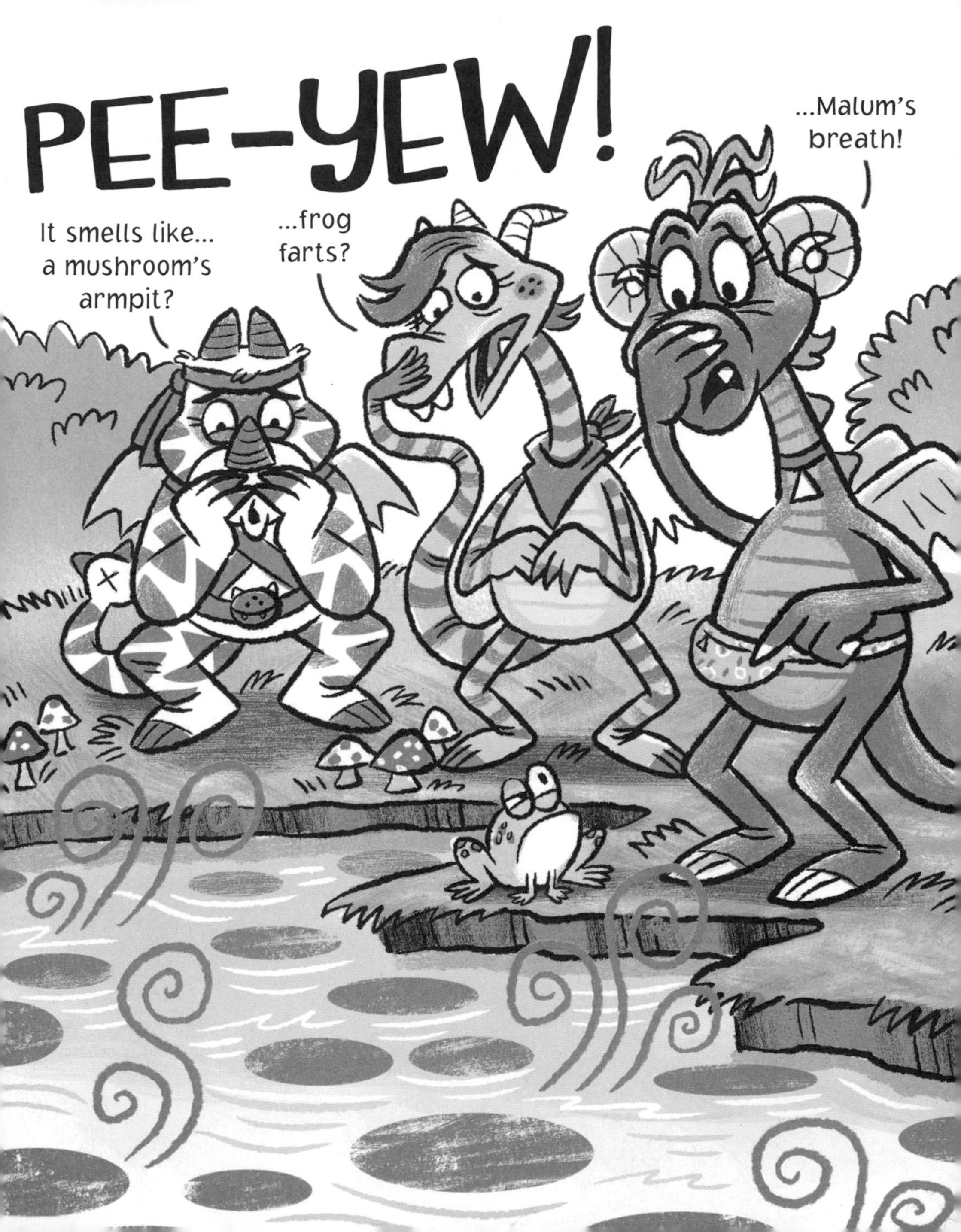
PEE-YEW!
It smells like... a mushroom's armpit?
...frog farts?
...Malum's breath!

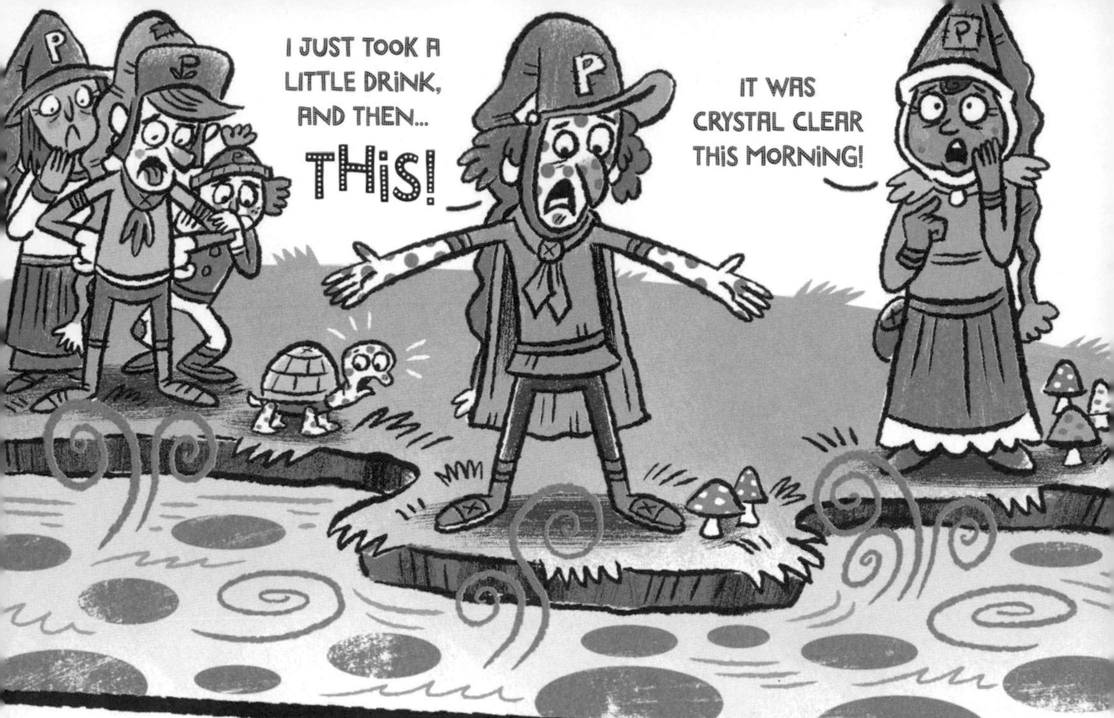
I JUST TOOK A LITTLE DRINK, AND THEN... THIS!
IT WAS CRYSTAL CLEAR THIS MORNING!

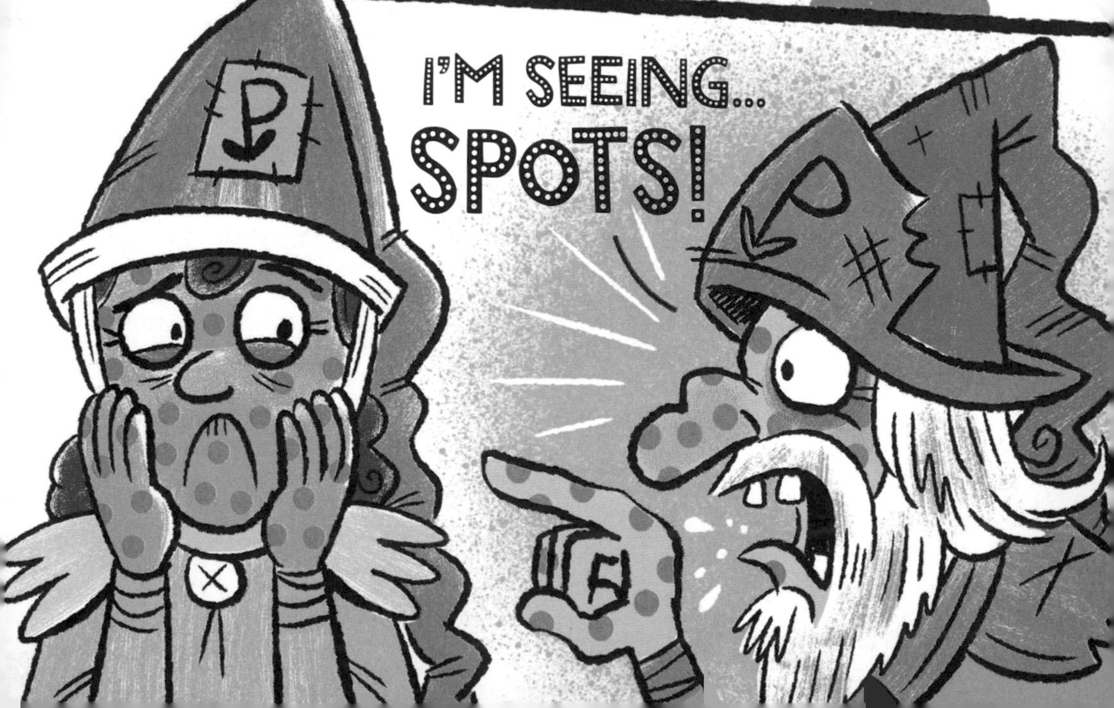
I'M SEEING... SPOTS!

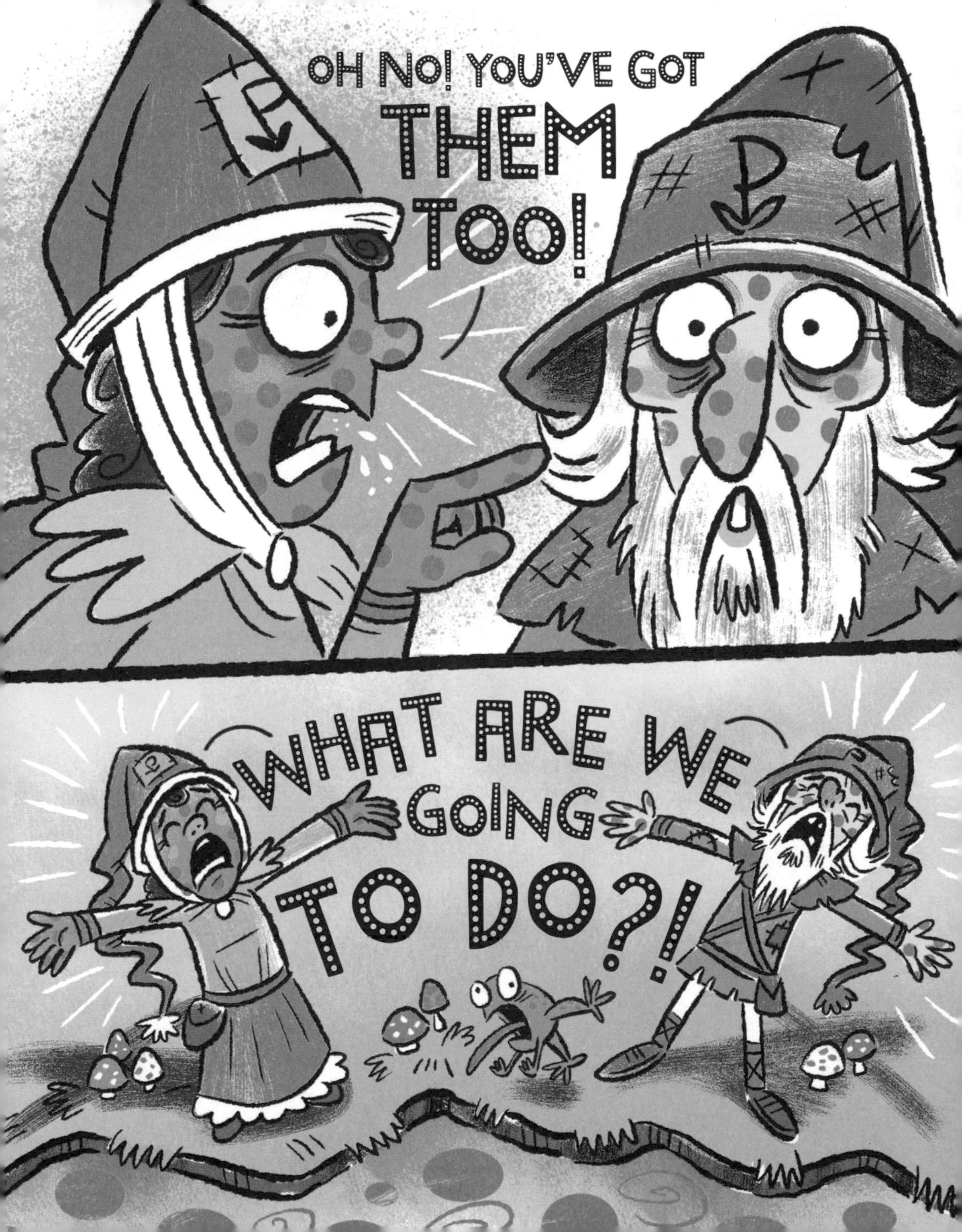
OH NO! YOU'VE GOT THEM TOO!
WHAT ARE WE GOING TO DO?!

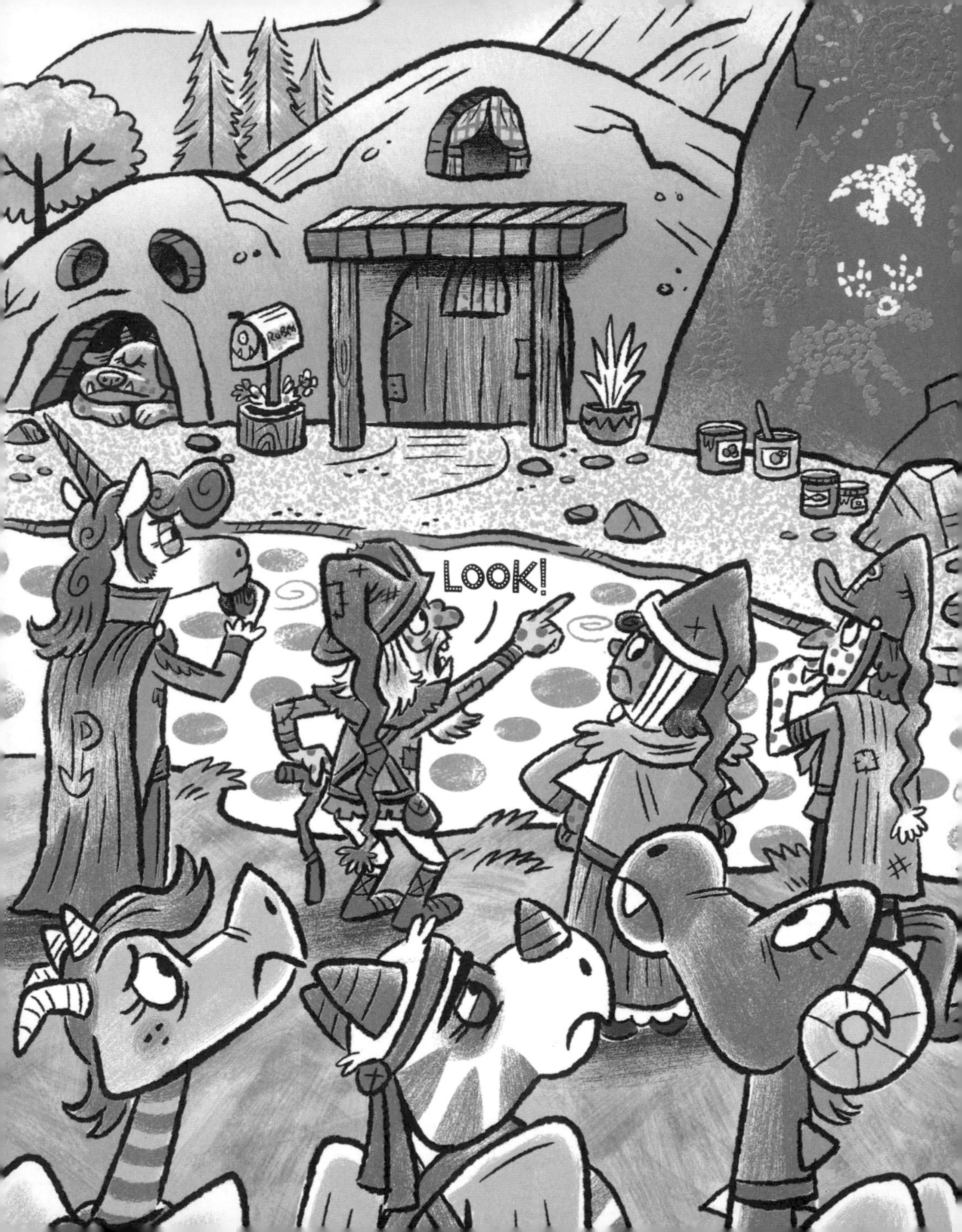
LOOK!

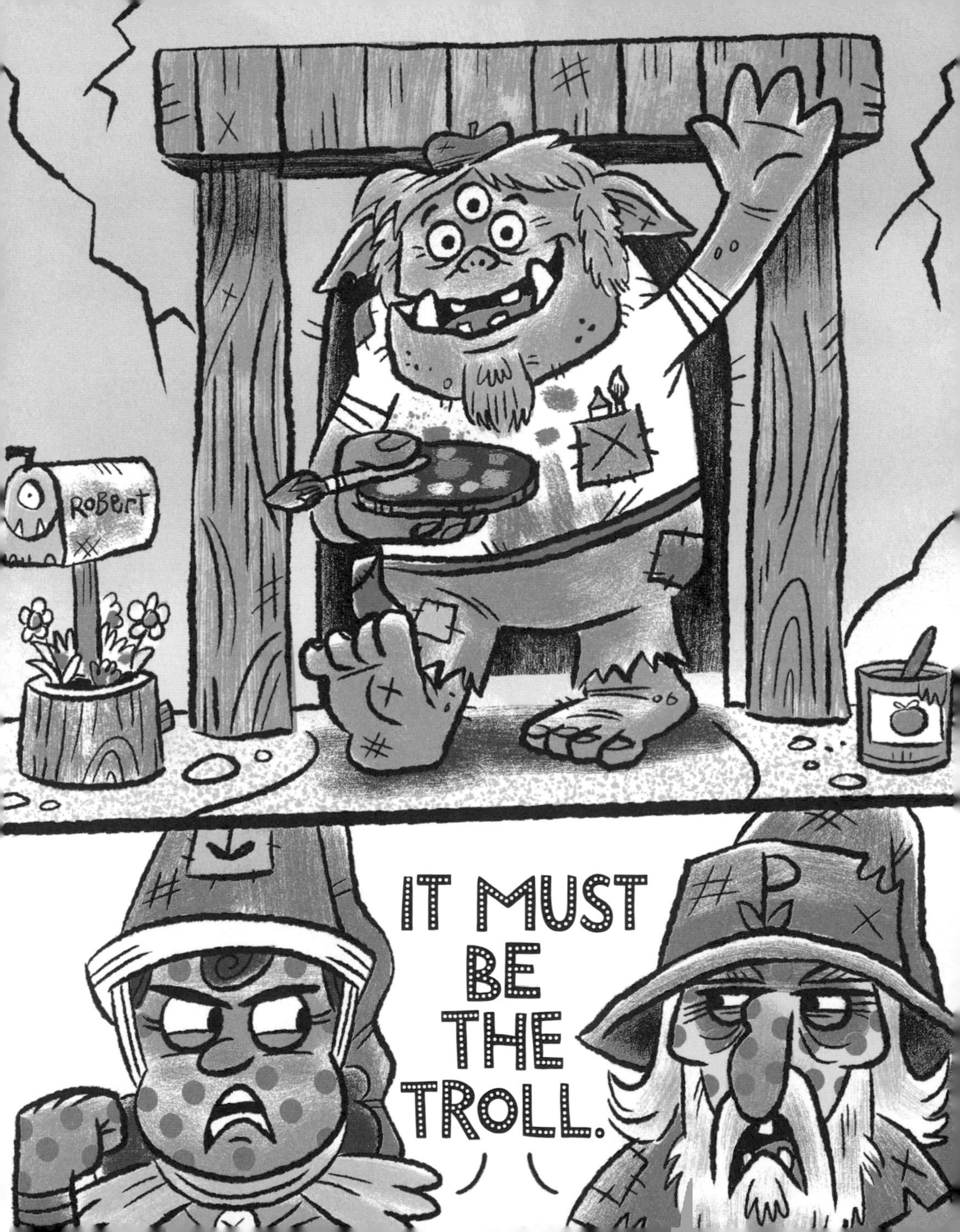
ROBERT
IT MUST BE THE TROLL.

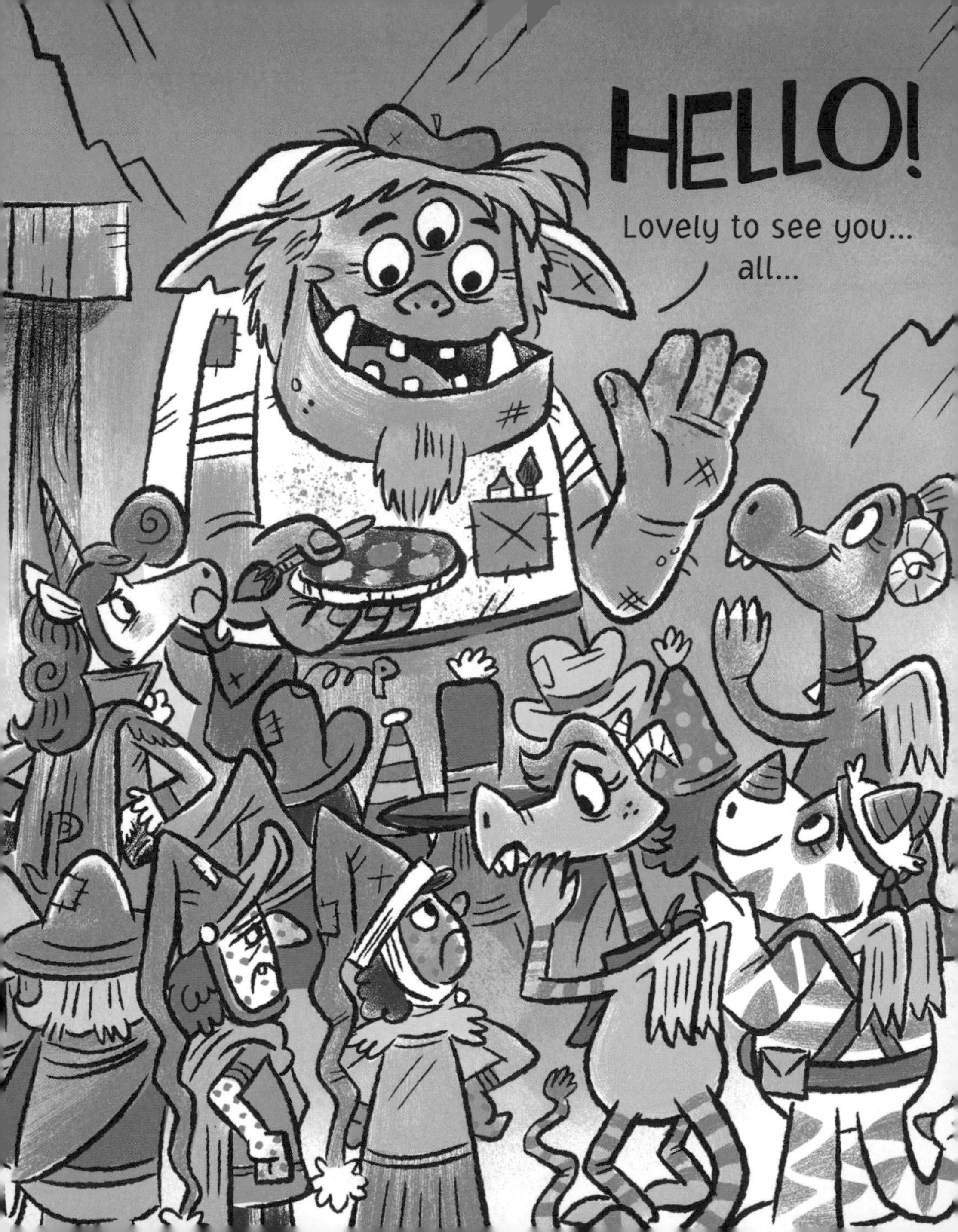
HELLO!
Lovely to see you...
all...

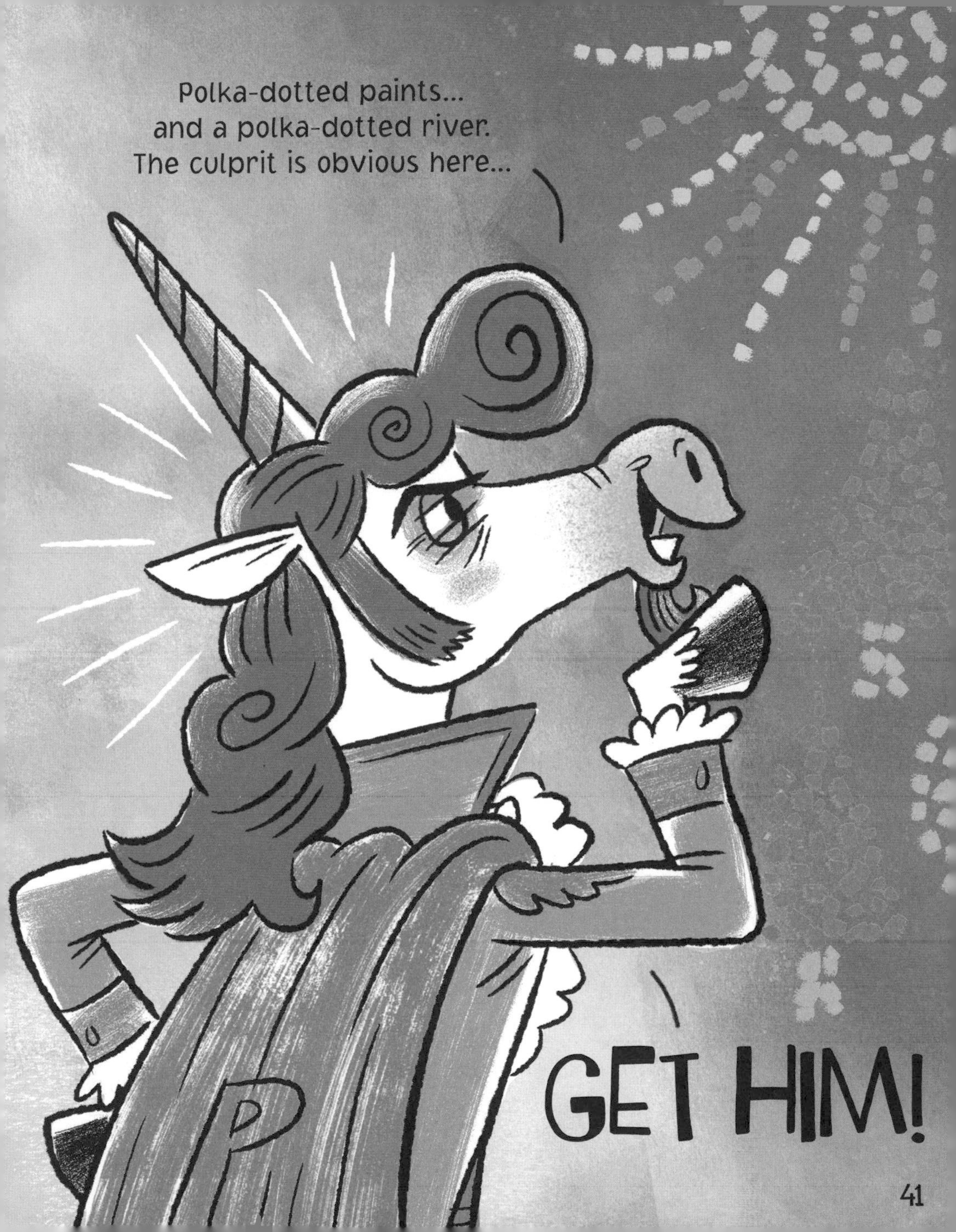
Polka-dotted paints...
and a polka-dotted river.
The culprit is obvious here...
GET HIM!

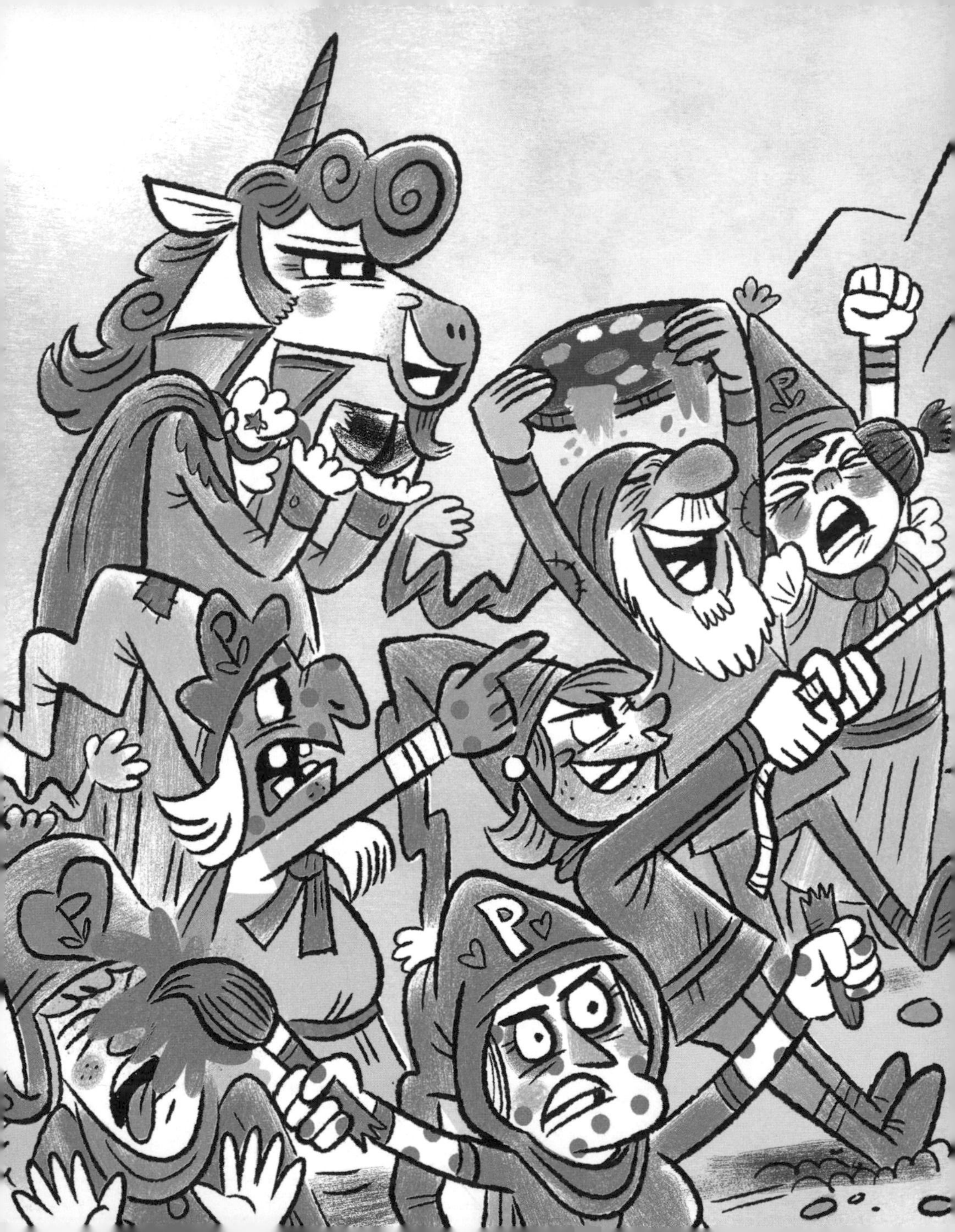
P
P
P
P

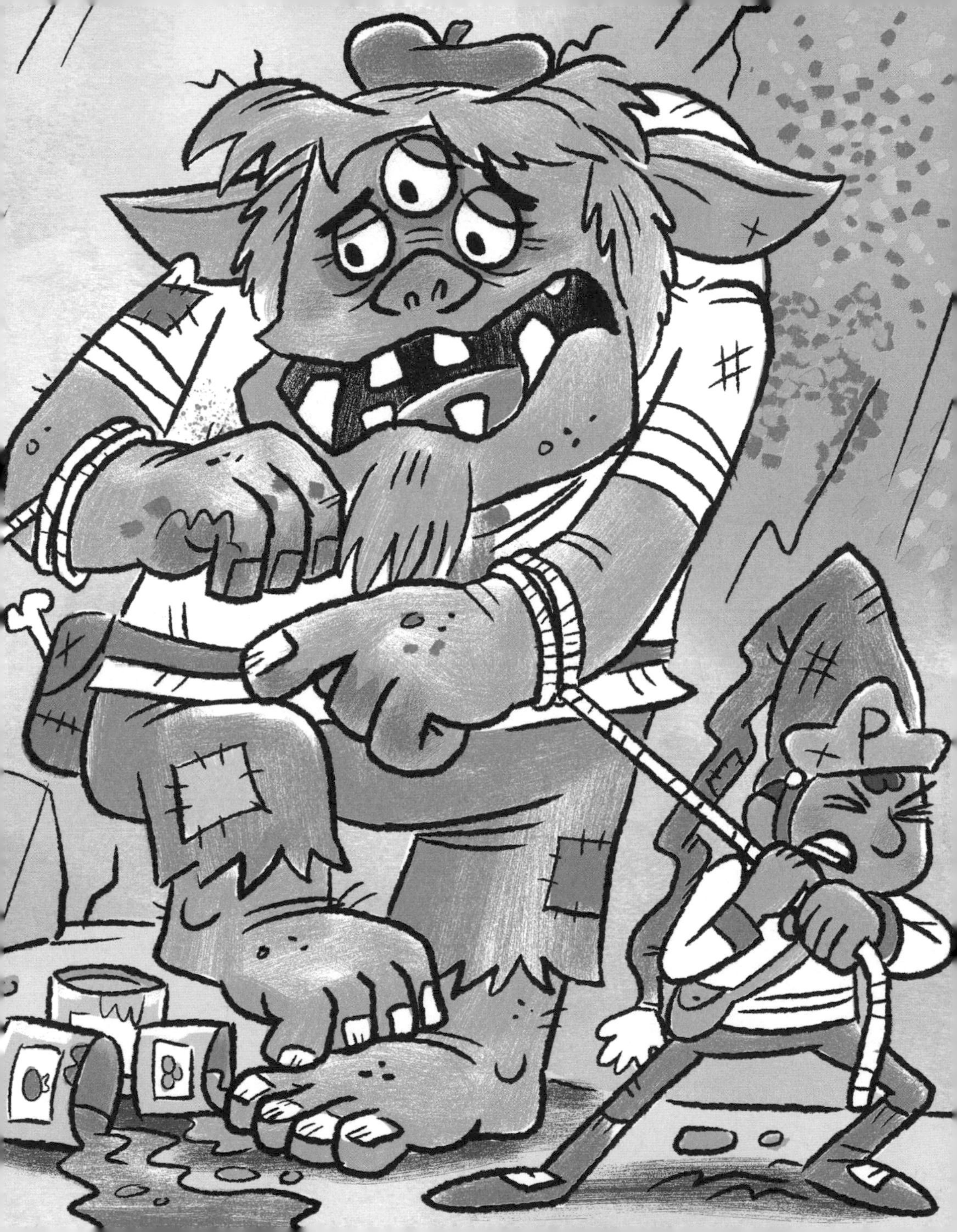
P

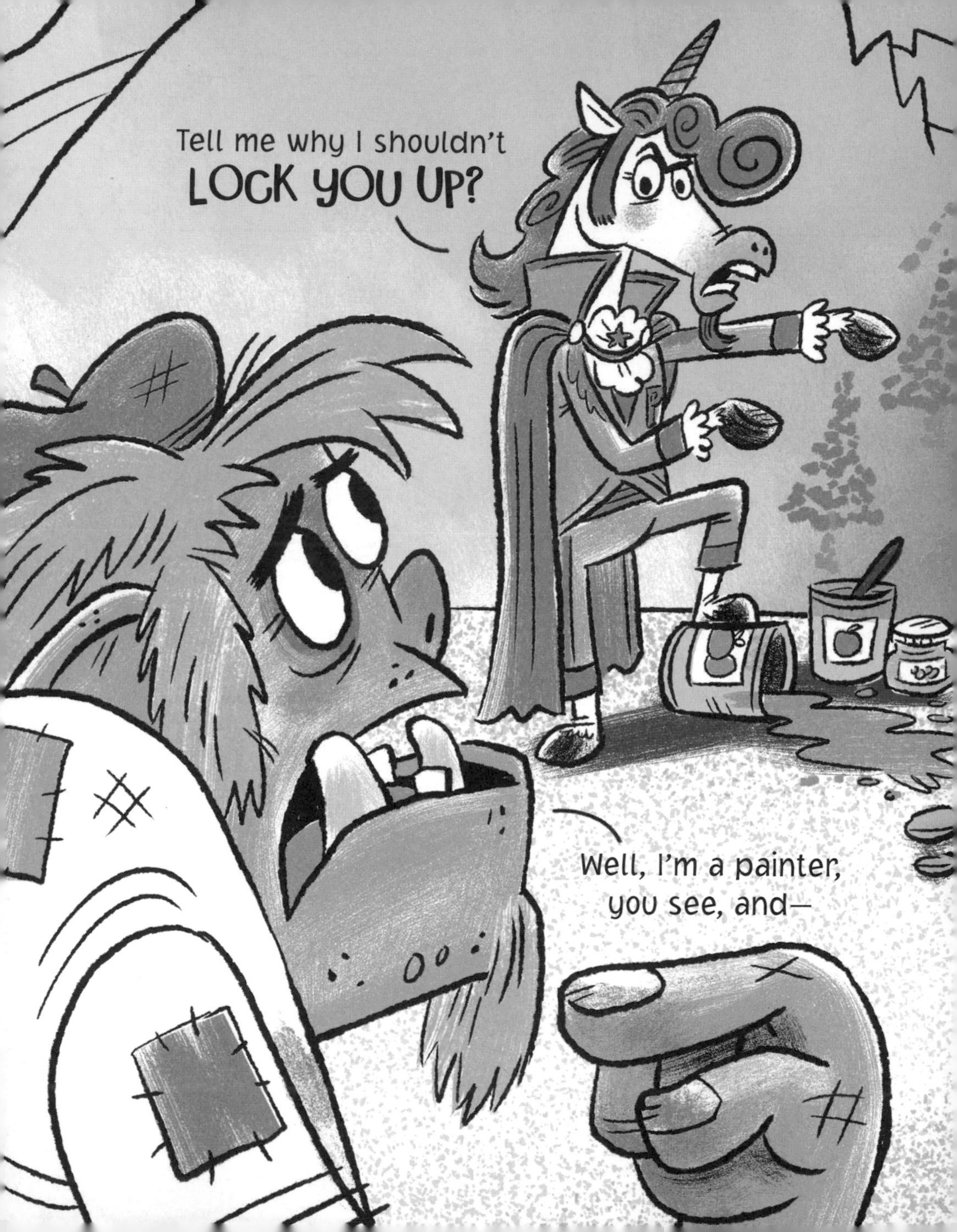
Tell me why I shouldn't
LOCK YOU UP?
Well, I'm a painter,
you see, and—

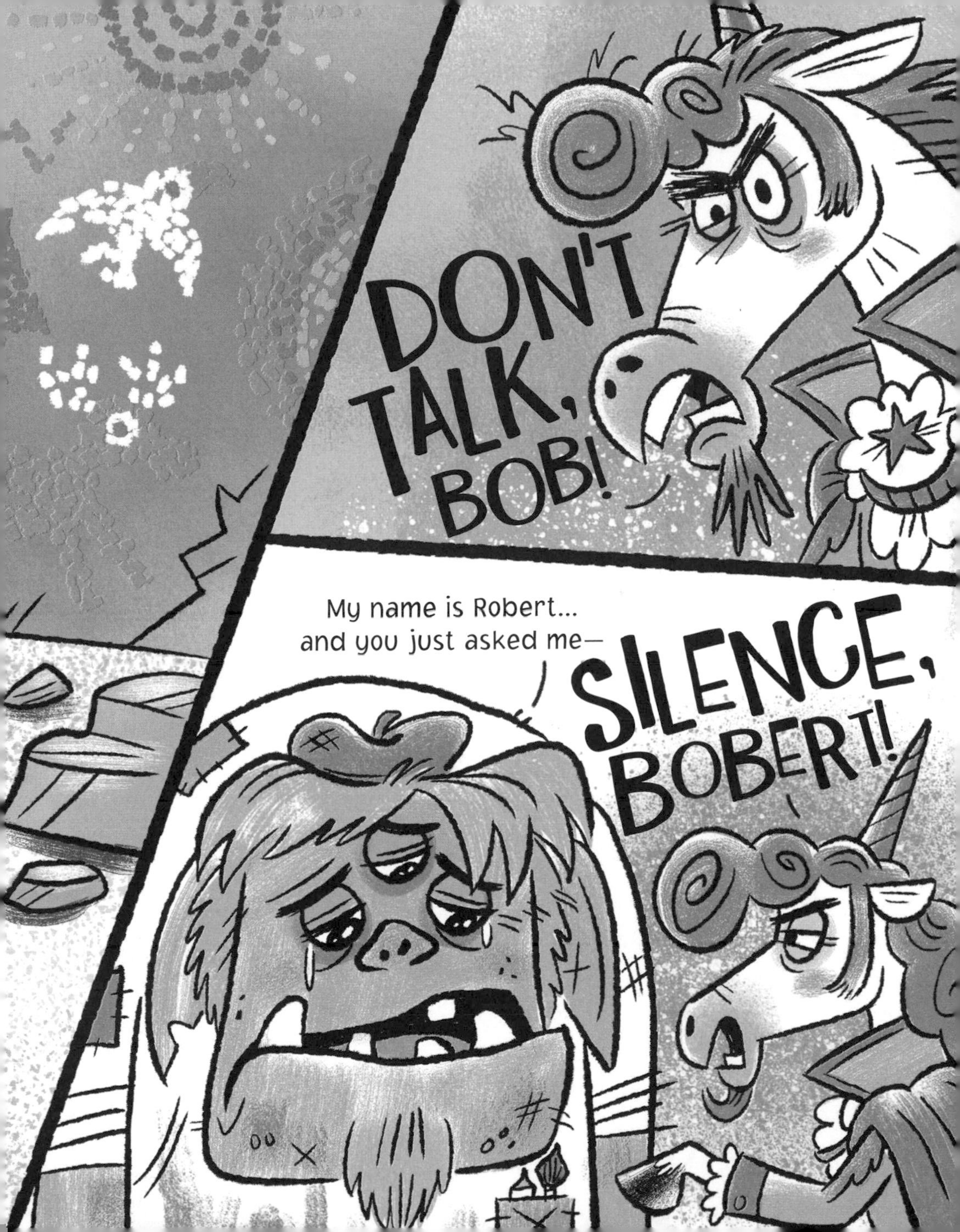
DON'T TALK, BOB!
My name is Robert... and you just asked me—
SILENCE, BOBERT!

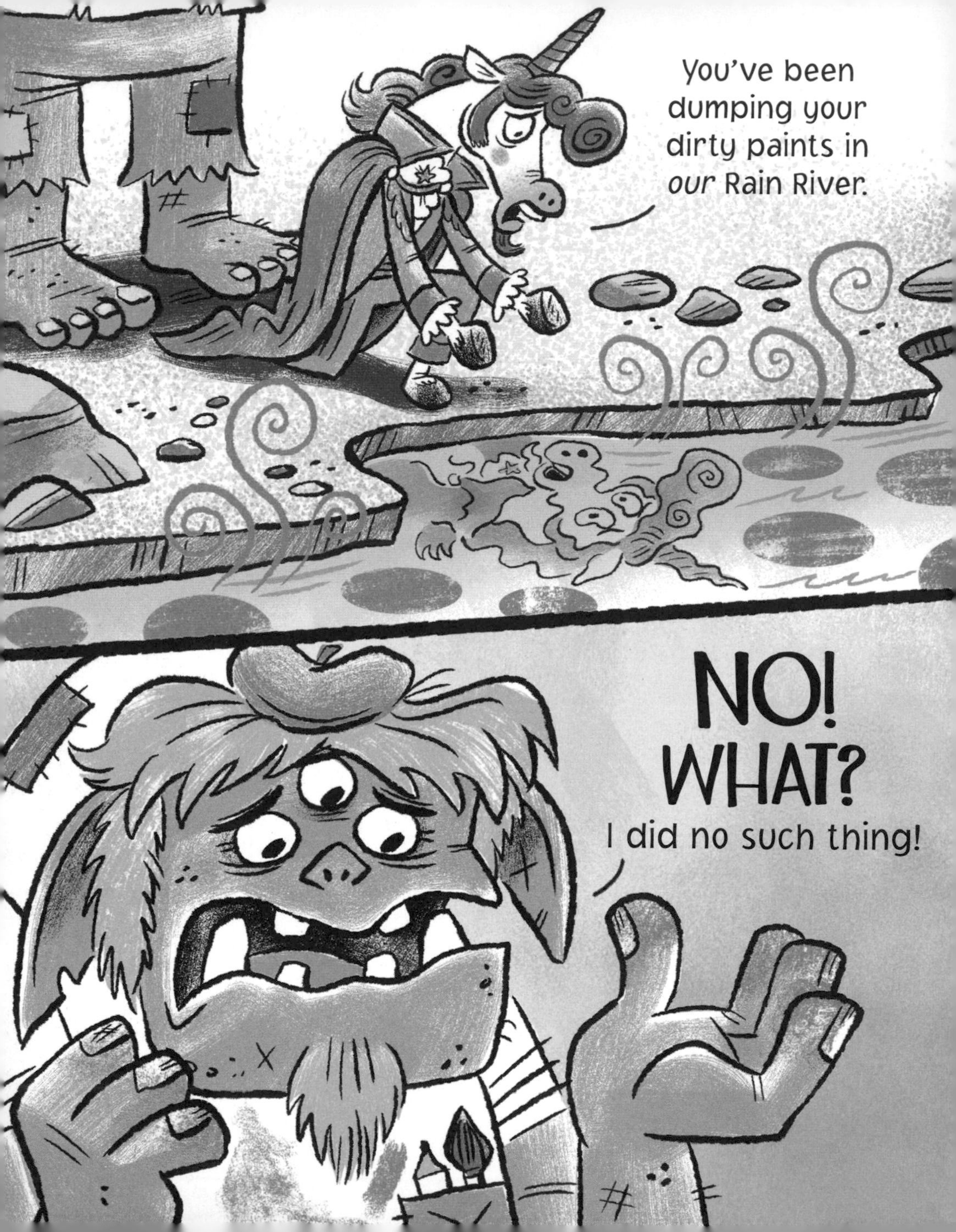
You've been dumping your dirty paints in *our* Rain River.
NO! WHAT? I did no such thing!

We all know how

DIRTY

and

MESSY

trolls are—

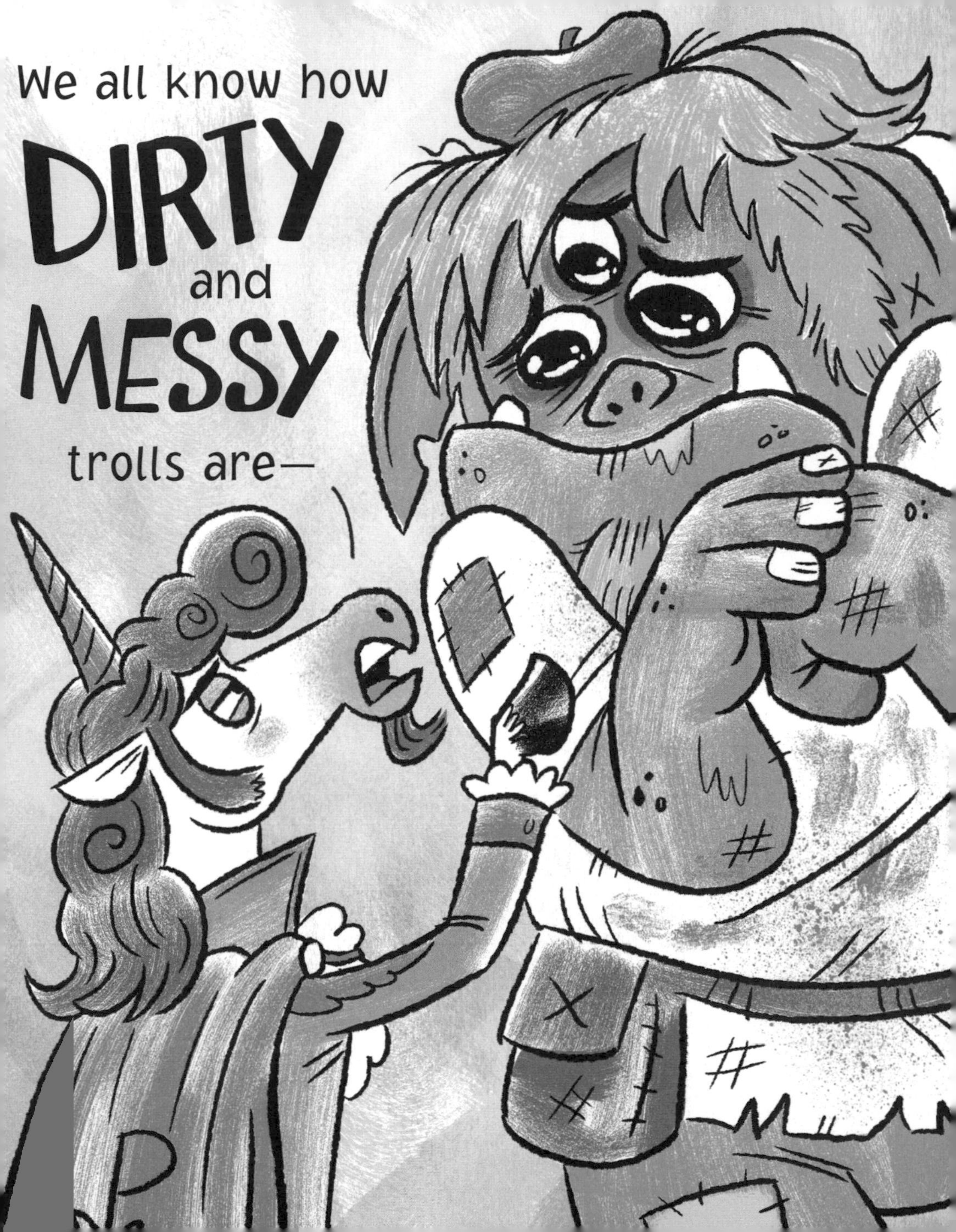

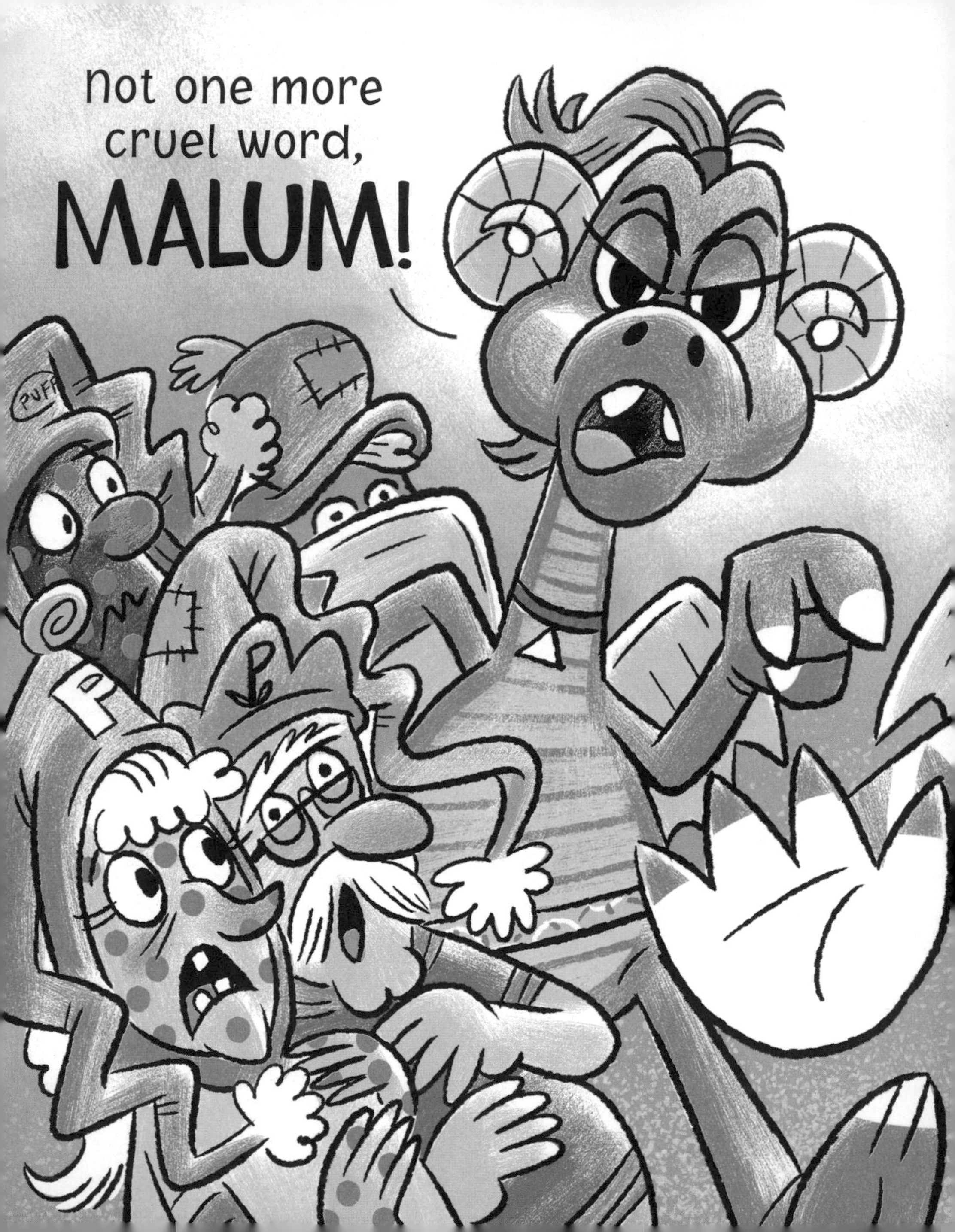
Not one more cruel word, MALUM!

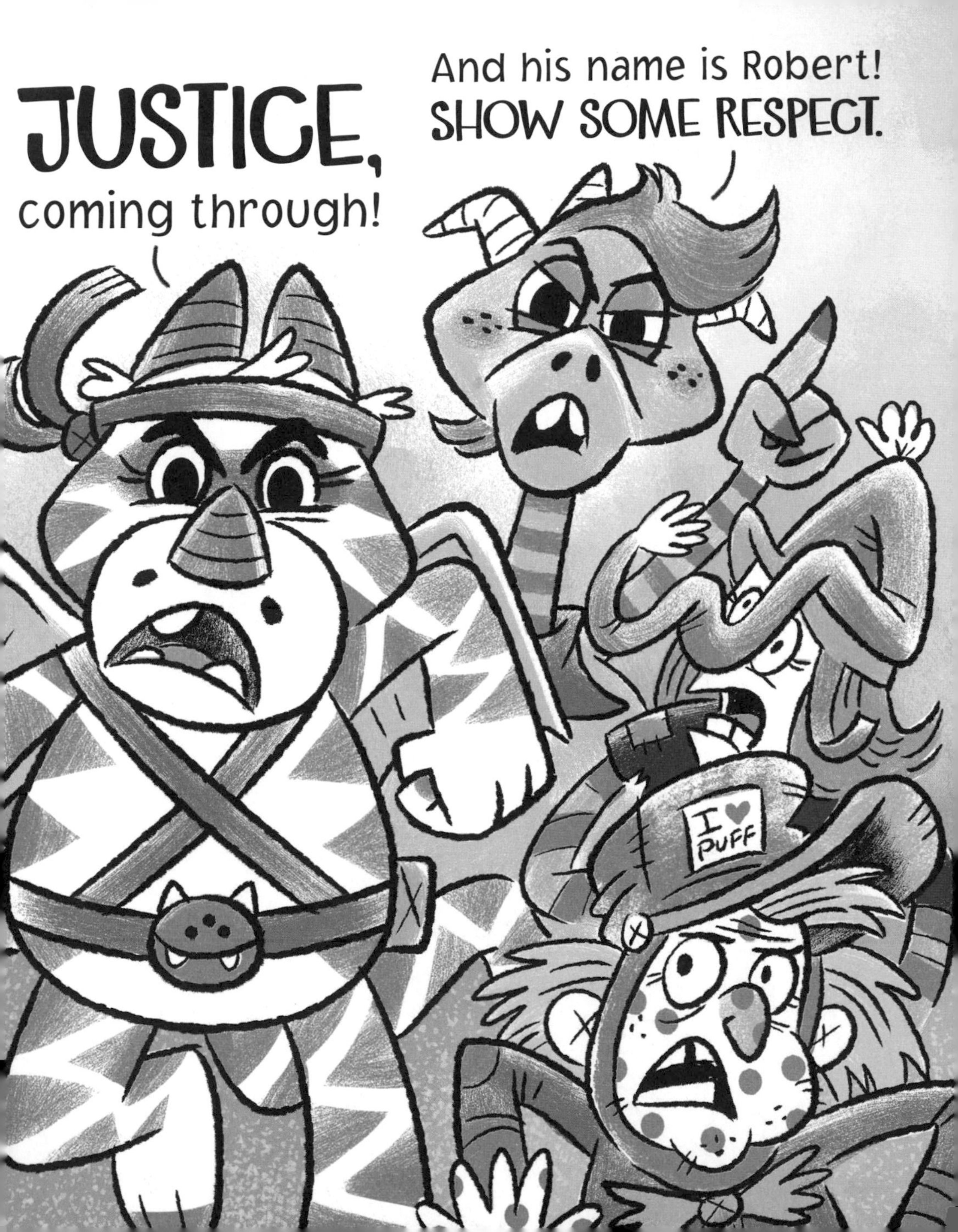
JUSTICE, coming through!
And his name is Robert! SHOW SOME RESPECT.
I ♥ PUFF

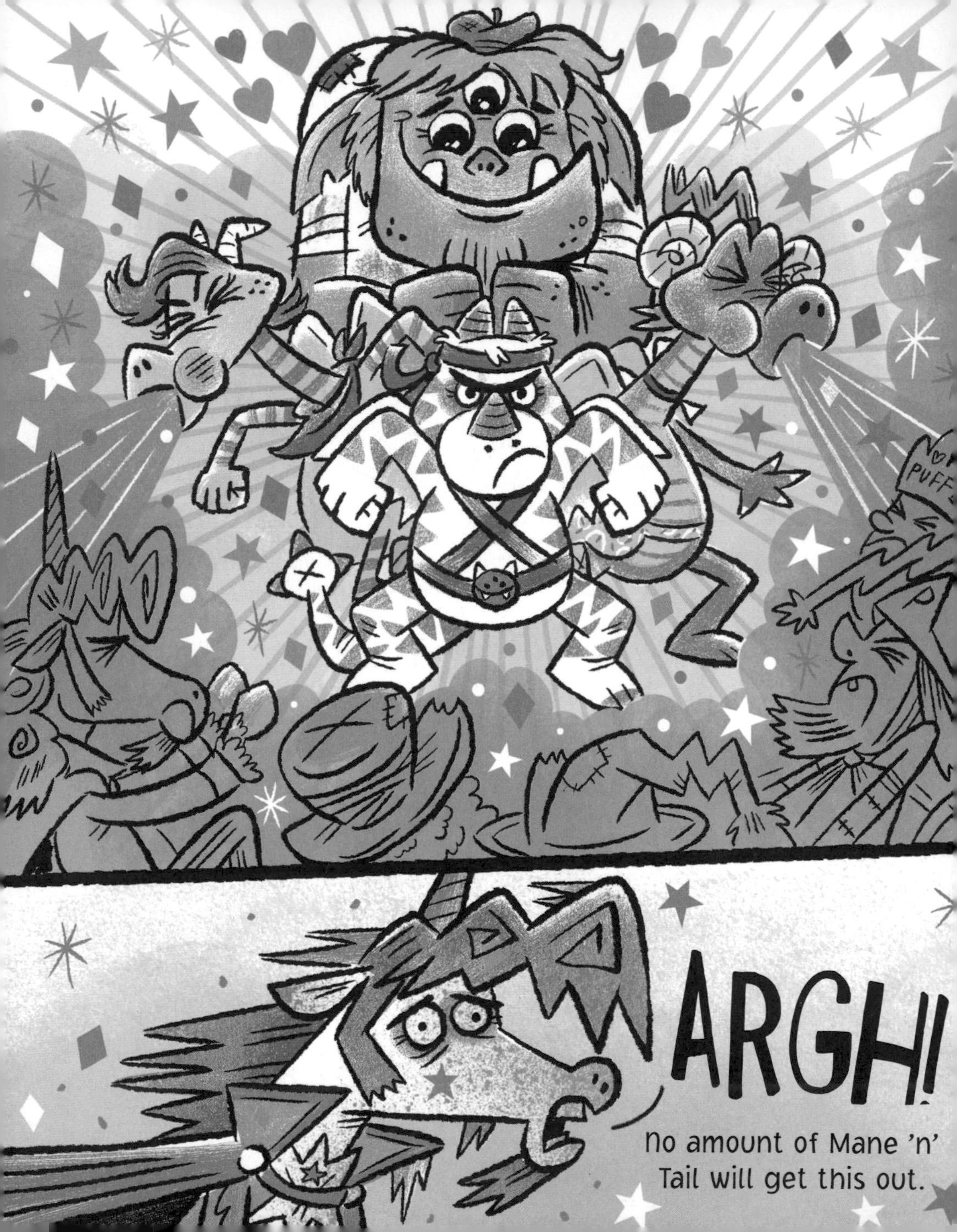
ARGH!
No amount of Mane 'n' Tail will get this out.

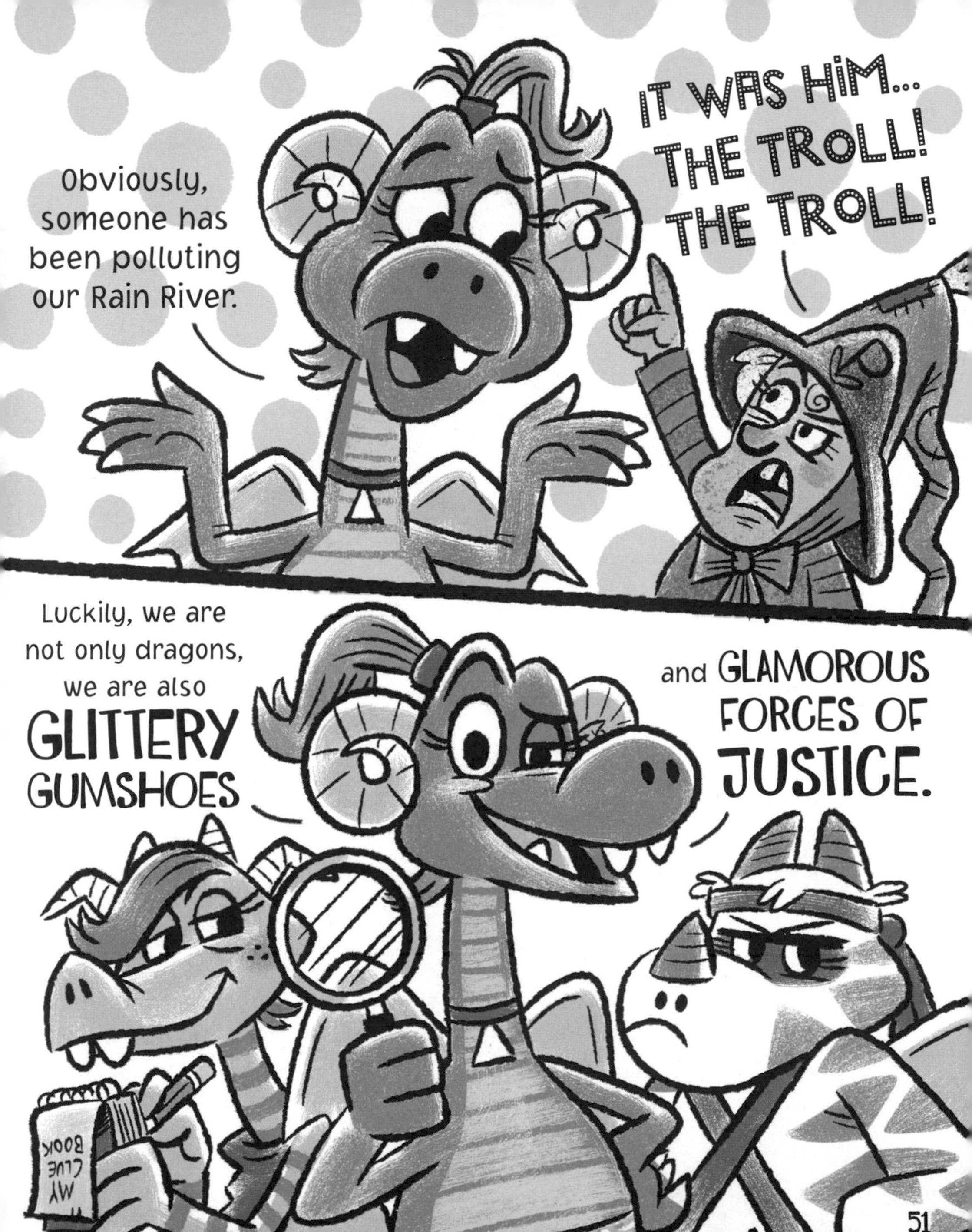
Obviously, someone has been polluting our Rain River.
IT WAS HIM... THE TROLL! THE TROLL!
Luckily, we are not only dragons, we are also GLITTERY GUMSHOES
and GLAMOROUS FORCES OF JUSTICE.
MY CLUE BOOK

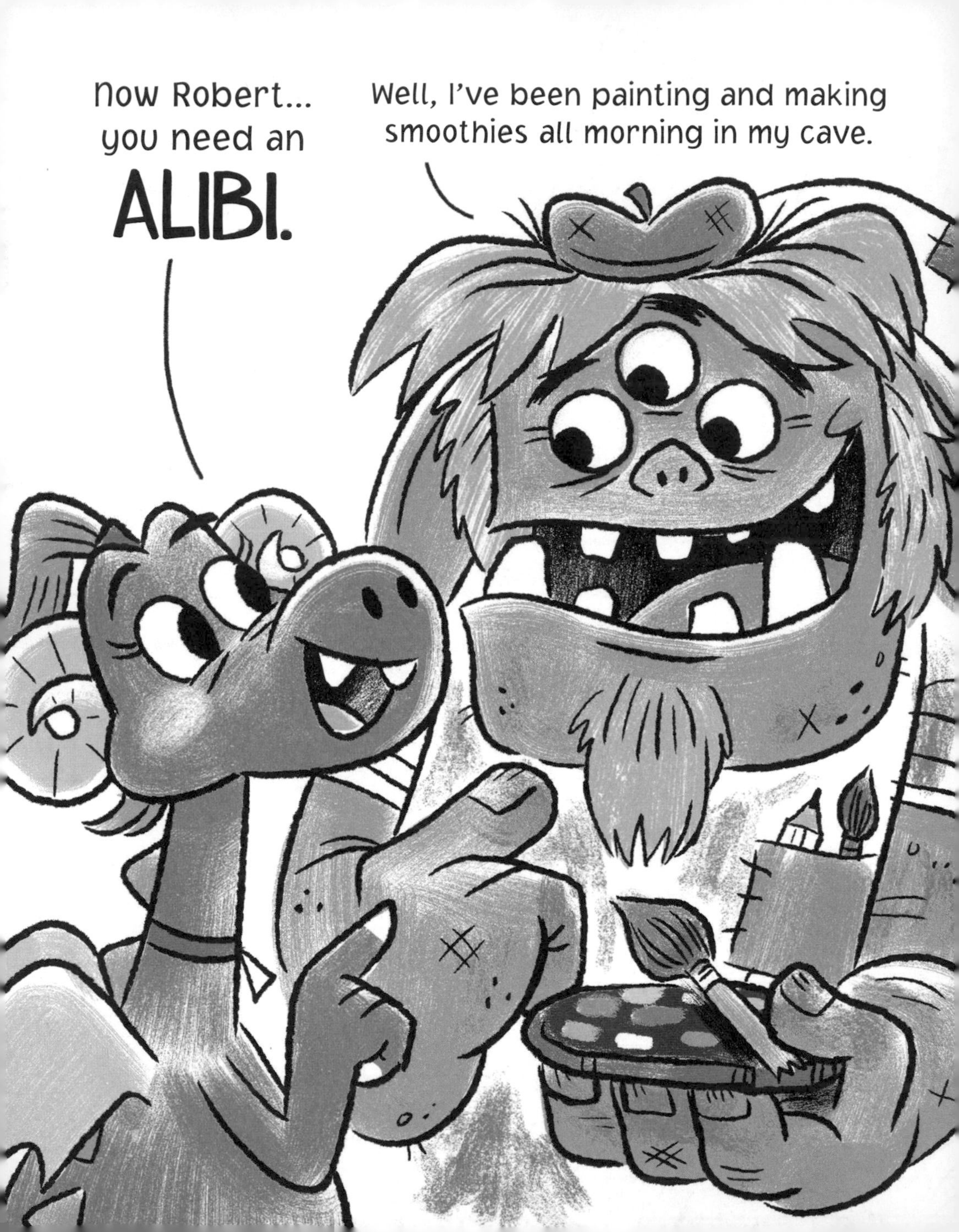
Now Robert... you need an ALIBI.
Well, I've been painting and making smoothies all morning in my cave.

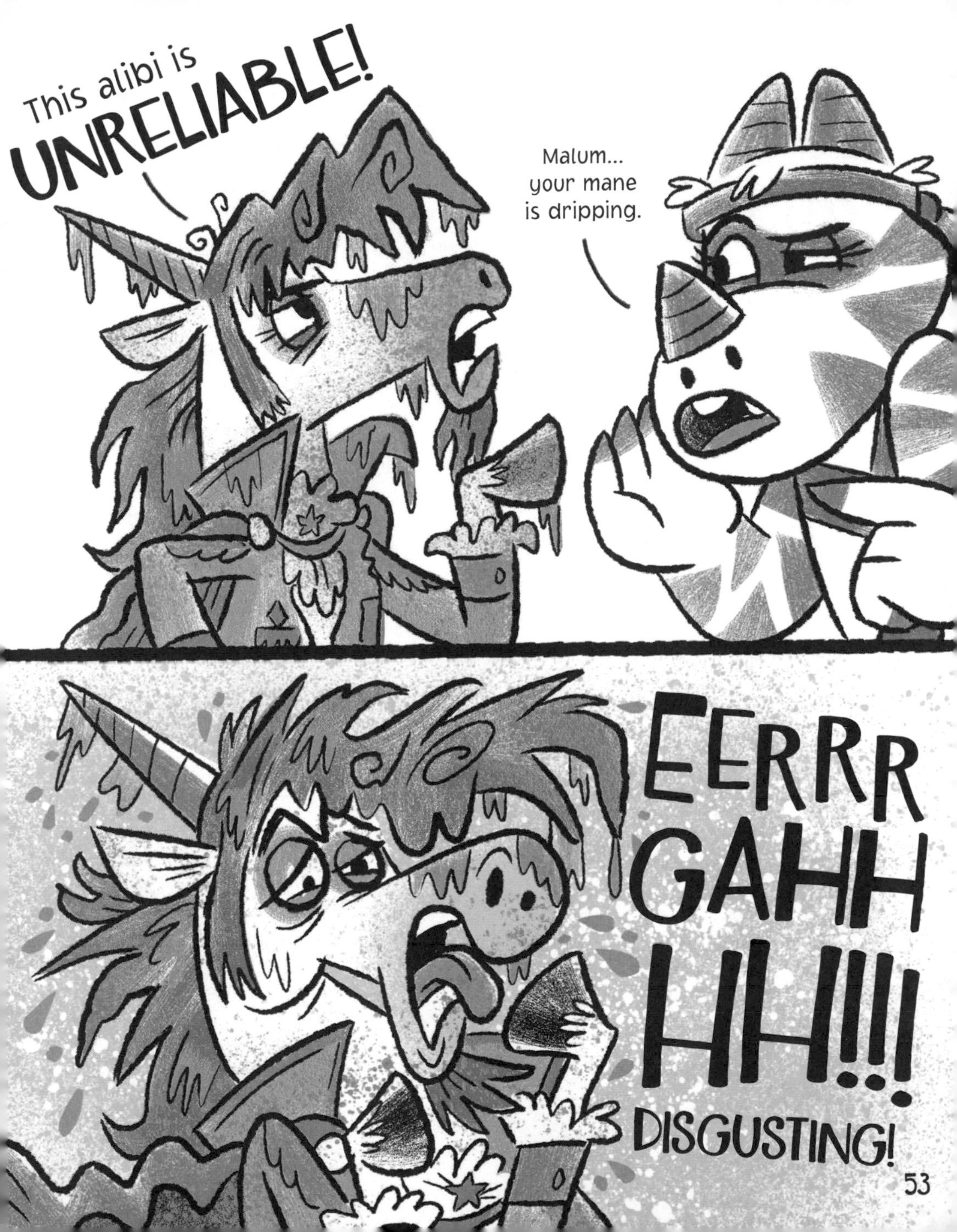
This alibi is UNRELIABLE!
Malum... your mane is dripping.
EERRRR GAHH HH!!!
DISGUSTING!

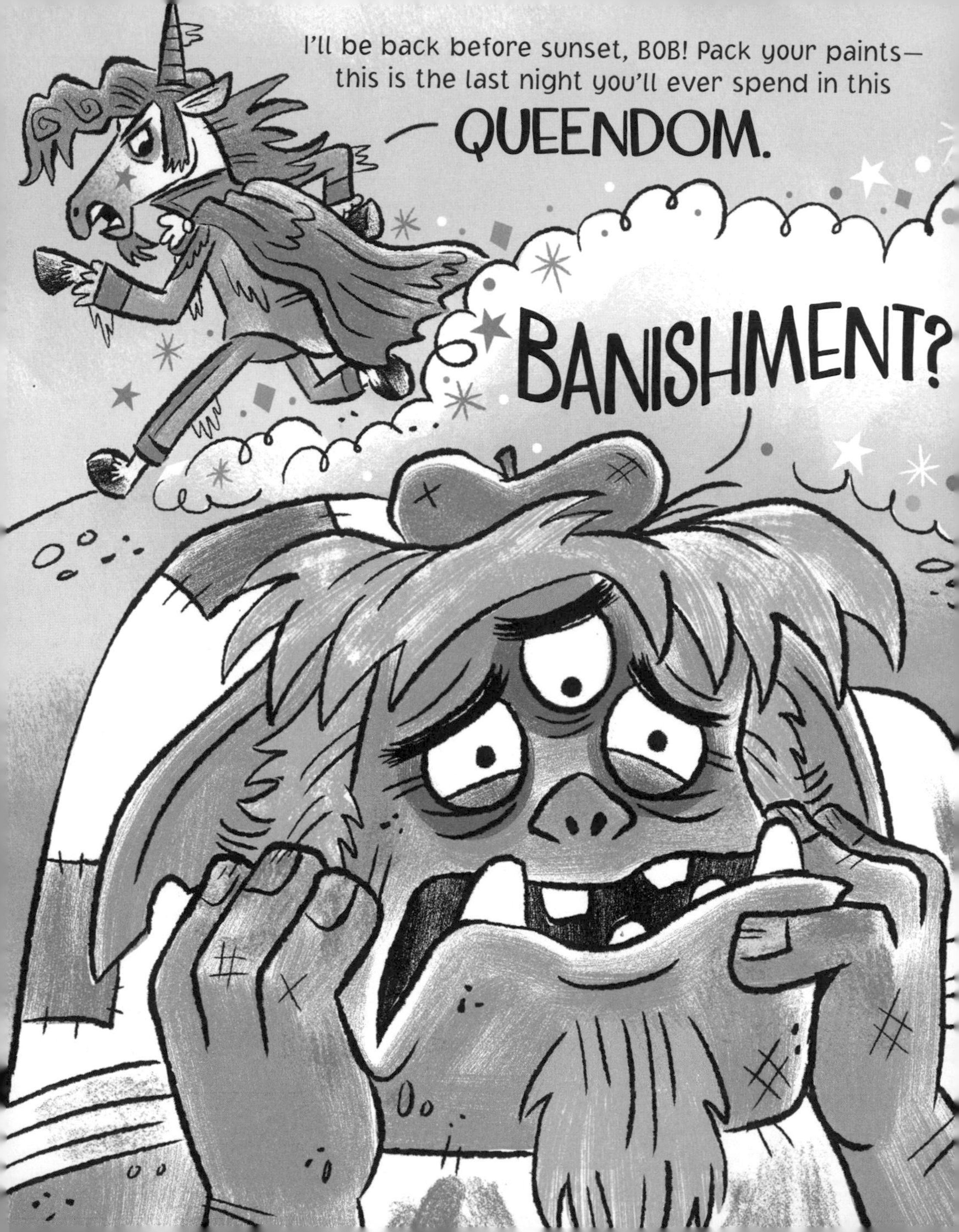
I'll be back before sunset, BOB! Pack your paints—this is the last night you'll ever spend in this QUEENDOM.
BANISHMENT?

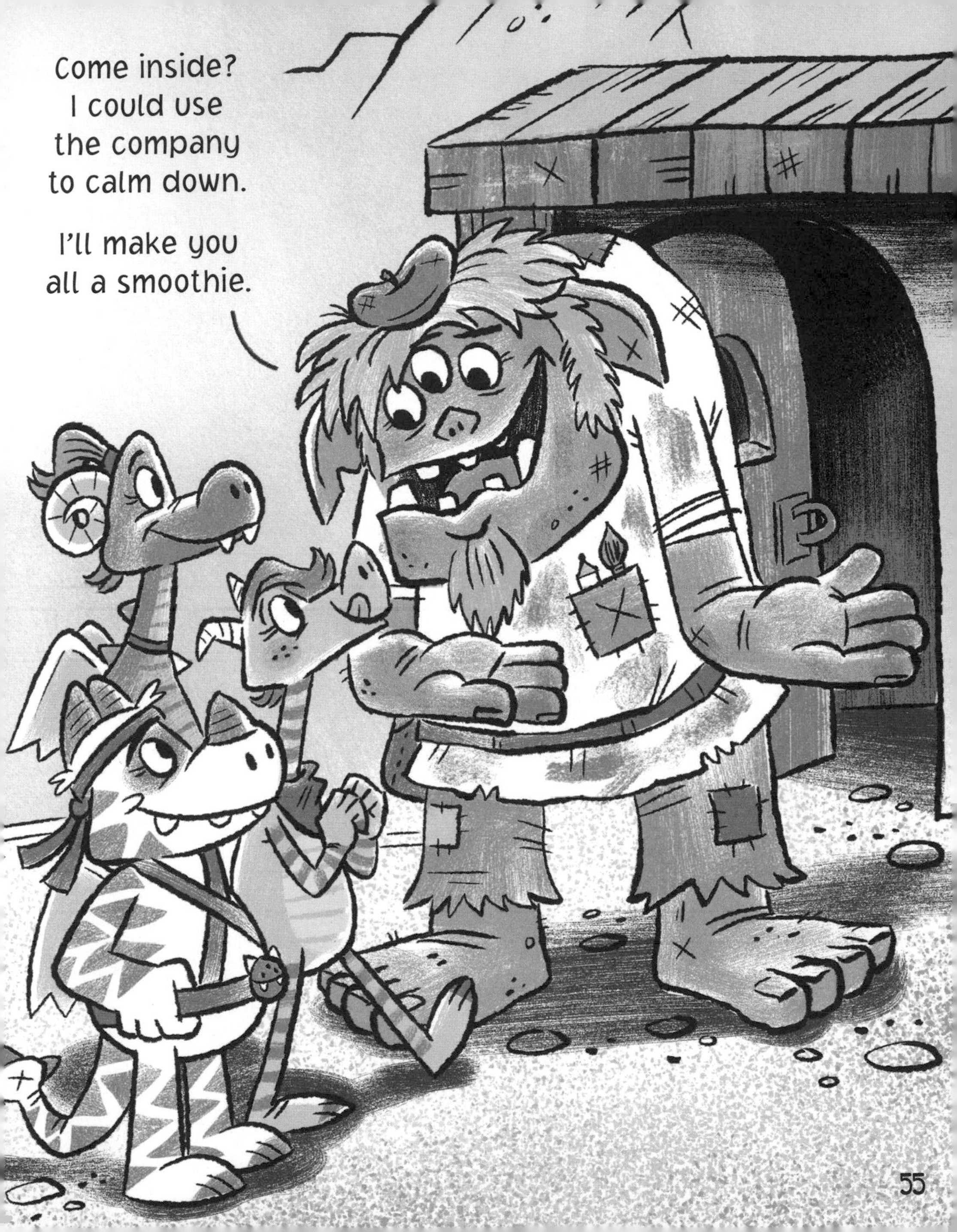
Come inside? I could use the company to calm down.
I'll make you all a smoothie.

CHAPTER FOUR
THE PROOF'S IN THE SMOOTHIE

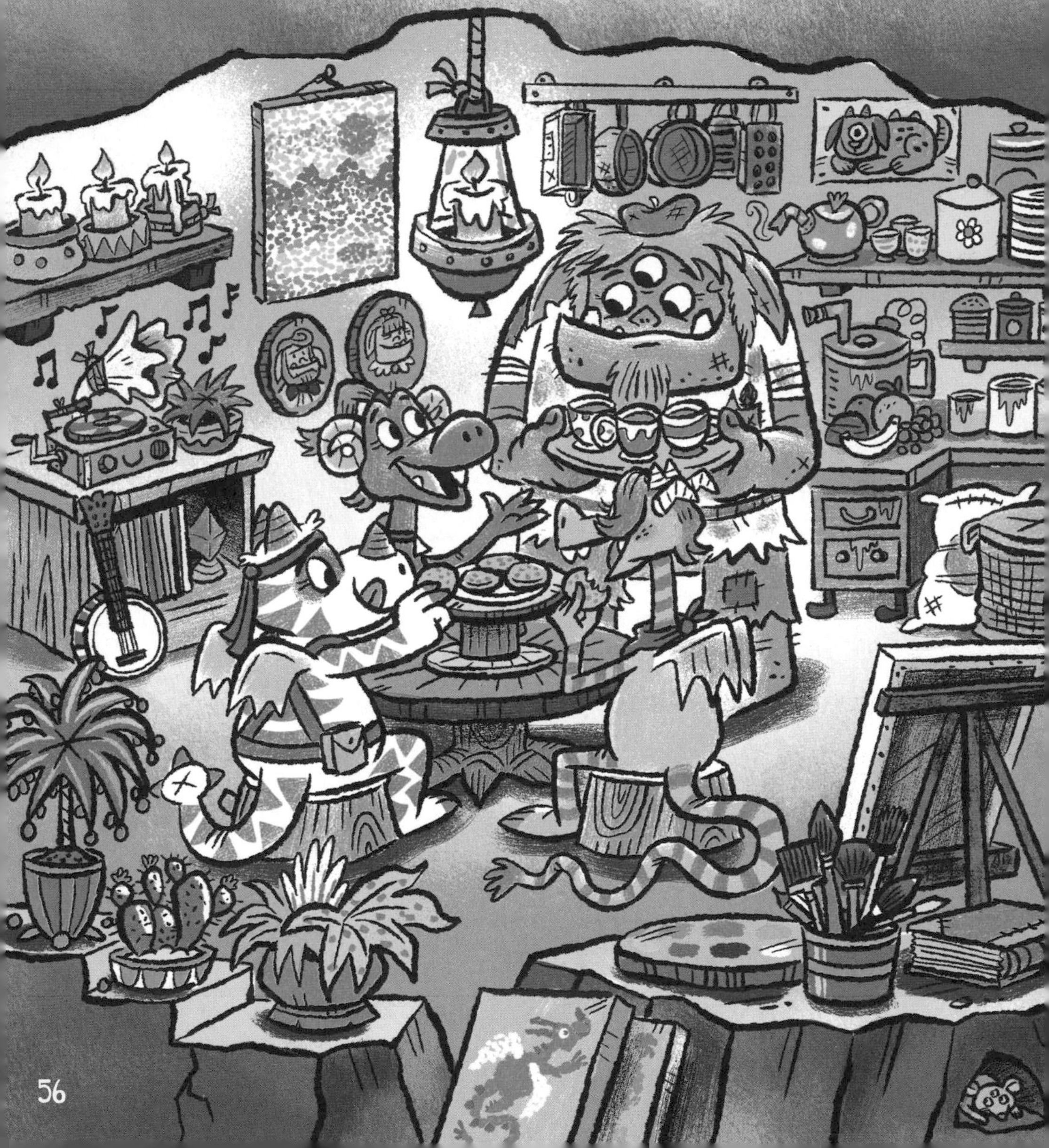

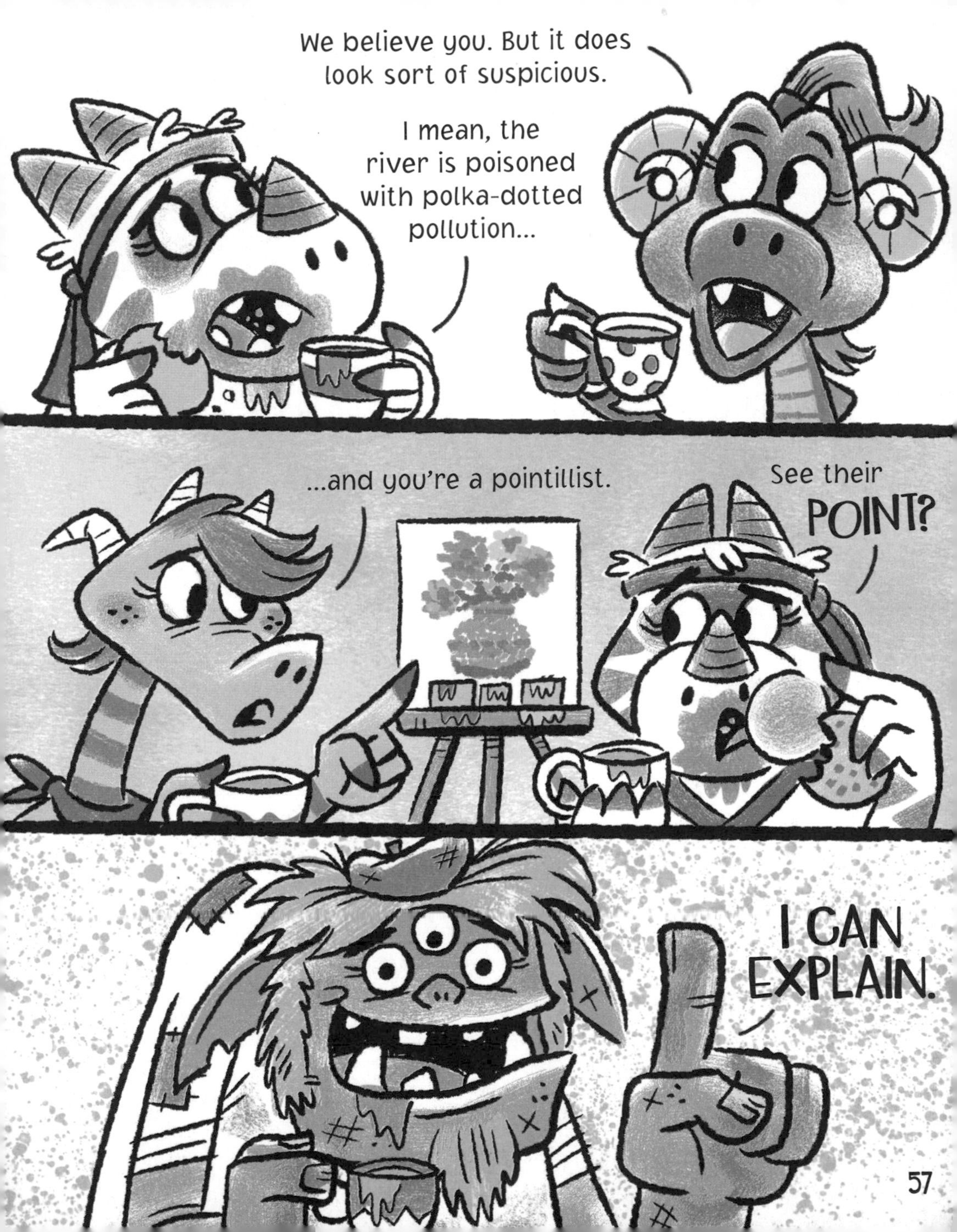
We believe you. But it does look sort of suspicious.
I mean, the river is poisoned with polka-dotted pollution...
...and you're a pointillist.
See their POINT?
I CAN EXPLAIN.

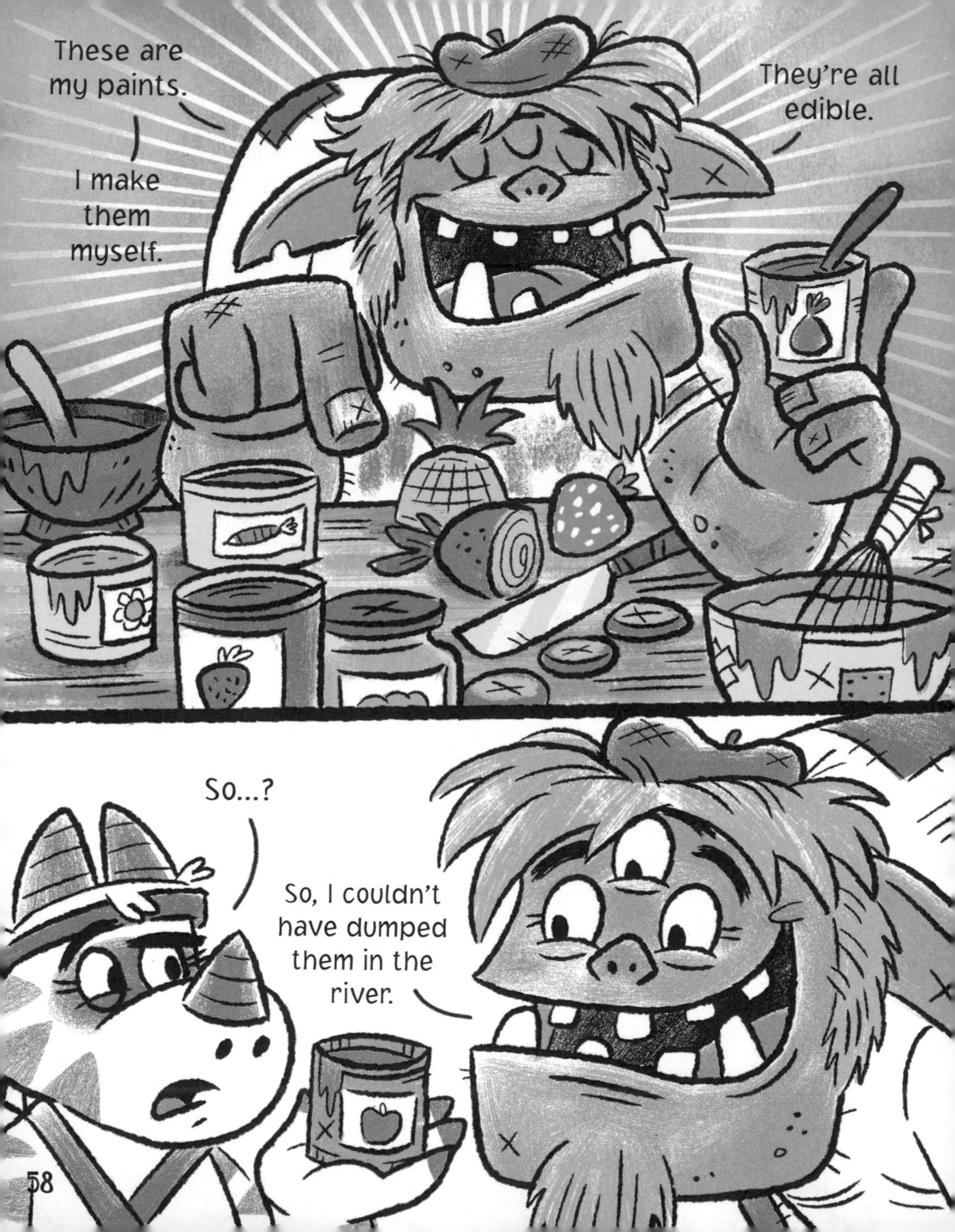
These are my paints.
I make them myself.
They're all edible.
So...?
So, I couldn't have dumped them in the river.

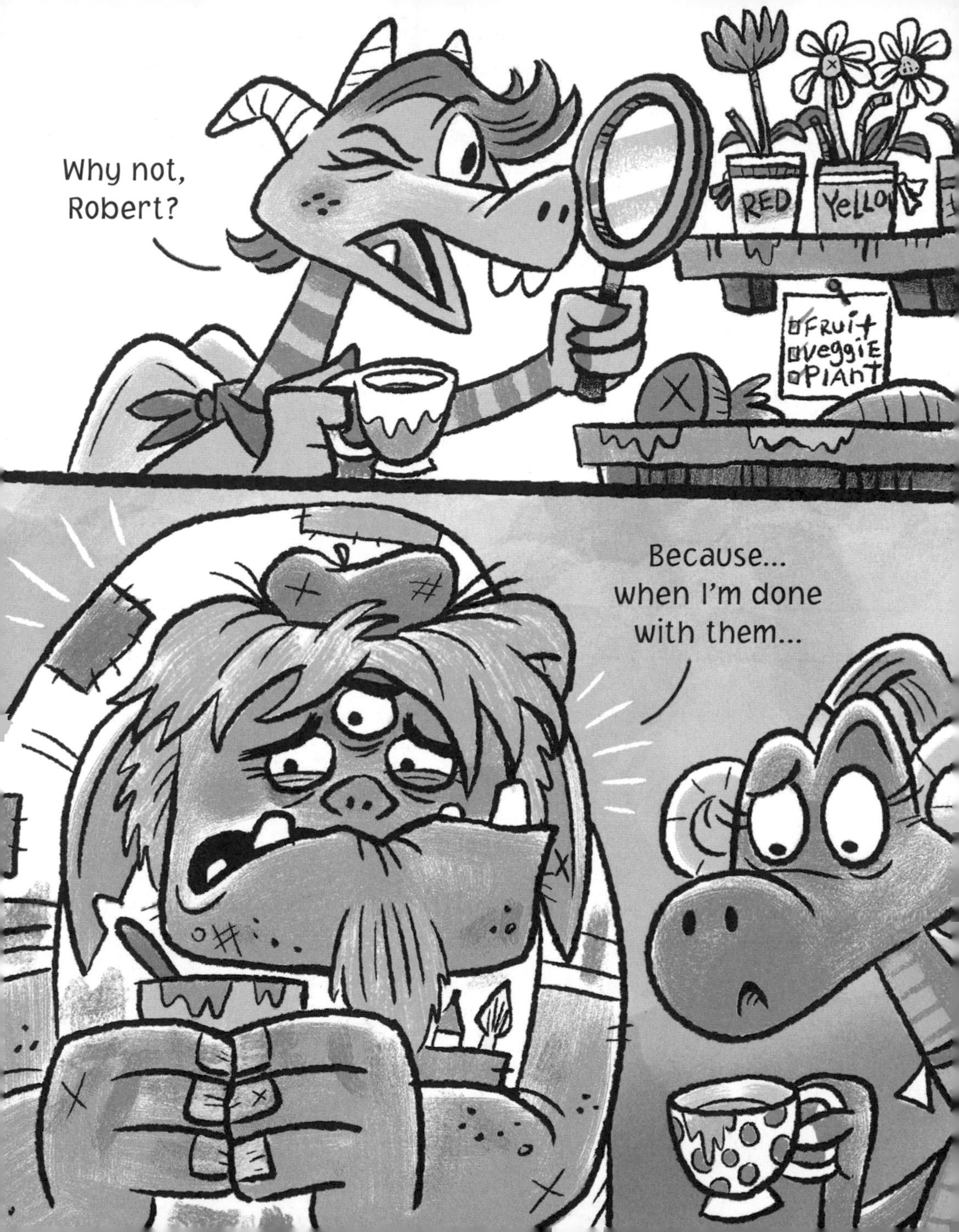
Why not, Robert?
RED
YELLO
FRUIT
VEGGIE
PLANT
Because... when I'm done with them...

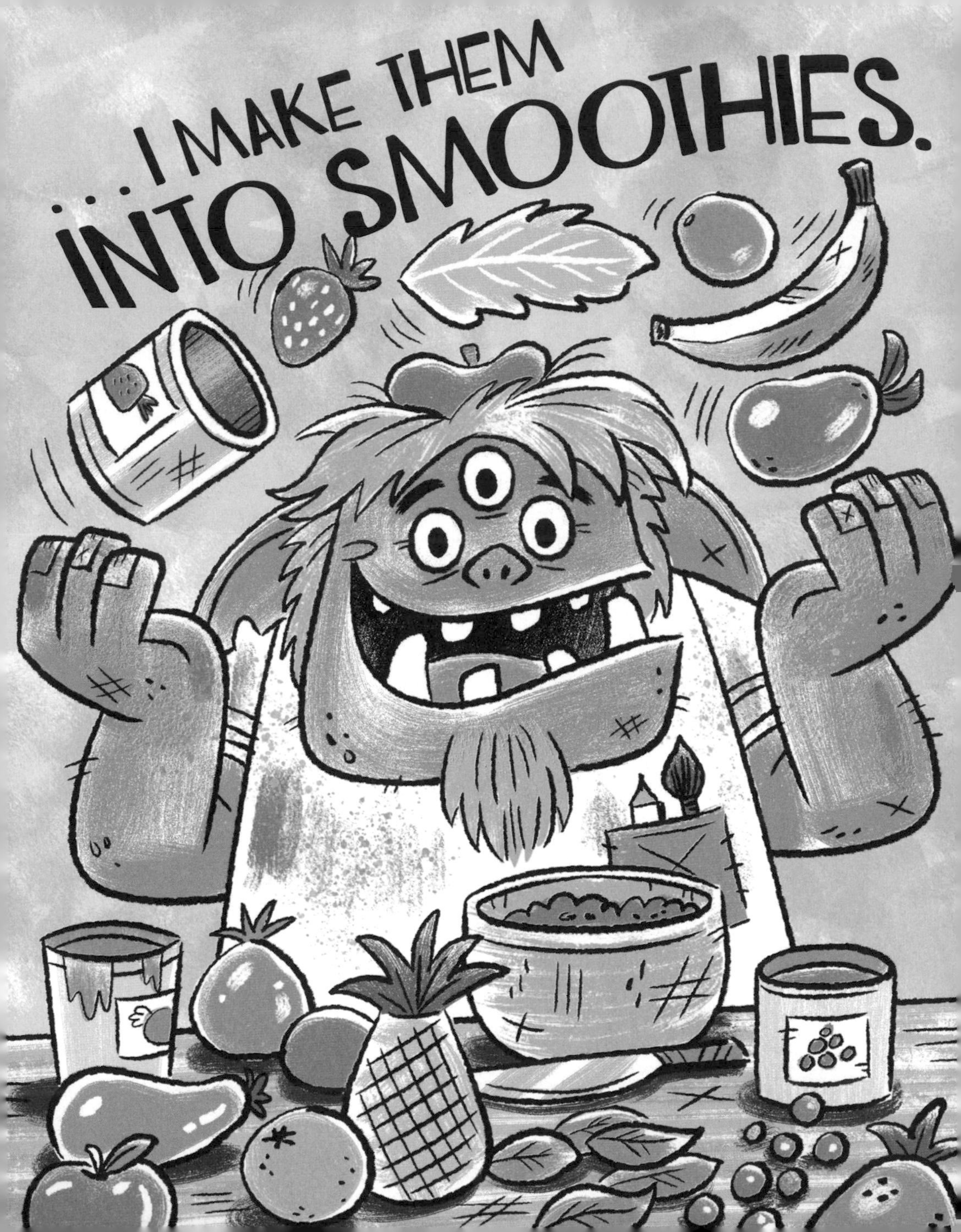
. . . I MAKE THEM INTO SMOOTHIES.

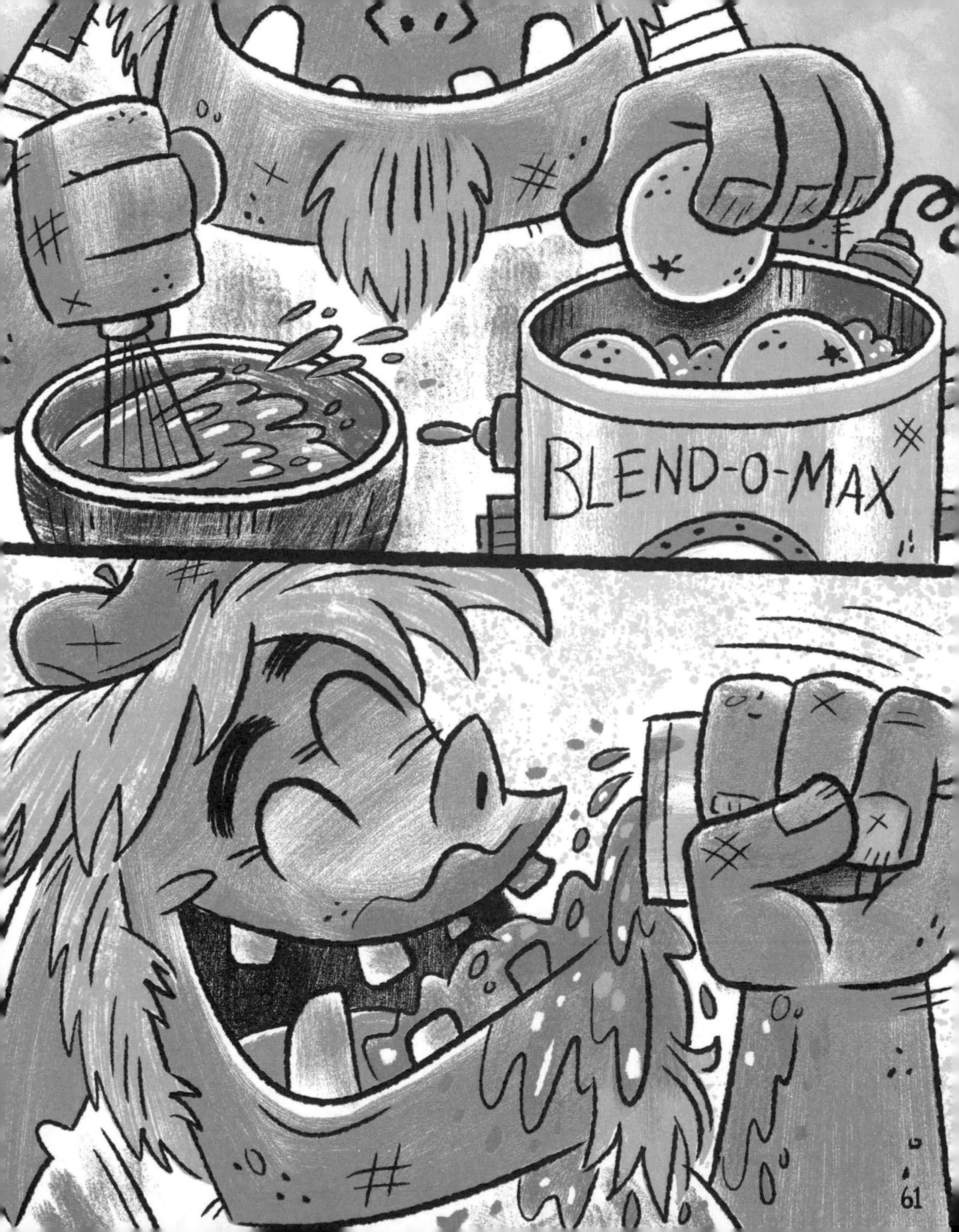
BLEND-O-MAX

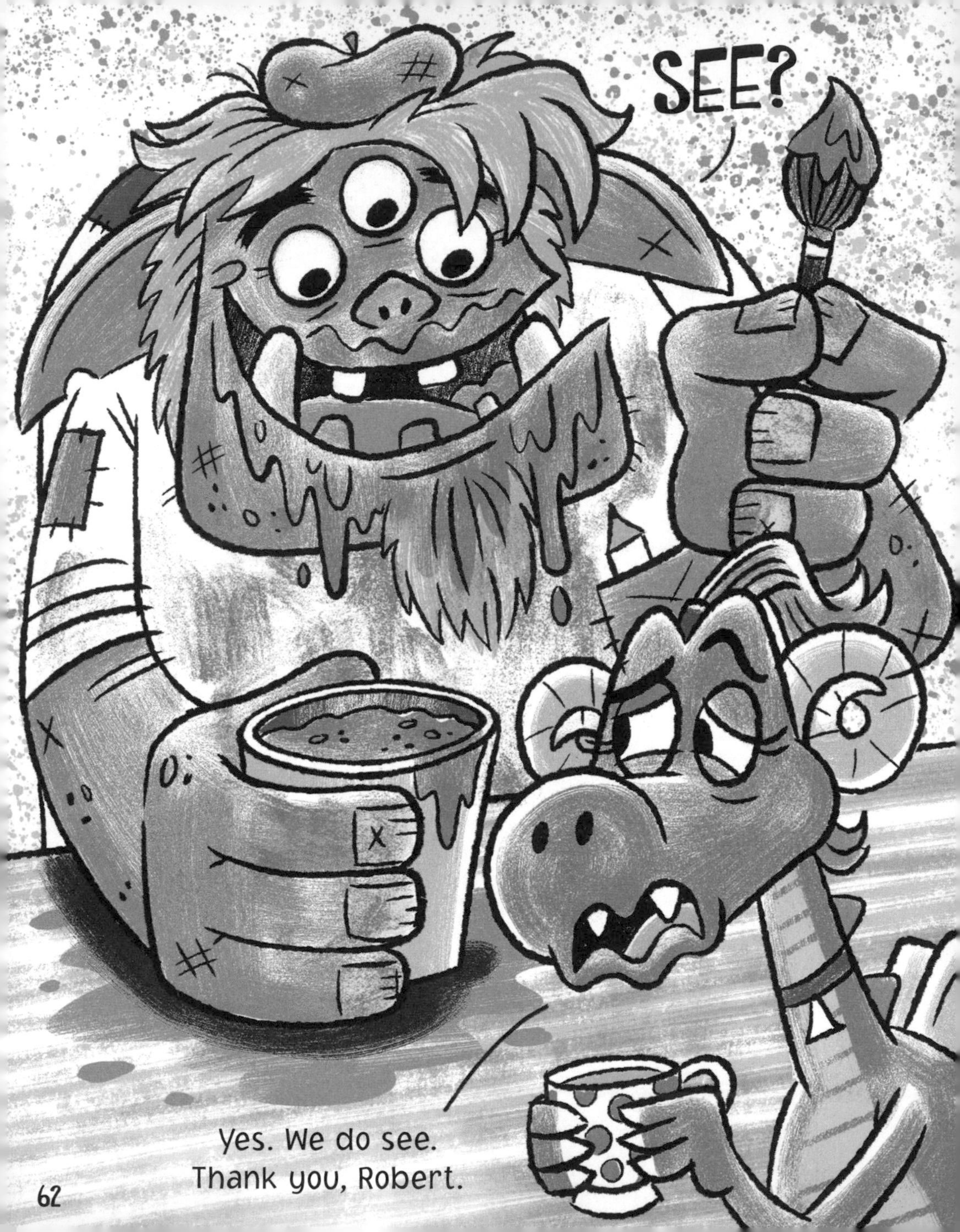
SEE?
Yes. We do see.
Thank you, Robert.

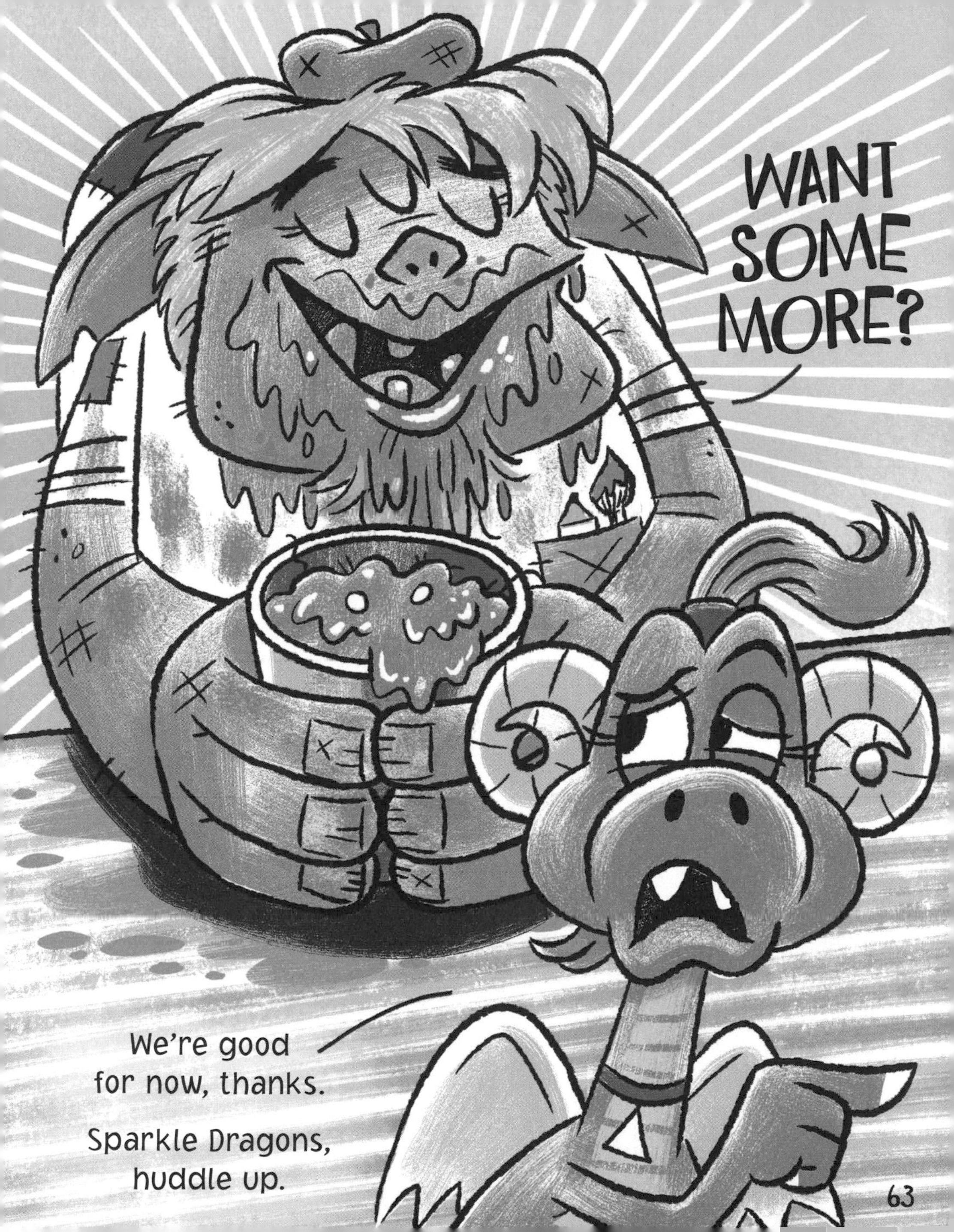
WANT SOME MORE?
We're good for now, thanks.
Sparkle Dragons, huddle up.

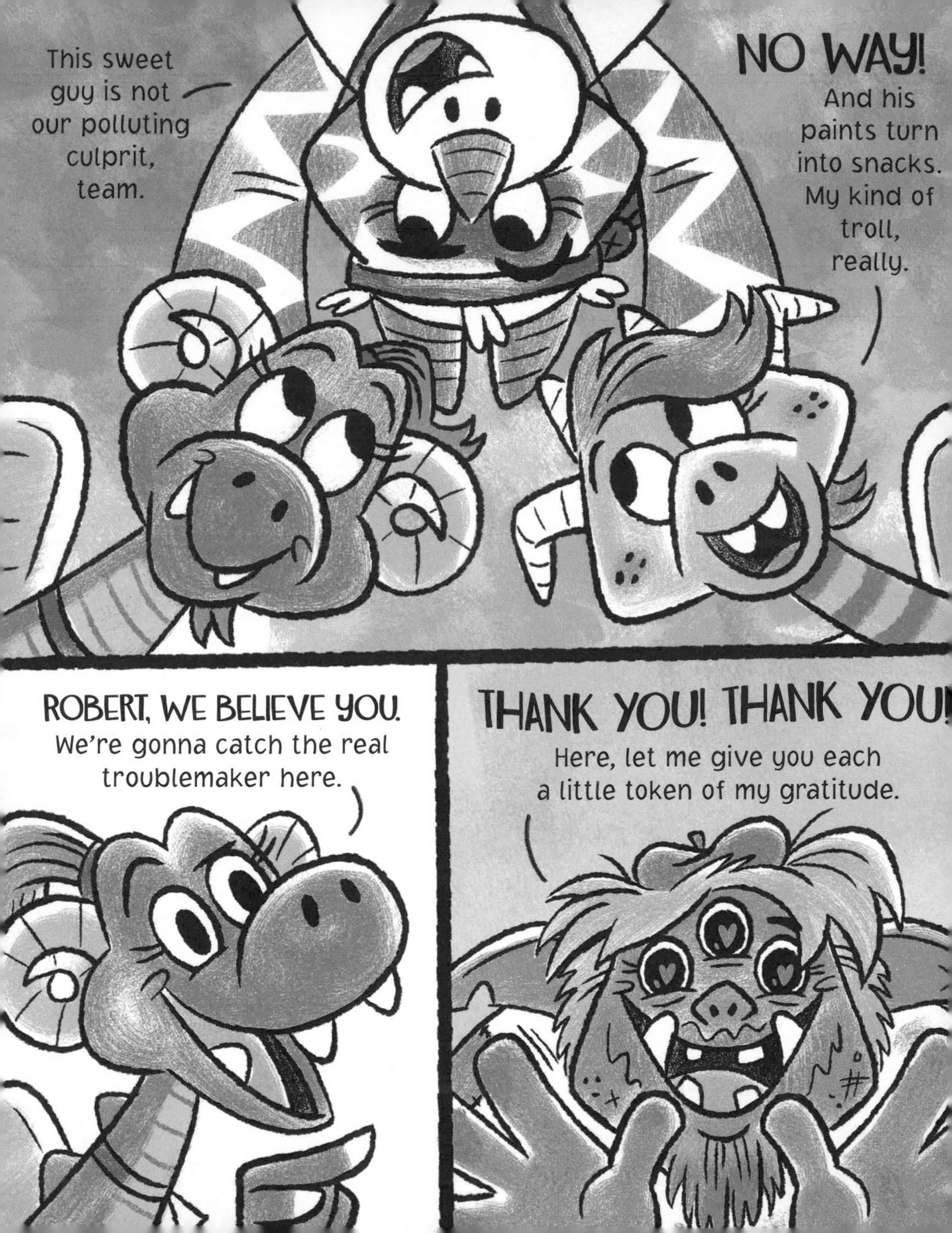
This sweet guy is not our polluting culprit, team.
NO WAY!
And his paints turn into snacks. My kind of troll, really.
ROBERT, WE BELIEVE YOU.
We're gonna catch the real troublemaker here.
THANK YOU! THANK YOU!
Here, let me give you each a little token of my gratitude.

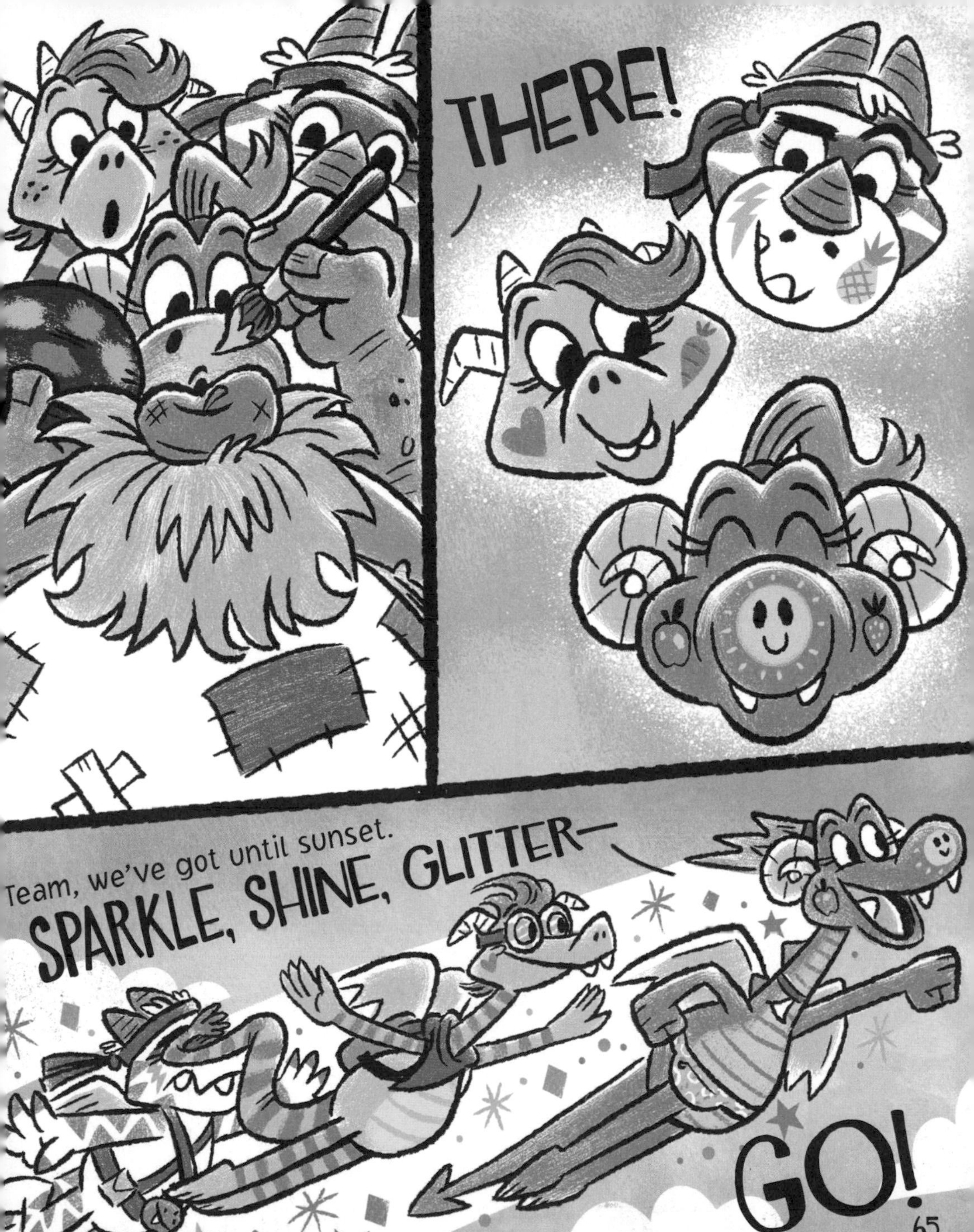
THERE!
Team, we've got until sunset.
SPARKLE, SHINE, GLITTER—
GO!

CHAPTER FIVE
CAVE SWEET CAVE

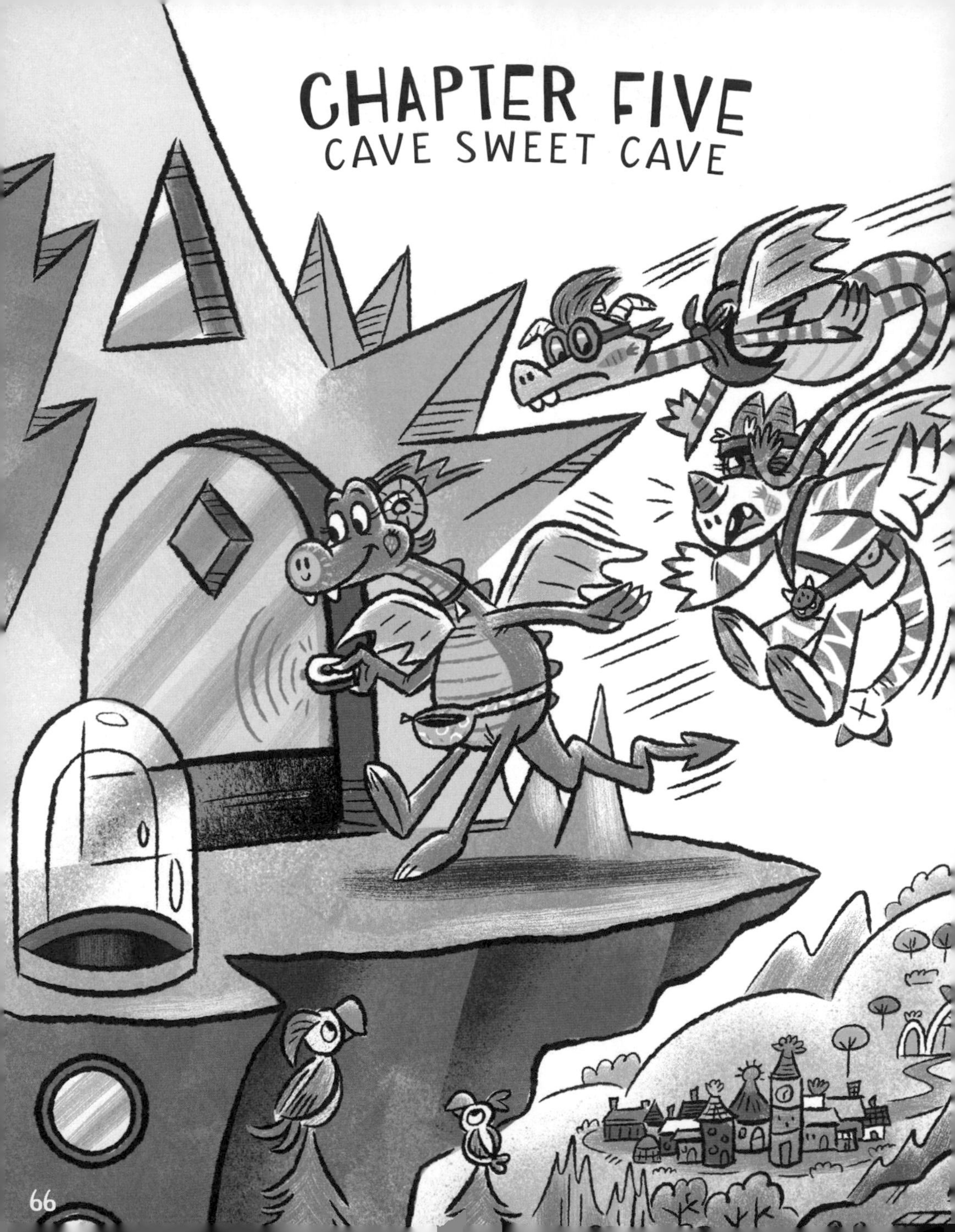

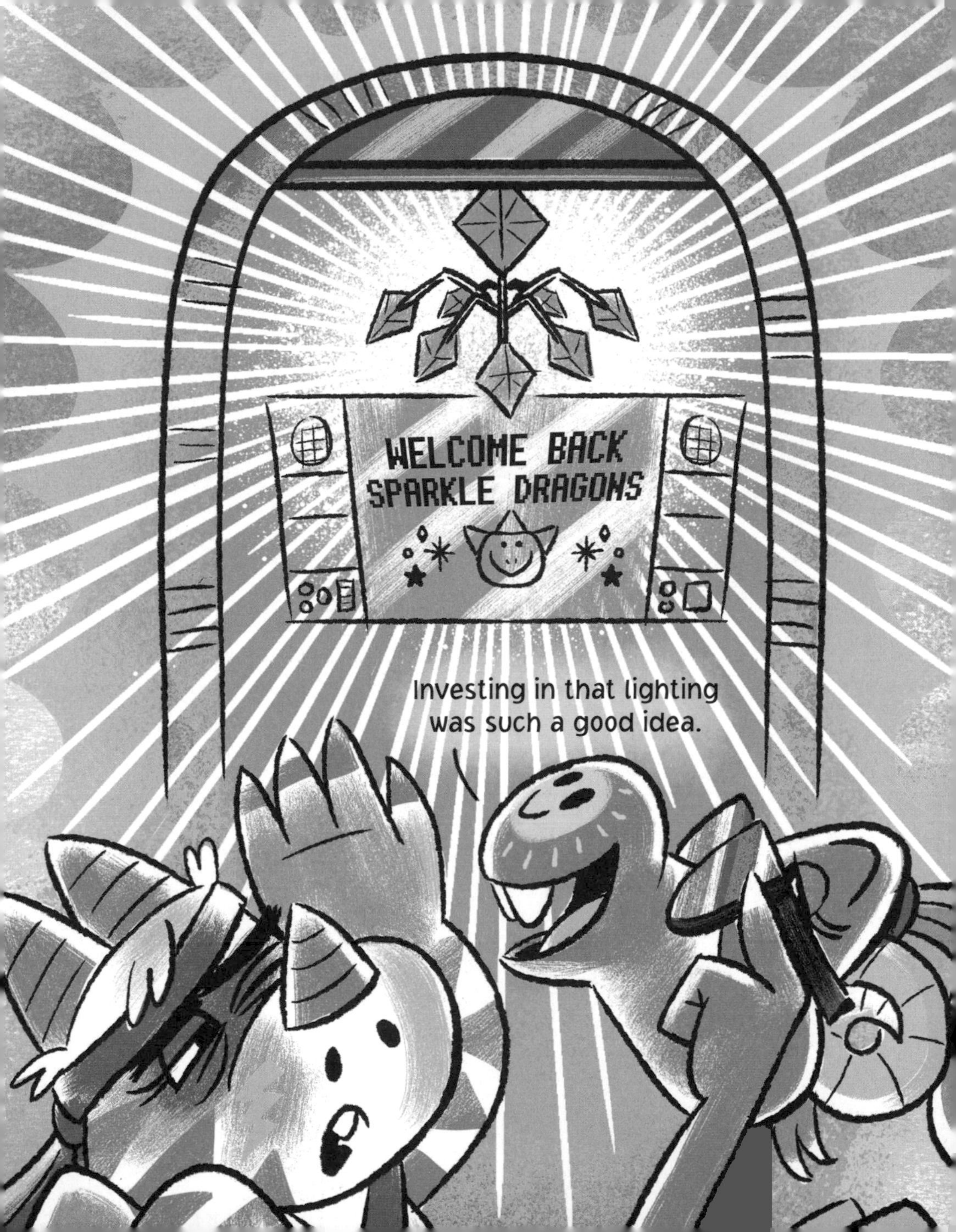
WELCOME BACK SPARKLE DRAGONS
Investing in that lighting was such a good idea.

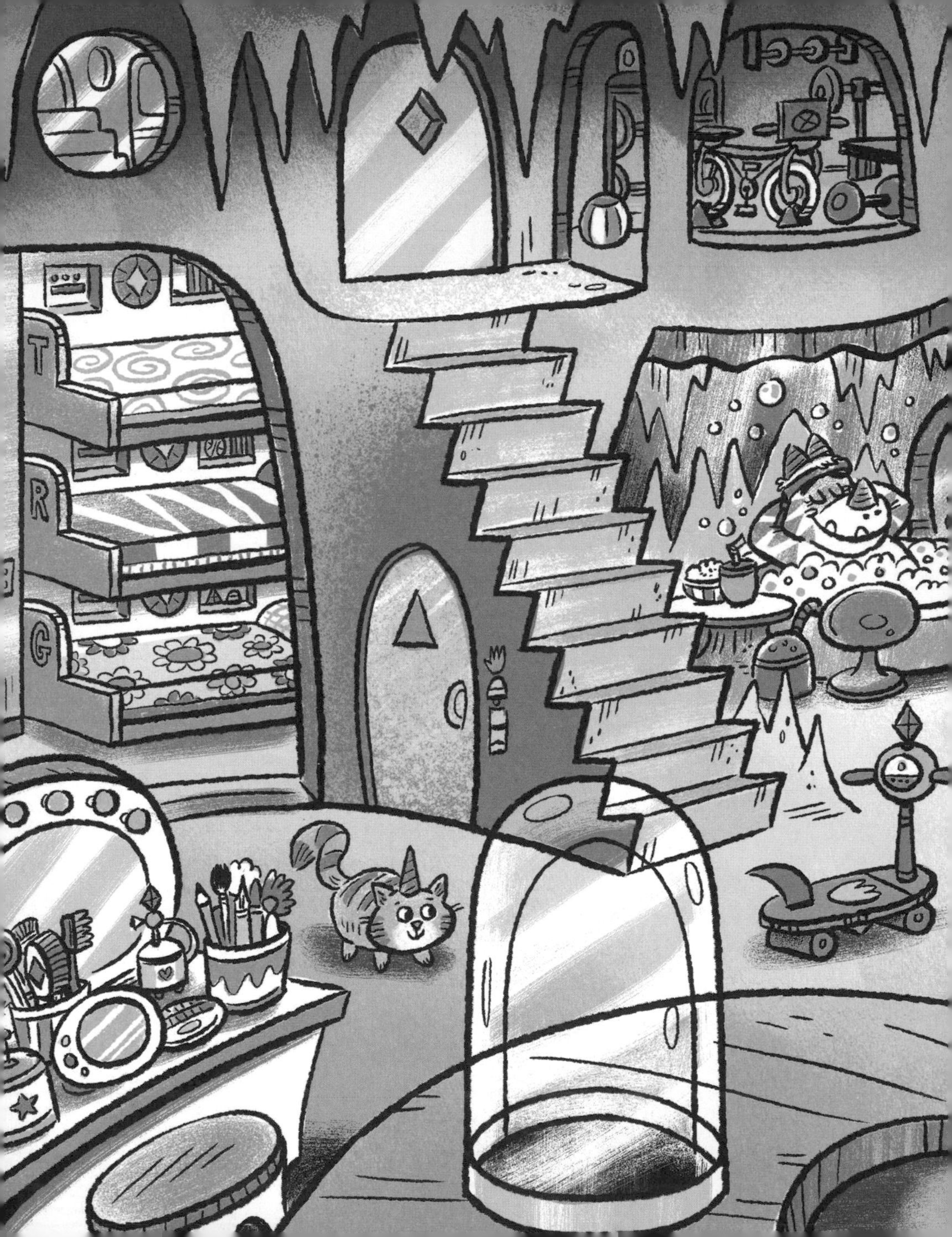
T
R
G

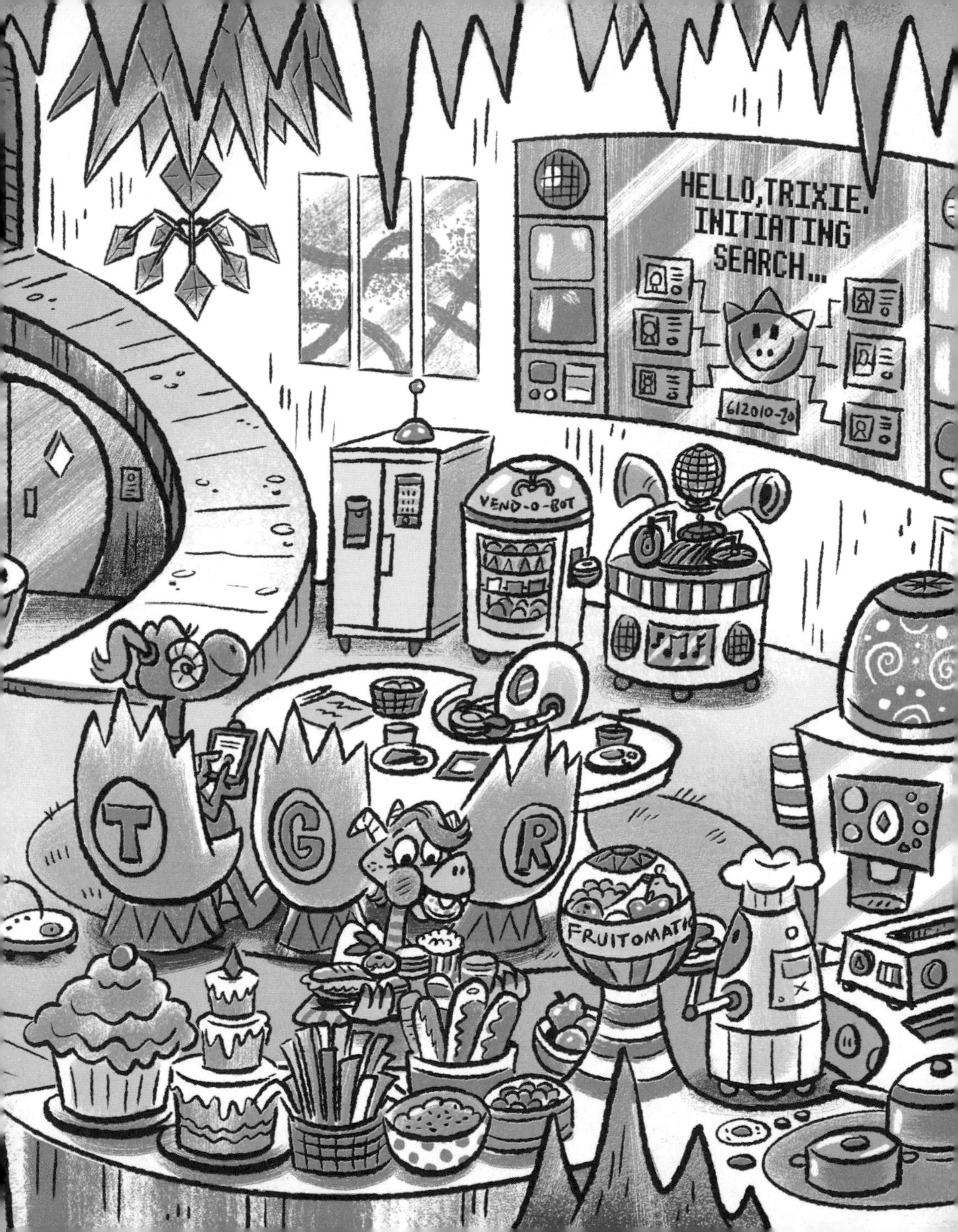
HELLO, TRIXIE.
INITIATING
SEARCH...
612010-70
VEND-O-BOT
FRUITOMATIC
T
G
R

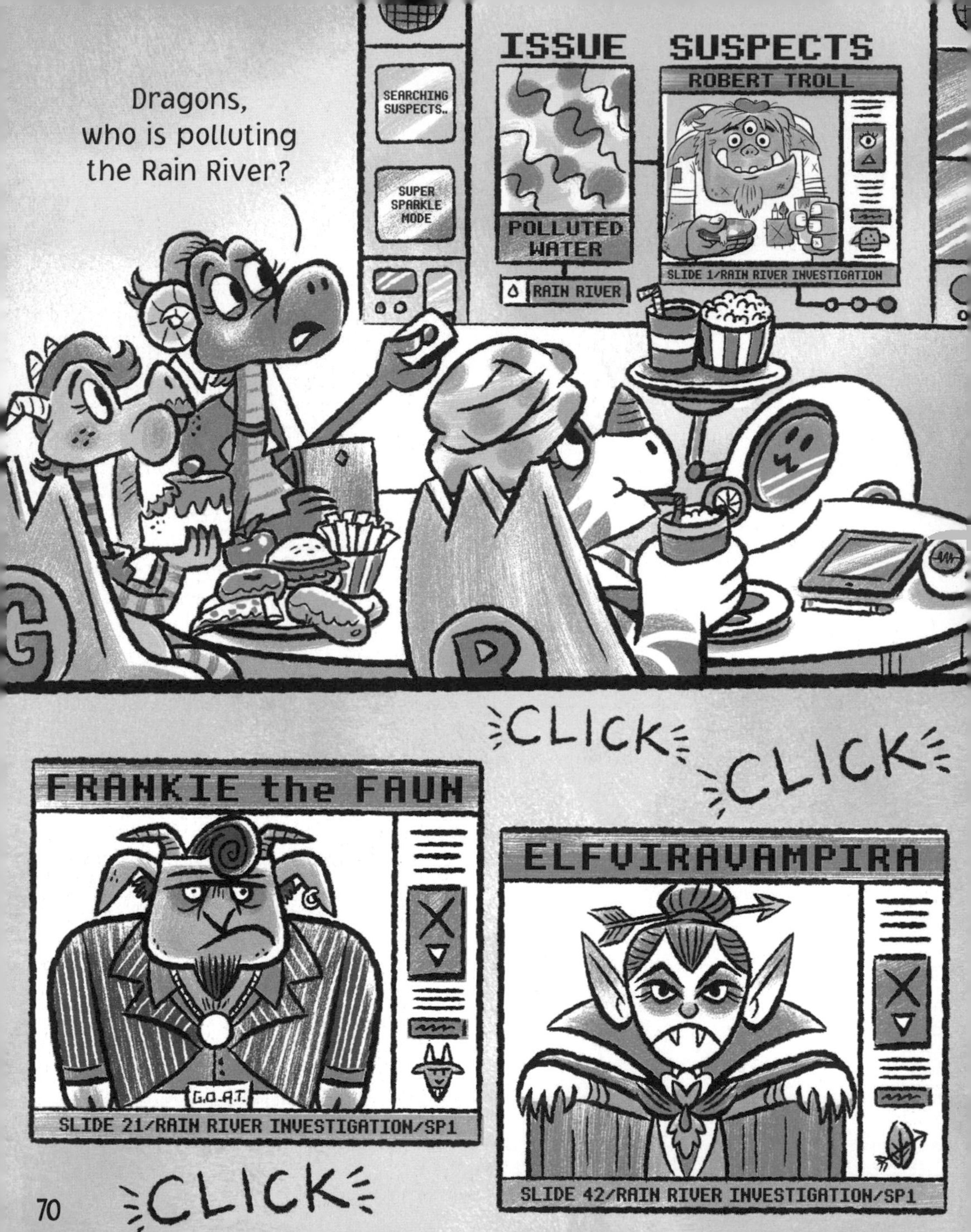
Dragons, who is polluting the Rain River?
SEARCHING SUSPECTS..
SUPER SPARKLE MODE
ISSUE
POLLUTED WATER
RAIN RIVER
SUSPECTS
ROBERT TROLL
SLIDE 1/RAIN RIVER INVESTIGATION
CLICK
CLICK
FRANKIE the FAUN
G.O.A.T.
SLIDE 21/RAIN RIVER INVESTIGATION/SP1
ELFVIRAVAMPIRA
SLIDE 42/RAIN RIVER INVESTIGATION/SP1
CLICK

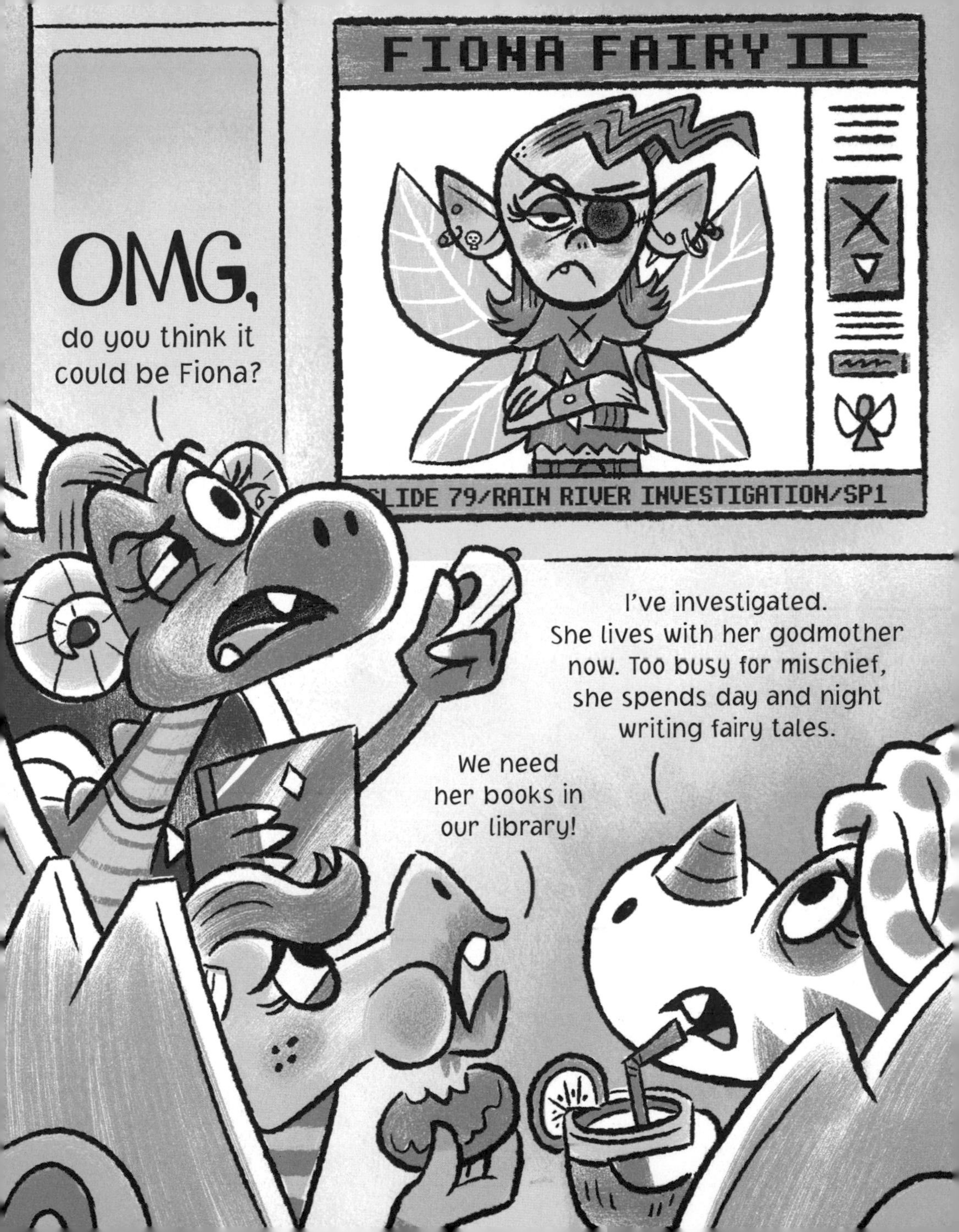
FIONA FAIRY III
SLIDE 79/RAIN RIVER INVESTIGATION/SP1
OMG, do you think it could be Fiona?
I've investigated. She lives with her godmother now. Too busy for mischief, she spends day and night writing fairy tales.
We need her books in our library!

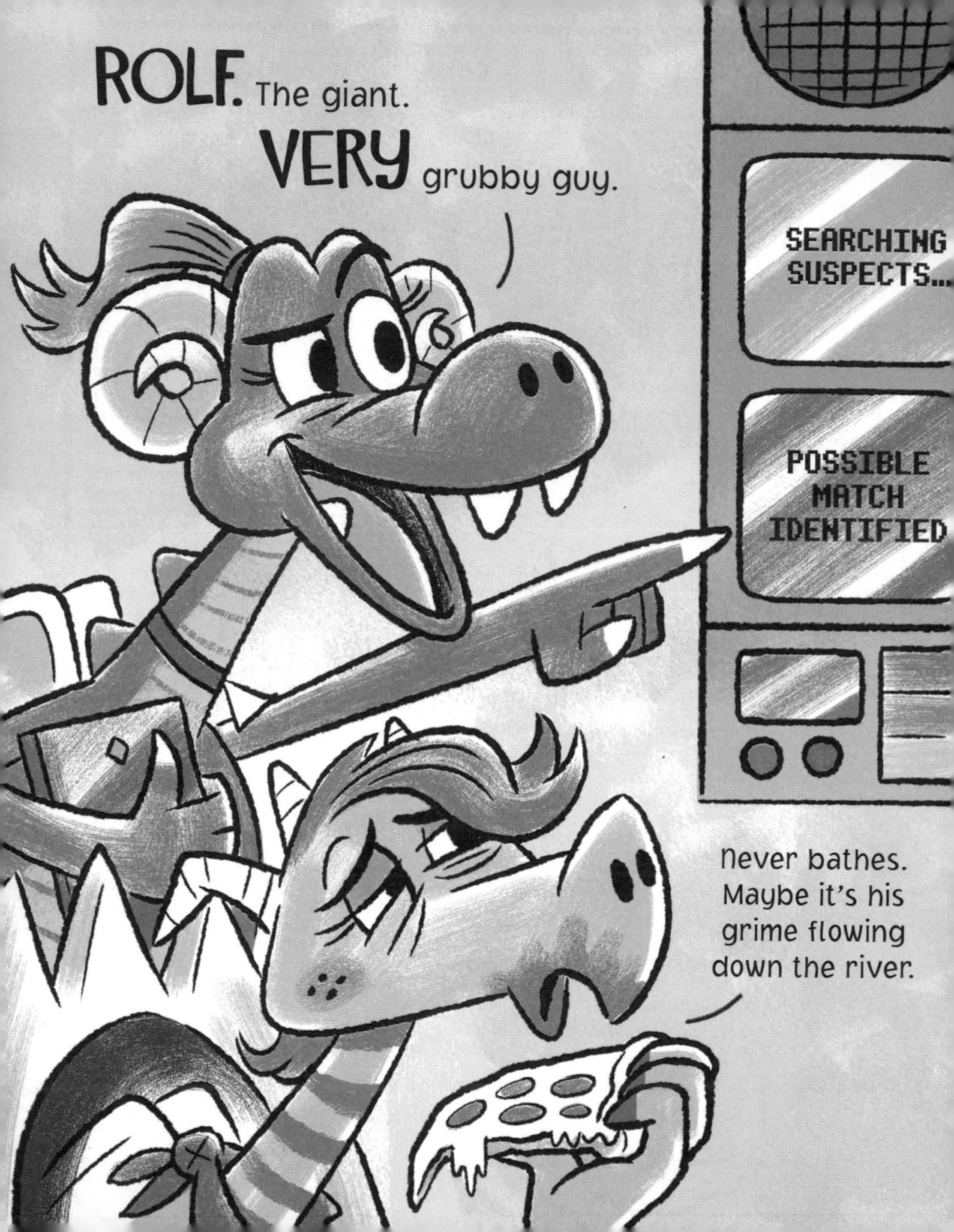
ROLF. The giant.
VERY grubby guy.
SEARCHING SUSPECTS...
POSSIBLE MATCH IDENTIFIED
never bathes. Maybe it's his grime flowing down the river.

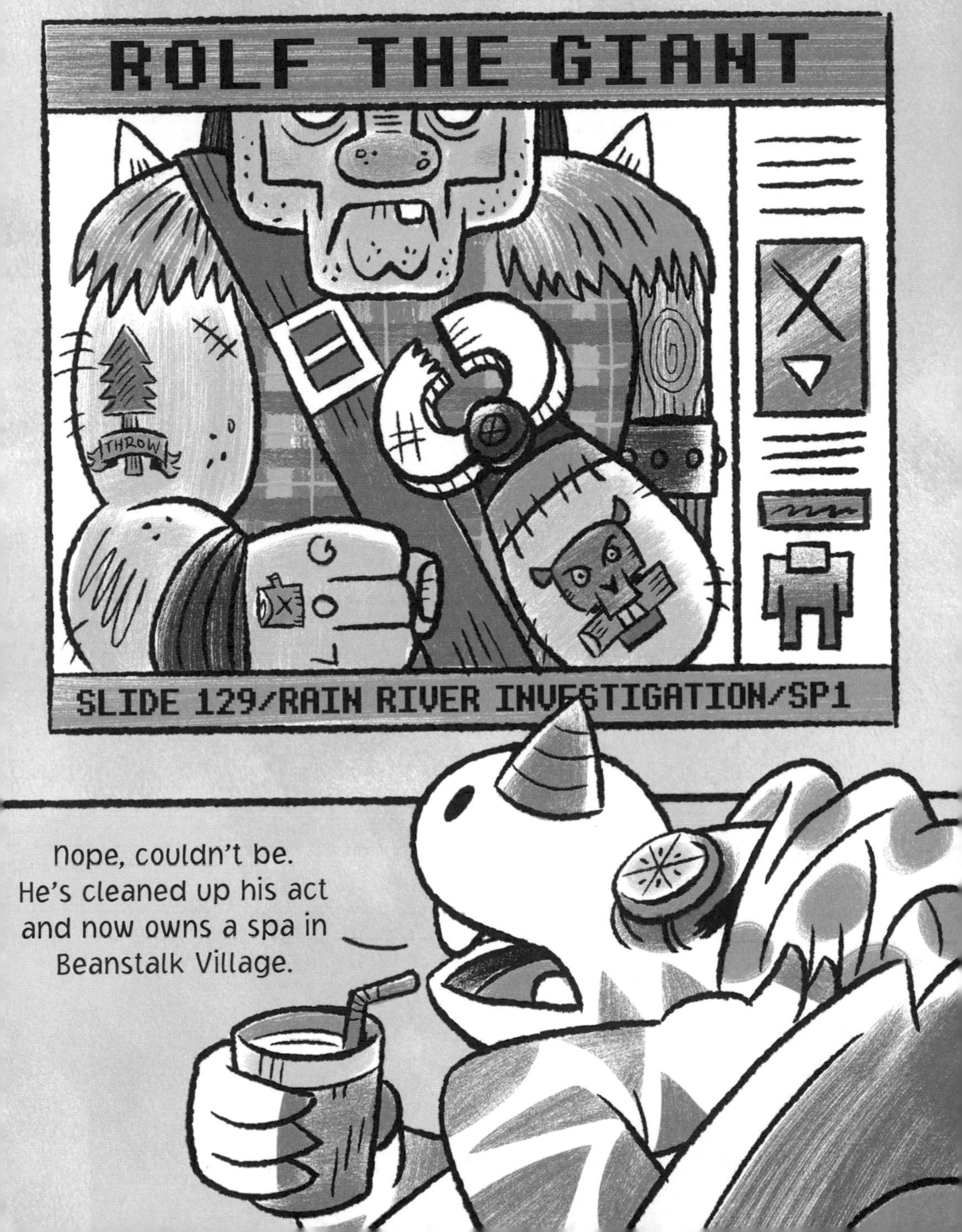
ROLF THE GIANT
THROW
SLIDE 129/RAIN RIVER INVESTIGATION/SP1
Nope, couldn't be. He's cleaned up his act and now owns a spa in Beanstalk Village.

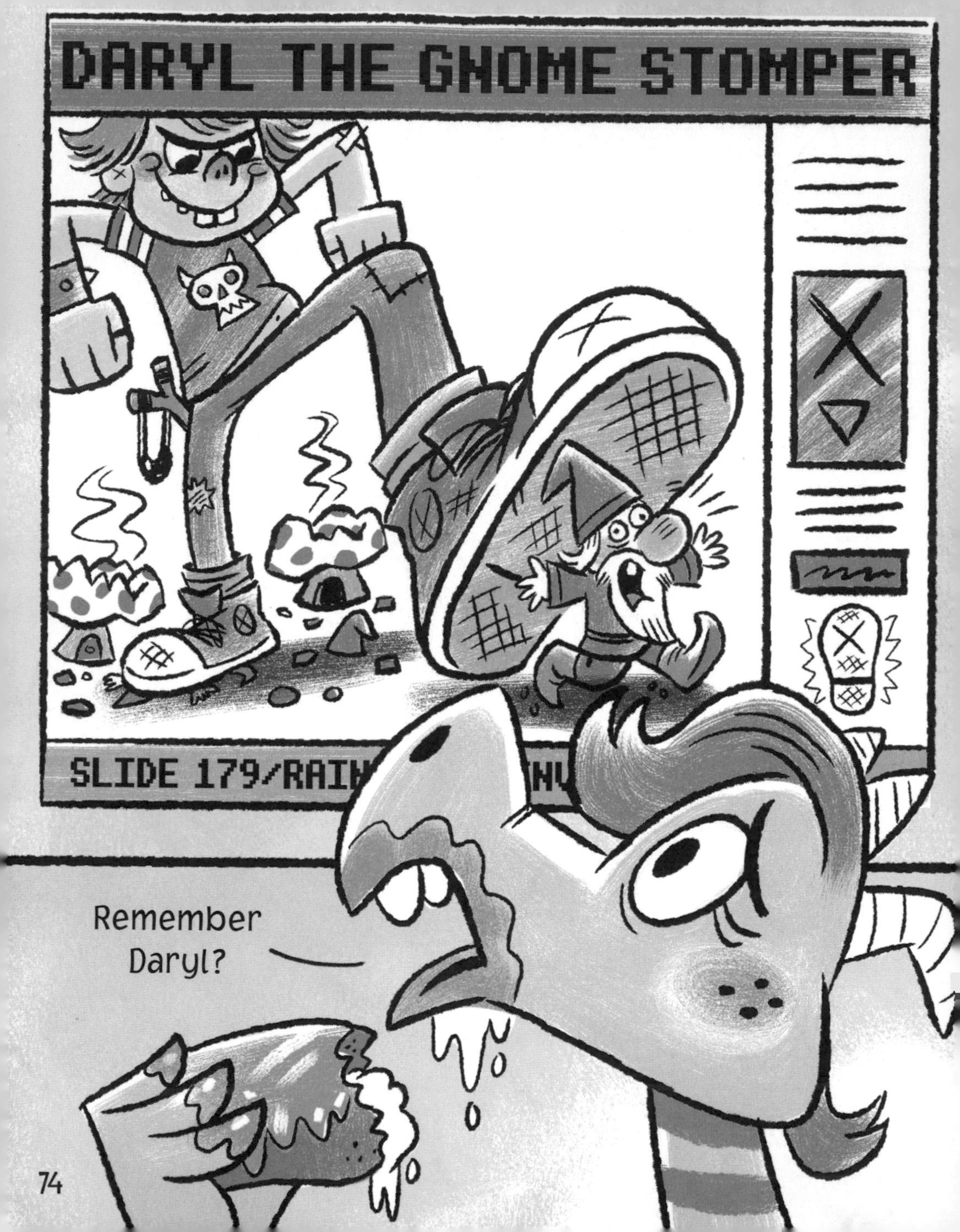
DARYL THE GNOME STOMPER
SLIDE 179/RAIN
Remember Daryl?

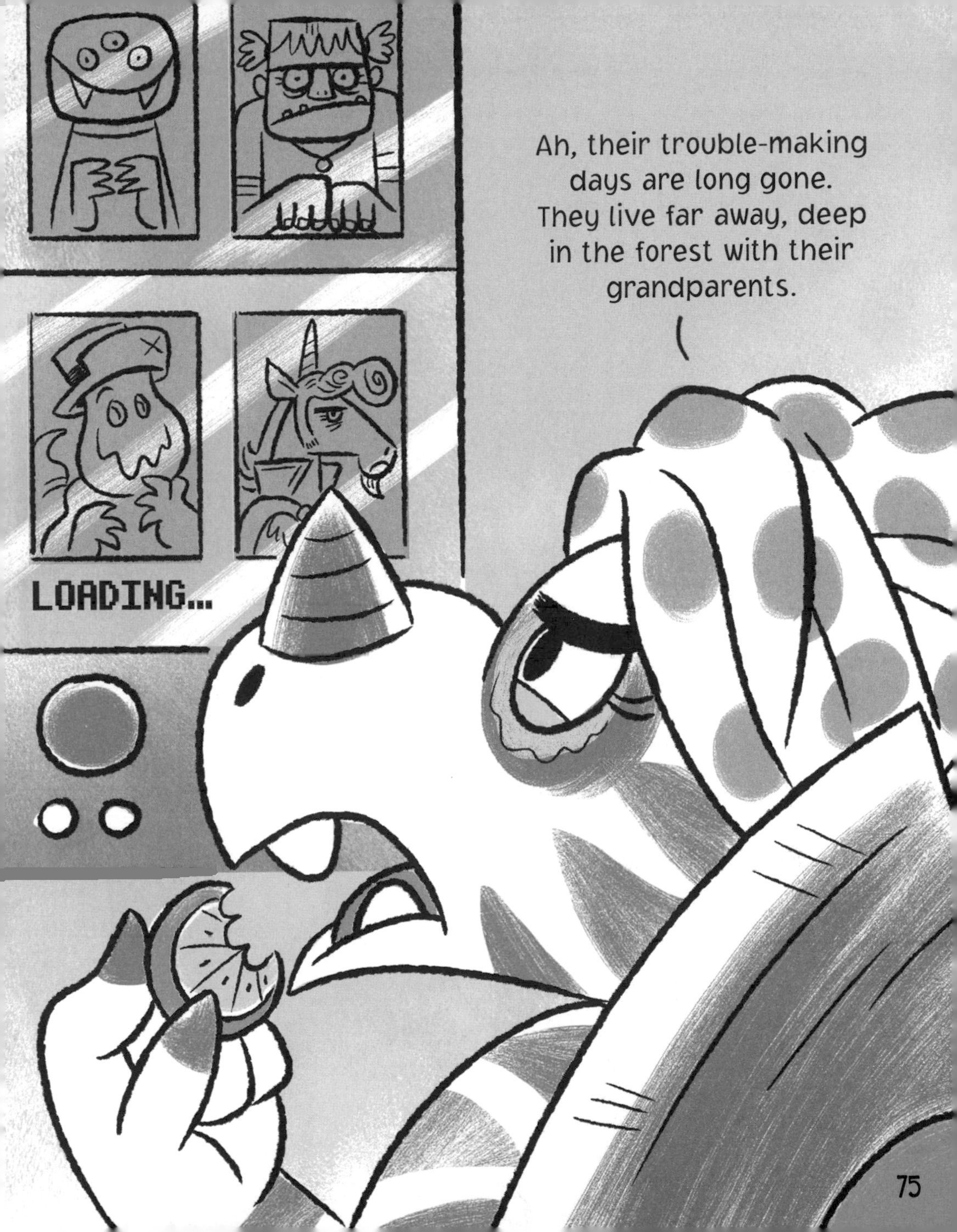
LOADING...
Ah, their trouble-making days are long gone. They live far away, deep in the forest with their grandparents.

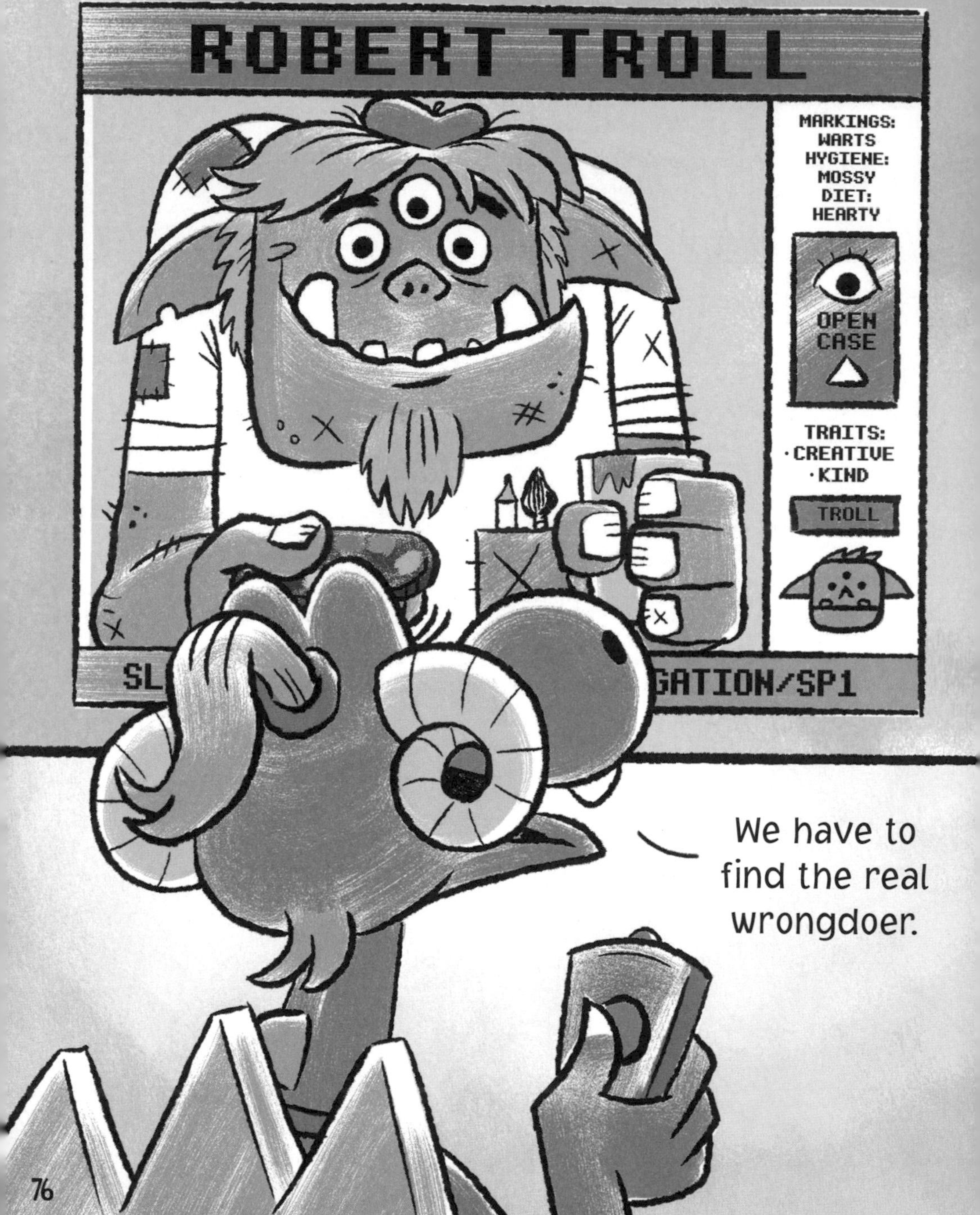
ROBERT TROLL
MARKINGS:
WARTS
HYGIENE:
MOSSY
DIET:
HEARTY
OPEN
CASE
TRAITS:
· CREATIVE
· KIND
TROLL
SL
GATION/SP1
We have to find the real wrongdoer.

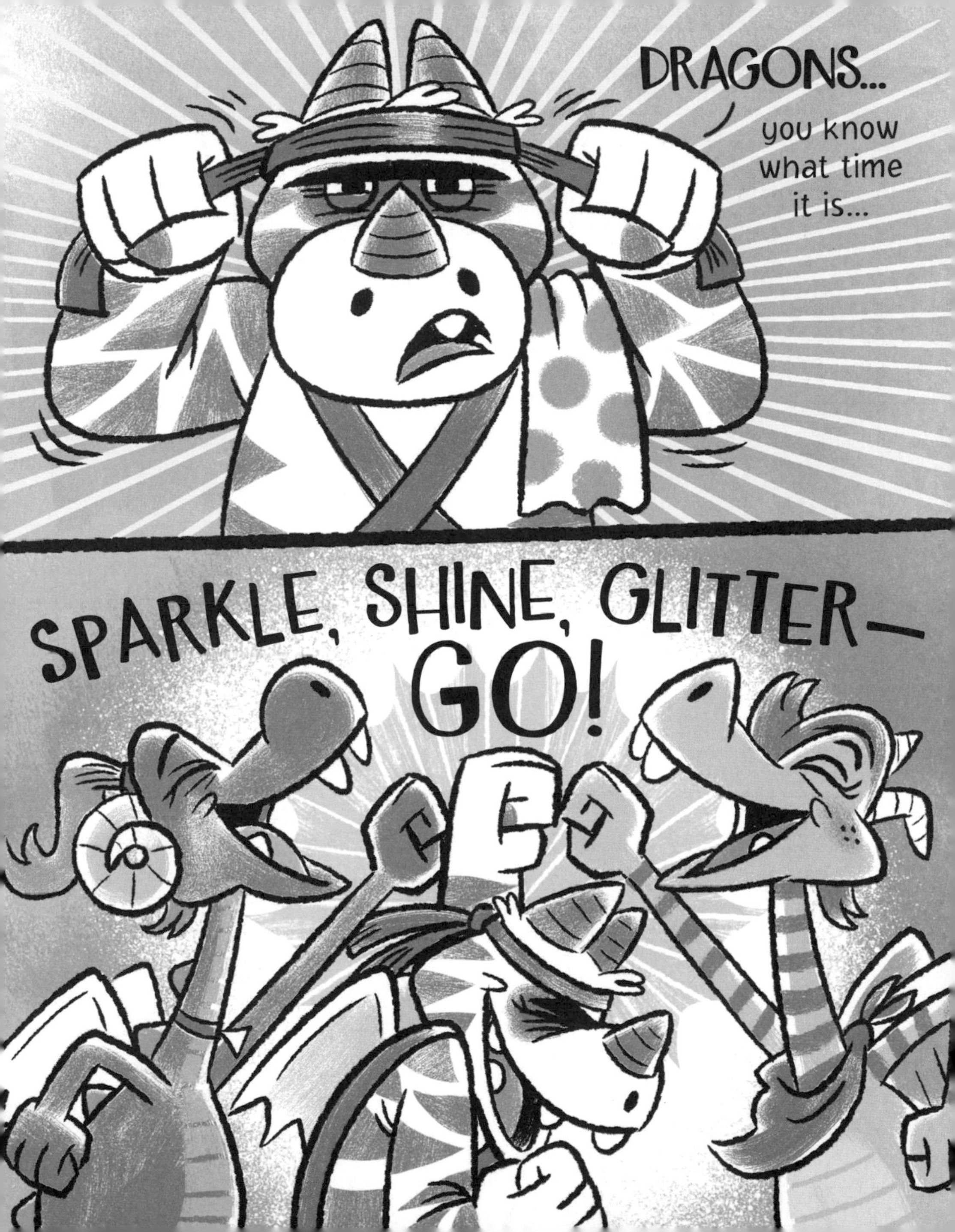
DRAGONS...
you know what time it is...
SPARKLE, SHINE, GLITTER—GO!

CHAPTER SIX
GLITTERY GUMSHOES INVESTIGATE

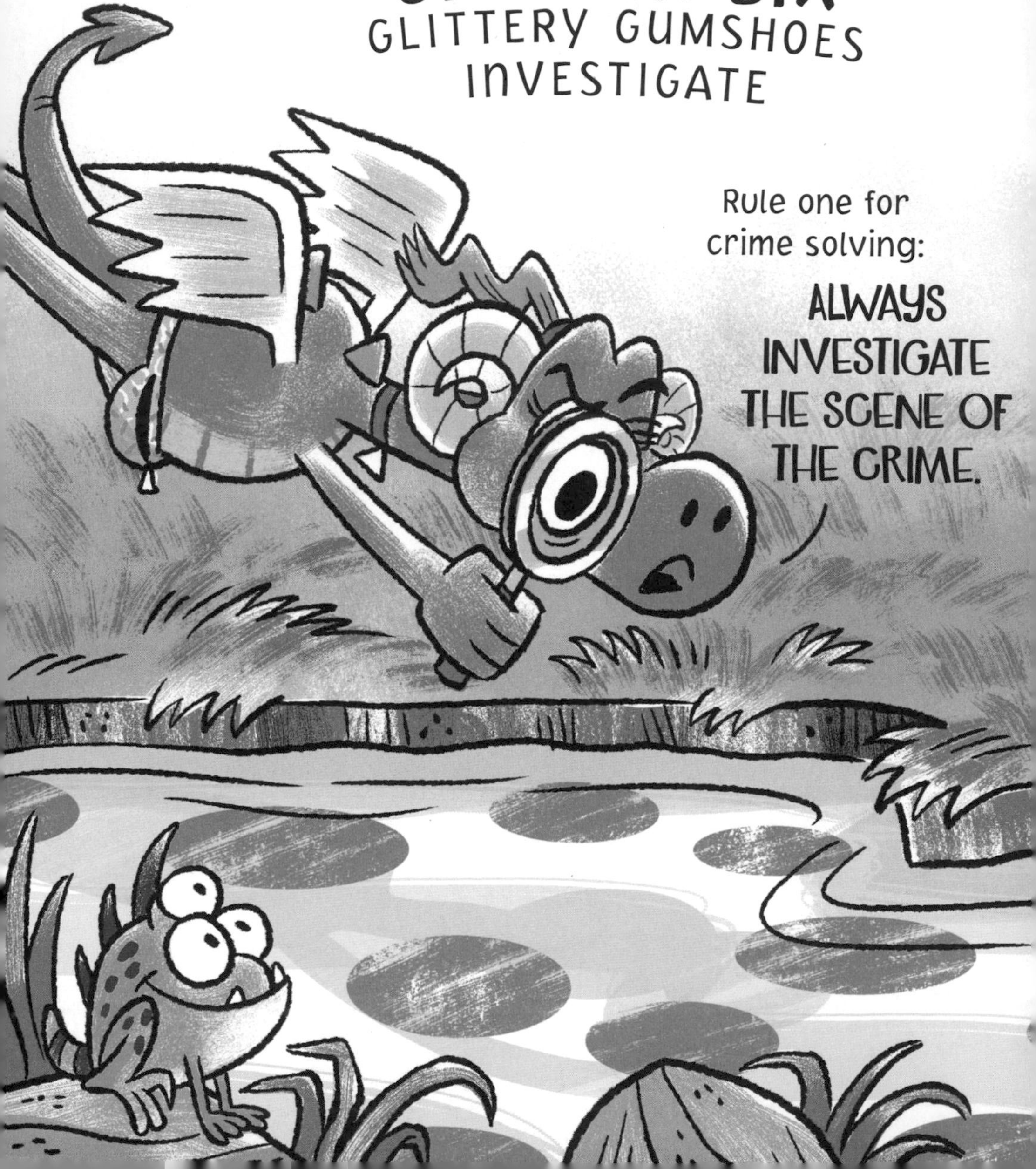
Rule one for crime solving:
ALWAYS INVESTIGATE THE SCENE OF THE CRIME.

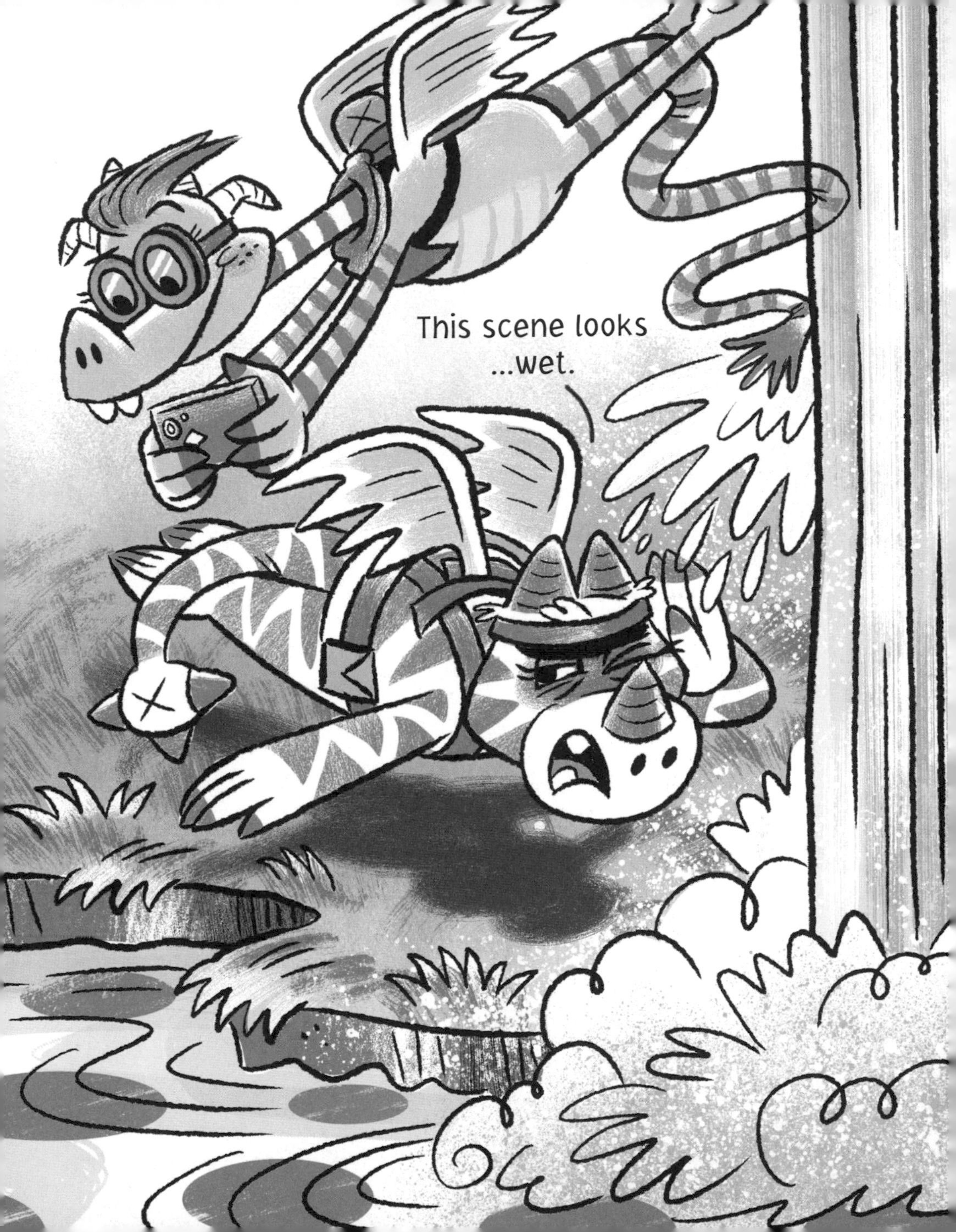
This scene looks
...wet.

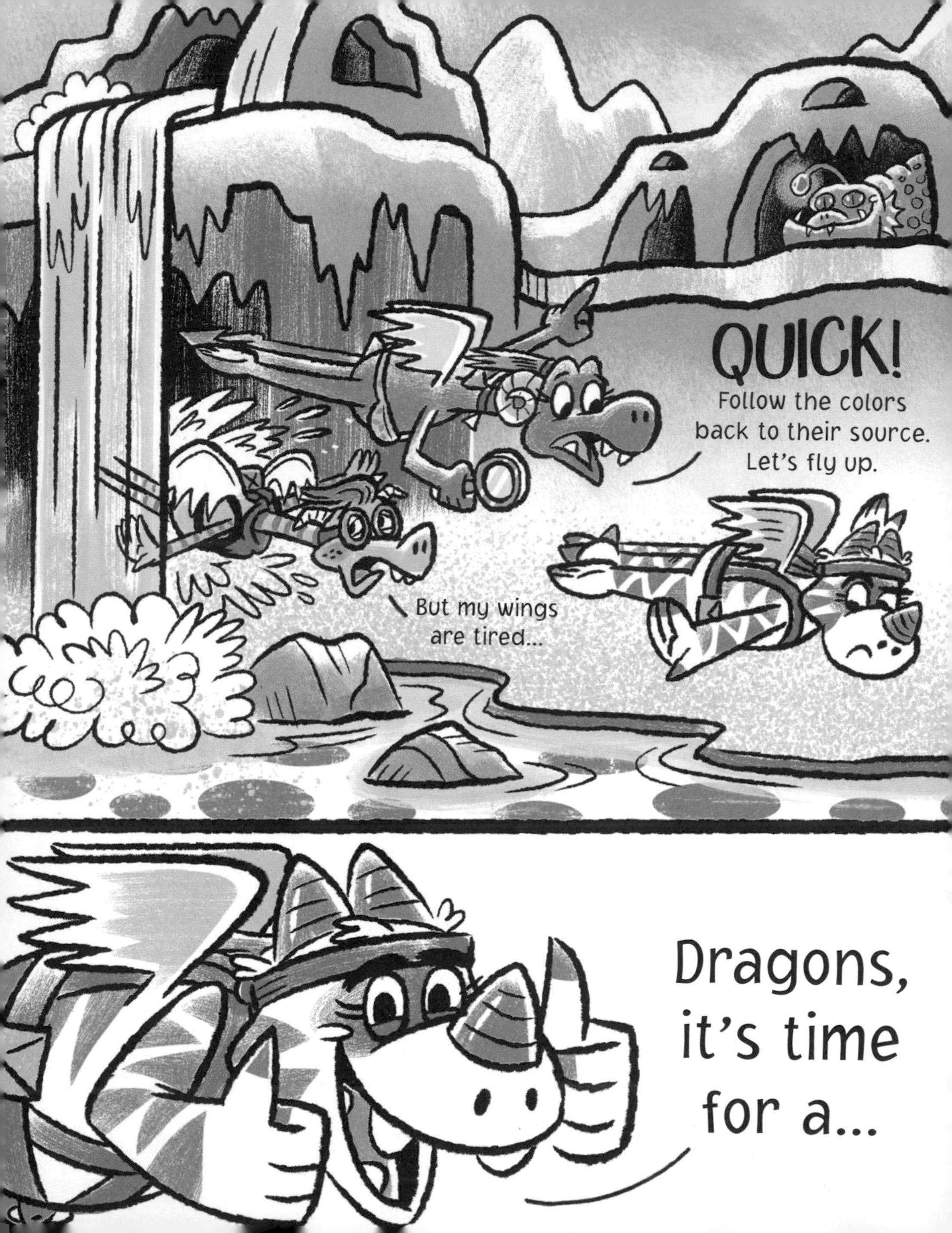
QUICK!
Follow the colors back to their source. Let's fly up.
But my wings are tired...
Dragons, it's time for a...

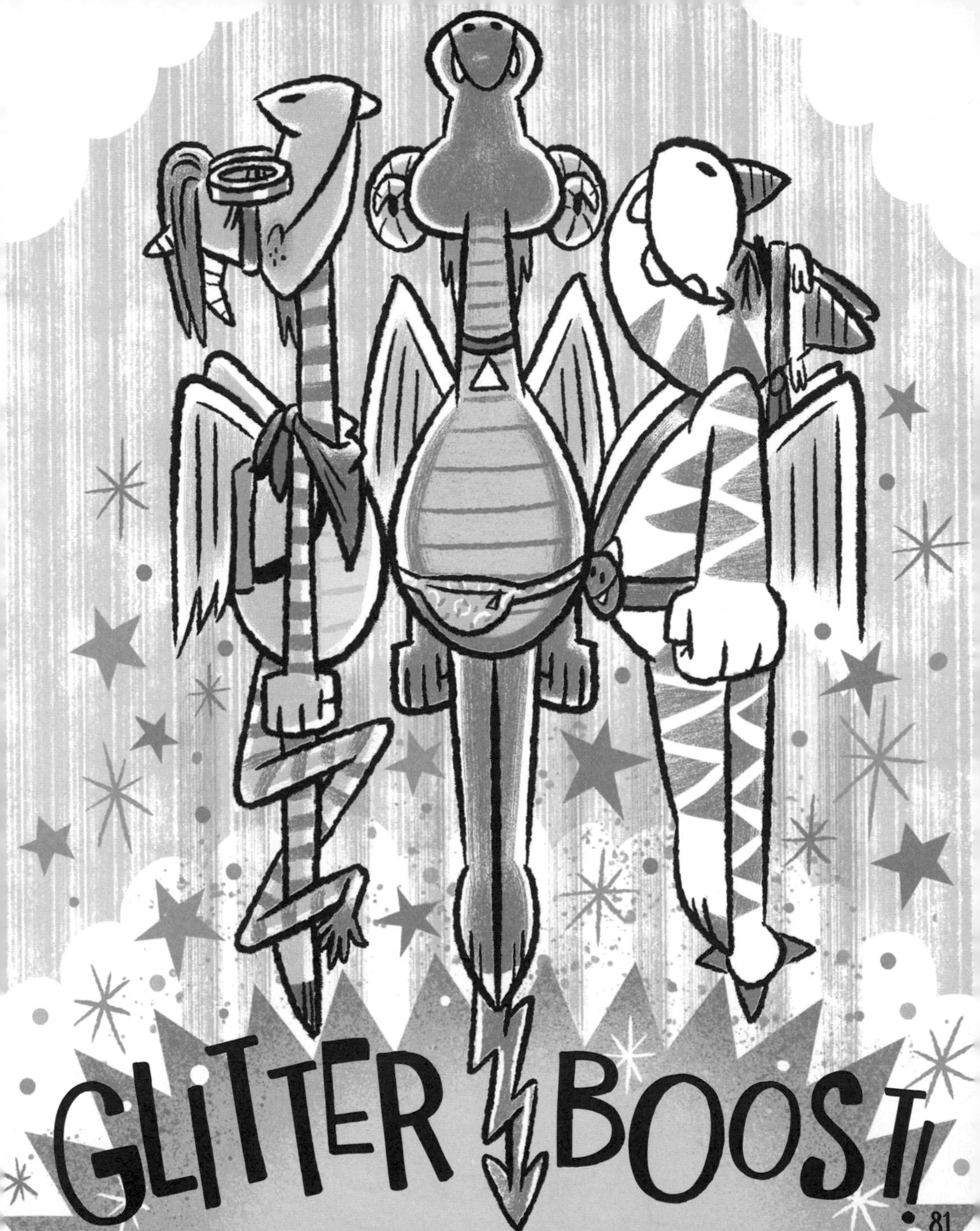
GLITTER BOOST!

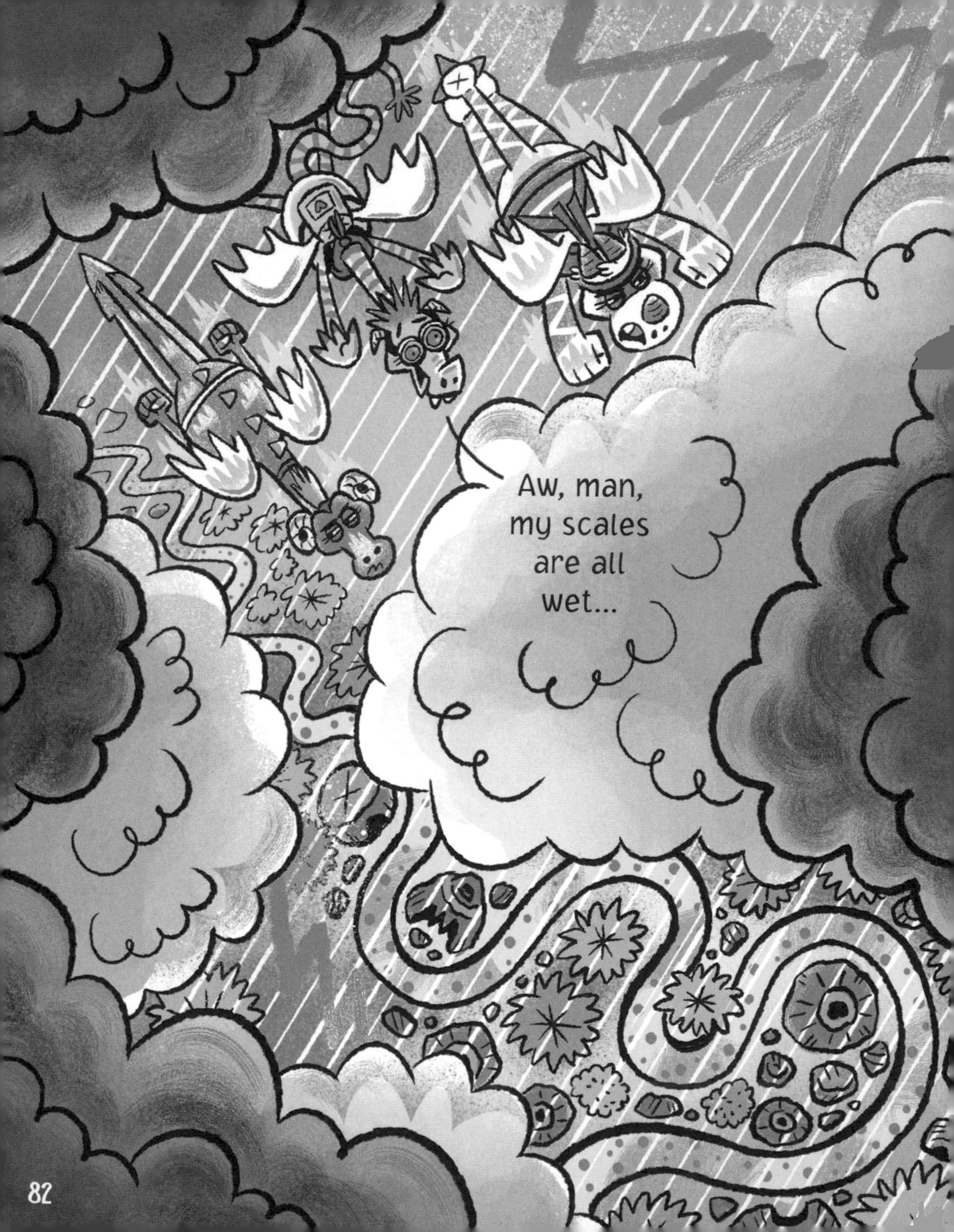
Aw, man, my scales are all wet...

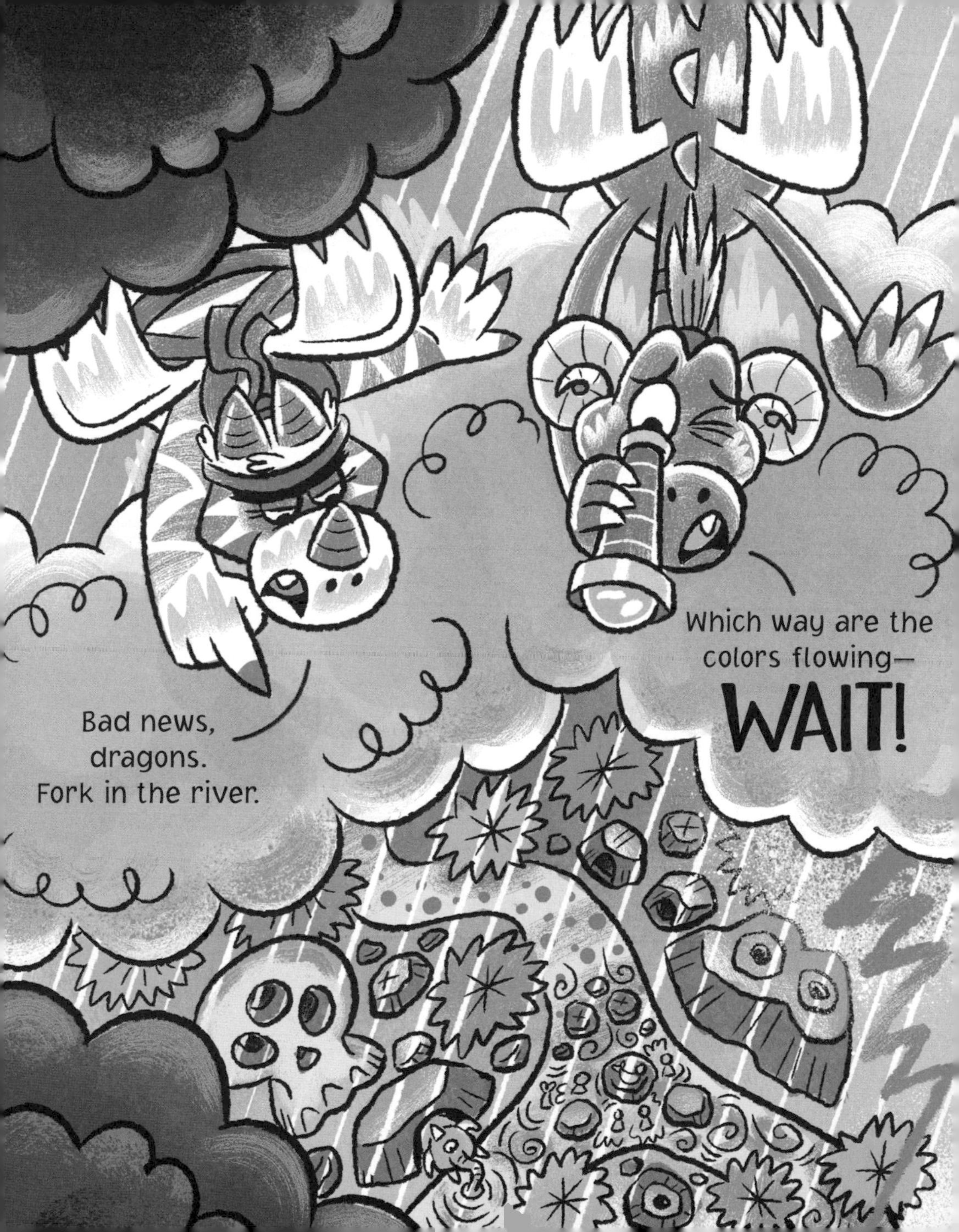
Bad news,
dragons.
Fork in the river.
Which way are the
colors flowing—
WAIT!

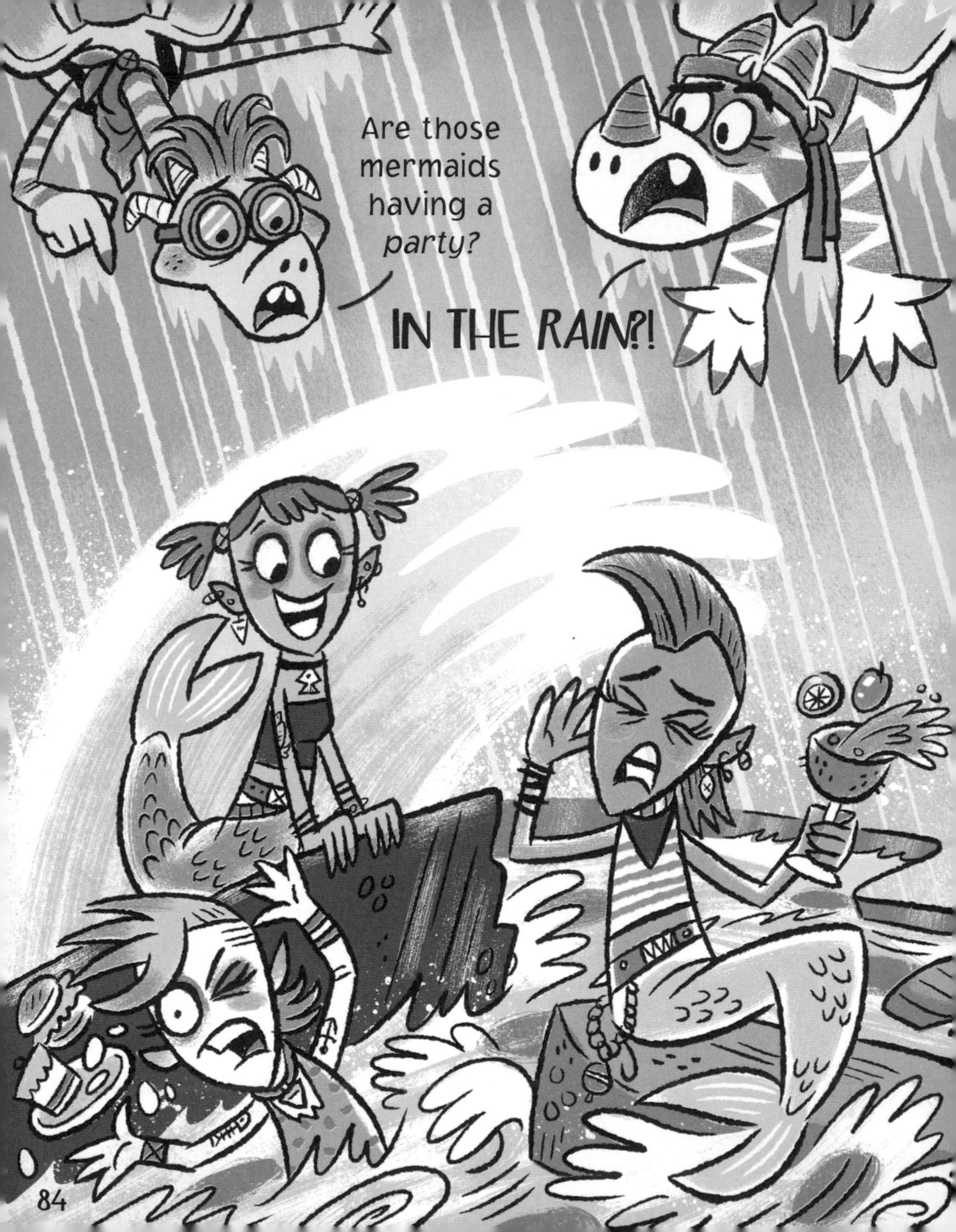
Are those mermaids having a *party?*
IN THE *RAIN*?!

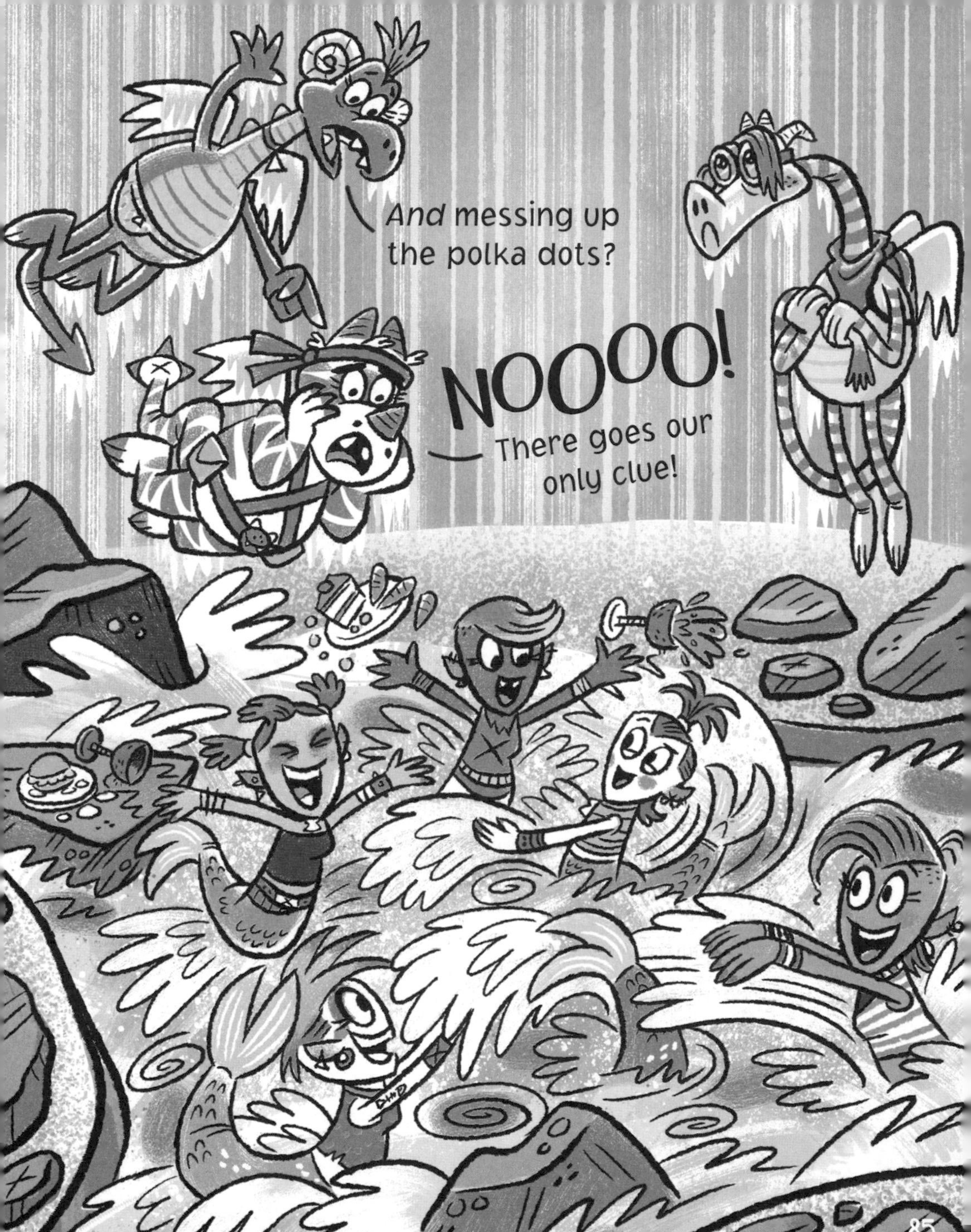

And messing up
the polka dots?
NOOOO!
There goes our
only clue!

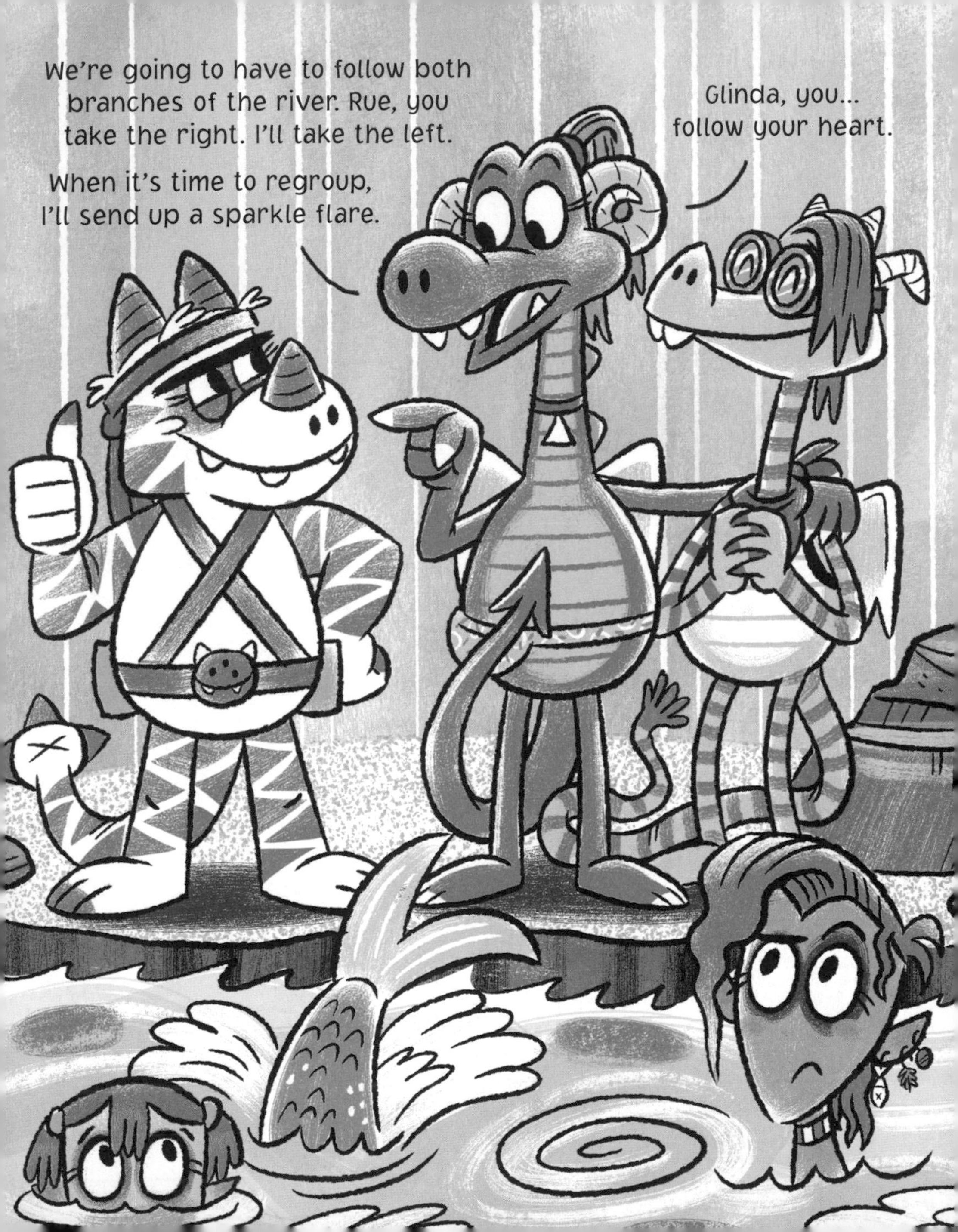
We're going to have to follow both branches of the river. Rue, you take the right. I'll take the left.
When it's time to regroup, I'll send up a sparkle flare.
Glinda, you... follow your heart.

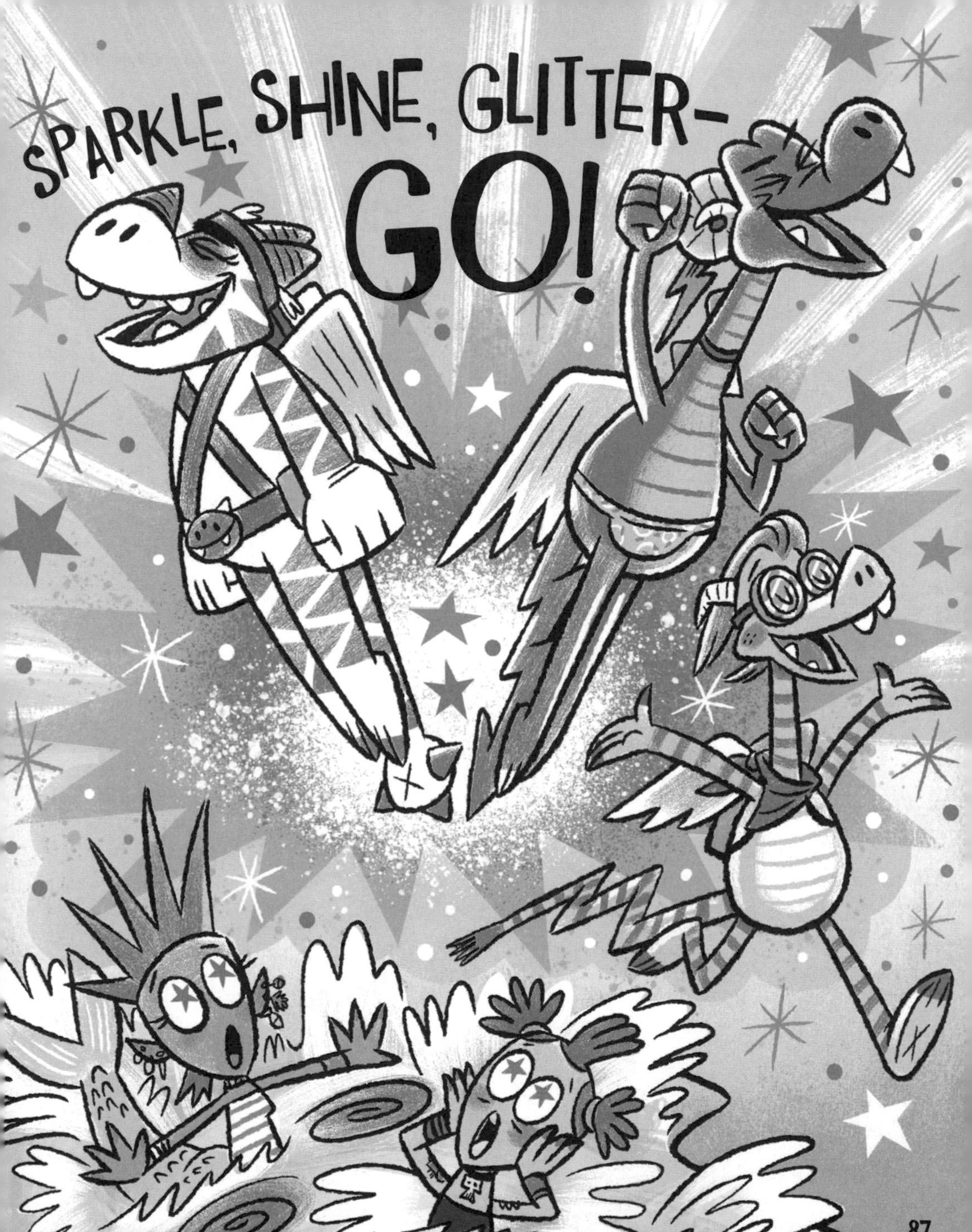
SPARKLE, SHINE, GLITTER–
GO!

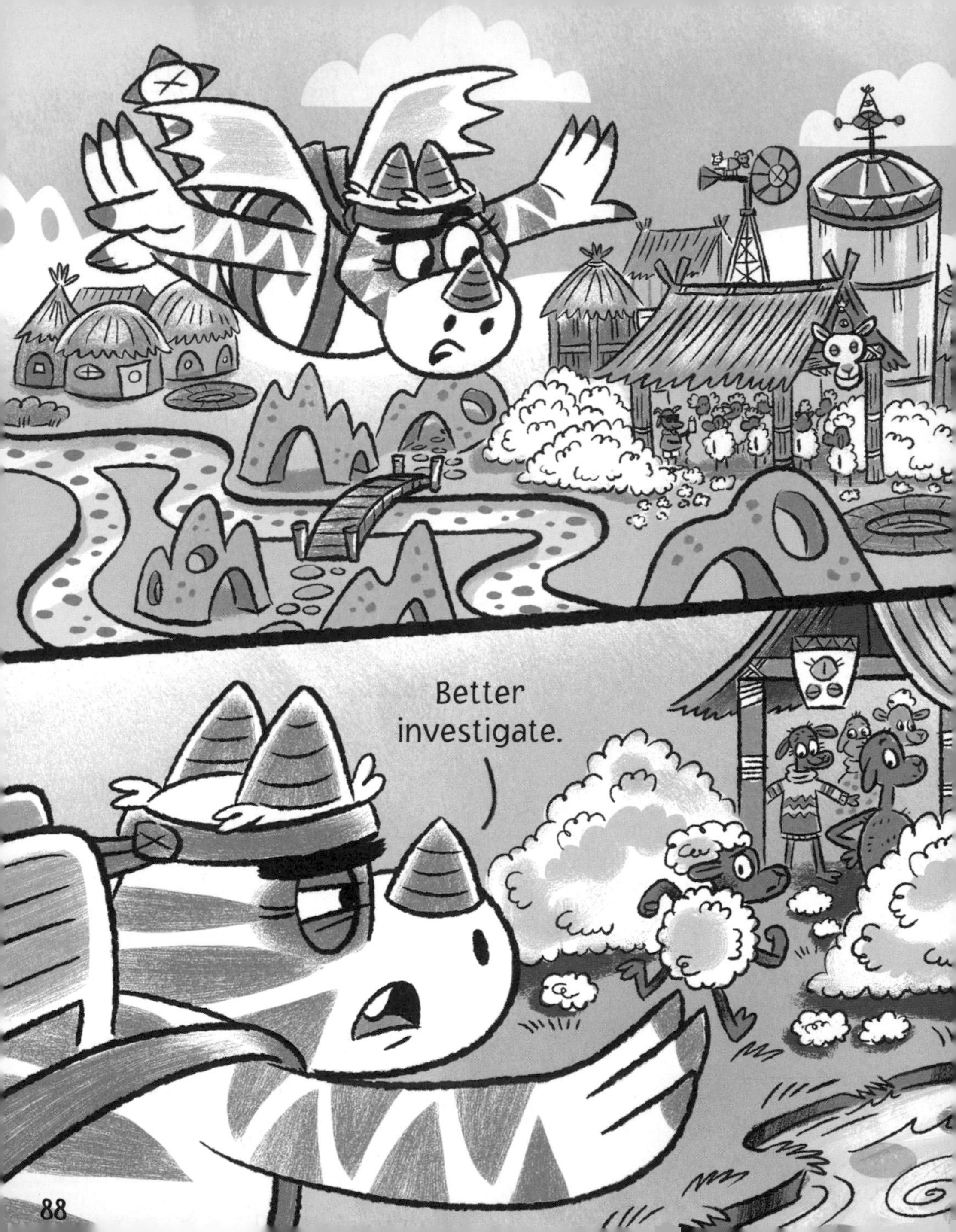
Better investigate.

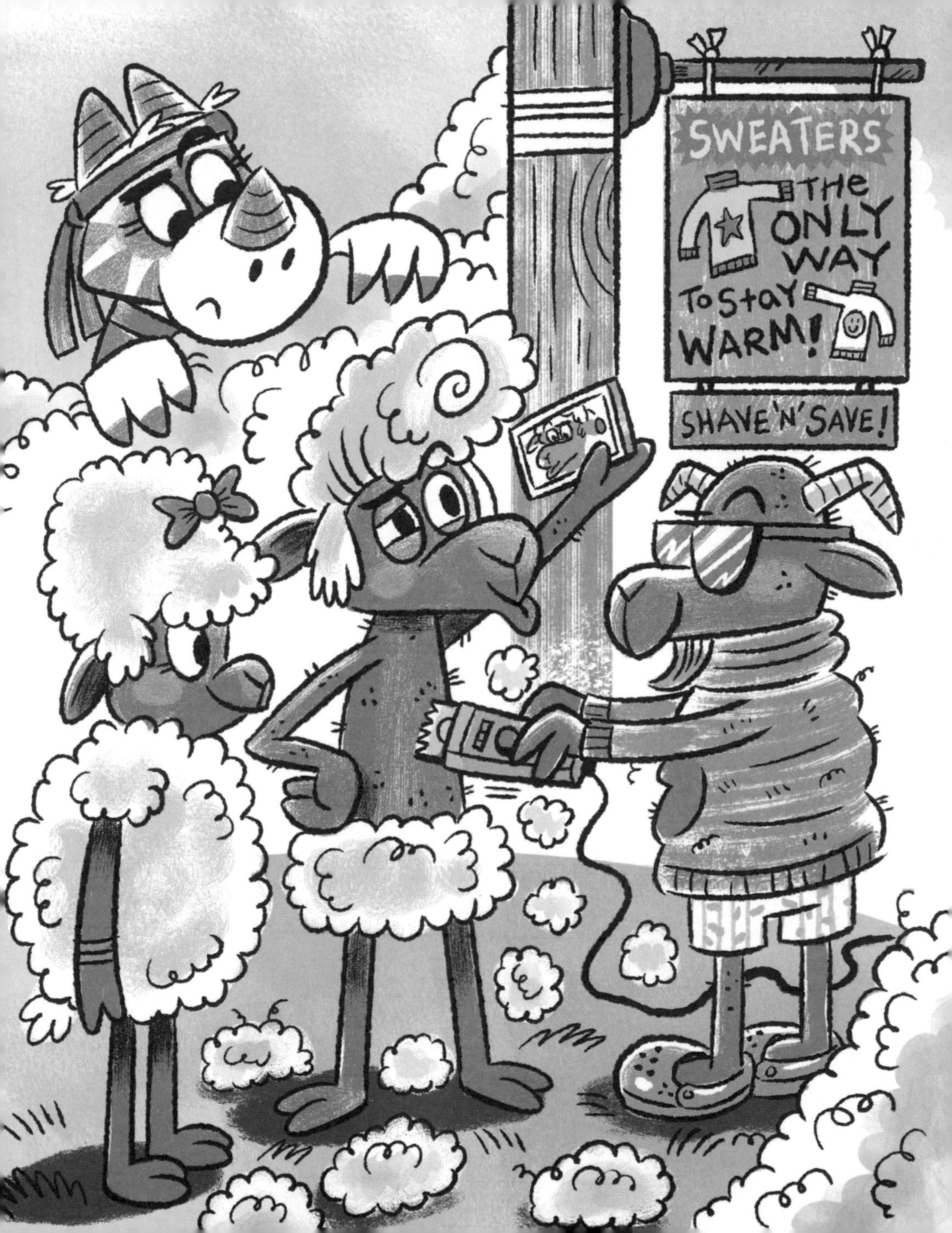
SWEATERS
THE ONLY WAY TO STAY WARM!
SHAVE 'N' SAVE!

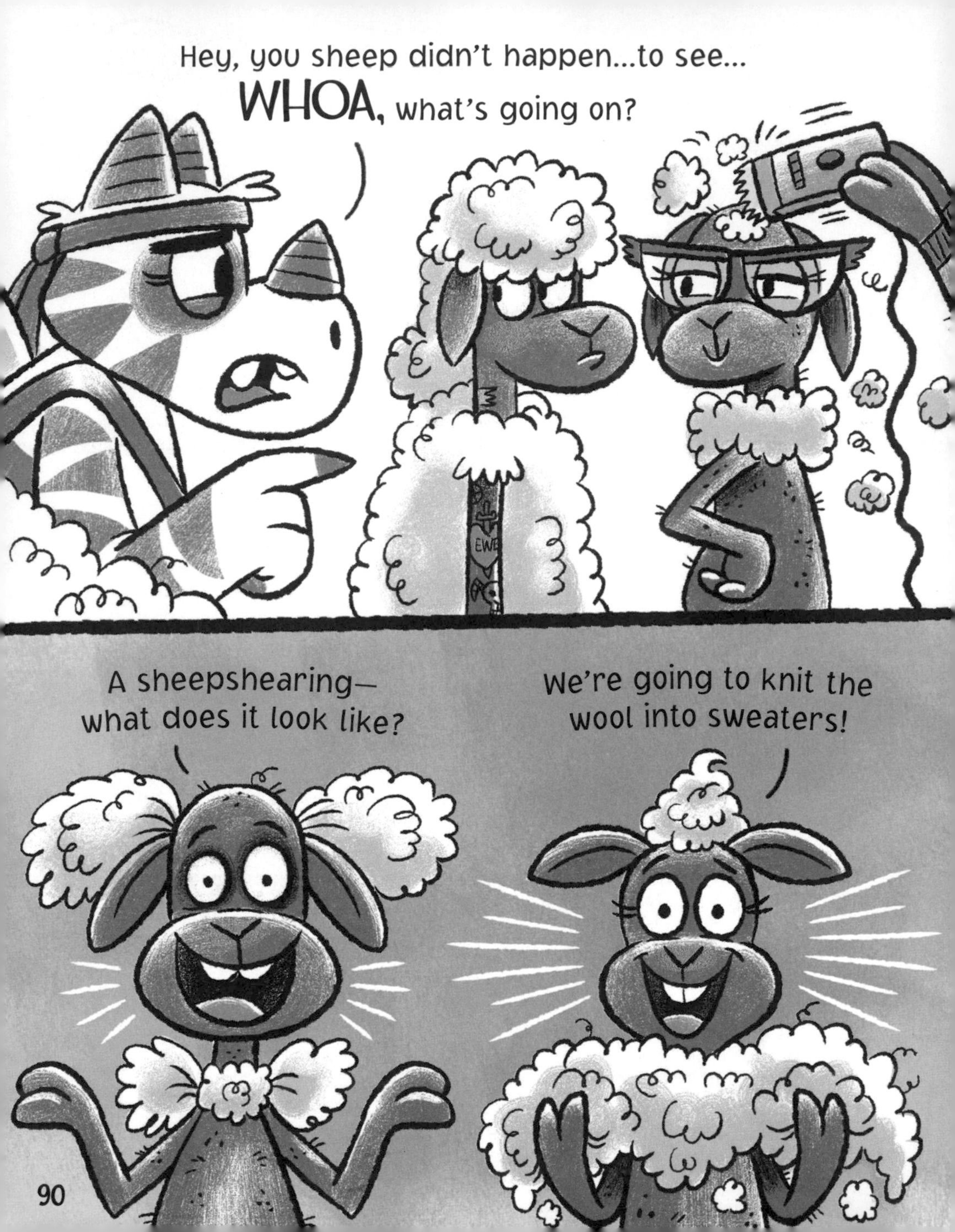
Hey, you sheep didn't happen...to see... WHOA, what's going on?
EWE
A sheepshearing— what does it look like?
We're going to knit the wool into sweaters!

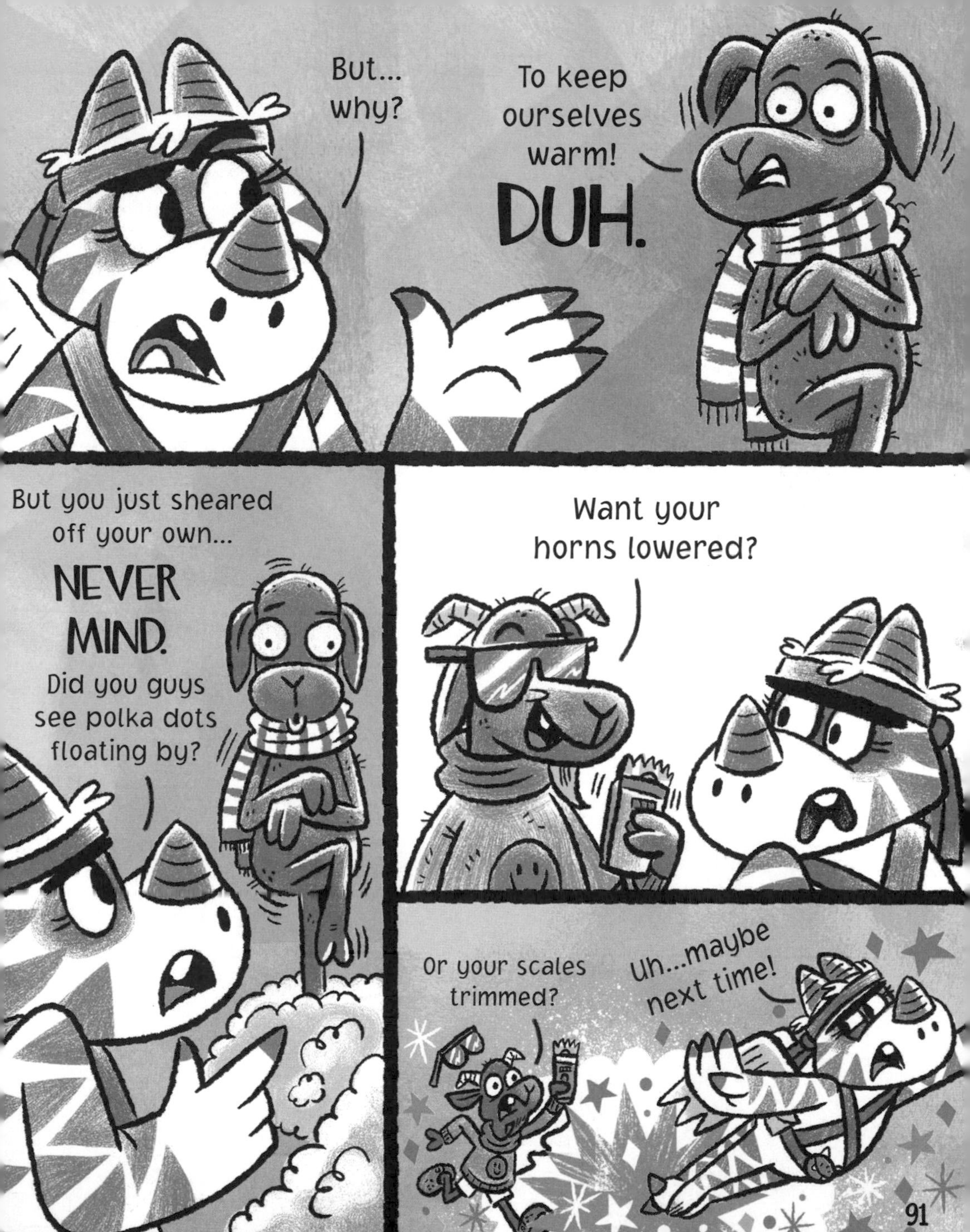
But... why?
To keep ourselves warm!
DUH.
But you just sheared off your own...
NEVER MIND.
Did you guys see polka dots floating by?
Want your horns lowered?
Or your scales trimmed?
Uh...maybe next time!

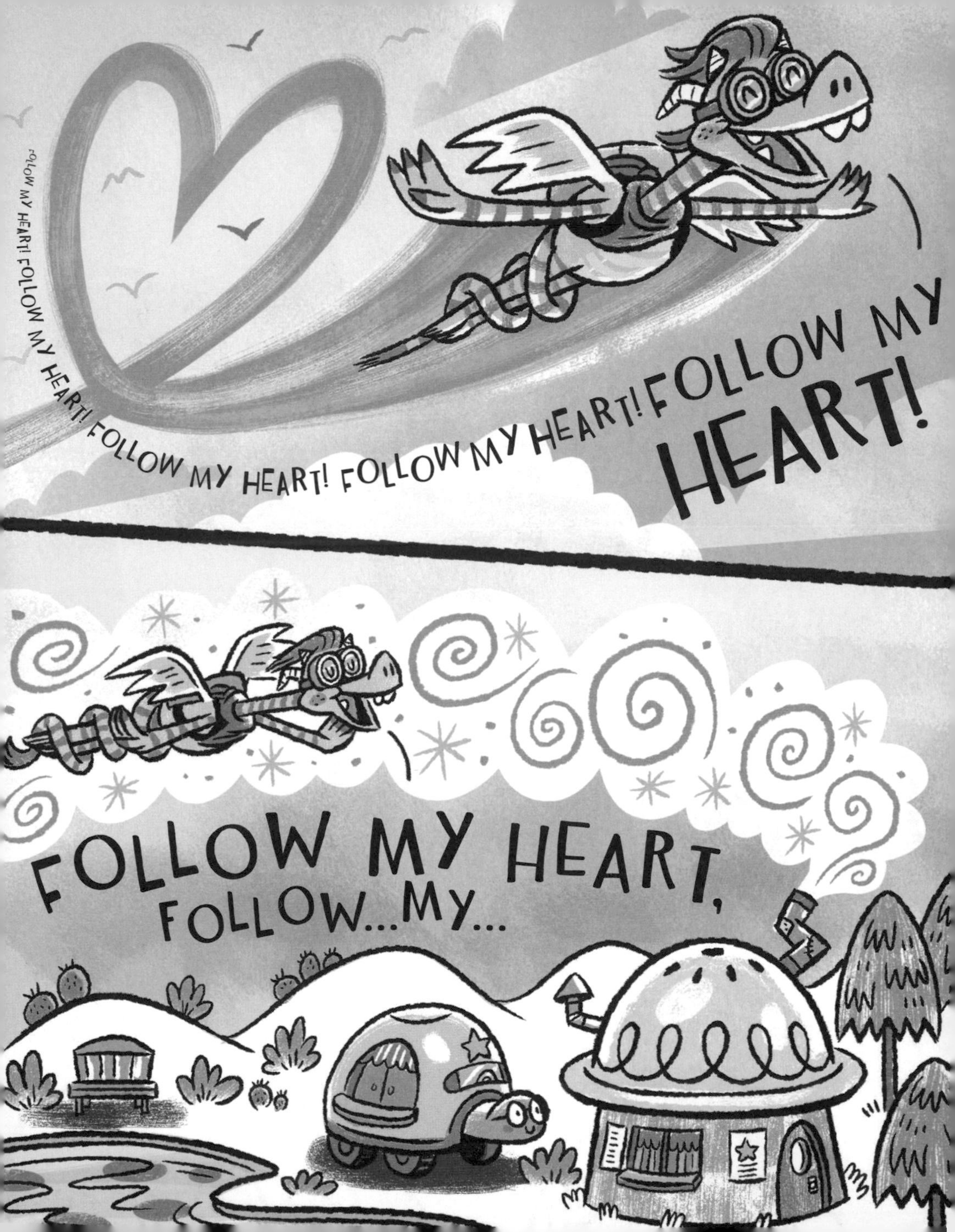
FOLLOW MY HEART! FOLLOW MY HEART! FOLLOW MY HEART! FOLLOW MY HEART! FOLLOW MY HEART!
FOLLOW MY HEART,
FOLLOW...MY...

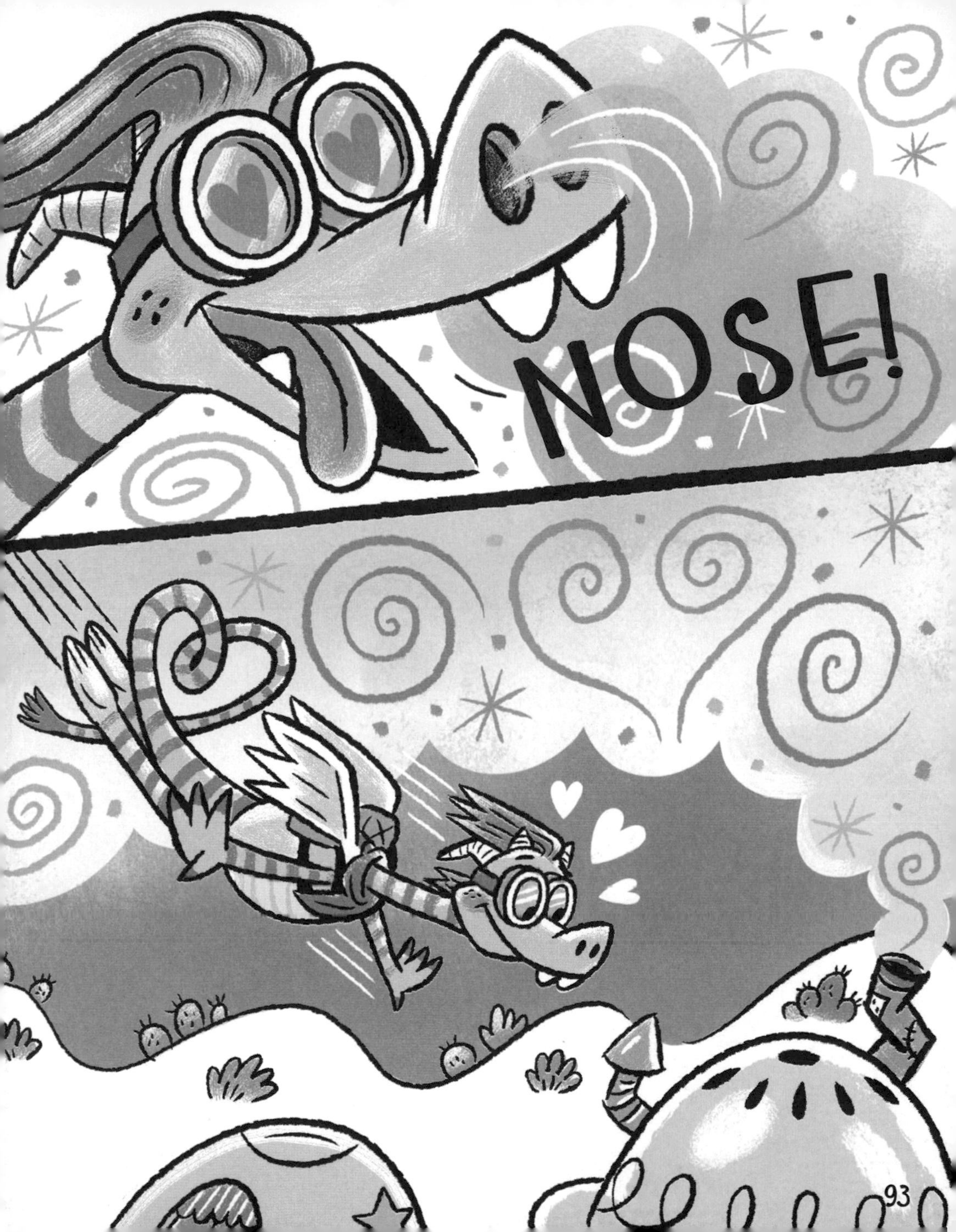
NOSE!

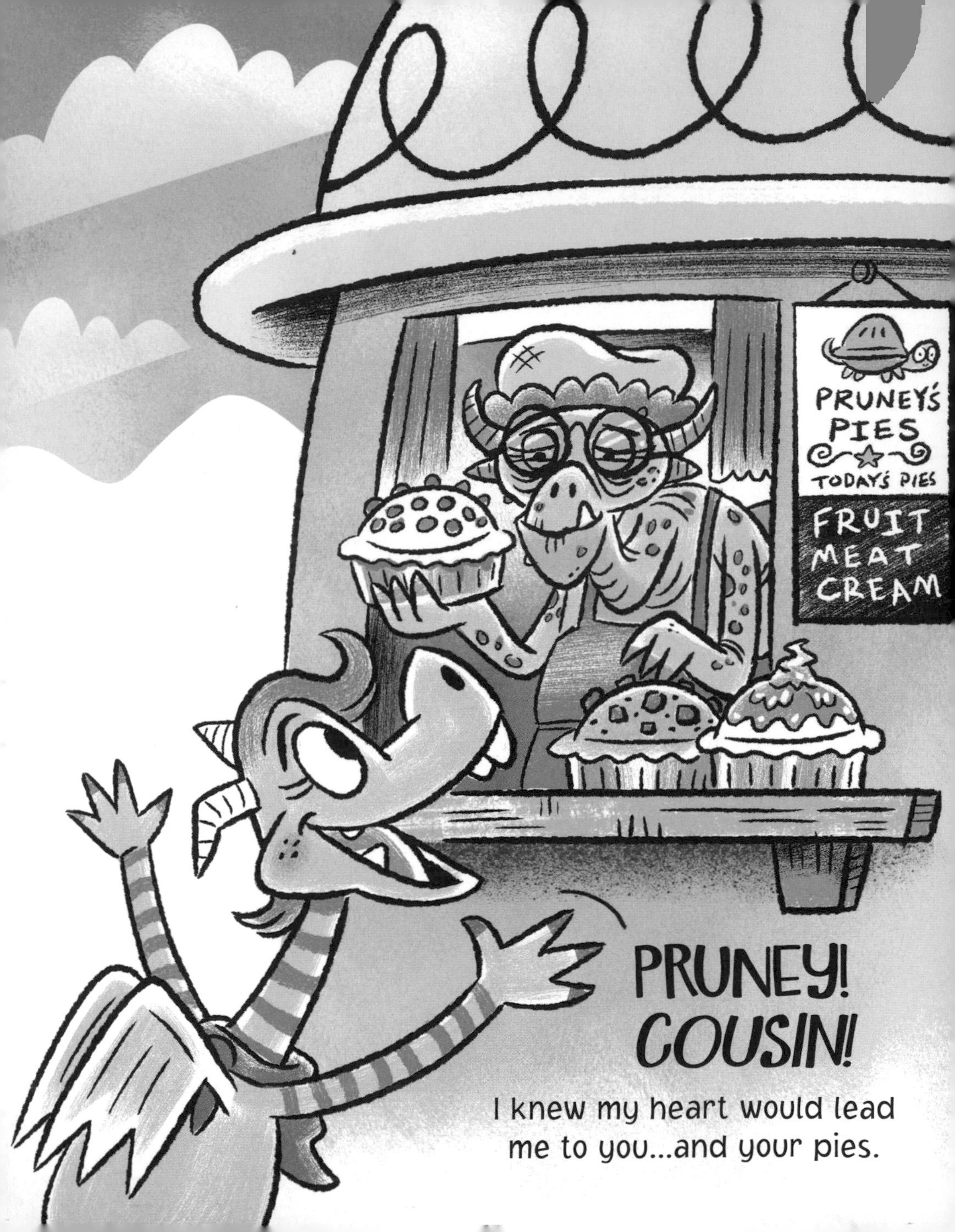
PRUNEY'S PIES
TODAY'S PIES
FRUIT
MEAT
CREAM
PRUNEY!
COUSIN!
I knew my heart would lead me to you...and your pies.

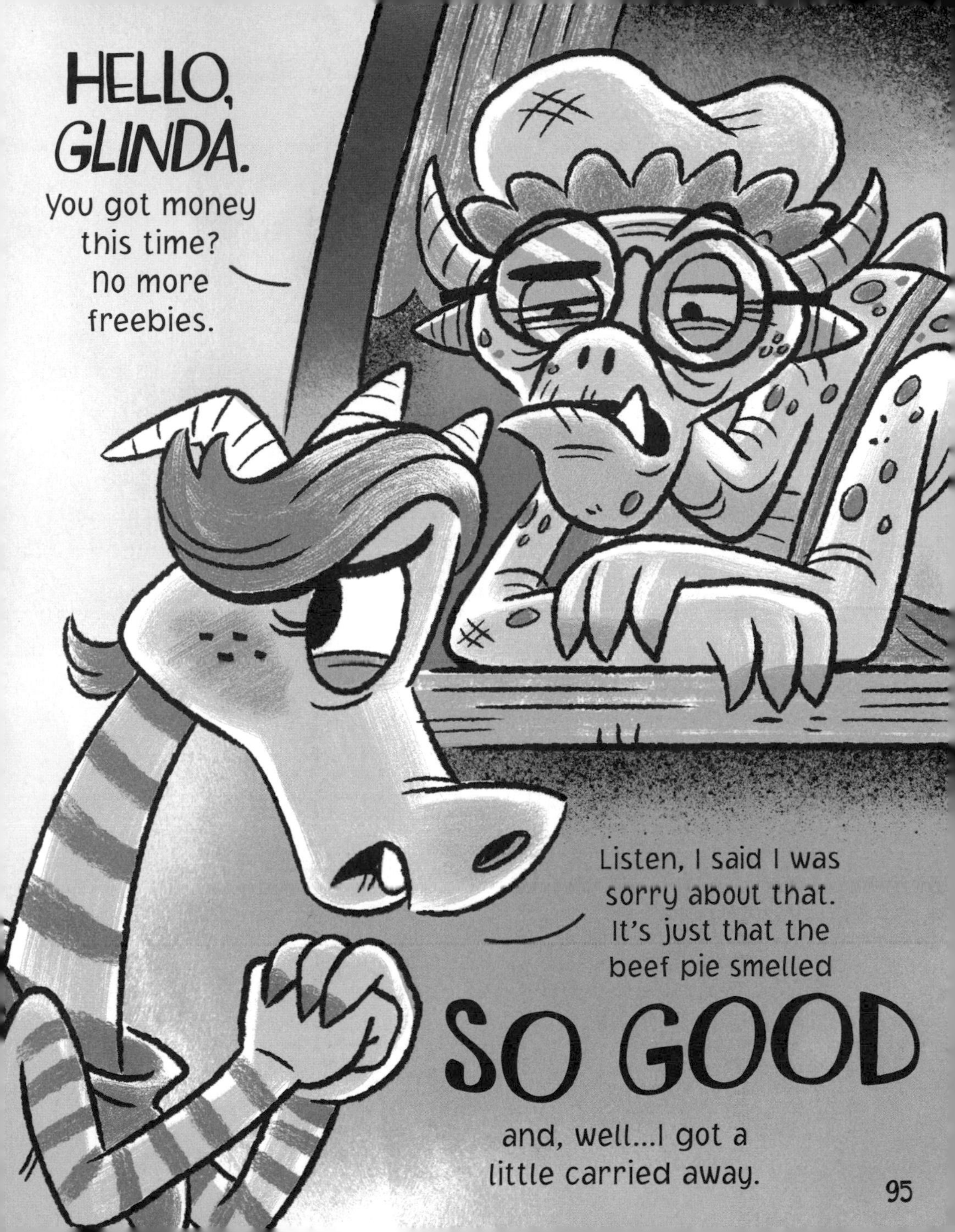
HELLO, GLINDA.
You got money this time? No more freebies.
Listen, I said I was sorry about that. It's just that the beef pie smelled
SO GOOD
and, well...I got a little carried away.

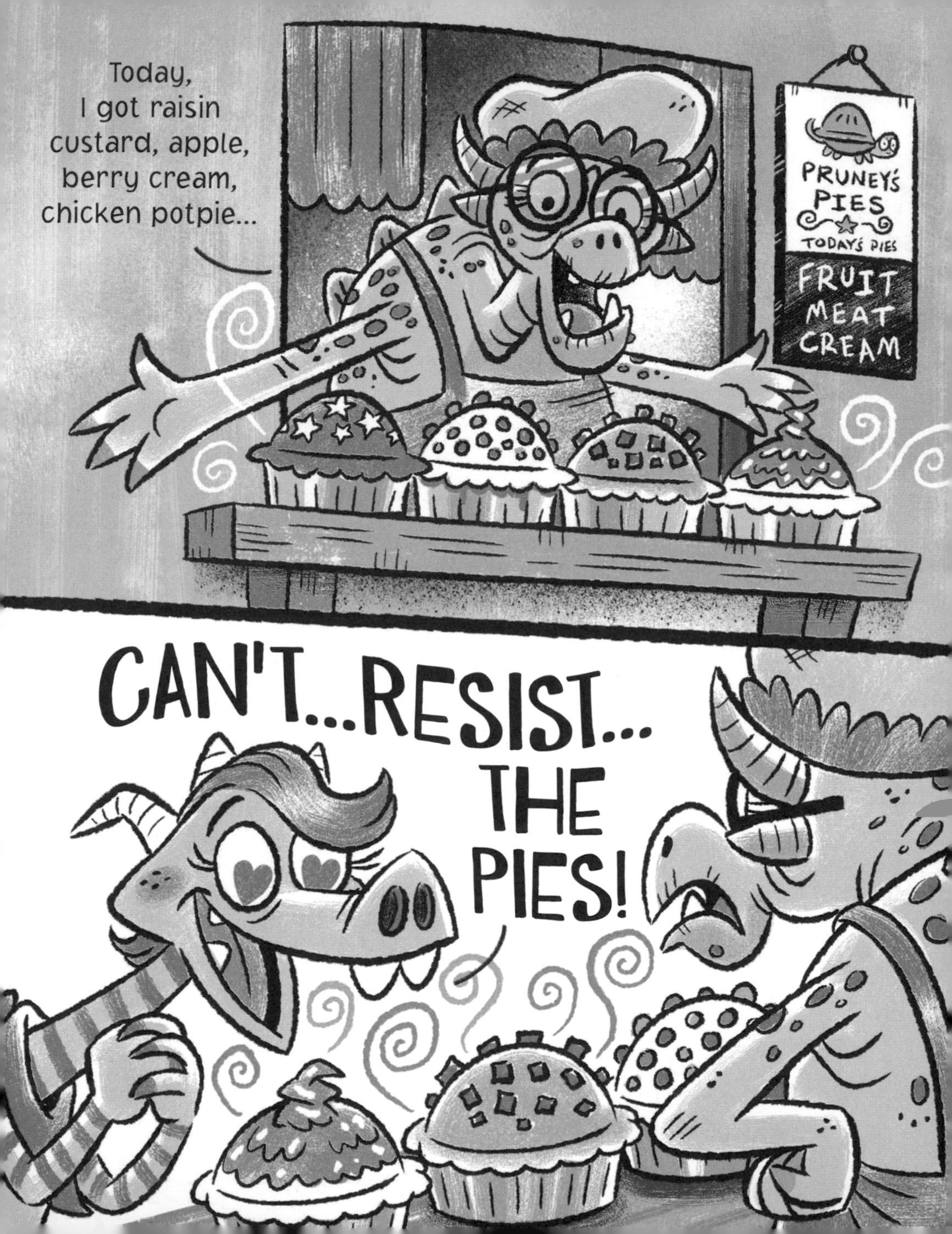
Today, I got raisin custard, apple, berry cream, chicken potpie...
PRUNEY'S PIES
TODAY'S PIES
FRUIT
MEAT
CREAM
CAN'T...RESIST... THE PIES!

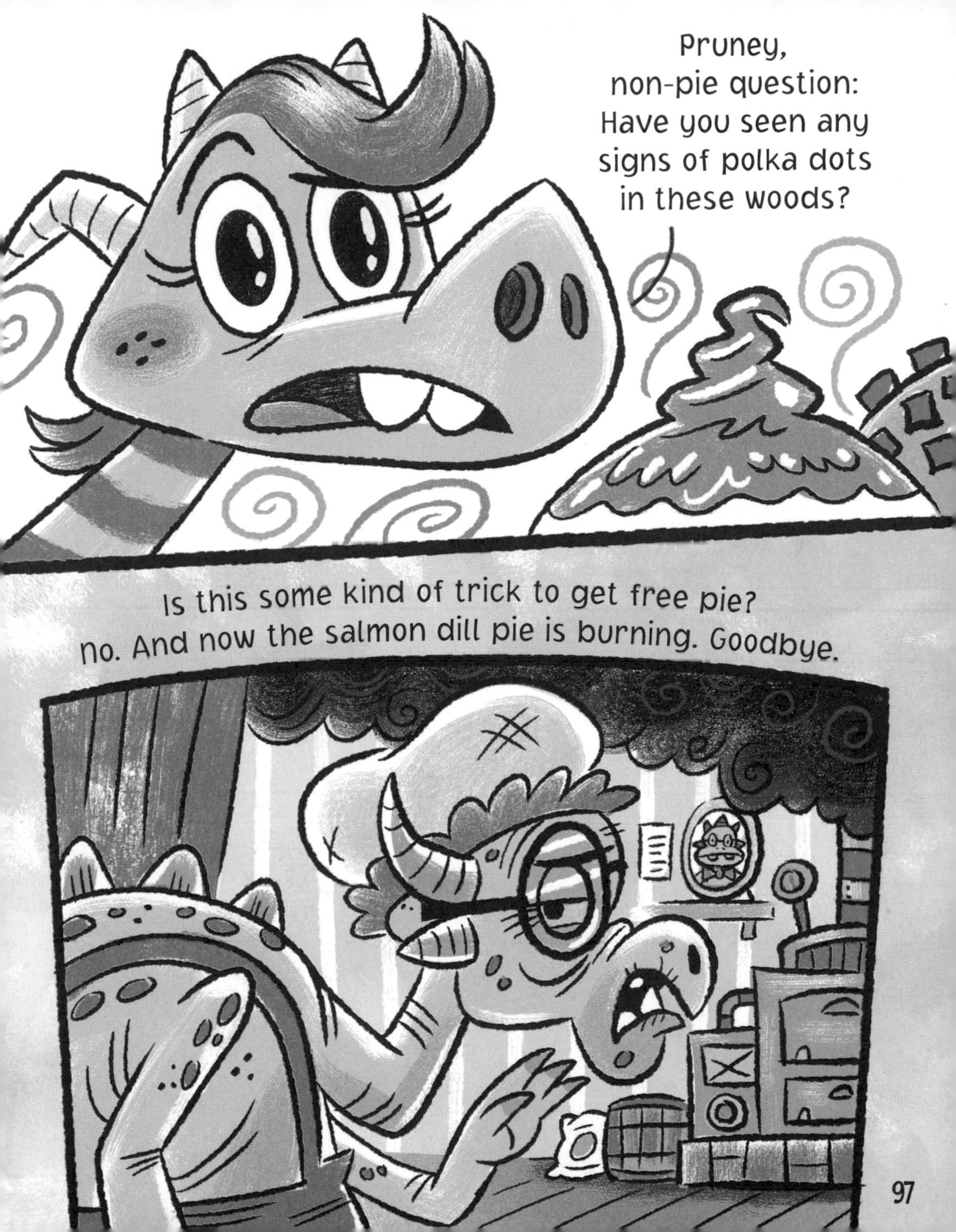
Pruney, non-pie question: Have you seen any signs of polka dots in these woods?
Is this some kind of trick to get free pie?
No. And now the salmon dill pie is burning. Goodbye.

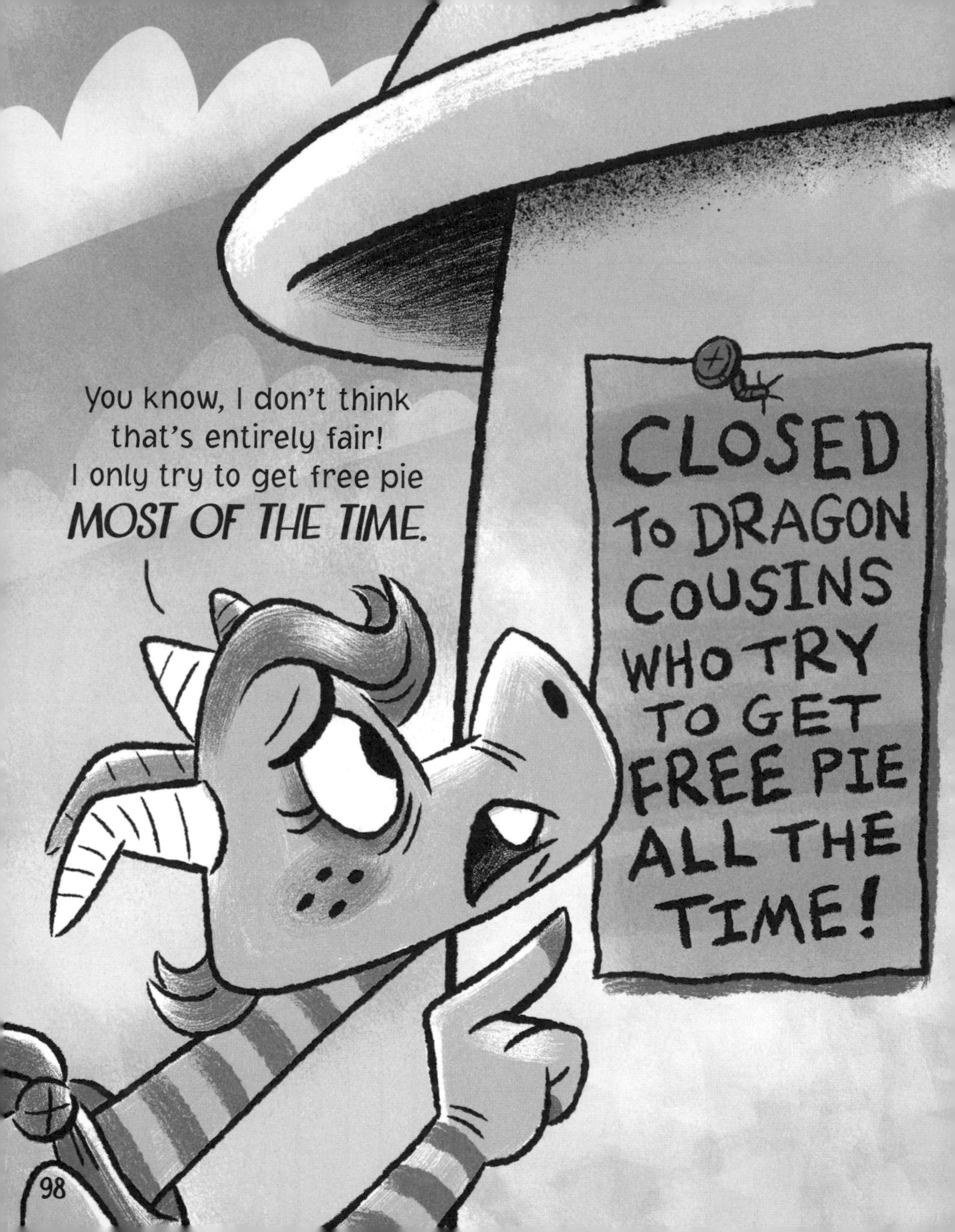
You know, I don't think that's entirely fair! I only try to get free pie *MOST OF THE TIME.*
CLOSED To DRAGON COUSINS WHO TRY TO GET FREE PIE ALL THE TIME!

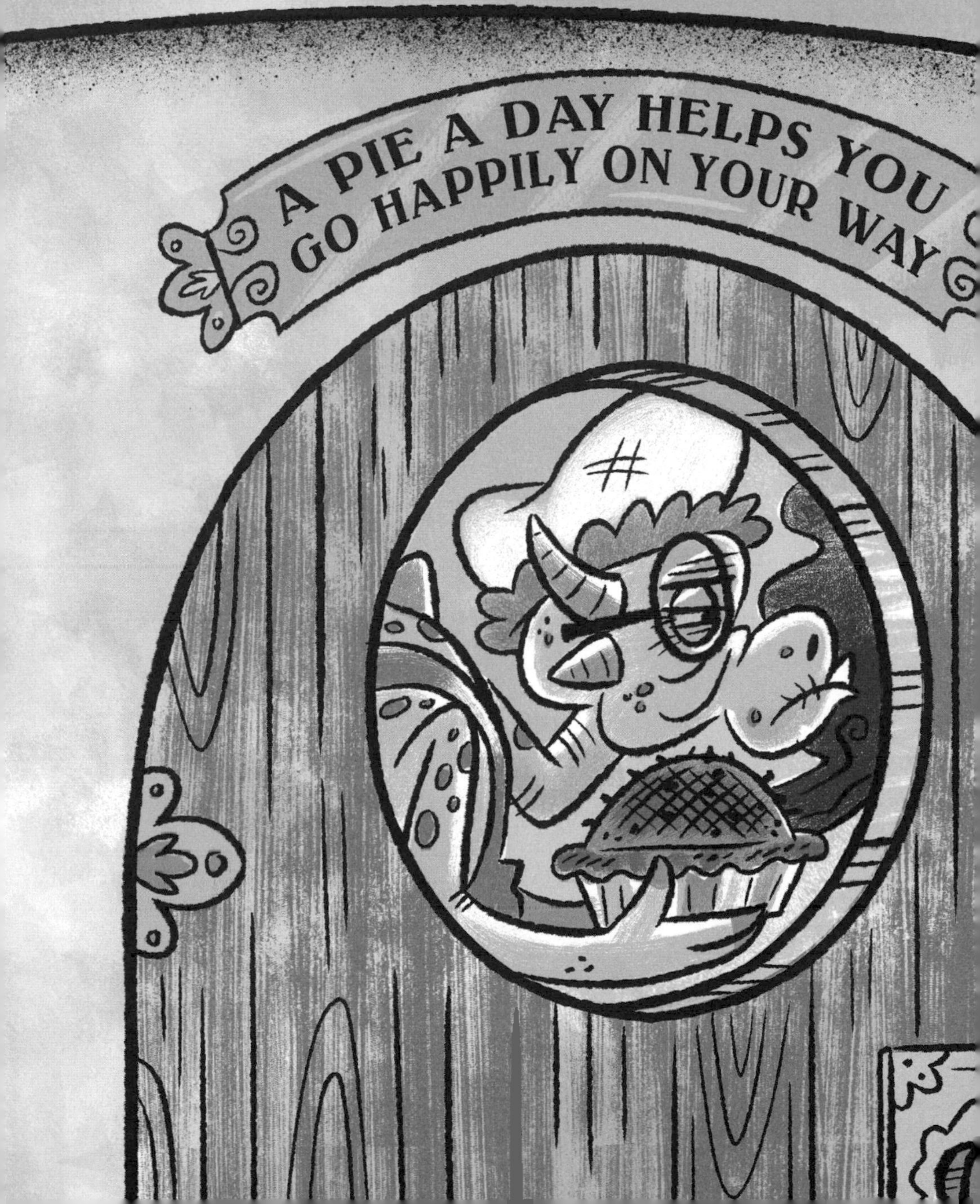
A PIE A DAY HELPS YOU
GO HAPPILY ON YOUR WAY

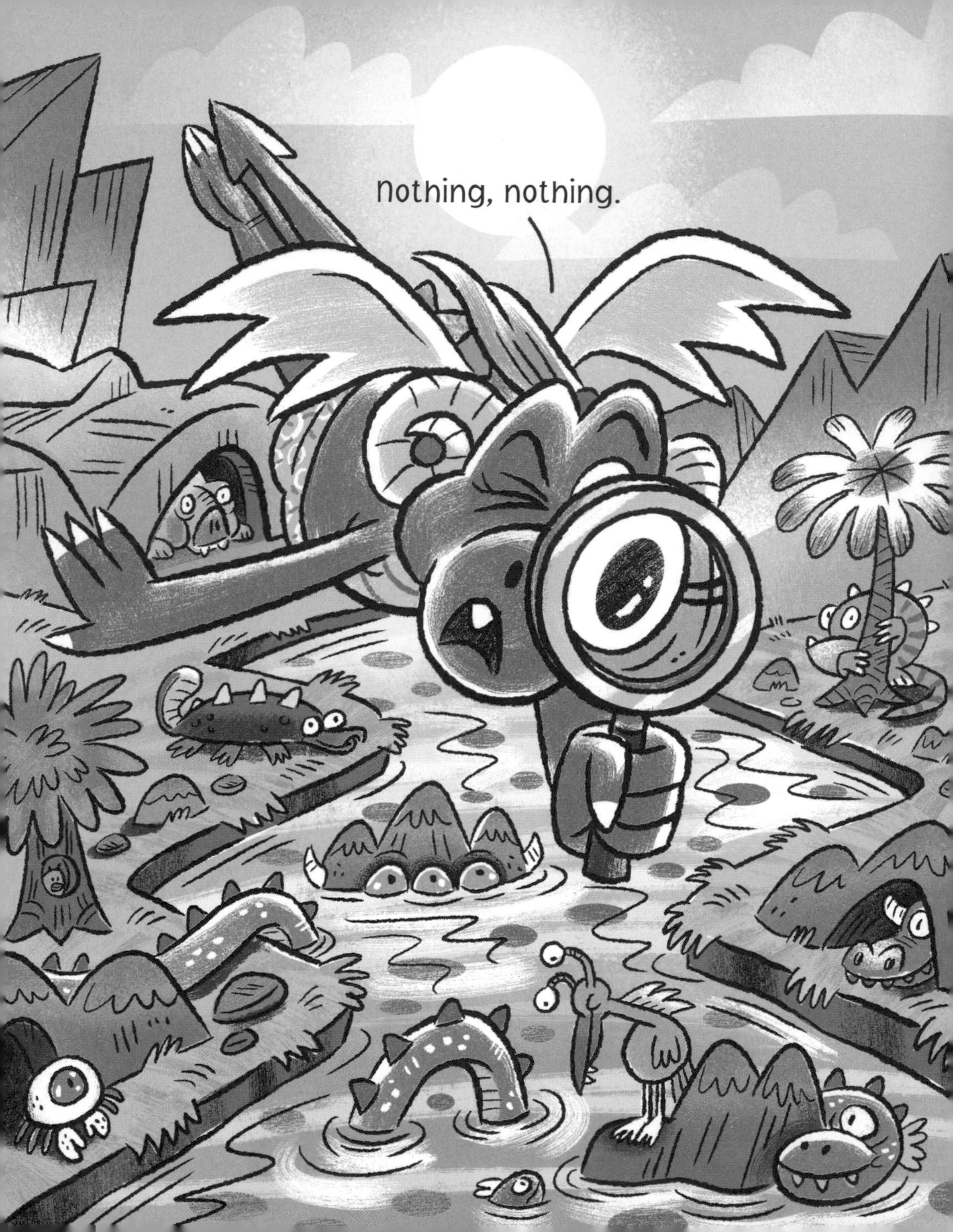
nothing, nothing.

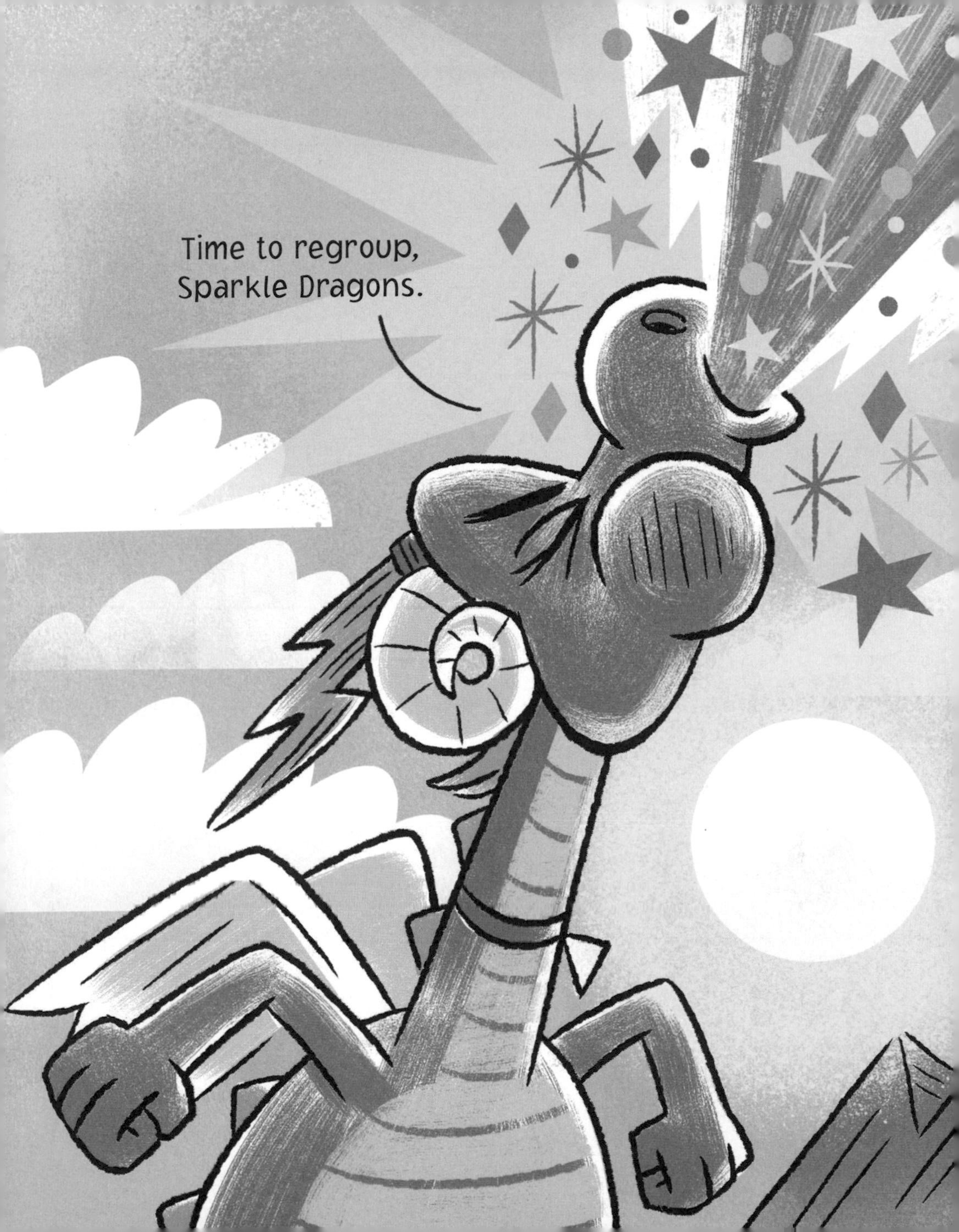
Time to regroup,
Sparkle Dragons.

CHAPTER SEVEN
FOLLOW THAT RAINBOW

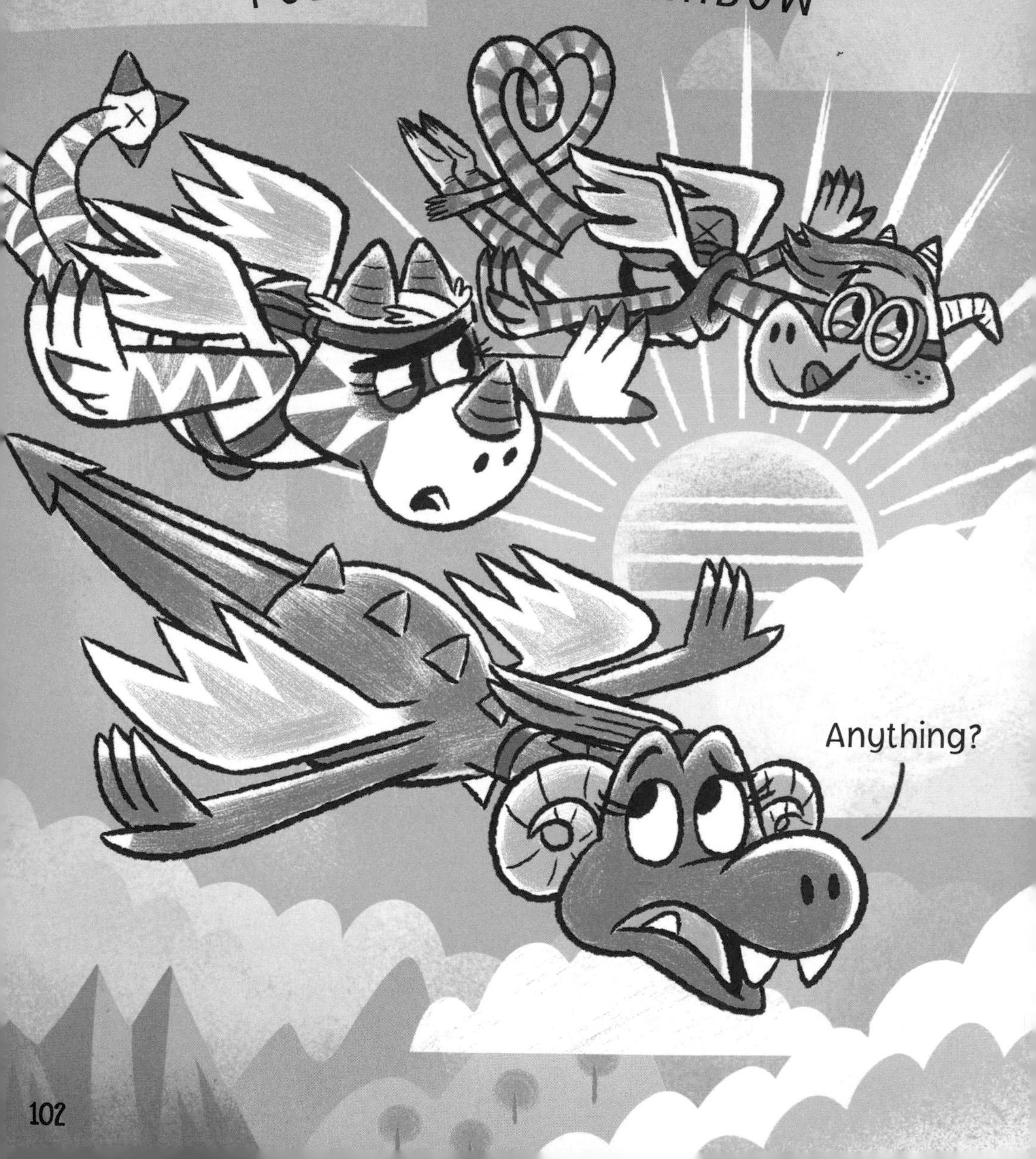

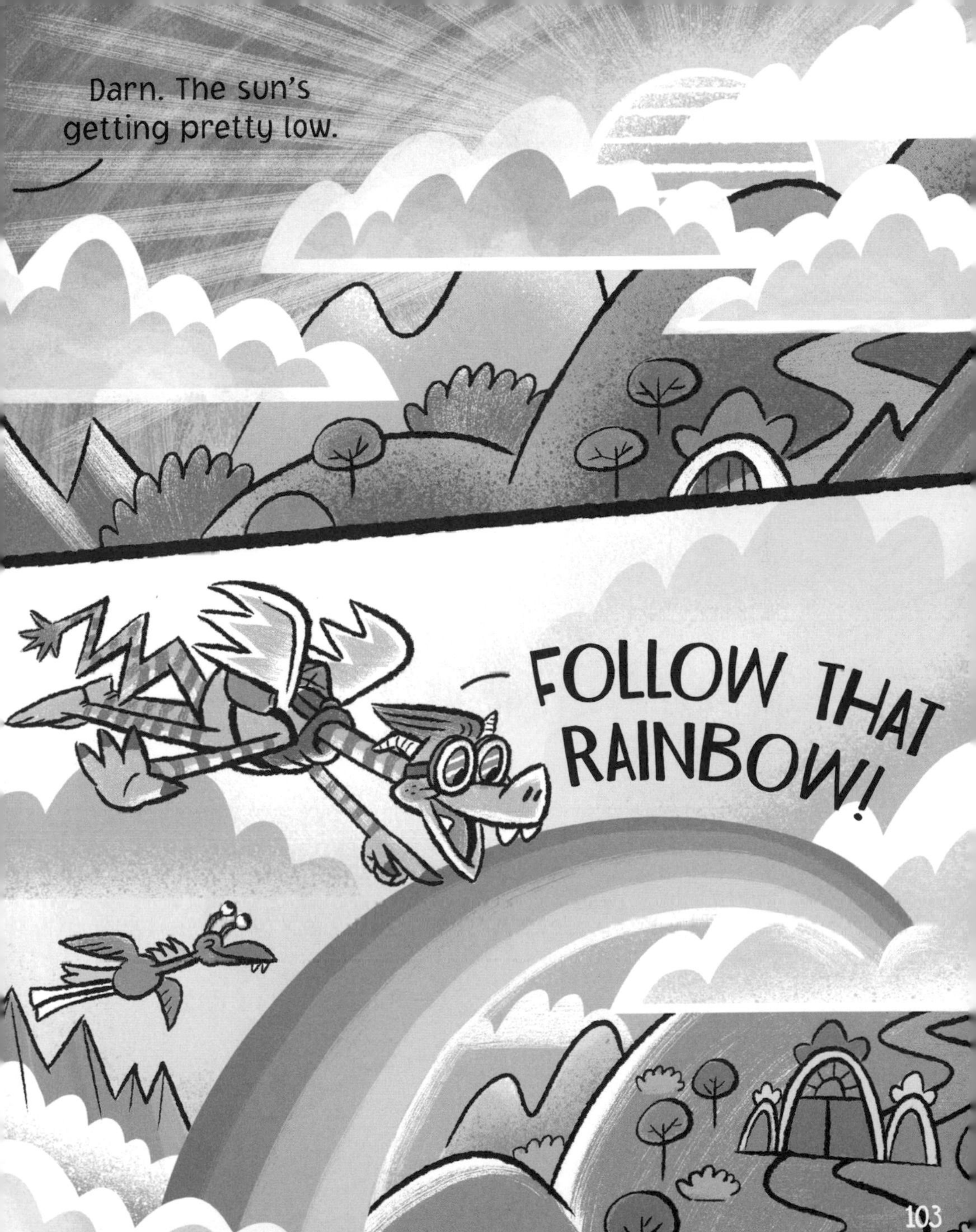
Darn. The sun's getting pretty low.
FOLLOW THAT RAINBOW!

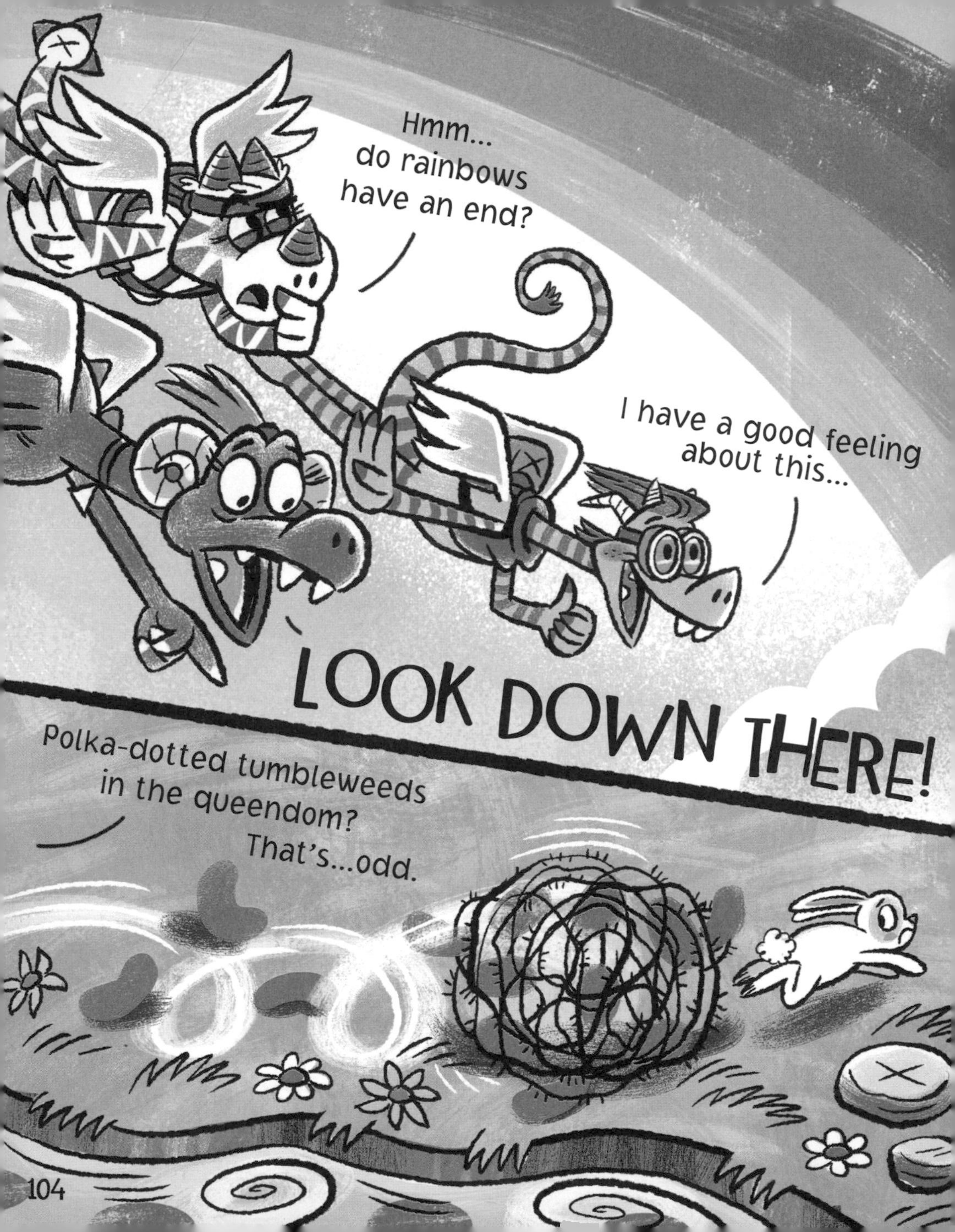
Hmm... do rainbows have an end?
I have a good feeling about this...
LOOK DOWN THERE!
Polka-dotted tumbleweeds in the queendom? That's...odd.

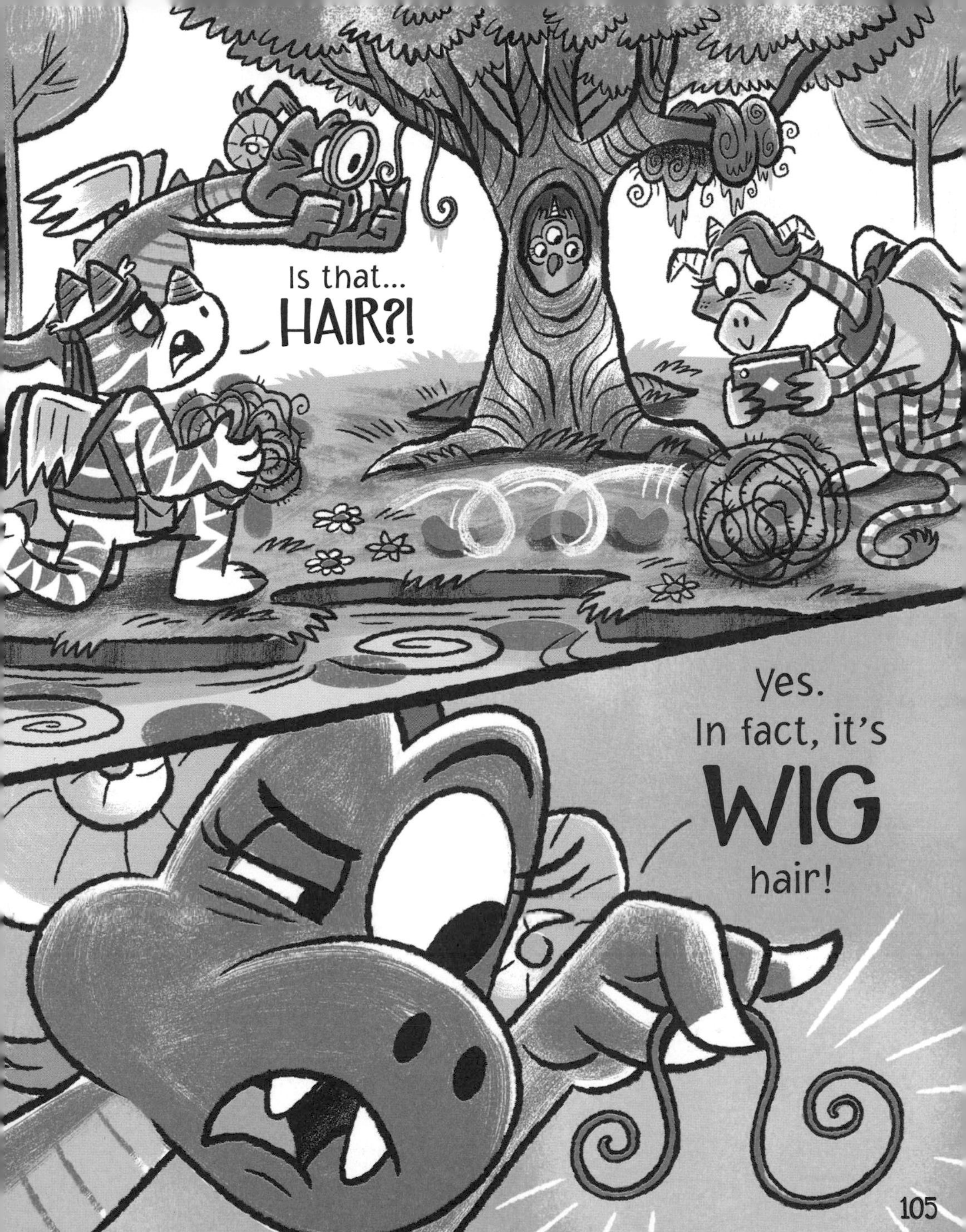
Is that... HAIR?!
Yes. In fact, it's WIG hair!

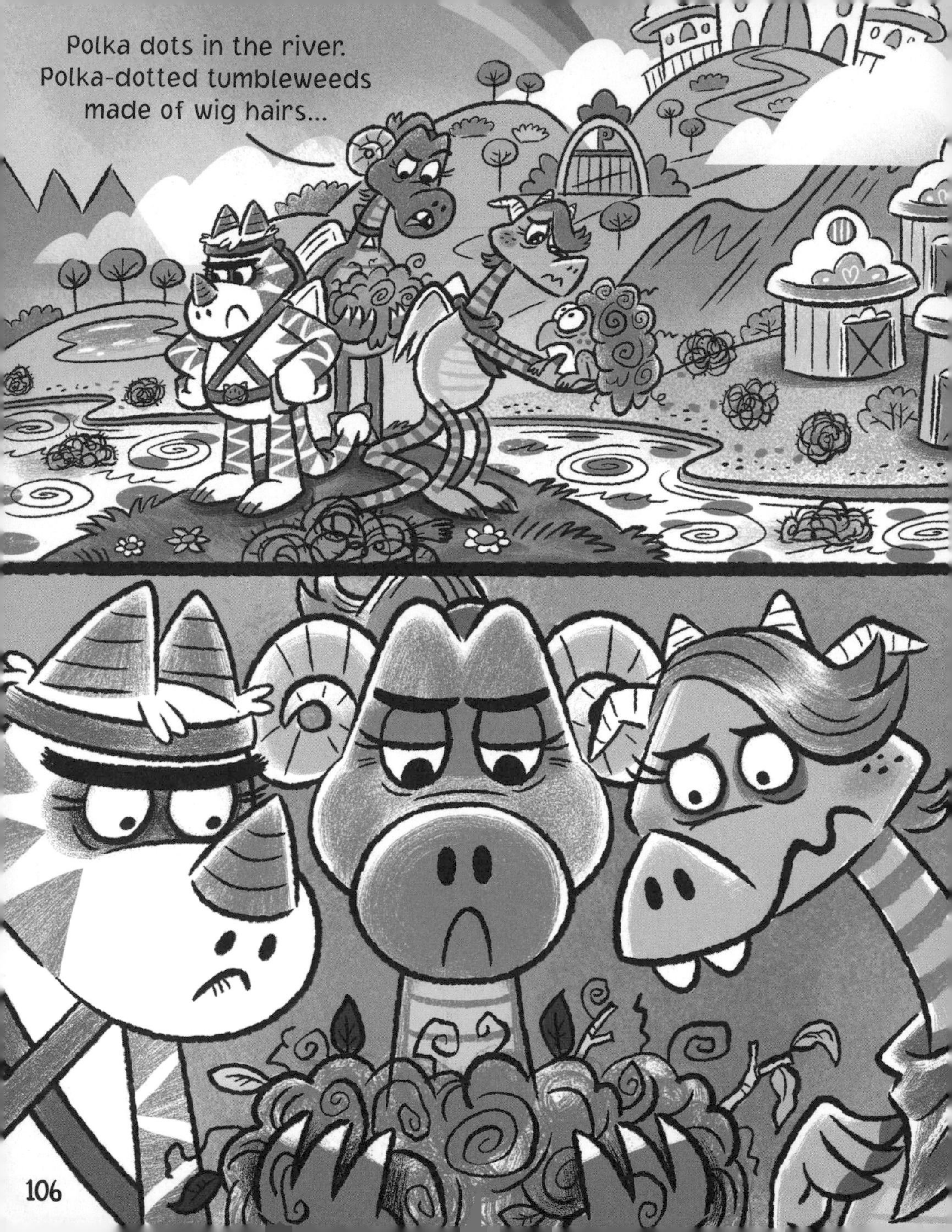
Polka dots in the river.
Polka-dotted tumbleweeds
made of wig hairs...

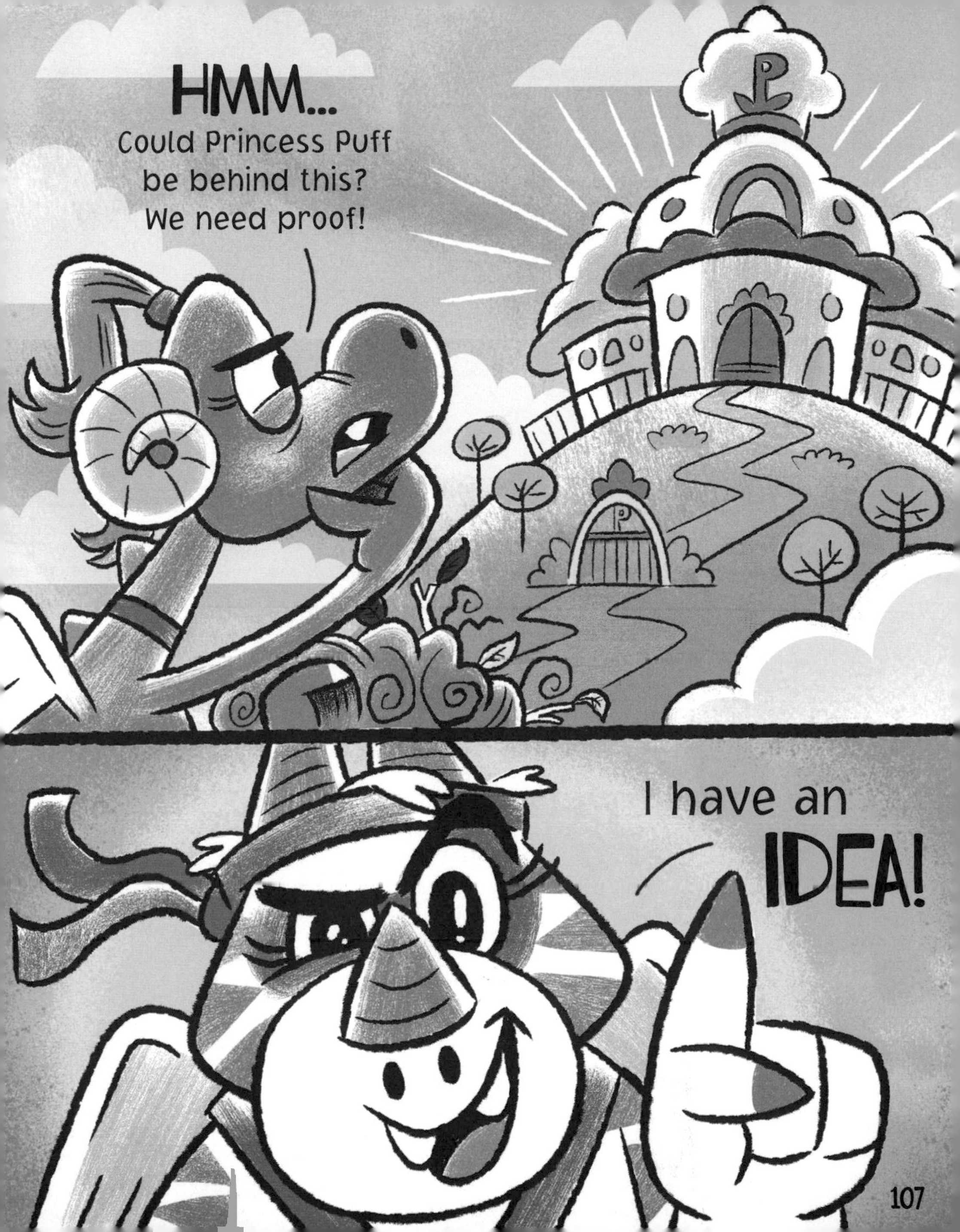
HMM...
Could Princess Puff be behind this? We need proof!
I have an IDEA!

CHAPTER EIGHT
THE UNINVITED GUEST

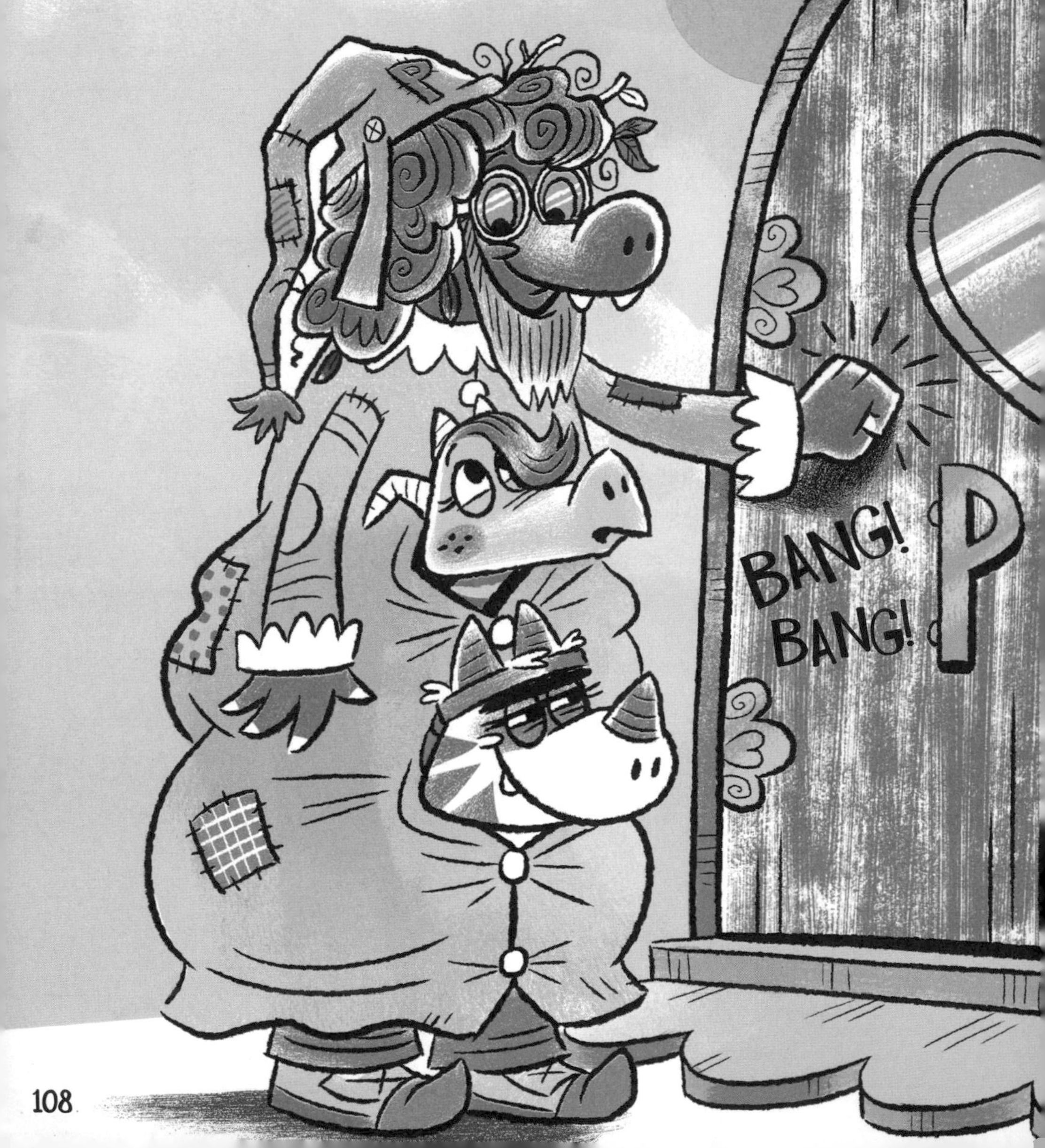
BANG!
BANG!

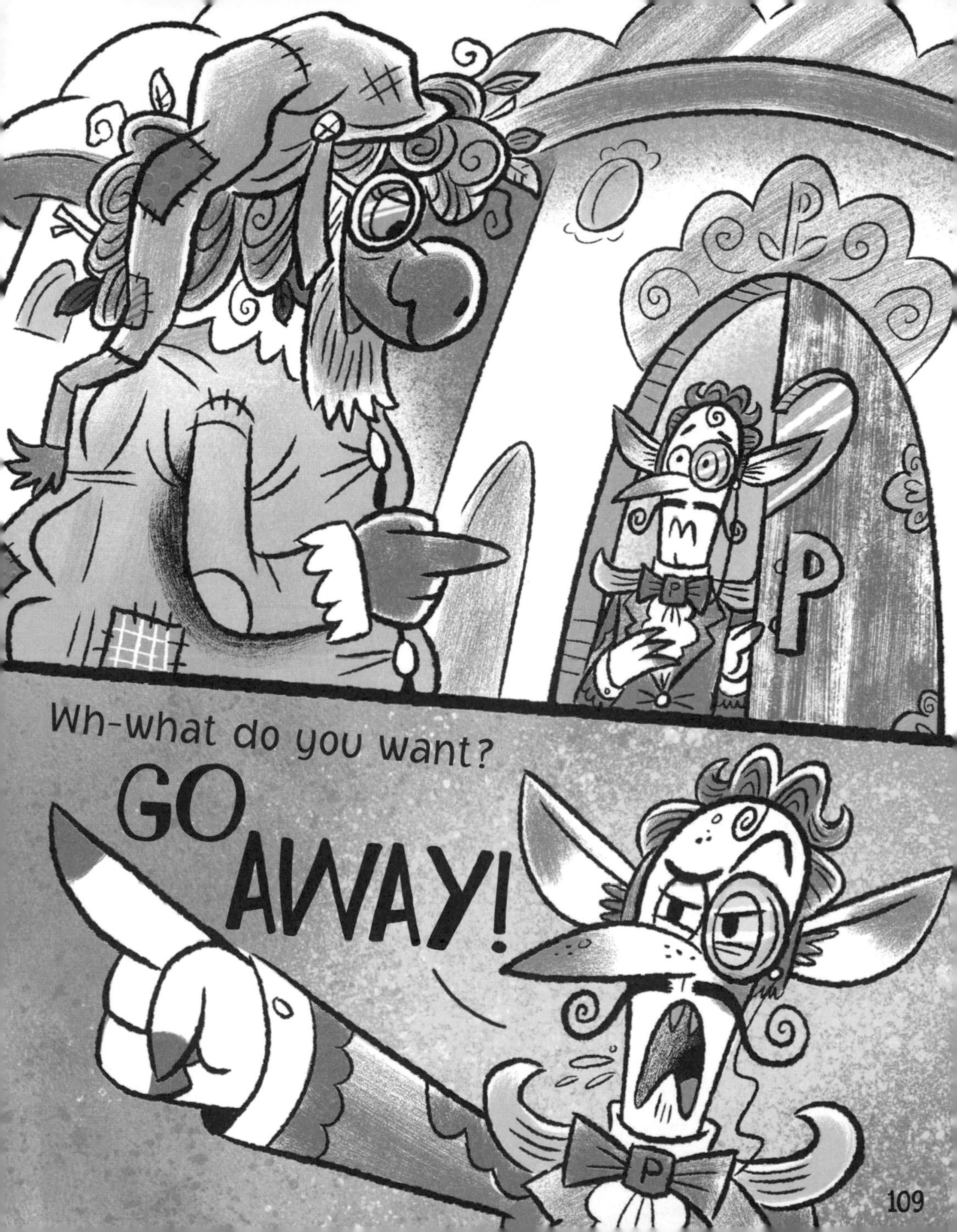
Wh-what do you want?
GO AWAY!

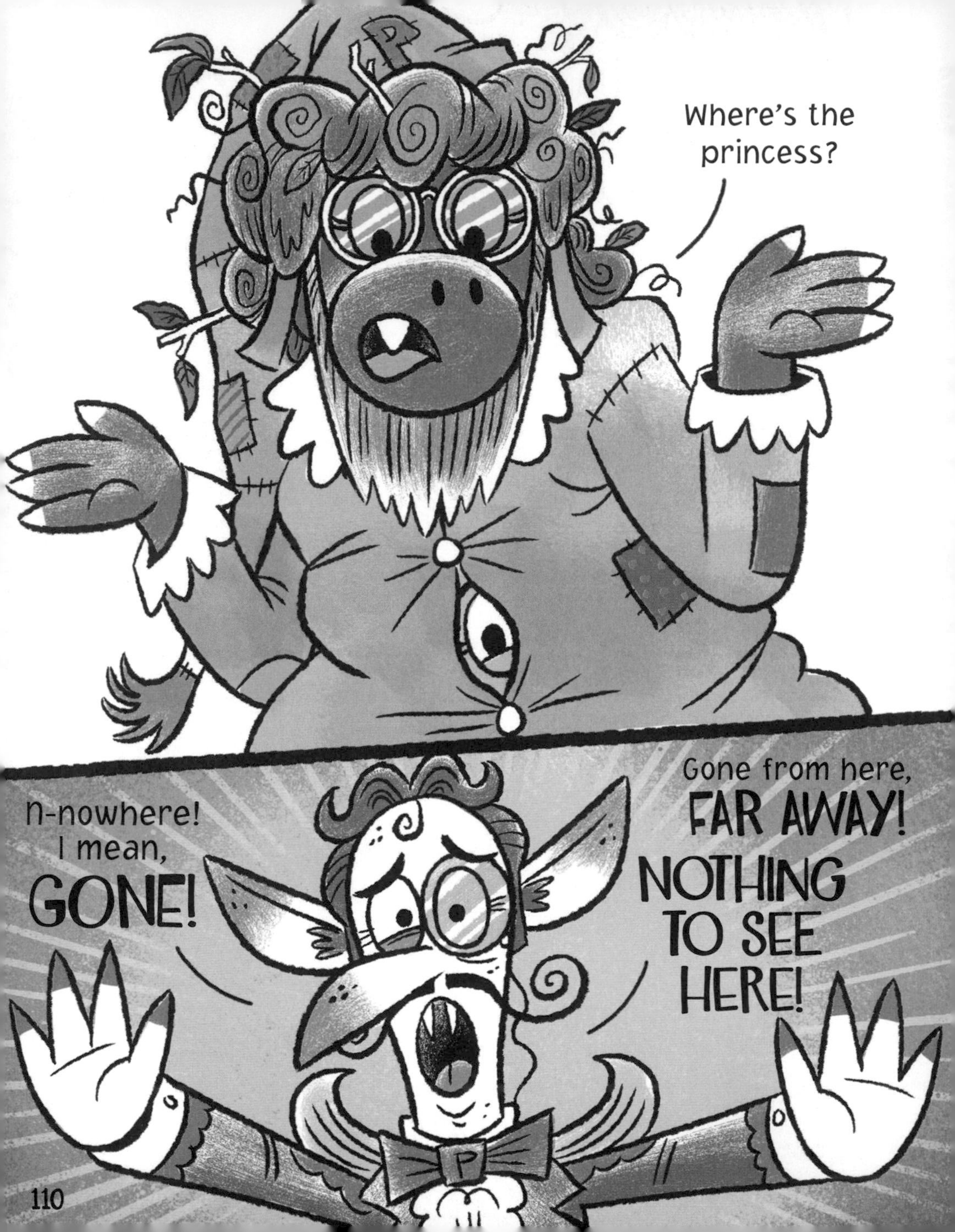
Where's the princess?
N-nowhere! I mean, GONE!
Gone from here, FAR AWAY!
NOTHING TO SEE HERE!

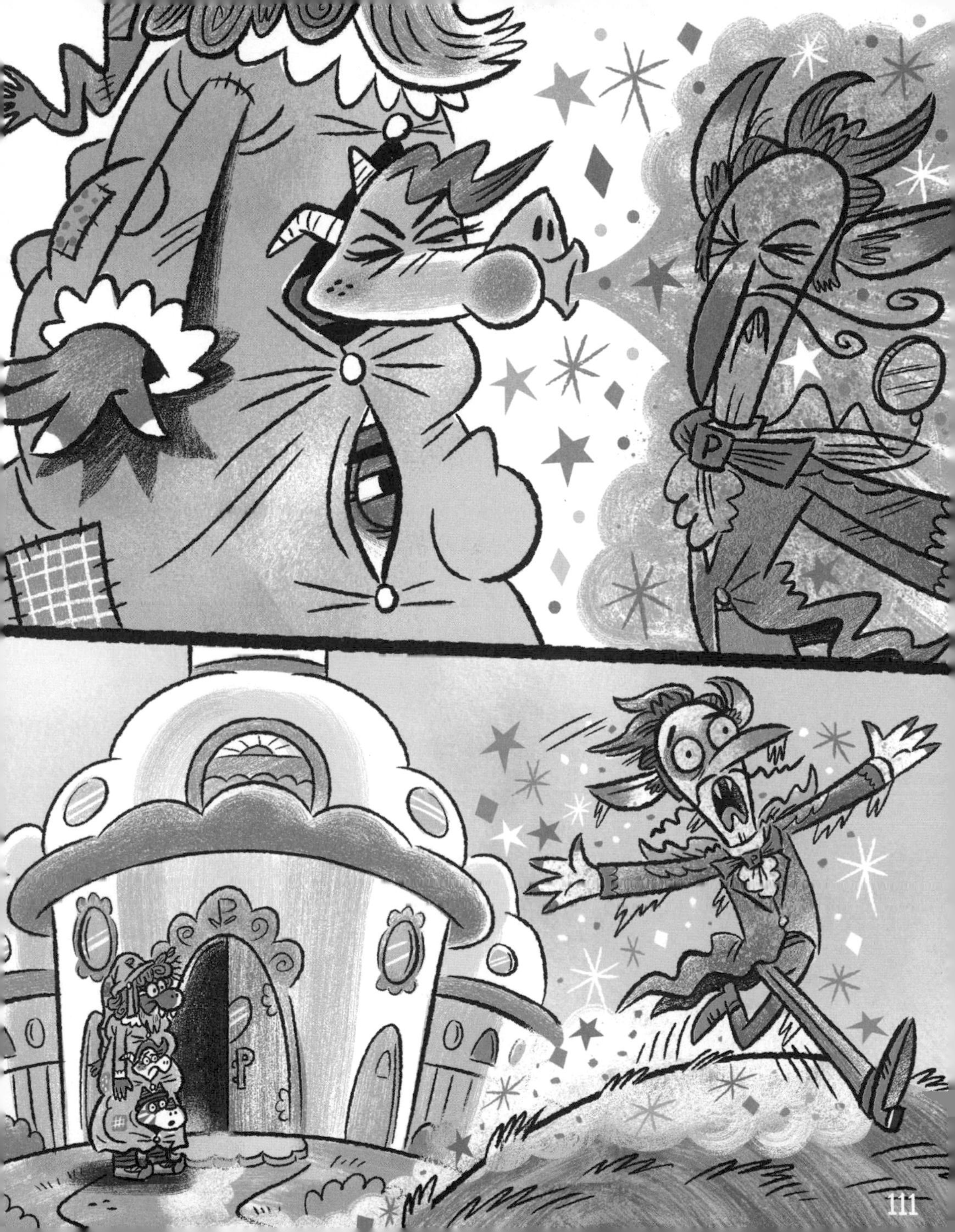

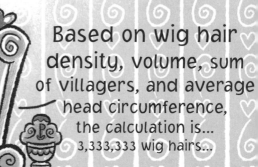

That was easy.

PERFECTIO

PUFF

Based on wig hair density, volume, sum of villagers, and average head circumference, the calculation is... 3,333,333 wig hairs...

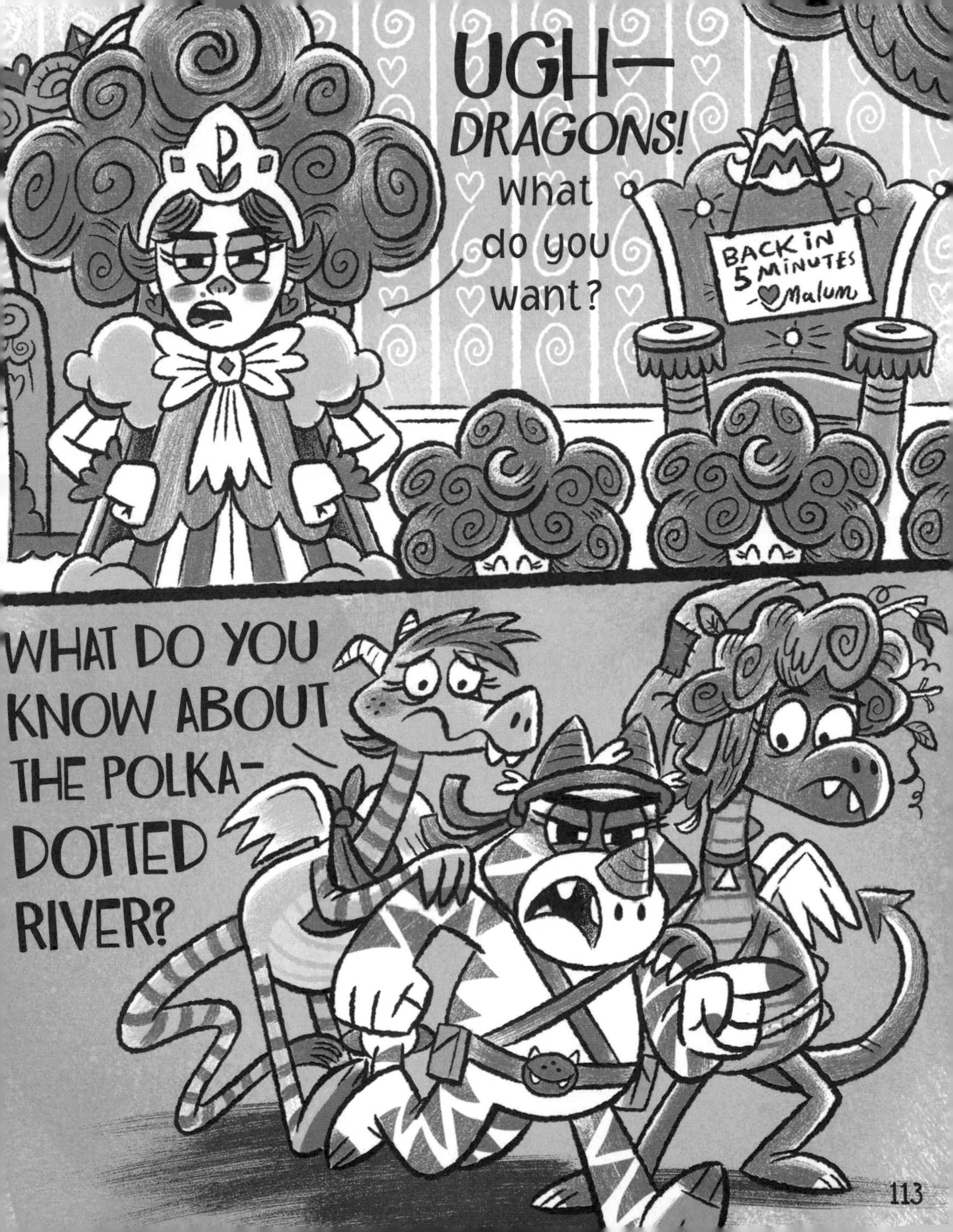
UGH—
DRAGONS! What do you want?
BACK IN 5 MINUTES -♥Malum
WHAT DO YOU KNOW ABOUT THE POLKA-DOTTED RIVER?

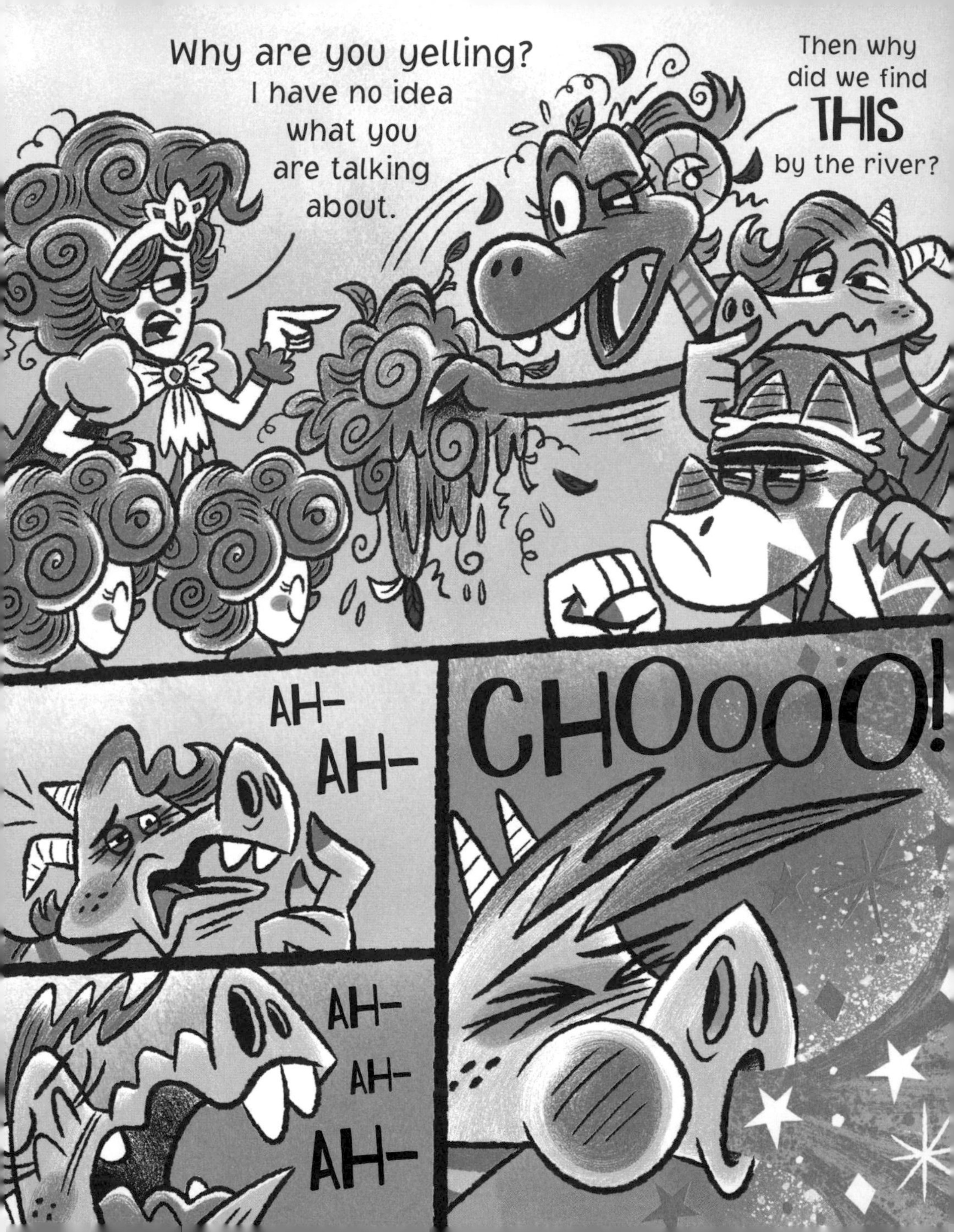

Why are you yelling? I have no idea what you are talking about.
Then why did we find THIS by the river?
AH- AH-
AH- AH- AH-
CHOOOOO!

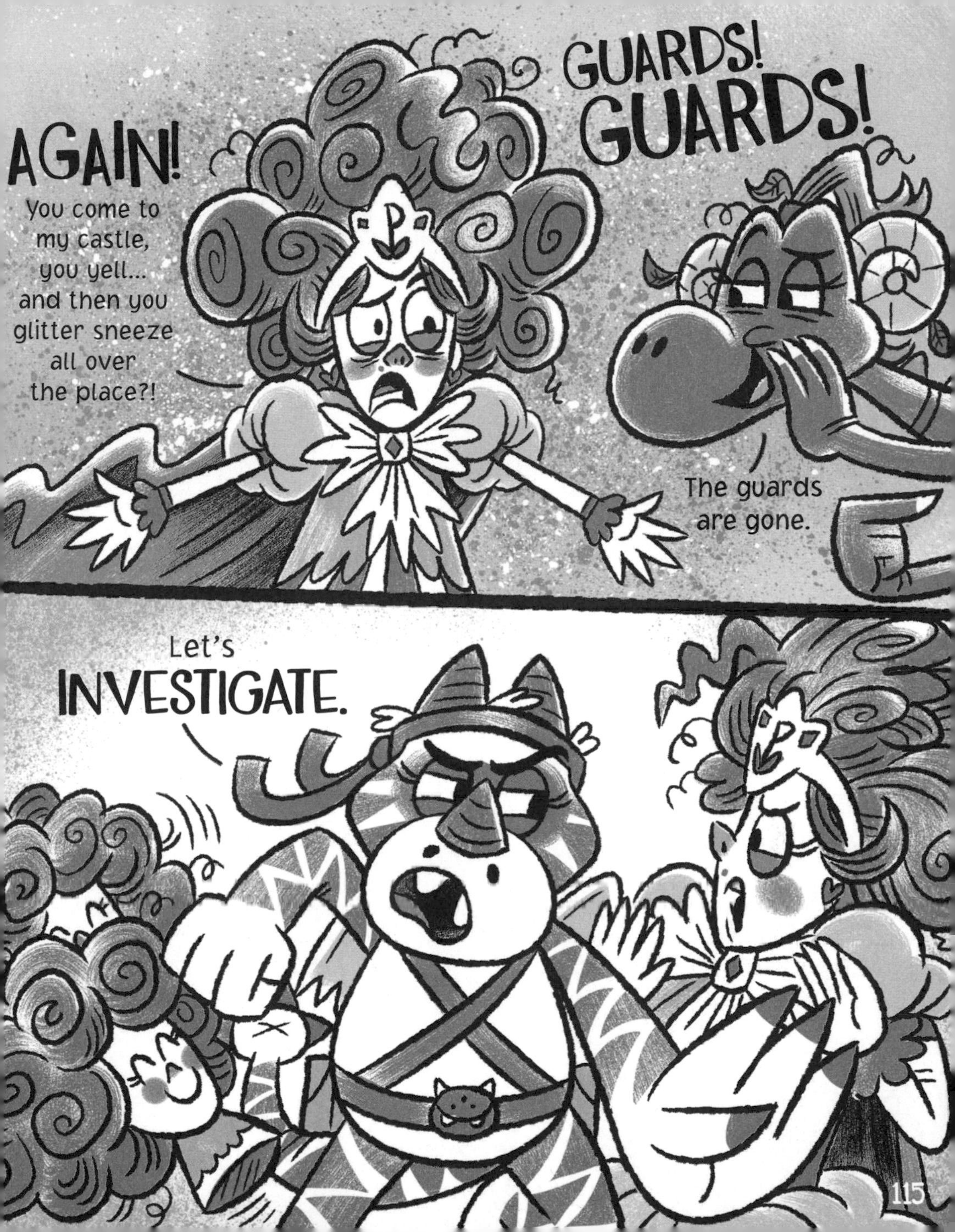
AGAIN!
You come to my castle, you yell... and then you glitter sneeze all over the place?!
GUARDS! GUARDS!
The guards are gone.
Let's INVESTIGATE.

CHAPTER NINE

HER PUFFINESS IS...DEFLATED.

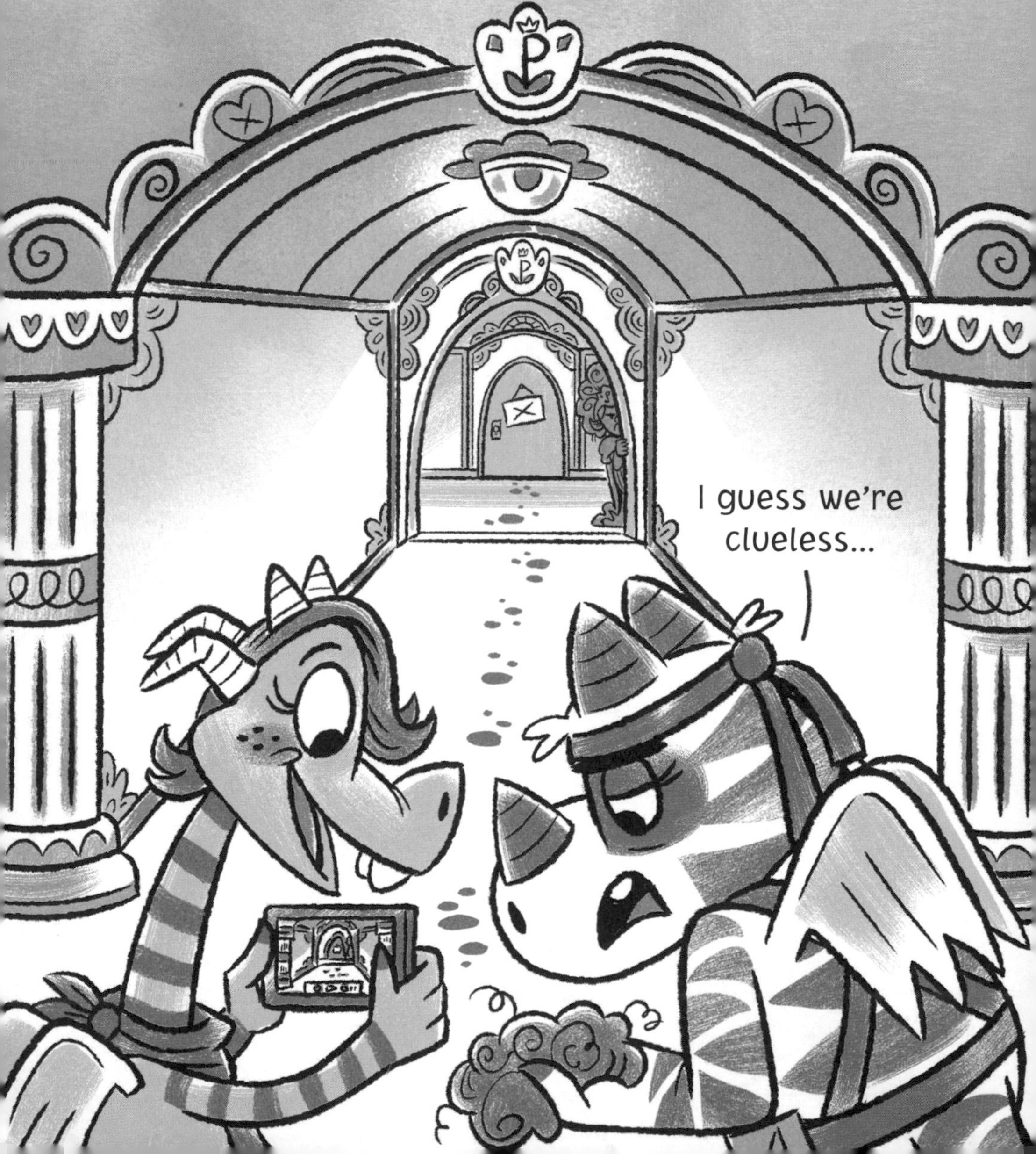
I guess we're clueless...

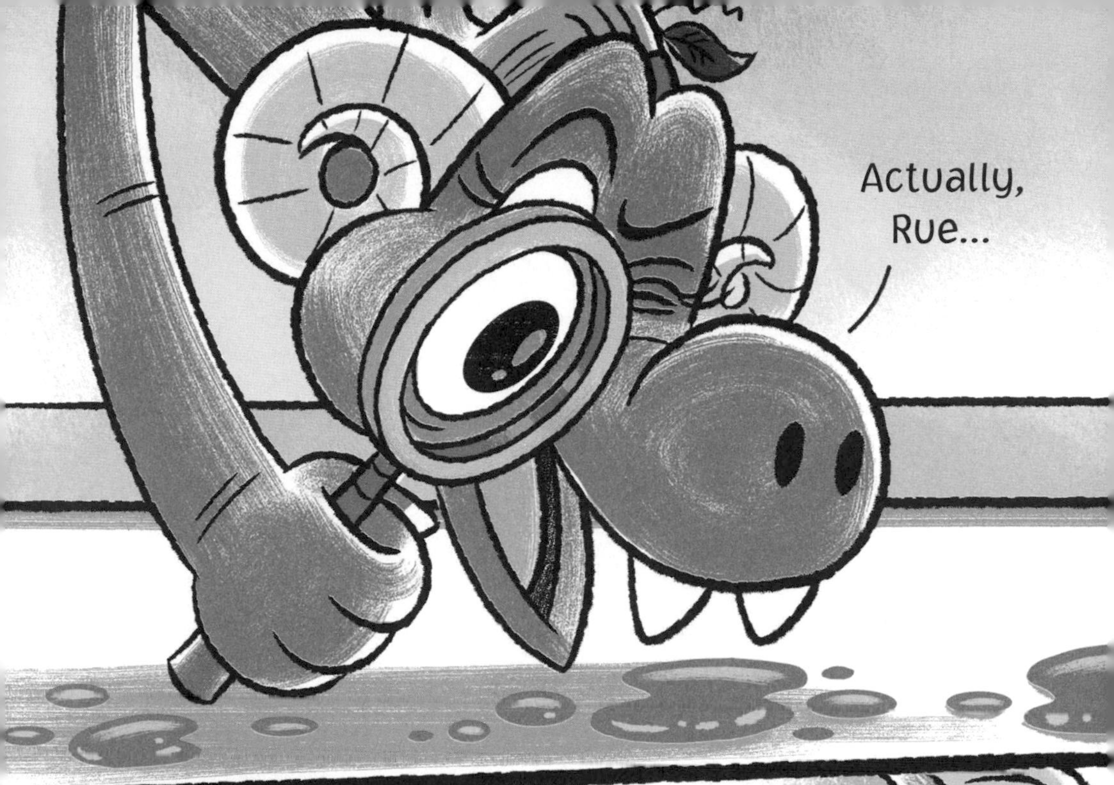
Actually, Rue...

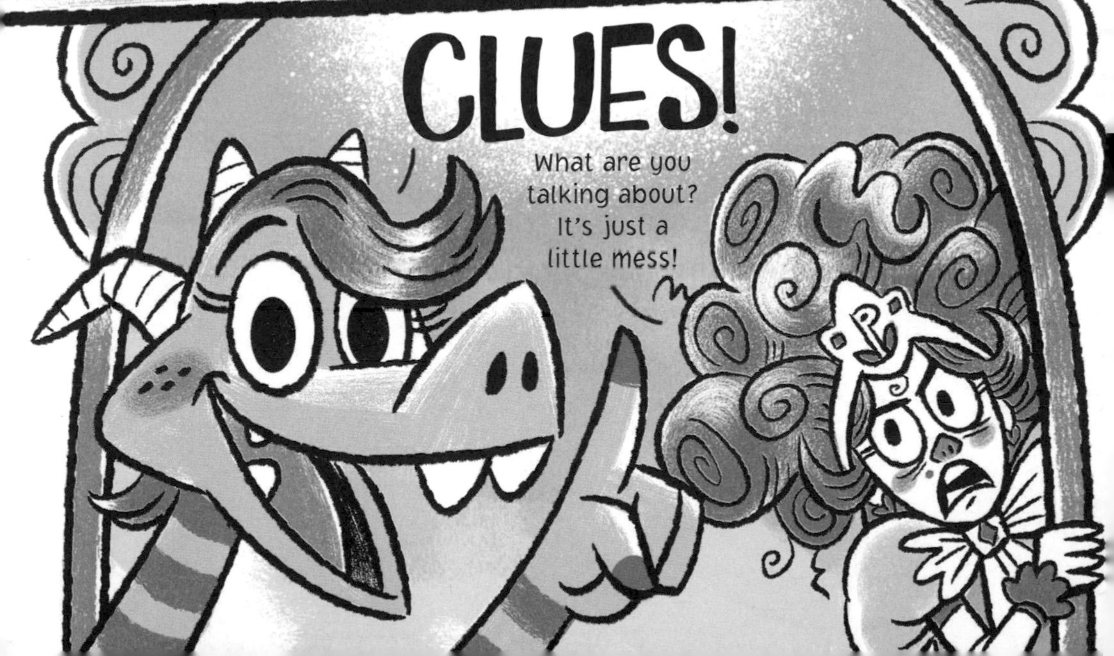
CLUES!
What are you talking about? It's just a little mess!

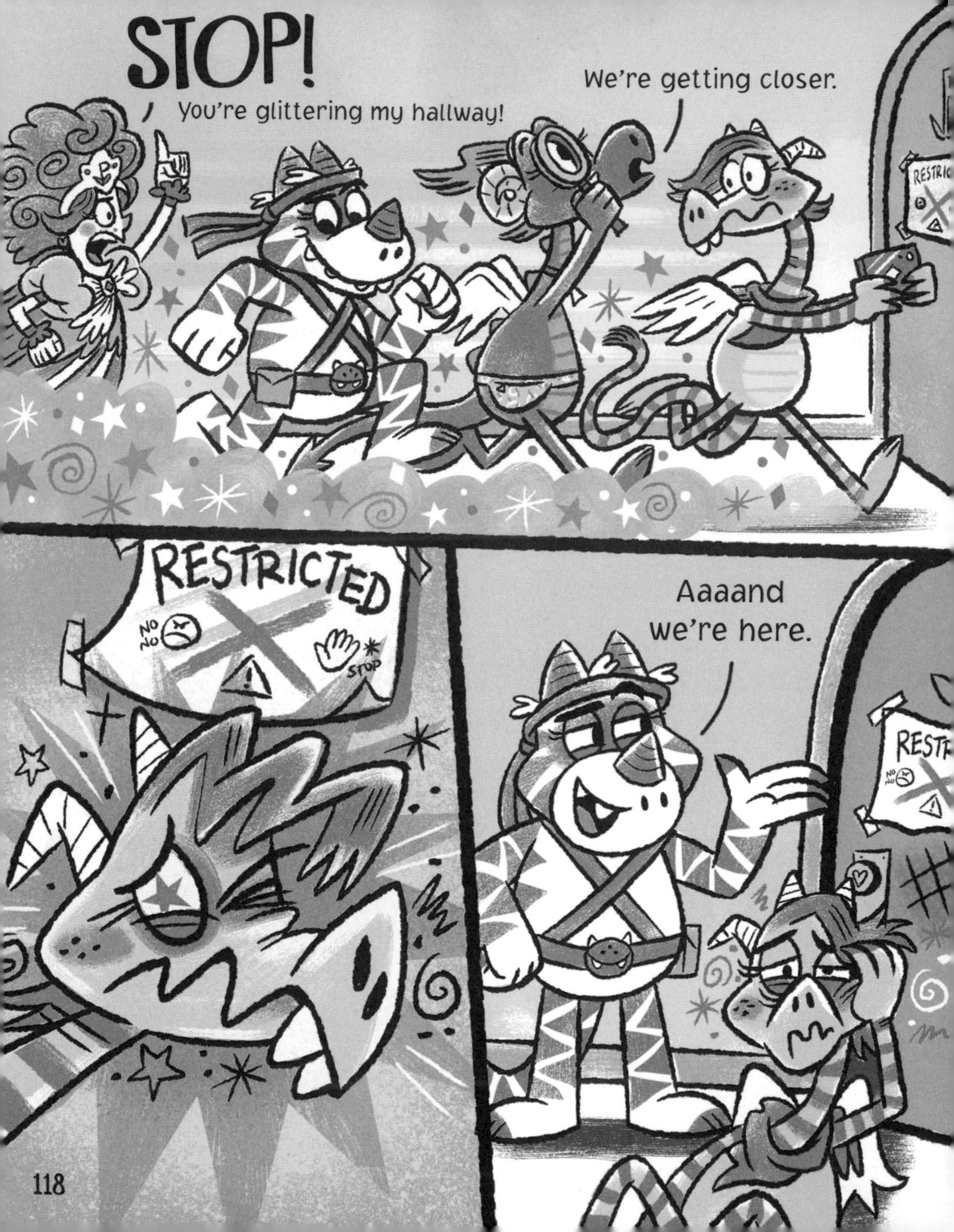
STOP!
You're glittering my hallway!
We're getting closer.
RESTRICTED
NO NO
STOP
Aaaand we're here.

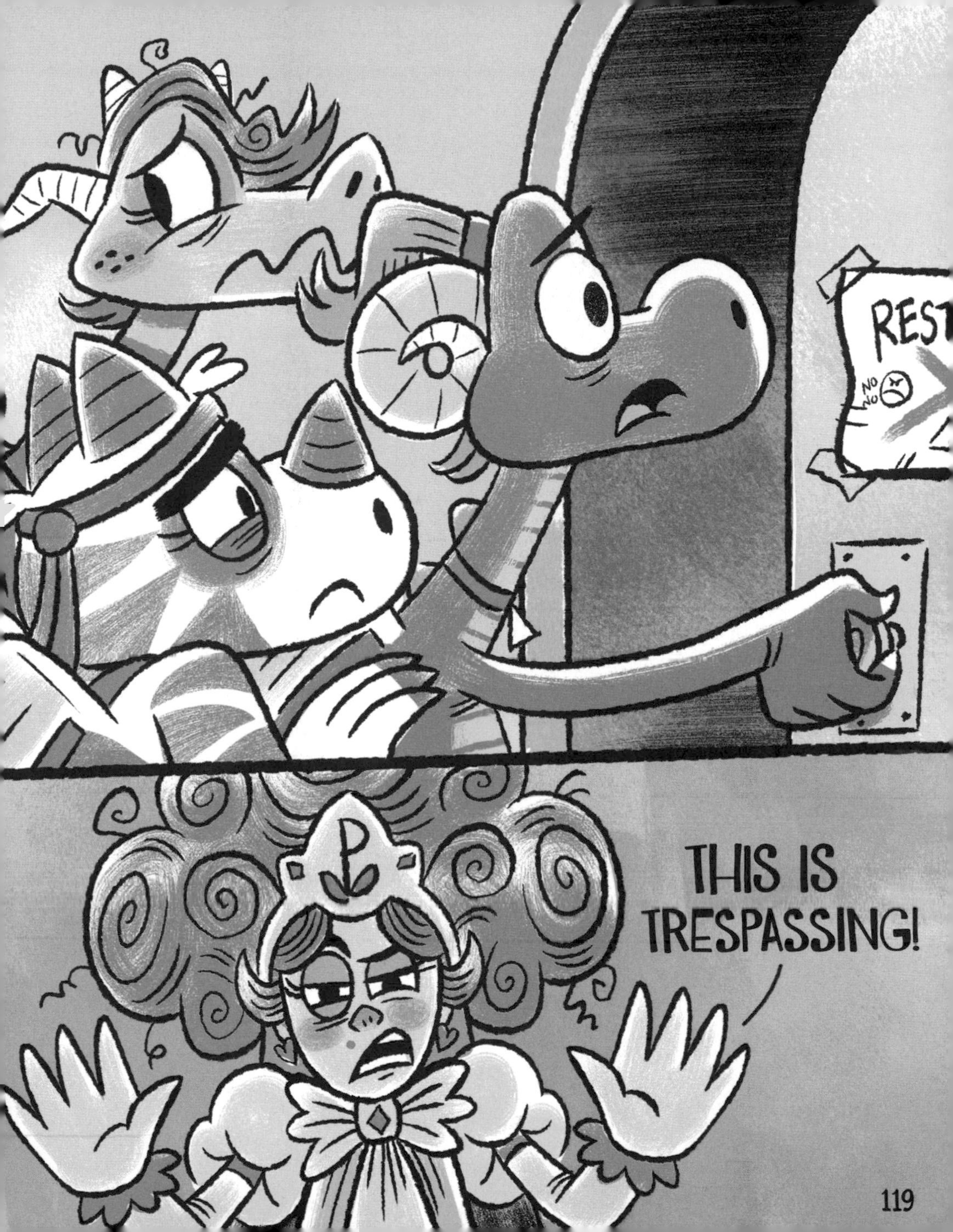
REST
NO
NO
THIS IS TRESPASSING!

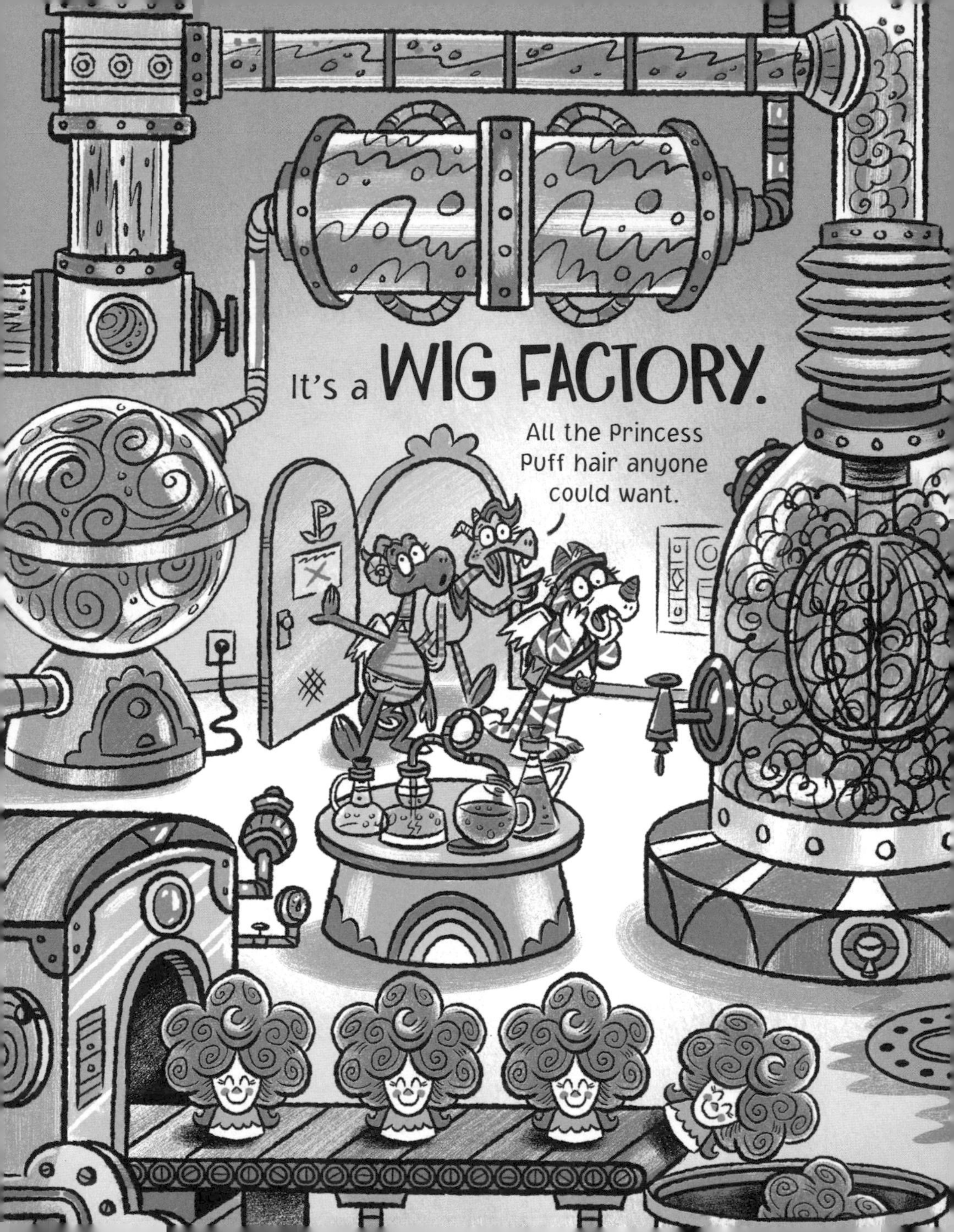
It's a WIG FACTORY.
All the Princess Puff hair anyone could want.

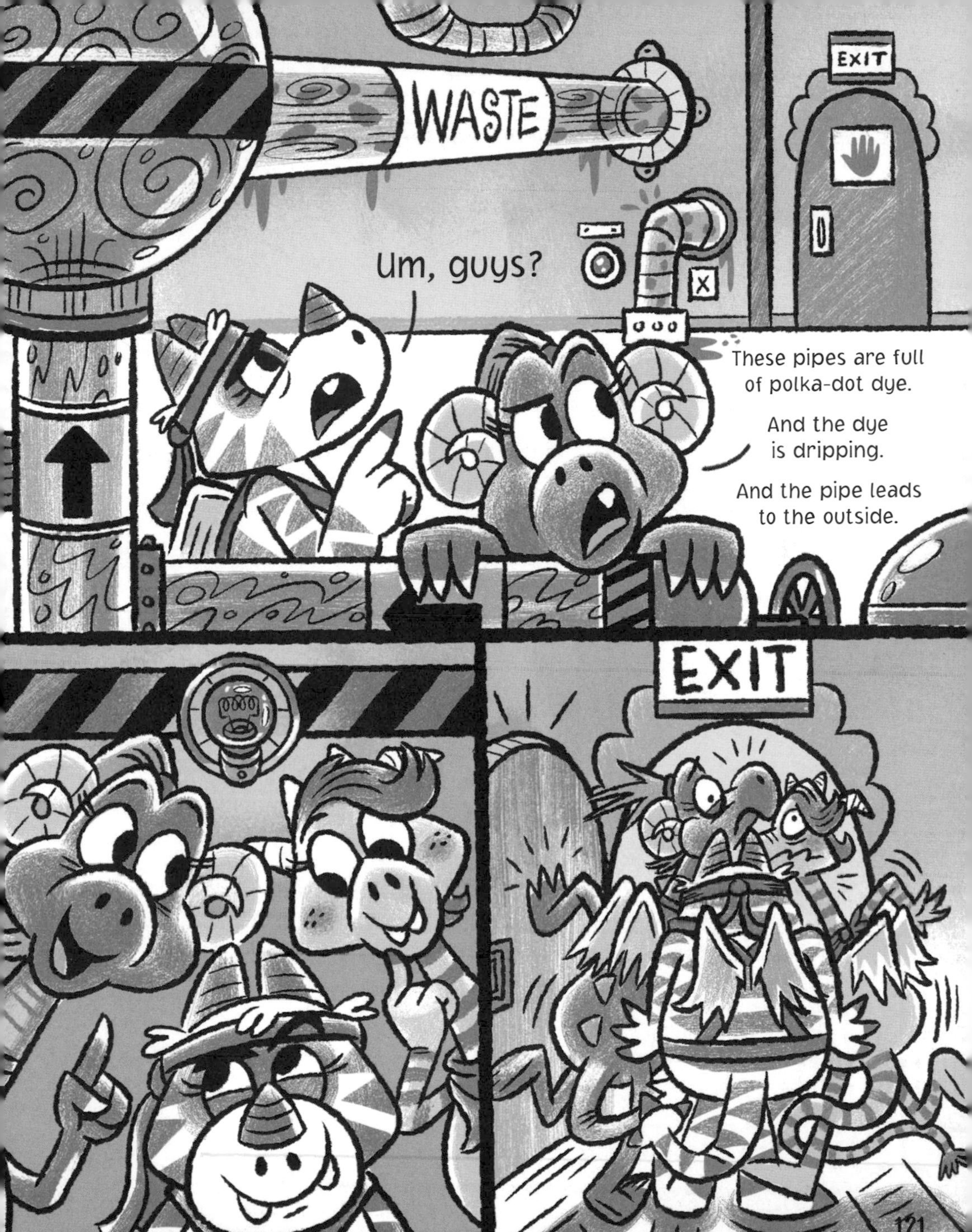
WASTE
EXIT
Um, guys?
These pipes are full of polka-dot dye.
And the dye is dripping.
And the pipe leads to the outside.
EXIT

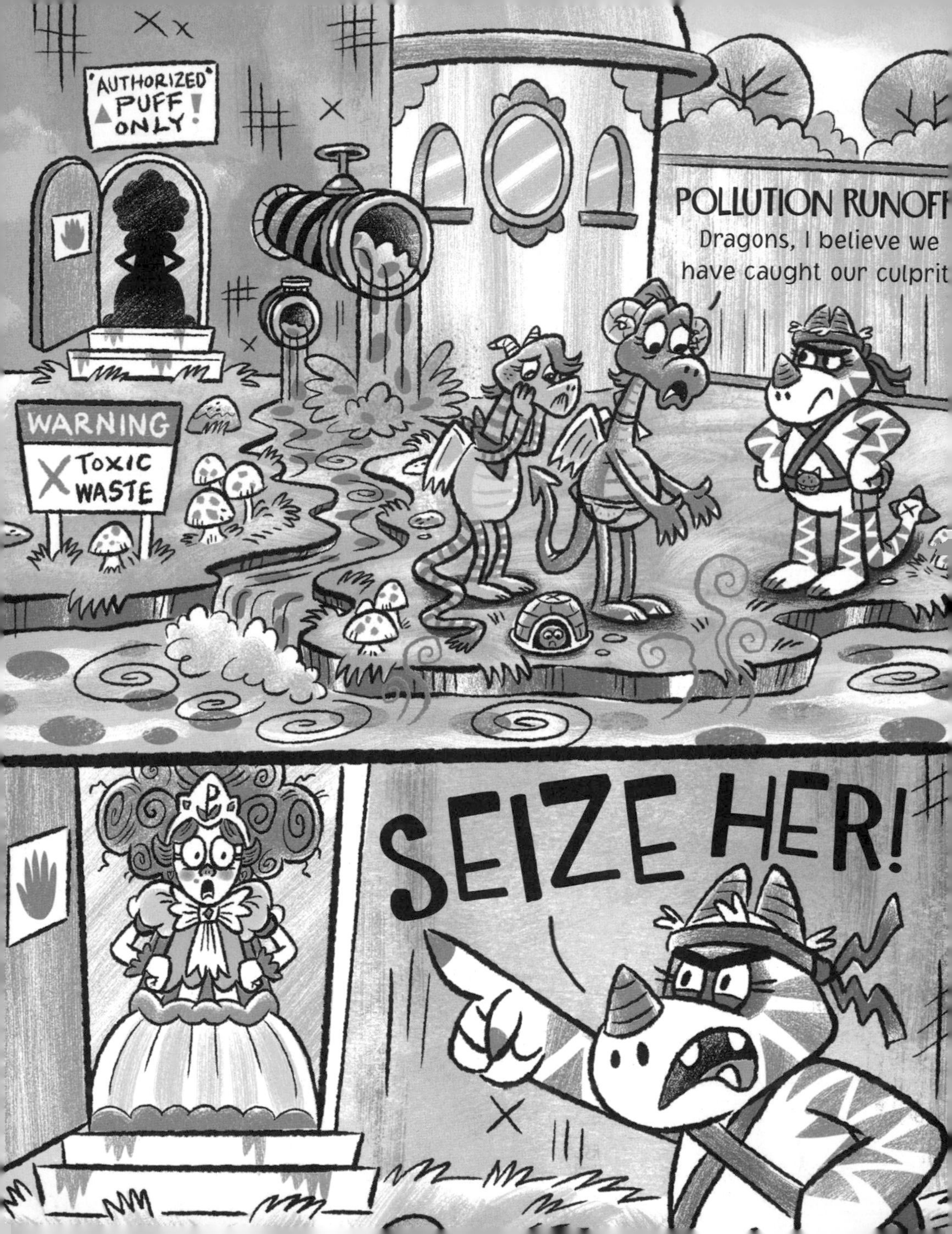
AUTHORIZED PUFF ONLY!
WARNING
TOXIC WASTE
POLLUTION RUNOF
Dragons, I believe we have caught our culprit
SEIZE HER!

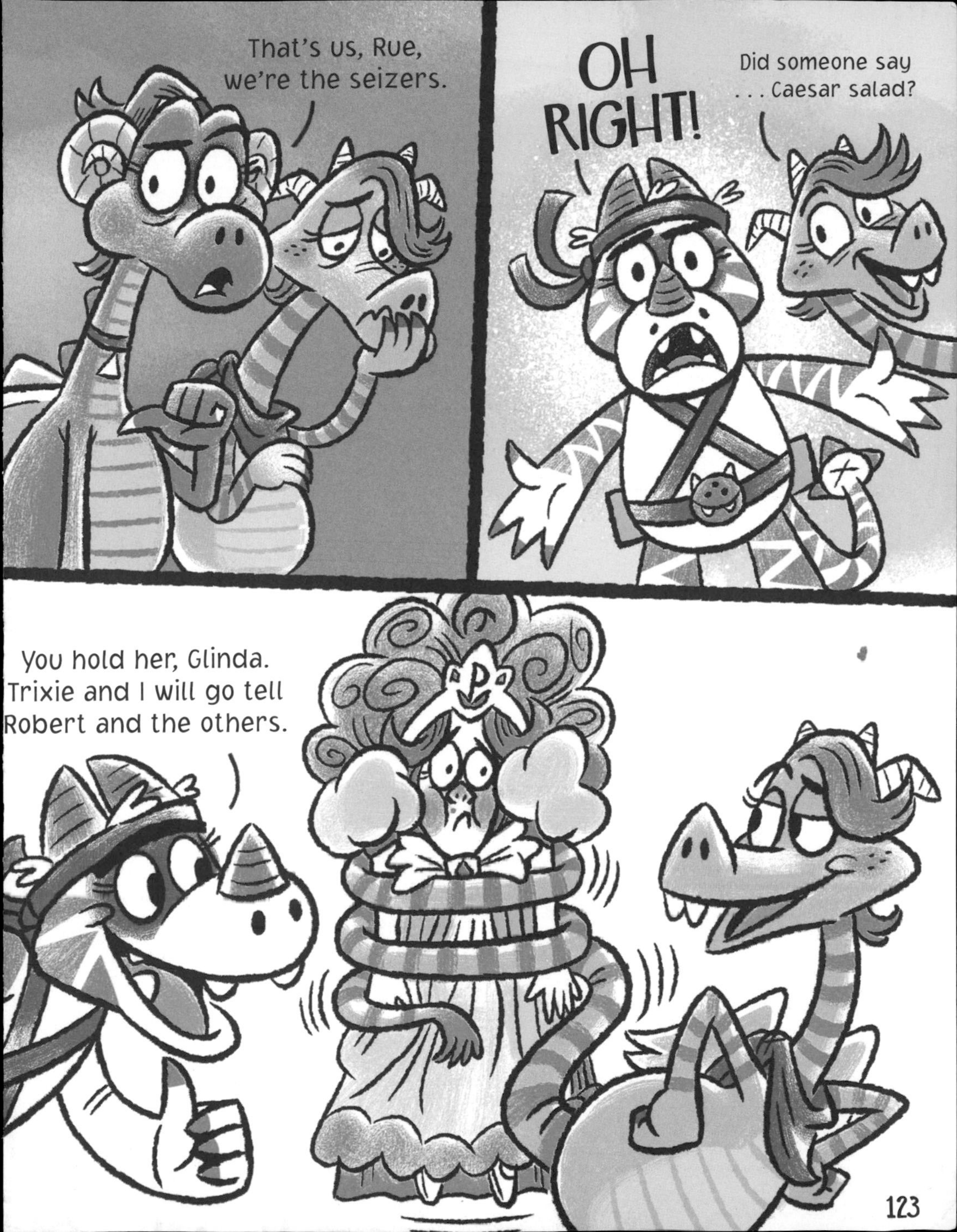
That's us, Rue, we're the seizers.
OH RIGHT!
Did someone say . . . Caesar salad?
You hold her, Glinda. Trixie and I will go tell Robert and the others.

CHAPTER TEN
JUSTICE, COMING THROUGH

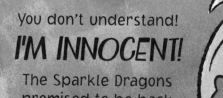

You don't understand!

I'M INNOCENT!

The Sparkle Dragons promised to be back by sunset—

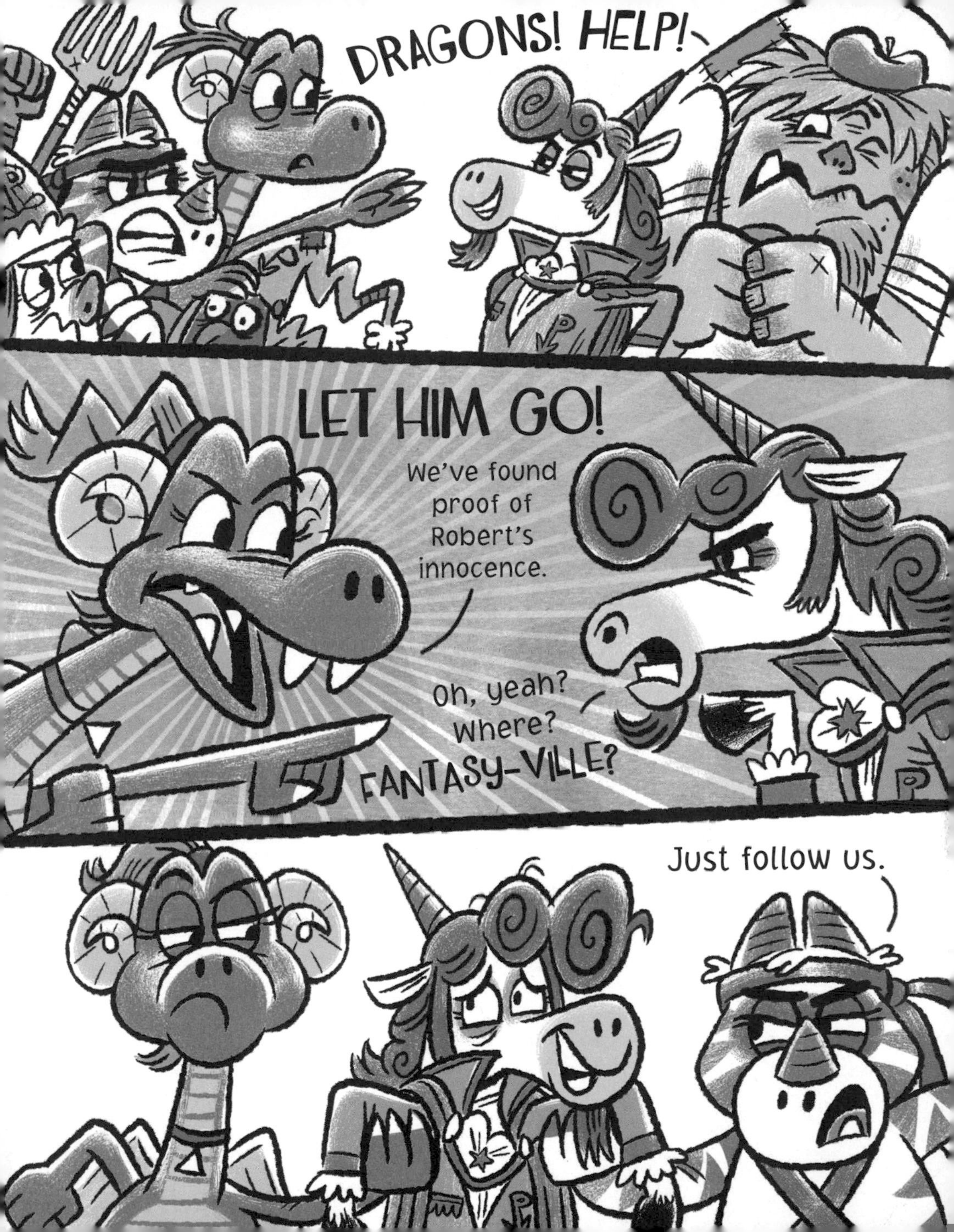
DRAGONS! HELP!
LET HIM GO!
We've found proof of Robert's innocence.
Oh, yeah? Where? FANTASY-VILLE?
Just follow us.

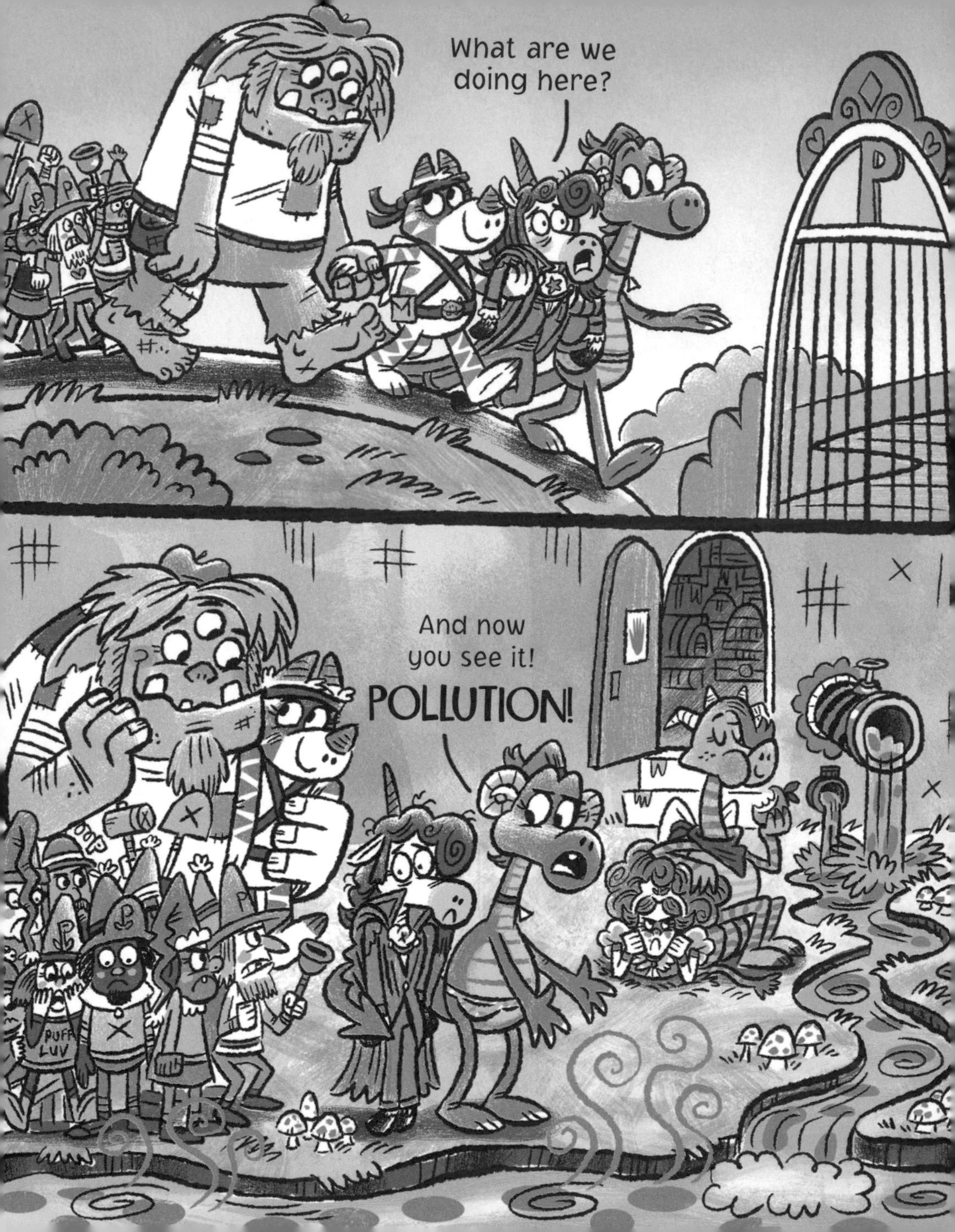
What are we doing here?
And now you see it! POLLUTION!
PUFF LUV

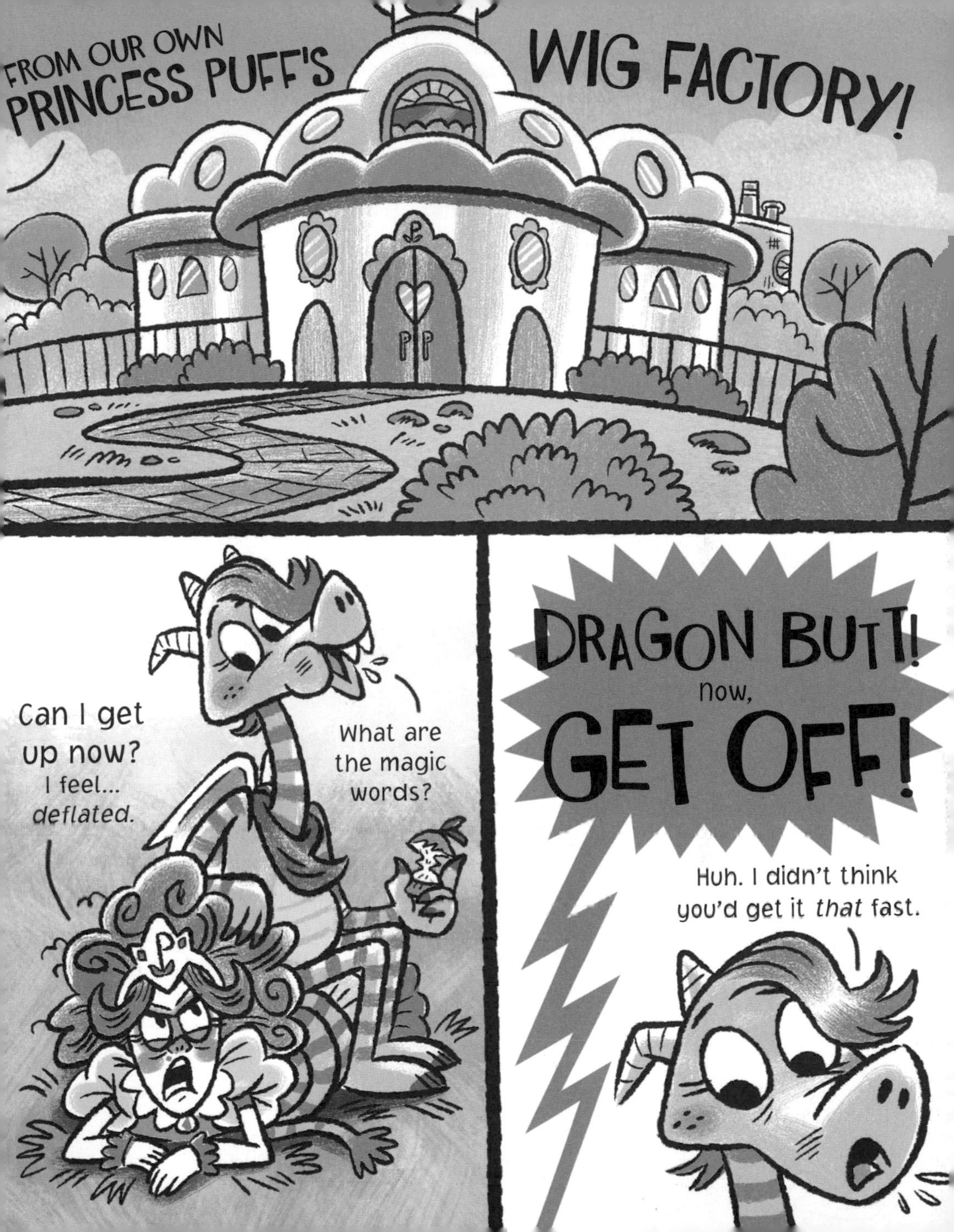
FROM OUR OWN PRINCESS PUFF'S
WIG FACTORY!
Can I get up now? I feel... *deflated.*
What are the magic words?
DRAGON BUTT! now, GET OFF!
Huh. I didn't think you'd get it *that* fast.

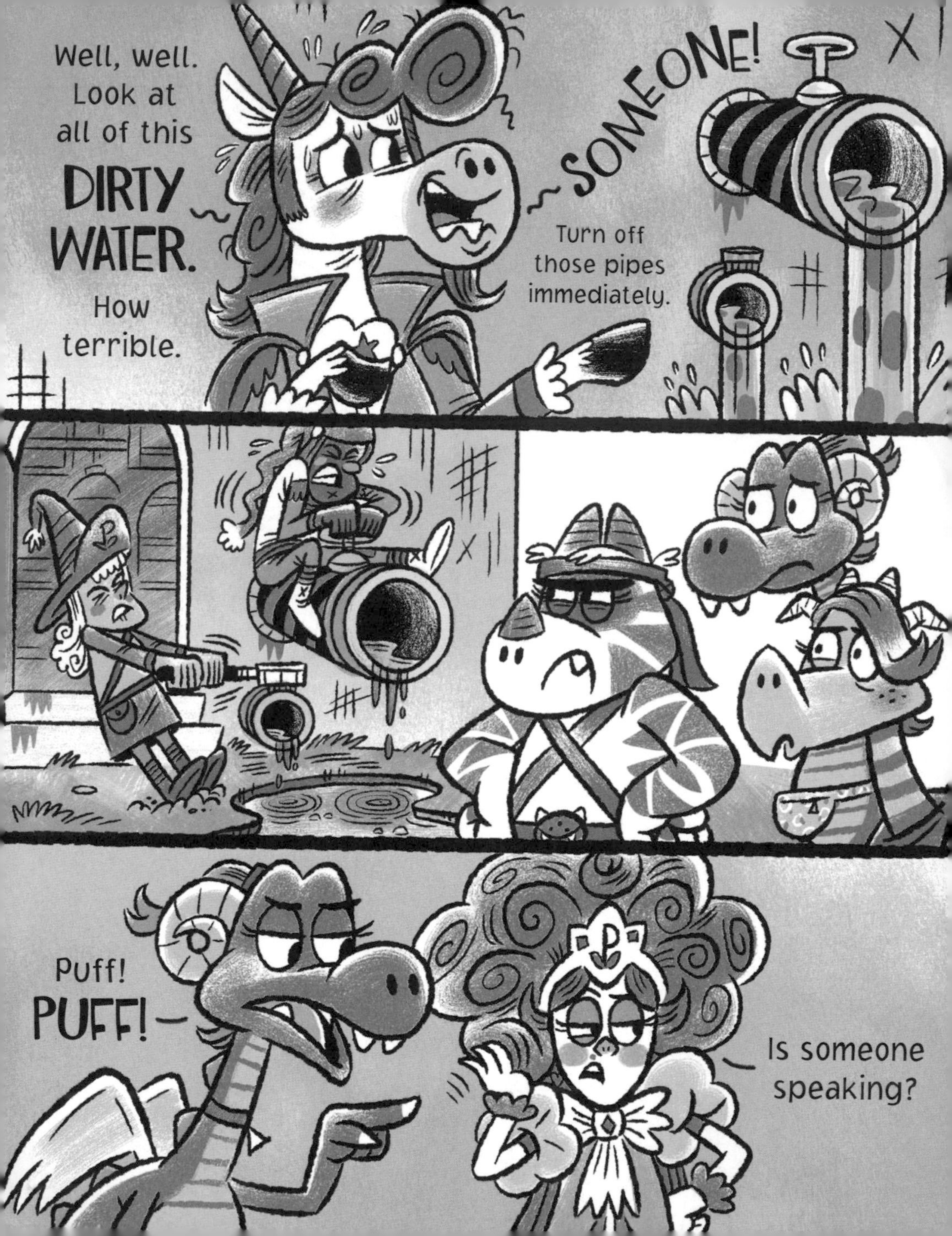
Well, well. Look at all of this DIRTY WATER.
How terrible.
SOMEONE!
Turn off those pipes immediately.
Puff! PUFF!
Is someone speaking?

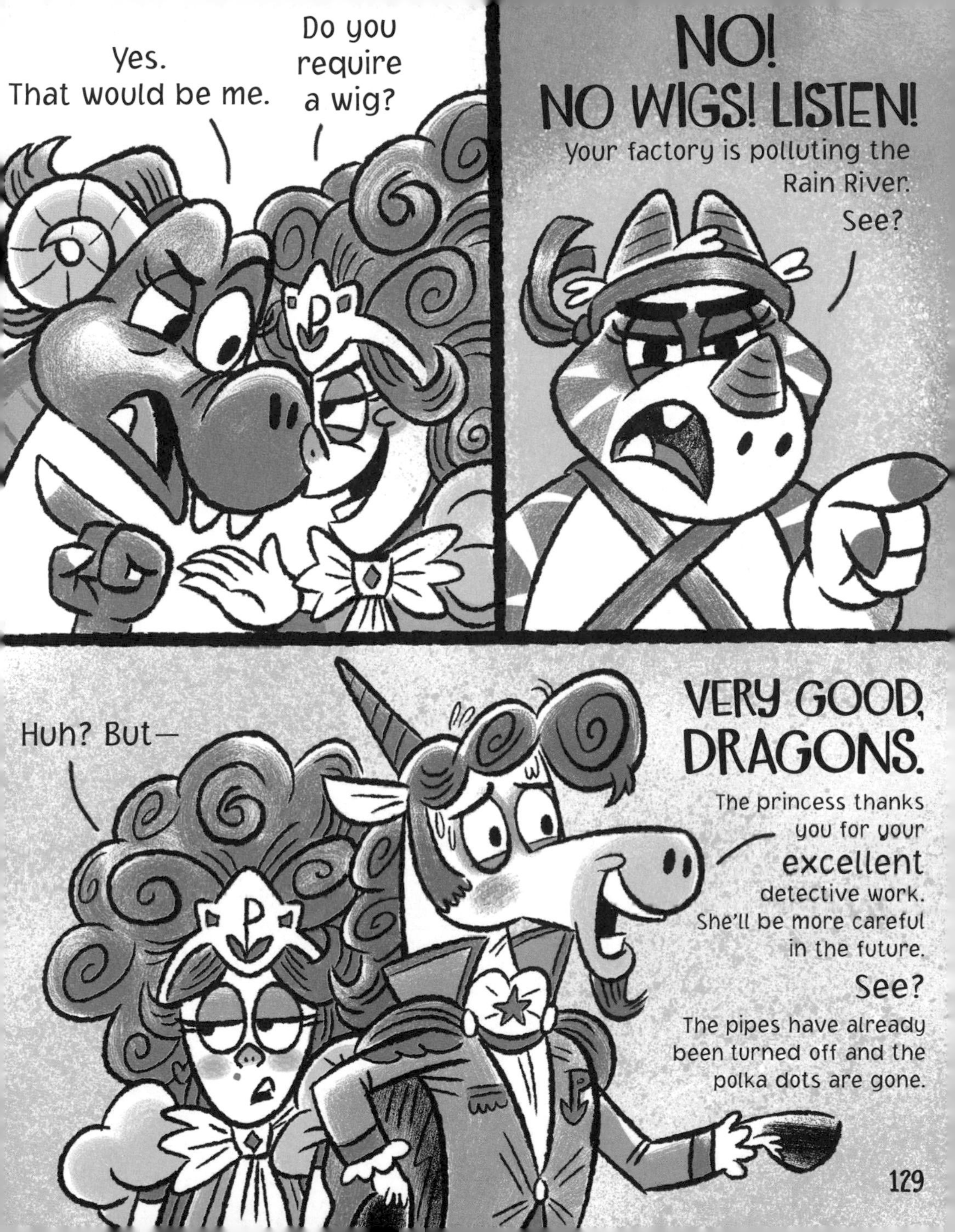
Yes.
That would be me.
Do you
require
a wig?
NO!
NO WIGS! LISTEN!
Your factory is polluting the
Rain River.
See?
Huh? But—
VERY GOOD,
DRAGONS.
The princess thanks
you for your
excellent
detective work.
She'll be more careful
in the future.
See?
The pipes have already
been turned off and the
polka dots are gone.

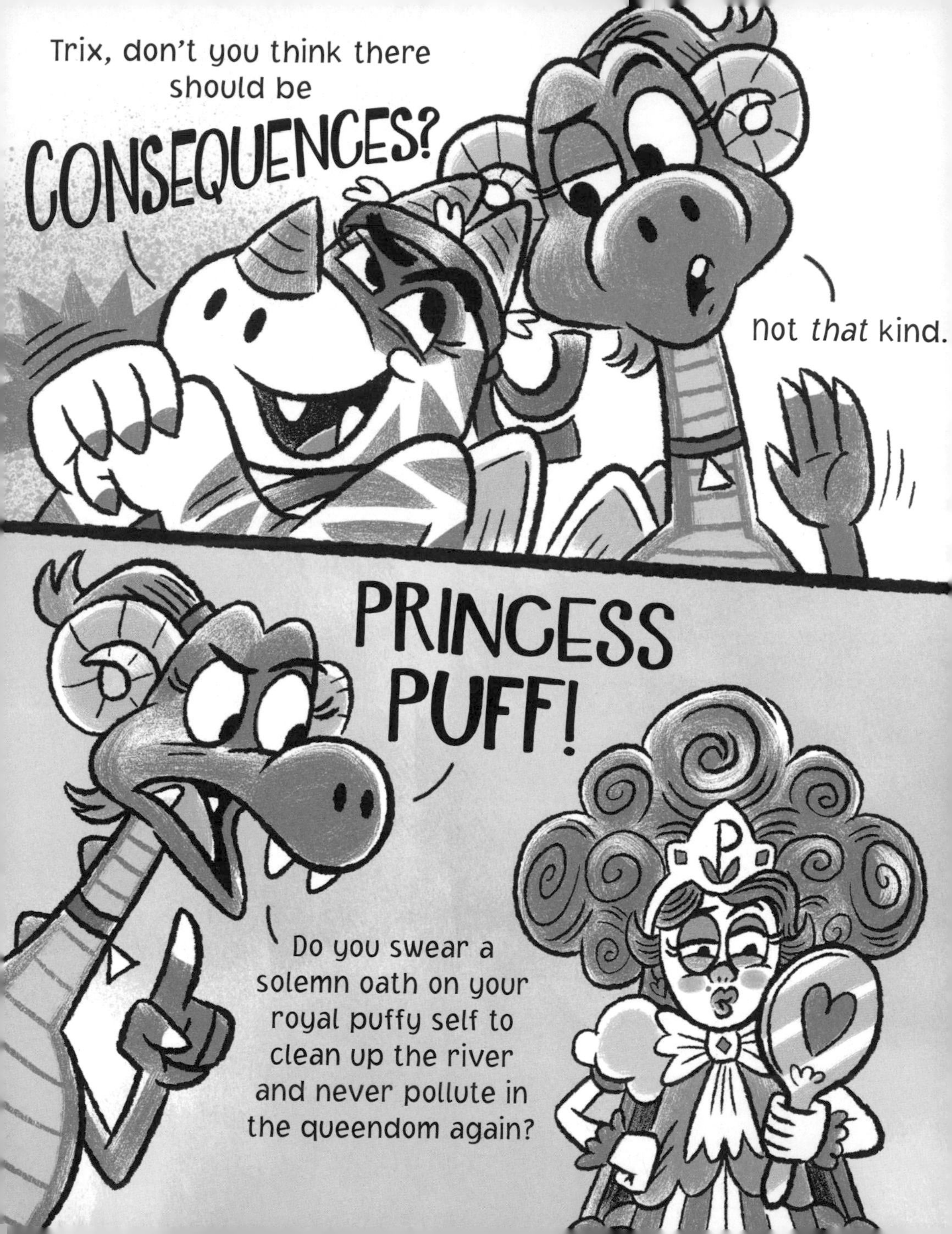
Trix, don't you think there should be
CONSEQUENCES?
not *that* kind.
PRINCESS PUFF!
Do you swear a solemn oath on your royal puffy self to clean up the river and never pollute in the queendom again?

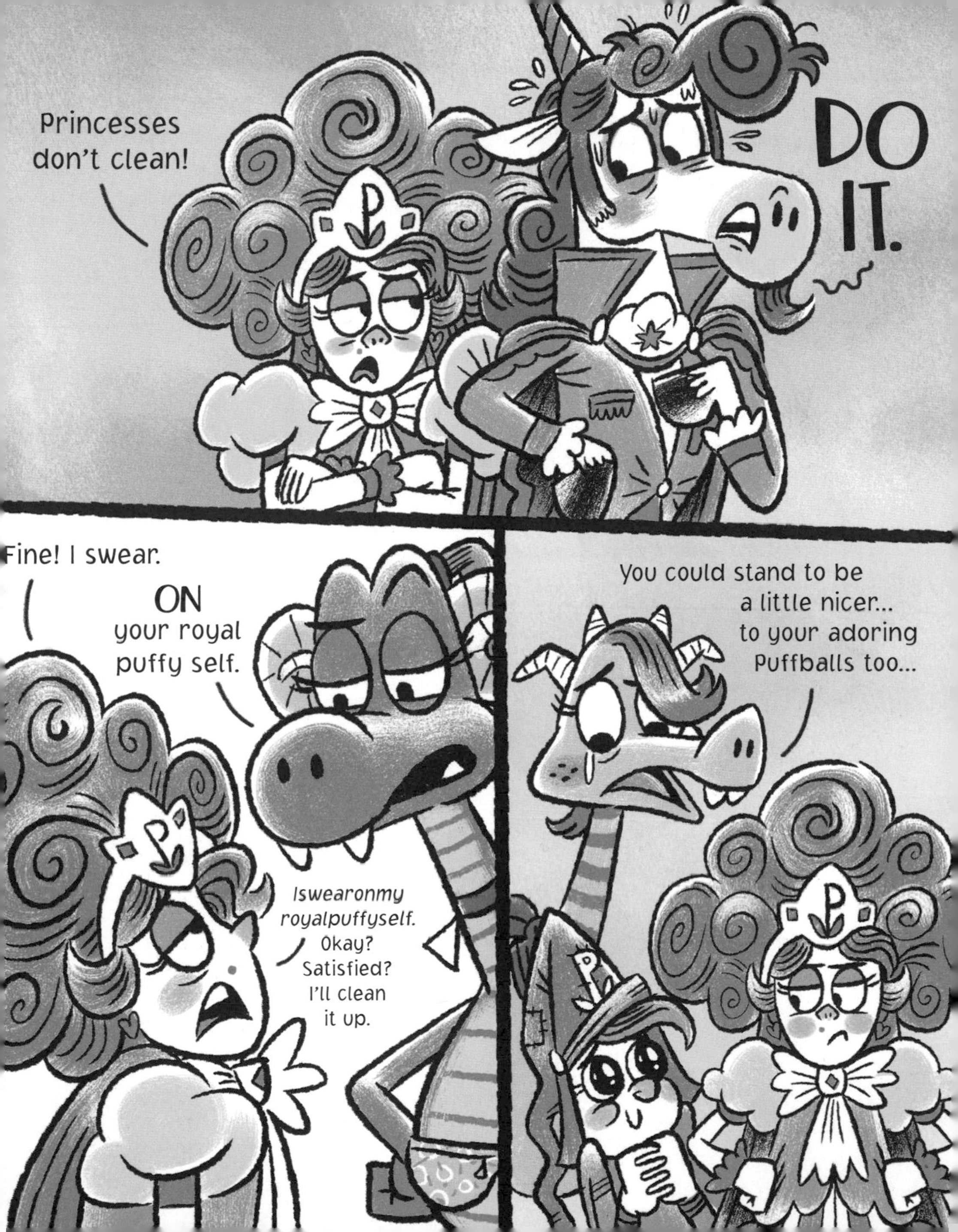
Princesses don't clean!
DO IT.
Fine! I swear.
ON your royal puffy self.
Iswearonmy royalpuffyself. Okay? Satisfied? I'll clean it up.
You could stand to be a little nicer... to your adoring Puffballs too...

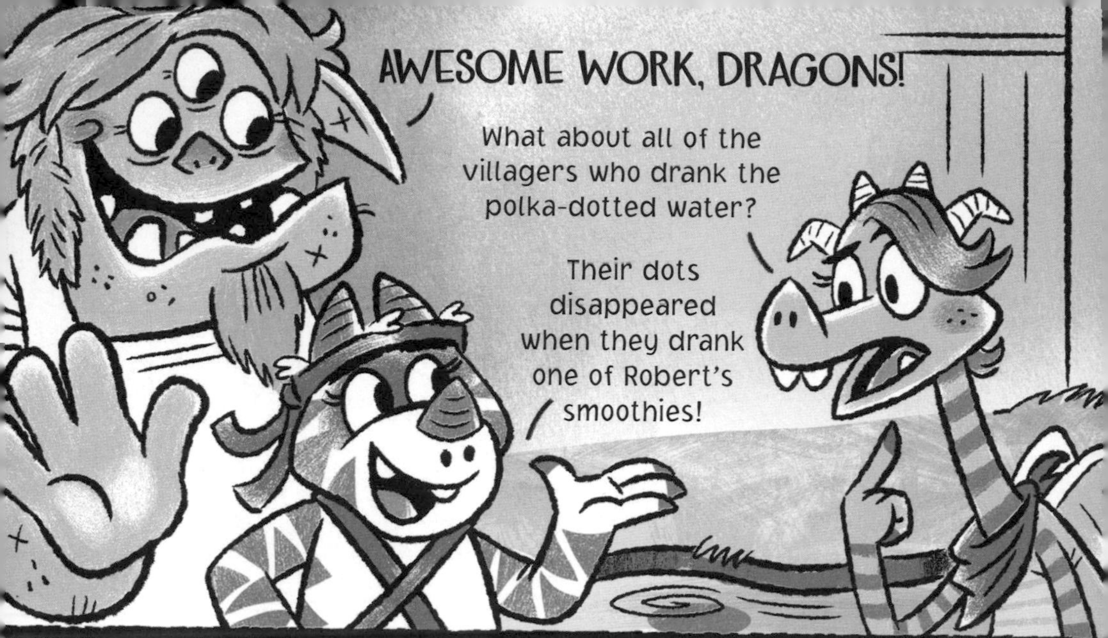
AWESOME WORK, DRAGONS!
What about all of the villagers who drank the polka-dotted water?
Their dots disappeared when they drank one of Robert's smoothies!

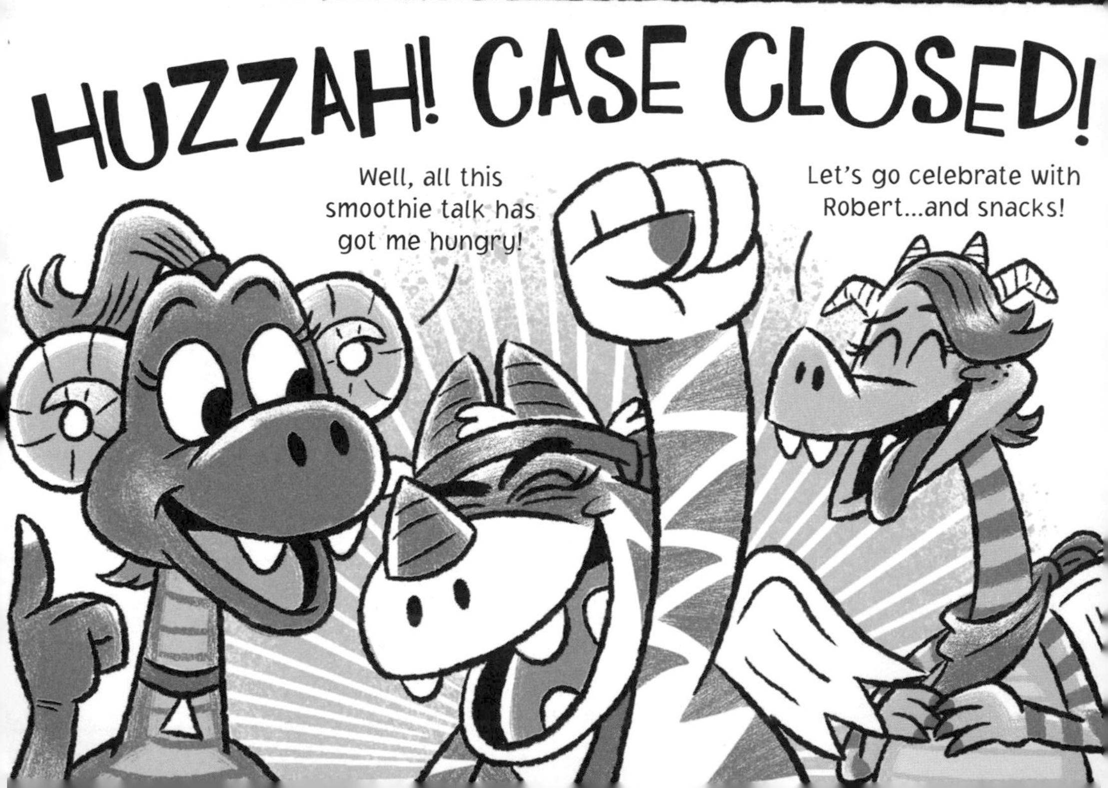
HUZZAH! CASE CLOSED!
Well, all this smoothie talk has got me hungry!
Let's go celebrate with Robert...and snacks!

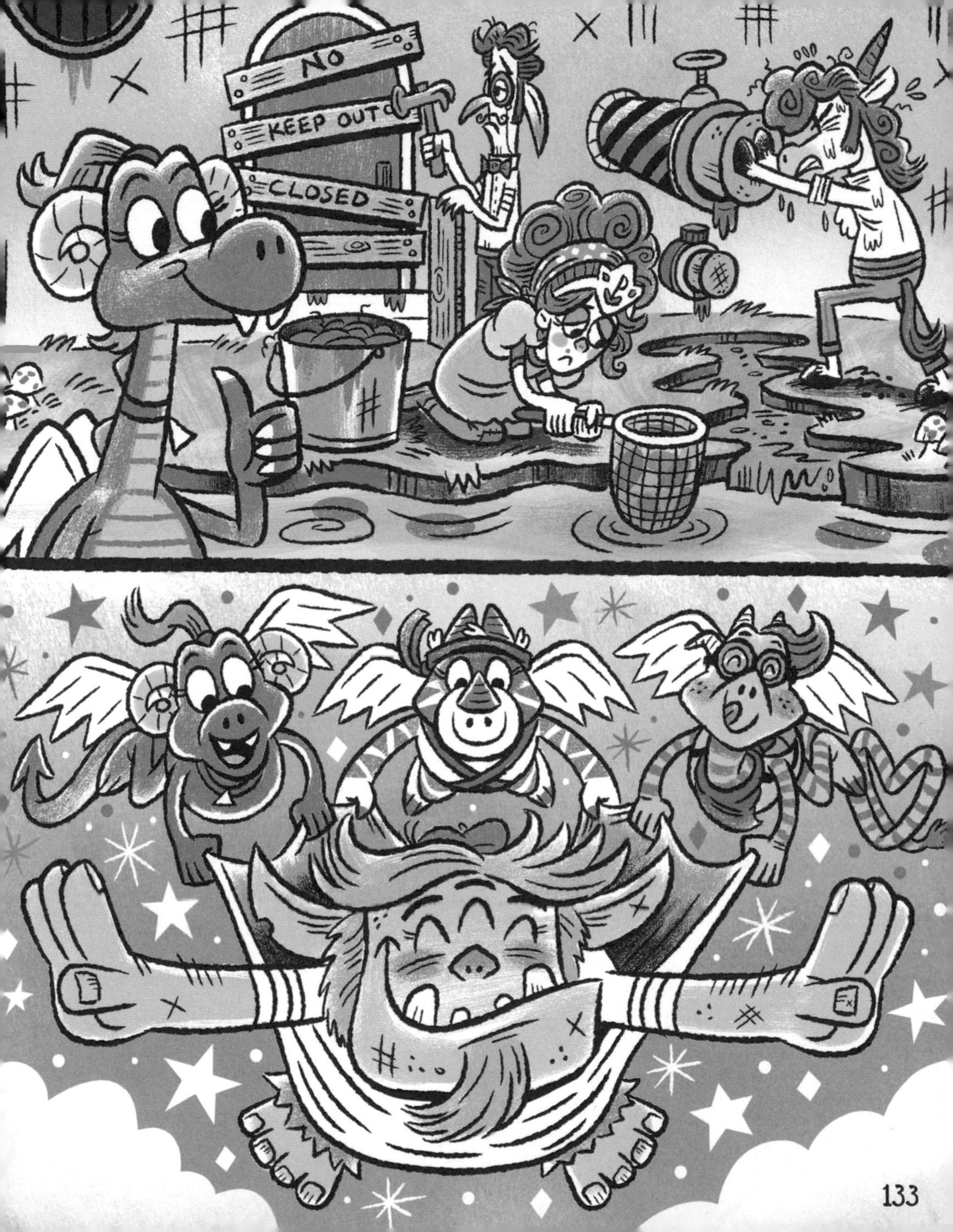
NO
KEEP OUT
CLOSED

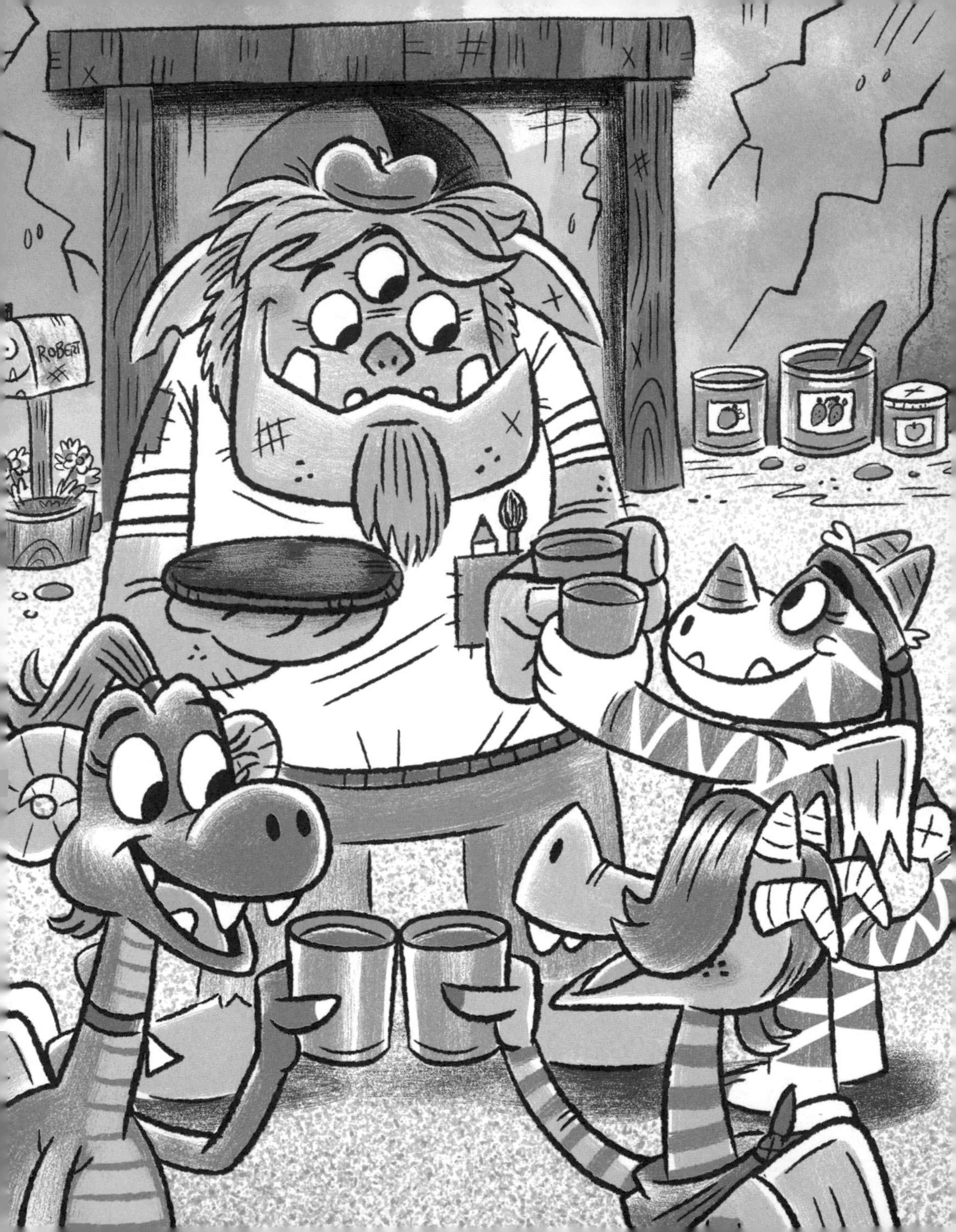
ROBERT

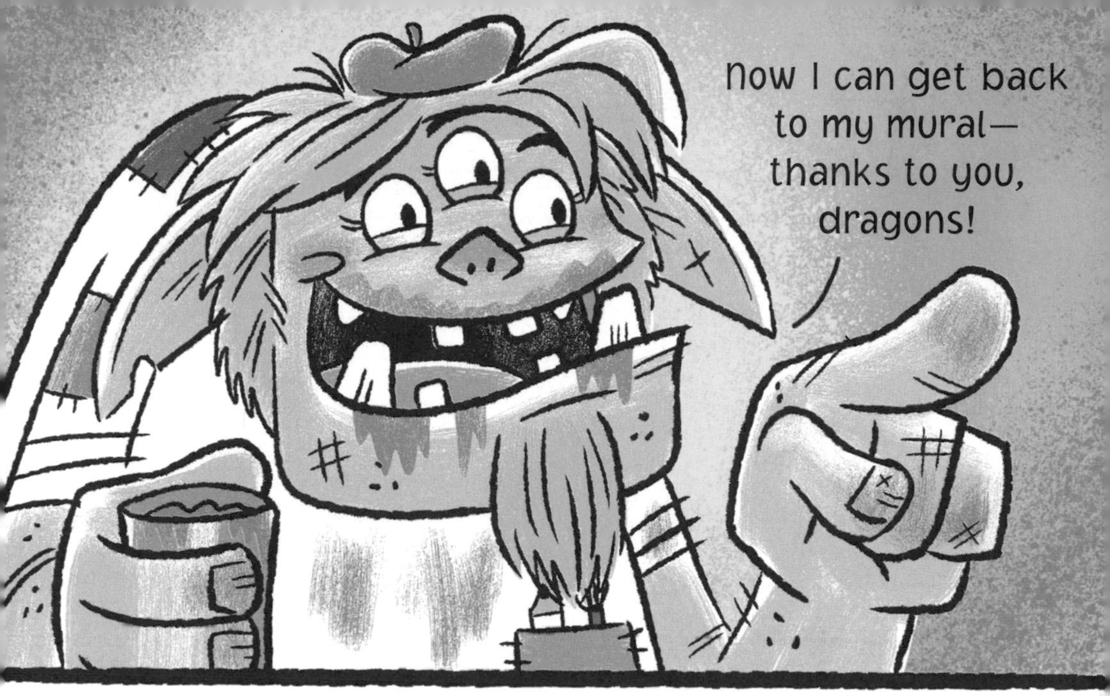
Now I can get back to my mural—thanks to you, dragons!

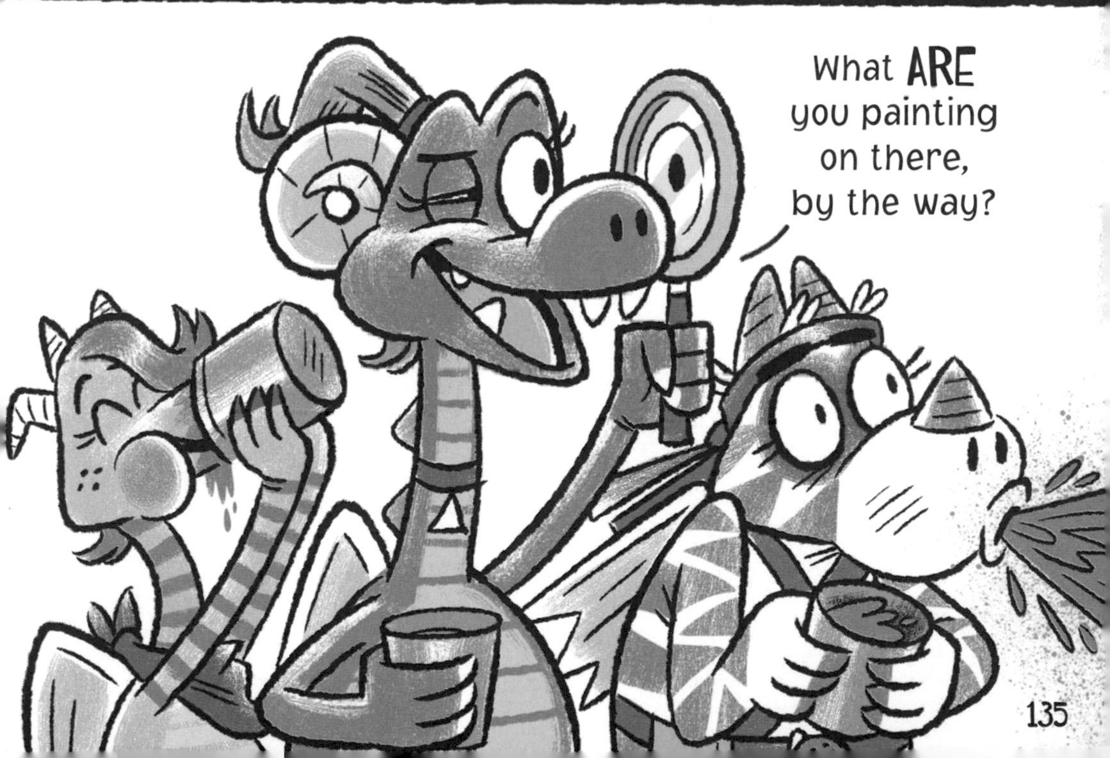
What ARE you painting on there, by the way?

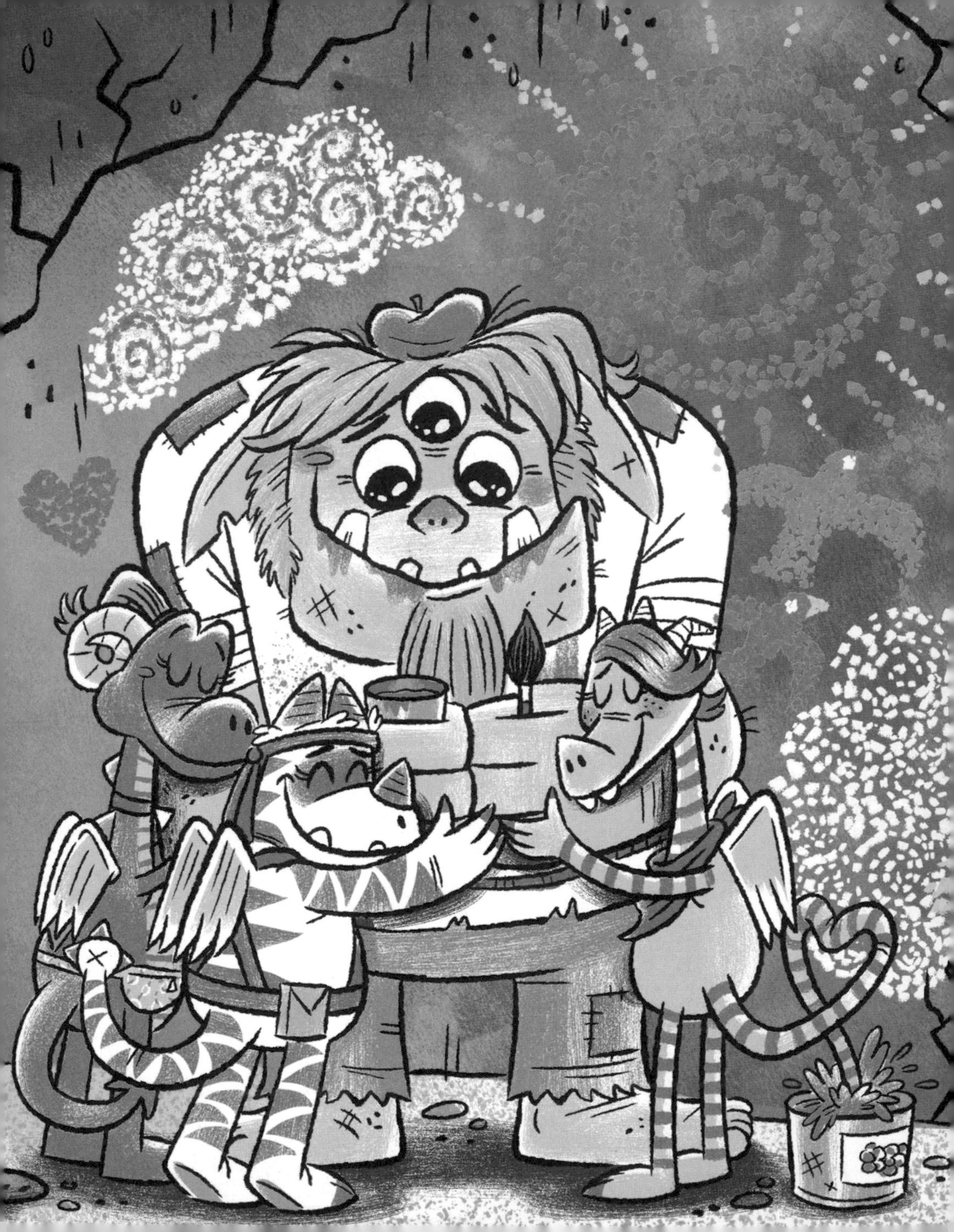

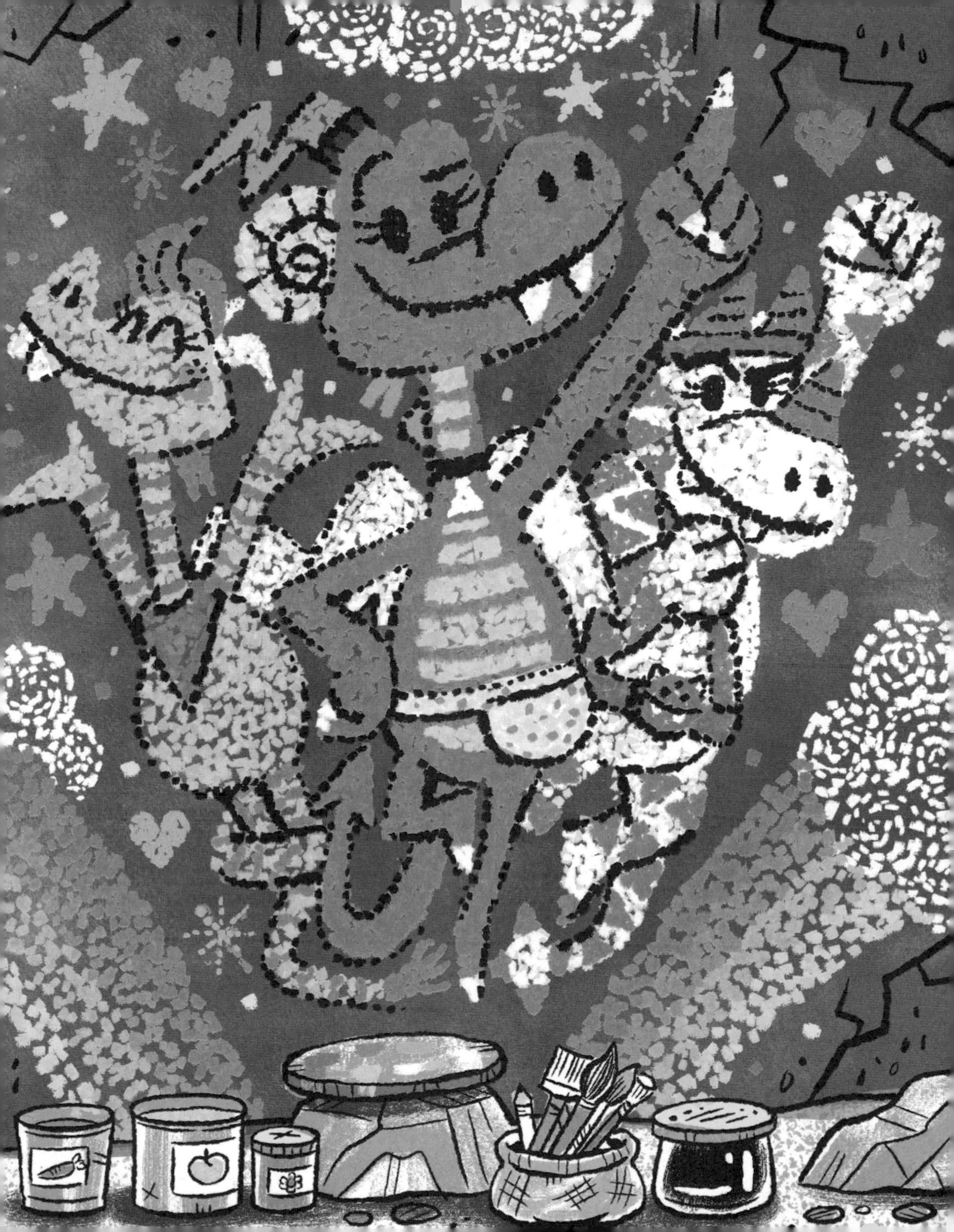

CHAPTER ELEVEN
RAIN RIVER RENEWED

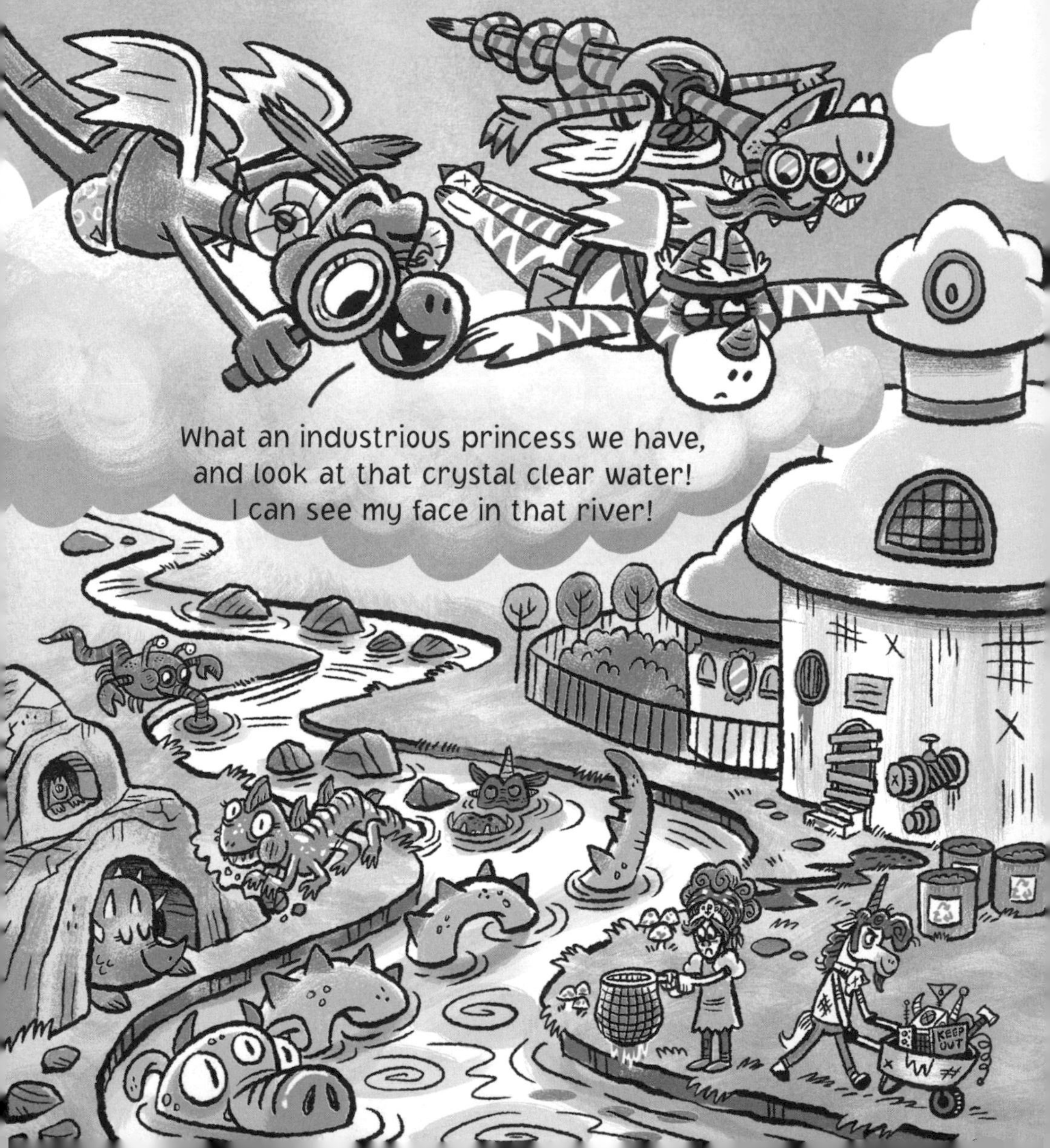
What an industrious princess we have,
and look at that crystal clear water!
I can see my face in that river!
KEEP OUT

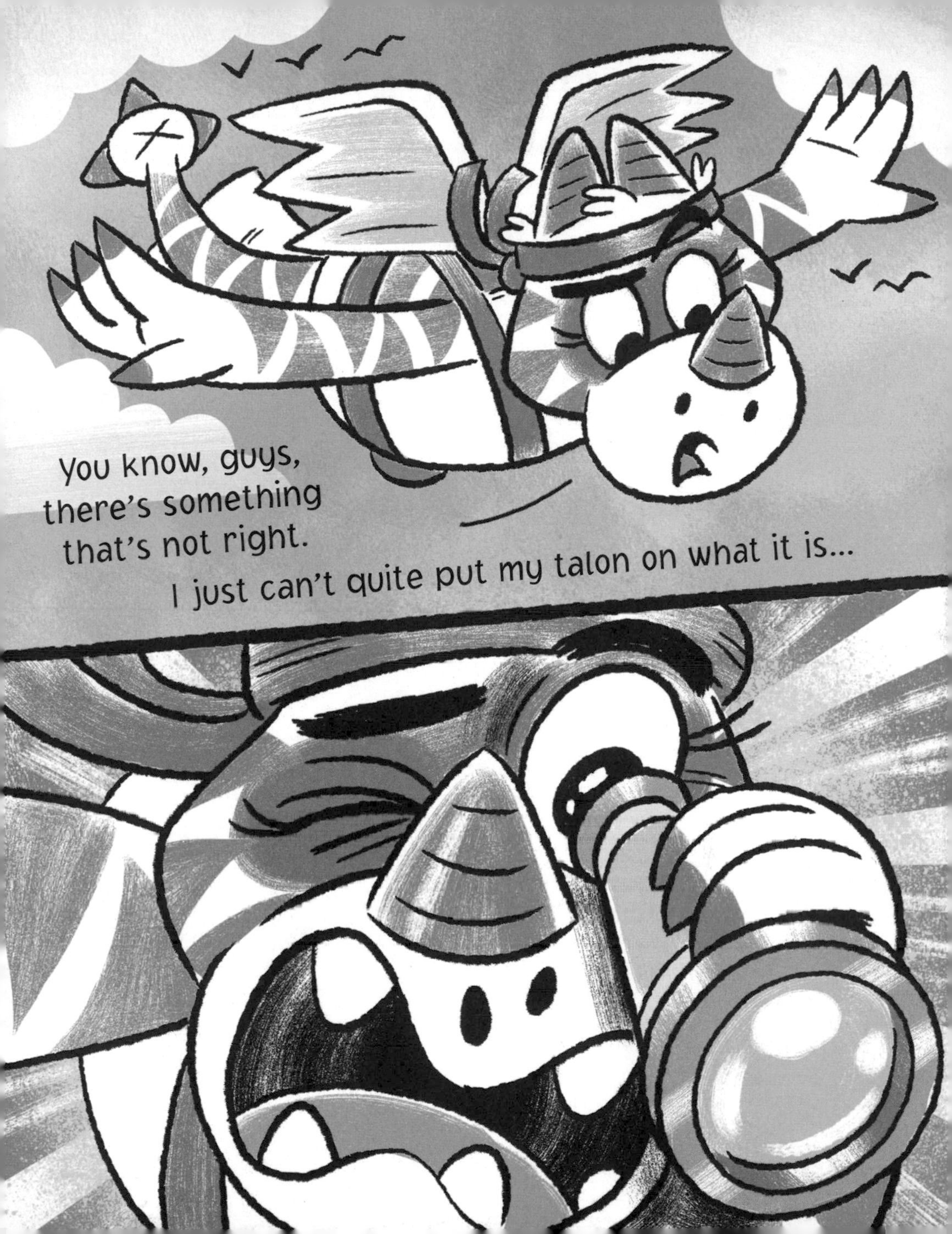
You know, guys, there's something that's not right.
I just can't quite put my talon on what it is...

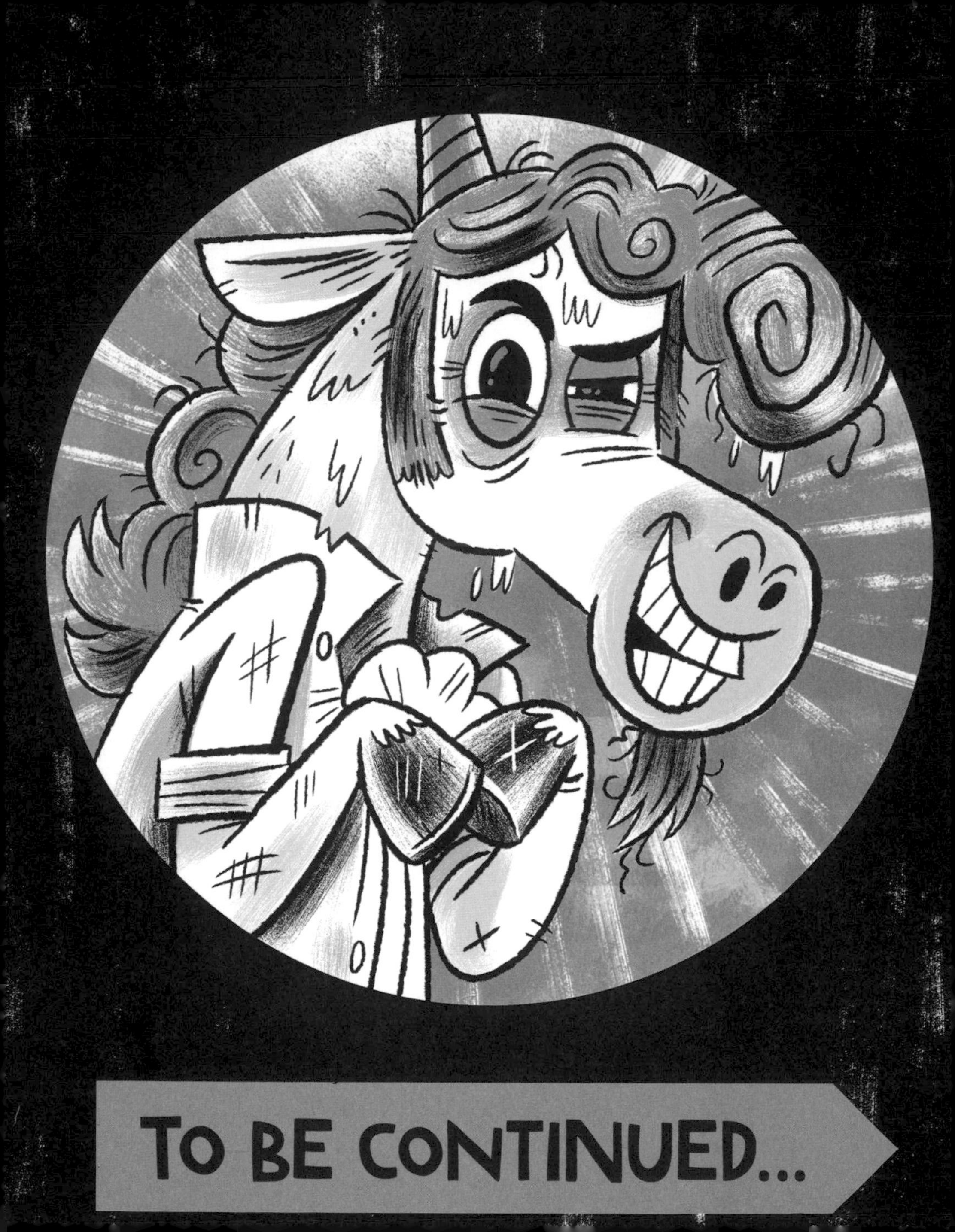

TO BE CONTINUED...